One tenet Teller Kendira had taught with painstaking care over the cycles came to Alysa's mind: *Let the needs of many overshadow the desires of a single one.*

Alysa replayed the phrase over and over in her thoughts. She found it made no sense. What were *needs*? What were *desires*? Was a need more important than a desire, or were they really the same thing? If dire circumstances were to affect everybody, only then would the same need — the need to survive — exist for all. But if one was alone in their need — or their desire — must it be ignored? *No.*

Every person's needs were important and should be fulfilled. Each should be able to live life as chosen. *Alysa desired — no,* needed *— to choose how she wanted to live!*

Her father's gentle face rose to mind. It seemed as if she saw him at the corner of her vision. Then she thought she heard a whisper which spoke but one word: "Individual." She startled and looked around; but there was no one else about.

Tish —

Find the champion who lives inside of you!

Best,
Terri Fedro Ithen
'10

A champion lives inside each one of us.

There is a lot of literature supposedly geared towards adolescents that should—and hopefully will—find its way to the bookshelves of adults as well, and I believe Tina Field Howe will join the ranks of J.K. Rowling, Stephenie Meyer, Cornelia Funke and the likes shortly.

Olivera Baumgartner-Jackson, Reader Views

I loved your book. It was the first fantasy I've ever read and I am so glad your book was the first. Even if readers don't like fantasies, they'll find the story engrossing and the characters so memorable.

Francine Silverman, author of *Book Marketing from A-Z*

Alysa of the Fields will enrapture you and you will be unable to put it down. Readers who enjoy post-apocalyptic events, cultural exchanges and unlikely heroes, will almost certainly enjoy this book.

Ian McCurley, Reader Views Kids

The journey continues in

The TrailFolk of Xunar-kun
Book Two in the Tellings of Xunar-kun

We are part of something greater than ourselves.

Once in a while you come upon a book the literally "knocks your socks off." In teen literature, it is reassuring to discover a well-developed plot with believable characters without violence, explicit sexual events, and constant use of profanity. The values of the characters instill morality and doing the right thing for yourself in difficult situations. Also, important in both novels is the underlying theme of there are different correct decisions for different people.

Teri Davis, BookSellerWorld.com

Tina Field Howe's *The TrailFolk of Xunar-kun* was another delightful and worthwhile read from a very talented and unique author. Although geared to young adults, those of us who remain curious and willing to learn should enjoy it greatly as well. A perfect read for a cold winter afternoon, the kindness of this story should warm you up nicely.

Olivera Baumgartner-Jackson, Reader Views

A look at the book's cover will give a fair idea as to its nature. The author's charming and intricate artwork reflect her writing style: articulate, but not overdone; detailed, but with a simple theme that does not become lost in the details. This is not a high-action book until the last few chapters, but it is an interesting and enjoyable read.

C.S. Marks, Author, The *Elfhunter* Trilogy

Tina Field Howe's writing style would best be described as fanciful. Her creative style of science fiction combining elements of the post-apocalyptic, foreign planets and fantasy is refreshing.

Ian McCurley, Reader Views Kids

Coming soon…

The Monx of the Roaming Star
Book Three in the Tellings of Xunar-kun

Together we can create a better world.

Alysa of the Fields

Book One
in the Tellings of
Xunar-kun

Tina Field Howe
PO Box 762
Corning, NY 14830

607-936-1455
info@AlysaBooks.com
www.AlysaBooks.com

Booklocker.com, Inc.
2006

Application submitted for Library of Congress Control Number: 2006909383

Alysa of the Fields

Book One
in the Tellings of
Xunar-kun

Tina Field Howe

The Glossary in the back contains references to characters, terminology, creatures, geography, and pronunciations.

SPECIAL THANKS

I heartily thank all who read the first drafts of *Alysa of the Fields*. I could not have completed this book without your honest comments, which inspired me to reach deeper and work harder to help this become a "true" story. Thank you all so much!

Simon Bailor, Kearston Campanelli, Kathie Christensen, Lynette Cornell, Meredith Gaylo, Caitlin Hatch, Laurissa Hatch, Rebecca Hatch, Matt Kapral, Jennifer Lorang, Sandra Margeson, Julie Paschal, Jeni Paquette, Ellen Passmore, Jan Przybylski, Babak Raj, Leigh Richardson, Janet Stafford, Sean Stearns, Rosemary Stevens, Pam Weachock, Jacqueline Welles, Sheila Wilson and Patricia Woodruff

Thank you, Caitlin, for posing for Alysa.
You struck the perfect pose!

— Tina Field Howe

Homesteads, Paths,
Trails & Landmarks
of Xumar-krin

Sladporn
Mountains

Far Reach
Mountains

Lowlands Camp

The
City

Sleeping Lands

Lowlands

Lakelands

Lowlands

Winding
Mountains

Honor
Pass

Ridge Camp

Trackground

High Point

Upper Path

Camp Path

Rocky Stream

Lower
Path

Falling Stream

Miranda
Ridge

Short Mountains

Ridge Path End

Yellow
Cliffs

Middle Path

Valley Ridge

Creek Path

Green Plateau

Far Path

Rolling Lands

CHAPTERS

THE LEGACY OF FATHER GORD'N –
AFTER CAT'CLYSM 36

From the darkness of outer space, a meteor whisked between the orbits of two moons circling Xunar-kun, a world that appeared largely brown and dead. Below the haze and scattered whorls of clouds in the atmosphere, short fingers of blue-white ice reached out from the polar caps, yielding to tall mountain peaks which appeared to hold them back. The world possessed scattered areas of blue water and forest, suggesting the possibility that it was able to bear life.

The meteor sped toward a battered space station. Spans of what were solar-collection grids were shot through with countless holes. The grids' broken metallic skeletons sprawled at odd angles to one another, torn from their original attachments.

Behind large, still-intact windows in the space station floated the lifeless bodies of several men and women. Raw, golden sunlight glared on the stiff gray bodies, accentuating stark expressions of frozen panic. A spacejet had collided with the station. Its hull had exploded on impact, piercing the station's outer shell. The mangled and charred tableau was a remnant of a battle lost long ago.

The speeding meteor struck the twisted space station and blew apart, propelling its fragments and pieces of the space wreckage in every direction. The meteor fragments showered upon the curve of the sky and sped downward, sparking into wild flames that consumed them.

By the time the debris reached mid-atmosphere, it turned to ash. Buffeted by high winds, the ash broke into smaller and smaller pieces until it became dust. Some of the dust was gradually drawn toward the planet's surface.

Golden sunlight gave way to darkness and darkness again to sunlight as a dust mote slowly drifted over the brown plains. Between breaks in clouds appeared fleeting views of ruined city structures, yellow-green bodies of water, and severely ravaged lands. Whirlwinds and dense storms raged here and there on the world, moving rapidly over the plains and abruptly dissipating as they slammed into mountainsides. Patches of green and blue tucked within vast mountain ranges drew closer.

A harsh current of wind caught the dust and whisked it into a mountain chain, whirling it down through dispersing clouds. It was rushed between harsh peaks and above verdant, misty valleys; through flocks of screeching birds and over rushing streams; and between stands of tall trees.

Eventually the dust was freed by the high breezes. It floated down over gushing waterfalls, where it rose and fell above turbulent waves, then was released to calmer air above a sunny hillside meadow. The warm air, dotted with iridescent-winged insects, carried the dust downslope. Smaller updrafts threaded it through steep terraces of neat, tilled plants and, finally, toward a cottage of log and stone built into the side of a hill.

The dust drifted closer to the cottage's rough plank door, which bore a carving of three mountain peaks with two moons rising above them. The dust slowed nearly to a halt as it approached the door and was drawn through a crack between planks.

Within the dark cottage, a wisp of incense wafted through the soft flame of a hanging lamp. The lamplight reflected off the grim, dark-golden faces of men standing in a circle. Their mournful chanting filled the room with sadness. The low, non-syllabic drone was punctuated now and then by higher tones joining in.

Their eyes focused on Father Gord'n—a frail, dark old man—who lay on a narrow cot in the center of the circle. His long white hair spilled over the side of the cot. Not far from death, his breath was shallow, irregular. The men gazed upon him with unmistakable reverence.

Alvan—a man whose face was nearly as dark and as deeply etched as Father Gord'n's—stood in a corner. Alvan's gray hair braid hung down to his waist. His dark eyes were heavy with sorrow and exhaustion. He leaned close to a man who stood opposite him and whispered, "My heart is heavy, Kahnton. I don't know what to say to Father Gord'n. How do I comfort one who has been such a strong leader, the one who saved us from the cataclysm? We all remember how great he used to be...what tremendous feats through great courage and wisdom he accomplished. Yet, that man lying there...*that* is not Father Gord'n..."

Kahnton, a younger man whose braid was beginning to gray, whispered, "Alvan, I don't know what you should say. I can't give you any advice but..." Kahnton glanced at the dying man. "You're wise and have known him the longest. You've been with him from the beginning! What do you think he would *like* to hear? What would he tell you if you were in his place? Tell him that." Kahnton gently pushed Alvan toward the dying man and followed.

Alvan knelt beside Father Gord'n and adjusted the coarse-woven blanket covering his shivering torso, as if this comfort would keep the old man from slipping away. Alvan struggled to find words.

Father Gord'n raised his weak eyelids. His feeble hand searched the surface of the blanket and found Alvan's. Father Gord'n attempted to speak. Alvan bent to hear his words. The chanting ceased. The men strained to hear Father Gord'n's words.

"These are my final...instructions," gasped Father Gord'n. "You, Alvan of Falling Stream...I appoint First Teller of the Laws." Dutiful Alvan nodded. Father Gord'n, gulping air, gathered the strength to continue. "You must commit to memory...all I have spoken...all I have written." His weak hand indicated the shelves of books against the walls of the cottage, vaguely visible in the dim light. "Teach those from the other homesteads...so generations to come...will know the ways...that are best...to follow."

Alvan replied, "Father Gord'n, trust that your instructions will be carried out. Your Law will live forever! Know that, despite the Laws you have given us, we'll be lost without you..." Alvan knelt beside the dying man and bowed his head. The others followed Alvan's lead and resumed their melancholy chant.

Father Gord'n's eyes looked at the lamp flame. His breathing ceased, but his eyes continued to stare, unfocused, at the flame.

A.C. 3013

Golden sunshine burned through white mist. A filigree of leaves and branches shattered the rays into bright streaks that cascaded down through the tall, ancient forest. High above the ground, an adolescent boy suddenly came swinging through the trees. His motion cut a swath through the light and mist, and with little effort he glided from vine to vine. It seemed as though the greenery lent itself to his reach, even as he altered direction and height.

The youth—dressed in close-fitting hide tunic and breeches, boots that rose to his knees, and a hide helmet that fit snugly to his head—landed on a heavy branch and ran up to the tree's huge trunk. Breathing hard, he peeked from behind the tree, watching in the direction from which he had come. Other boys and girls, dressed in kind, were in pursuit. They dipped and soared from tree to tree, yelling to each other as they glided through the air.

The boy stifled a laugh as the others passed his hiding place yelling phrases like, "Where did he go?" and "There he is!" It seemed as soon as they appeared they were gone again, on to another part of the forest.

As the hiding boy regained his breath, he heard the rush of a stream and another sound that he couldn't quite place. He hopped to a lower branch and walked toward the sound. He lay prone, shinnied to the end of the branch, parted the leaves, and peered out.

On the opposite shore of a rushing stream, crouched a small figure framed by large boulders and tall, soft-branched foya trees. It was a slender girl. She hugged her chest to her knees.

The boy stared at the girl in bewilderment. He lost his balance and instantly wrapped his legs around the branch to regain it. He pulled the helmet from his sweaty, short mop of dark-streaked hair. Colorful tattoos covered the tops of his ears and trailed down the back and sides of his neck. Pale-blue eyes stared from his smudged, light-golden face. He squinted at the girl.

Clear, sparkling water splashed and roiled in deep pools as it cascaded down steps of flat rock, melting into the boulder-strewn stream on its course through the forest. Pink briarwood petals, caught up by the stream as they floated from the high archway of overhanging branches, bobbed like tiny rafts on the water as they, too, began their journey downstream.

The girl—Alysa—lifted her small oval face. It was wet and dirt-streaked, and her large, brown eyes brimmed with tears. Her soft, rounded chin quivered as she wiped her face with a sleeve. If her face was clean, it too would have been golden like the boy's. The skin of all younglings this age was colored thus. In Alysa's grain-hued hair, held in a single, untidy long braid, pieces of leaves and moss were tangled in unruly strands. Her blue, coarse-woven smock was also quite dirty.

She wiped her eyes again and rested her chin on her knees. Her angry eyes took no notice of the playful, purple water bugs skittering in the shallows near the edge of the stream, nor of shy, golden shimmerfish peeking out from fringes of swaying waterweed.

Seda, a plump, red-haired girl, climbed up a steep path behind Alysa. Seda's blue eyes peered warily into the undergrowth. With one hand she held up her heavy, yellow skirt so the hem rested across her shins, thus easing her steps. With the other hand she held her dark shawl tight about herself. The distant sound of a joyful flute and playful drum drifted up the path behind her. "Ho, Alysa...Ah-LIH-sah!" She spotted her crying friend. "There you are! Don't you hear it? They've started the music. You don't want to miss all the fun, do you?"

Out of breath, Seda flopped down. Alysa turned her head away to hide her flushed cheeks and tearful eyes. Seda said, "I've been tromping all over High Point looking for you. I should've known to look here first!" She picked pieces of leaves from Alysa's hair and looked her over. Seda shook her head. "Look at you. What a mess!"

Seda looked around, nervous, suspicious of the surroundings. She glanced up at the trees and into the water. Not far from her foot, a large, blue-green rockhopper popped onto the shore. Its large, protruding orange eyes circled in opposite directions as it surveyed the ground. In one continuous motion, the scaly creature thrust out two sharp-clawed fingers, hooked a large, orange beetle wobbling close to her foot, stuffed it into its wide mouth, and plopped back into the water. Seda caught sight of the capture, shivered and recoiled. She hurried to her feet, brushed herself off, and pulled the back of her skirt around to examine it for possible vermin. She shook and released the skirt and stomped her foot. "You and your stream, Alysa! You know how I hate it up here, in this odd hiding place of yours...so far from the homestead. I'll never figure you out!" Seda sighed. "Have you even been home to see your new little sister yet? No. Do you even know what name's been given to her? No."

"Doesn't matter anyway," Alysa said through her tears. "Nobody cares about me, Seda. All they care about is that newborn..."

"So *that's* what this is about. Your new sister. That is not true, Alysa. You know how much you're loved. Why do you let the birth of one little youngling upset you so?" Seda sighed, exasperated. "You are so spoiled!"

Alysa turned her streaked face to Seda and glared at her.

Looking at her pointedly, Seda scolded, counting on her fingers, "Do you have a mother, father, brother, cousin, grandfather and two aunts to share everything with like I do, all in one little cottage? You've had your parents *and* your bed to yourself for ten whole cycles. So now you have to share. Poor thing! Come on now."

Again, Alysa wiped her face, further smudging a streak of dirt. Stubborn, she turned away.

"We're all...worried, Alysa. What would Father Gord'n think?"

"Father Gord'n's been dead for almost three thousand cycles. What does he care?"

"What? You mustn't talk about the Ancient Founder like that!" Seda scolded, looking around with shame as if an Elder overheard. "That's not proper! That's so disrespectful to Father Gord'n! What...*what* makes you say such terrible things?"

Alysa shrugged.

Disgusted, Seda said, "You think too much. Sometimes it seems that you like to be sad!" She sighed. "Well, I'll tell them I found you. You can do what you like." She turned and hurried down the path.

Alysa called after her. "All right! I'm coming. But don't tell anyone where you found me!"

Seda turned back half-way. "Oh, you know I'll keep your little secret. I always have. But don't be long, because I will *not* make any excuses for you! I don't know why I put up with you..." And Seda was gone.

"Nobody understands me..." Alysa sighed, rose and again dabbed her eyes with a sleeve. She smoothed the long smock covering her slight young form and pushed her long braid over her shoulder. Her family was to be honored tonight and, even if she was not happy with her situation, she certainly did not want to shame them before the whole clan by looking untidy—or by continuing to be disagreeable.

Before turning to go back to the homestead, she looked up and down the stream admiring the many small waterfalls gushing over rocks, the tall trees that hugged the shore and curved overhead, and abundant flowers that reached toward sunlight. She inhaled a deep breath of the sweet-scented air. This was her favorite place, and she often came here to be alone. After a whole sun of working in the steamy fields, she liked to sit on the shore and dangle her feet in the cool water. Sometimes she tried to catch swishtails, but they were quick and usually escaped her scooping hands. She liked to come here anytime just to dream in the shade while sitting on a thick cushion of moss. This place was her refuge, her place to be alone when she wanted. And only Seda, her best friend, knew about it.

A faint flute melody drifted up through the trees. Soon another joined in, striking up an inspired counter-melody. A gleeful flatdrum quickened the pace. The celebration had begun. On Xunar-kun, every newborn was cause for celebration. Each was considered a blessed treasure. *When it's someone else's sister,* she thought.

Alysa would be required to share the affection her parents lavished on her alone for ten whole cycles. But she knew that she must accept this, because she did know, somewhere deep inside, that her parents loved her very much. Despite her sadness, she must make every effort to look happy to have a new sister. For them. From this sun forward. Forever and ever. It was her duty.

Once more she glanced back at the stream, closed her eyes and inhaled, filling her lungs with sweet air. She let the breath out and managed to curve her lips into a small smile. It wasn't a real smile, as when she felt truly happy, but it was the best she could do given the circumstances.

She opened her eyes and turned toward the path. No sooner did she turn than, sensing something was out of place, she spun back. Her surprised eyes darted to the stream and caught sight of the boy standing on a boulder on the opposite shore. He had replaced his helmet. She looked him up and down, incredulous. He was about her height and age, but she could not recollect seeing him at any Gatherings.

He said, "No, you do not know me, girl. Have not seen me before, nor I you."

Her brown eyes stared into his pale-blue ones, seeking recognition. "I'm not wondering so much *who* I'm looking at," she laughed, "but *what* I'm looking at. Why are you dressed like that, boy?"

"And I might ask what such a 'big girl' has to sob about on such an amazing eve. On such a splendid streamside, in the most glorious season of all. And in such a perfect part of Xunar-kun!"

Alysa sobered. "I wasn't crying."

"Yes, you were...look at your face!" He pointed at her and laughed. "It is an odd thing, seeing a youngling of our age cry. I have only heard such bellowing from newborns, never from someone as old as we are. You are, I am thinking, nearly a midling, as am I. At this age there is no reason to bellow so. I could hear your wailing above the rushing of the water!" The boy leapt on boulders until he stood in the middle of the stream.

"You didn't answer me. Why are you dressed like that?" Alysa demanded, "Where's your braid? *All* boys wear their hair in a braid. It's not possible that it could be tucked under that...thing on your head."

"This 'thing' is called a helmet. And what is a 'hair braid'?" He pulled off the helmet to reveal his short, dark-streaked hair.

His *short* hair! Alysa gasped and took a step back. She had never seen short hair on anyone before. And never having seen a tattoo, she strained to understand what the colorful patterns on his ears and neck meant.

He continued, "I am garbed as such so I can move...like this!" He jumped back and forth between boulders. "Like a greatclaw, from one place...to another. Could you do the same in that sack you are wearing?"

"Who'd want to?" Alysa retorted, flustered, once again turning to the path.

"A Trailmen would want to!" Alysa stopped short and turned back, a baffled look on her face. The boy said, "I am called 'Szaren'. These close-fitting hides that I wear are necessary when we are hunting. They allow us to move among the trees with ease. And in silence walk through brush. We always wear them when we are migrating. Which we are doing now. Heading to Winding Mountains for summering." He pointed upstream at the tall peaks in the distance that gave the appearance of winding up into the sky due to their angled cliffs.

Alysa said, "You're a...a..."

"Trailman!" the boy boldly proclaimed.

Then she remembered that the fierce hunter-warriors were often referred to as the *Painted Ones*. The designs on the boy's head and his short hair proved that he was, indeed, a Trailman!

He continued, "And you, I think, must not be a Trailman. Because a garment like the one you are wearing would be of no value to the women of my tribe." He paused and scrutinized her more carefully. "But if you are not Trailmen, then what are you? What tribe *do* you belong to?"

Hesitating, Alysa said, "I am a...I am of the Field Folk clan, if that's what you mean by 'tribe'." She stared at the youth as she recalled one of Teller Kendira's well-known teachings: *Field Folk and Trailmen never spoke to each other, nor were they able to, because they did not speak the same tongue.* Alysa knew full well that the only time the Folk and Trailmen came face to face was at Trade. Even then not a single word was spoken; tradesign was used. Alysa realized that she may have likely broken a Law by speaking to this Trailman. Suddenly she said, "I...but I must go!"

"Field Folk? Ah, you mean you are a 'Fielder'. That would explain your clothing. And the nakedness of your skin." He paused then asked, bewildered, "But how is it that we are speaking?"

"I...don't know. This can't be!" Alysa hurried to the path.

Szaren looked back at the forest with excitement. The boys and girls who were pursuing him moments before were returning, swinging back through the trees.

Alysa glanced back once more to where Szaren had stood, but he was gone. Relieved, she hurried down the long, twisting path and through a wide stand of trees, emerging into the open meadow. On the mountainous horizon beyond the terraced fields, the sky was turning pale purple and gold.

She drew nearer to the music, stopping once to glance back up the path. She shivered, shaking off the encounter with the strange Trailmen boy. What surprised her was that they understood each other. Through spoken words! She was taught that Field Folk and Trailmen spoke different tongues because they long ago descended from a different breed of being. She decided to forget about the encounter and never tell anyone—even Seda—for fear of ridicule. She hoped this traumatic event would vanish from her memory and that thoughts of the boy would not come to her again.

Crossing the meadow, Alysa approached her family's cottage. The Field Folk homesteaders—or 'steaders as they commonly called themselves—spent the sun draping the cottage's eaves with garlands of flowers and greenery, symbols of new life. They ringed the yard with lanterns that would burn well into the night.

The throng of 'steaders were dressed in festive garb, women and girls in skirts and smocks of many colors and men in their good tunics and trousers. Women's braids were coiled on top of their heads and the men's long, neat braids hung straight down the middle of their backs. All of the men, except for Alysa's father, wore beards.

Alysa wiped her face again and forced a smile. She entered the yard, aware that she looked disheveled but hoping that no one would notice. She was greeted with joy by Seda and the other girls who wore wreaths of flowers on their heads. Merry Seda, already having forgotten their squabble just a short while before, placed a wreath on Alysa's head.

Singing and giggling, the girls pulled Alysa into the center of the forming dance circle where she took her place beside her parents. Gray-haired Abso, Alysa's proud, smiling father, cradled in his arms the small bundle containing her new sister. Abso turned his dark, beardless face to Alysa and looked down at her. His blue eyes sparkled. He gestured to the new youngling. Alysa tried to look excited.

Loralle, Alysa's mother, held her hands out to welcome her elder daughter and drew her close. Loralle's soft, green eyes looked into Alysa's with loving understanding. She bent down and kissed Alysa on the forehead and tucked a loose piece of her grain-colored hair behind her ear. Loralle turned Alysa toward her father and gently guided her to him.

Abso's deep voice urged, "Her name is 'Ellee'. Come, good Daughter. Hold your new sister."

After a brief hesitation, an awkward but careful Alysa received the newborn. Her father pulled back a fold of blanket to reveal Ellee's tiny, pale-golden face. Alysa could already see that the youngling resembled her father, with wide-set eyes and round face. Ellee's hair was like her mother's—thick and the color of spicenuts.

With one look at the newborn's sweet expression, Alysa's breath caught, and a soft, genuine smile stretched across her face. She raised her suddenly happy eyes to her parents and snuggled the precious new life she held in her arms. With a gentleness that rose from within, a feeling that was new to her, Alysa kissed the wee one, finally accepting that not only did she have a little sister—but delighting in the realization that she was now someone's big sister.

Loralle and Abso embraced their daughters as the 'steaders, with hands linked, danced and sang in a joyous circle around them. The flutes and drums struck up a merry new melody, one of many that would celebrate new life and echo over the terraced fields until long after the sun set.

BITTER WINTERTIDE

A chill wind blew from Winding Mountains, and many-colored leaves swirled within it. Billowing, gray clouds extended across the horizon. Leaffall was progressing. Cruel wintertide would soon be in the mountains, accompanied by harsh, crunching snows and long, frigid nights.

A more mature Alysa stood at streamside. She shivered and gathered her hooded cloak about her. Her shoulders shook with quiet tears. Six and a half cycles passed since she last wept beside this stream.

Shifts in Xunar-kun's weather often came unexpectedly. Without warning a sharp gust of wind burst down the stream and tore leaves from nearby trees, lifting them in a high spiral above Alysa. As they sailed upward and disappeared from sight, how she wished she could join them!

The wind whipped off her hood. Hair escaped her pale braid and flailed about her face, which darkened over the cycles to nectar-gold. The wind whisked away her tears.

It was during this time of cycle that she tended to feel sad, as the flowers had departed and the color in the trees was drifting away. The ground was too cold to sit upon. She watched the water as, here and there, a curled leaf tumbled into the stream, floated for an instant, and sank in the current.

Ellee's birth six and a half cycles before was a trying sun for Alysa, one that ended much happier than it began. In the time since then, she and her little sister formed a close bond and were nearly inseparable. Those cycles were good ones, yielding many happy moments. But two suns before, an unexpected sadness came upon her family; there was no chance this sun would end with the slightest hope for joy.

Her father had died, the victim of a mishap. Searchers found Abso's body downstream after two suns of absence from the homestead; just five suns after the joyful celebration of Leaffall Moonsfest, and two days before he was to participate in Trade. It seemed that he lost his footing and suffered a fatal head injury as he walked the shore. That was the conclusion reached by the Council Elders.

Earlier this sun, Alysa tried to watch as her mother and other 'steaders—relatives, friends and neighbors—prepared Abso for his final farewell. They washed his body, which was laid out on a cot in the cottage, and cleaned his hair of blood from the wound on the back of his head. Then they combed and braided his long, gray hair and wrapped him in a near-black robe, the color of the dead. She could not bear to see his coldness, his stillness; or to hear the continual sad chanting. The smell of incense—burned for those departed—made her feel ill.

The loss of a parent, or any loved one, is a shock that one can never prepare for. As she stared at his body, overwhelming grief washed over her. She would never be able to confide in him again; he would never again be able to console her, teach her, praise her—or love her. So she ran to her refuge beside the stream. But this time it did not provide the smallest measure of solace. How she wished that Orryn, her betrothed, could come from Falling Stream to be with her during this hardship; alas, his work—his all-consuming Teller apprenticeship—would not allow him to leave his homestead at this time.

Abso's funeral pyre would burn at dusk, and her family would have to bid final farewell to this wonderful, kind man who reared her and Ellee with a love as deep as their mother's. At tomorrow's dawning, Alysa would watch her mother, in pain beyond imagining, gather his ashes and sow them over the fields—every spouse's tribute to a lost partner and, ultimately, everyone's final contribution to the fields.

The sun began its journey into the hills a little earlier each evening as leaffall progressed. Dusk arrived; the time of her father's final farewell drew near. Thinking of this was almost too much for her. Still, her mind also dwelt on how he died. His death made no sense. Very few deaths were caused by mishaps such as this, and her father was always very careful when walking the paths to the other homesteads. It did not follow that he would have fallen and suffered such an injury while simply walking along a stream.

She looked to the sky, longing for an answer as to how this could have happened; the sky revealed nothing to her but wind and blowing leaves and cold. She lowered her tearful eyes to the ground, turned away from the stream and, in a sad, hesitating manner, began to pick her way down the path.

With sudden furor, she whirled back to Winding Mountains. As if to an invisible presence, she wailed, "Father Gord'n, why did you do this? Why did you take from us the person my family needed most in this world? There wasn't anyone on Xunar-kun as wonderful as my father! Mother is lost. Ellee is still so young..." Aching for answers, she asked, "How can I leave my mother and sister now? How can I leave to join with Orryn and move to his homestead next cycle, as has so long been planned?"

As she awaited an answer, the sky grew darker. Light snowflakes came on the wind. She heard a low whisper that said, *Fear not, Beloved One. All is well!*

Startled, she looked around for the one who whispered those words; she thought she saw someone, a dark figure standing in the shadows on the opposite shore of the stream. Almost as quickly as the figure appeared, it vanished. The whisper in her head and the figure's stature reminded her of — but could not possibly have been — her father. She shook her head and sighed, believing her longing must have devised both the words and the shadowy figure in an attempt to achieve some measure of solace.

She already missed her father with a desperate longing; his loss would be the most difficult challenge of their lives. But she knew she must find the courage to help her mother and sister through this time of sorrow. What did courage look like? Did having courage mean she must hide her tears from them? Did it mean she must provide whatever comfort she could? She did not know; what she knew was that her father would expect her to do what she could to help them.

She wiped her tears, took a deep breath, and pulled up her hood. Turning to the path she had trod many times, she began the descent. How she dreaded long wintertide's approach!

Tiny green, black-capped birds hopped on the snow-covered ground. Seemingly weightless, the birds whirled and jumped and *chee-cheed;* they pecked at stray field grains and wildflower seeds that sustained them through wintertide.

The birds scattered as Alysa walked along the curved dwelling terrace. Her heavy cloak swished along the snow-packed path that crossed in front of the cottage yards of High Point Homestead. The birds flew back and resumed work after she passed, making scores of tracks as they hopped and scratched.

It was bitter cold. As Alysa walked, she breathed the sharp air in shallow breaths and held her hood close to her head, covering her mouth. At times her exhales puffed clouds into the air that evaporated almost as soon as they escaped her lips. It was during this bitterest of weather that she wondered why her father had built their cottage so far from the Great Hall, her destination. The walk seemed to take forever!

The sky overhead was clear. Angled shadows indicated mid-morning. To the southeast, far beyond the homestead terraces jutting out from the steep hillside, and even beyond Field Folk territory, a shadow of dark clouds hovered. The clouds would be releasing a severe storm of some kind, dropping dense hail or ripping the land with whirlwinds or lightning. It was rare for such storms to climb into these sheltered mountains. But occasionally they did make their presence all too well known.

Her gaze passed over the landscape. All along the dwelling terrace, many neat cottages, sheds and hen coops were enclosed in low-walled yards. Smoke rose from chimneys poking through the centers of rooftops. All window shutters were closed tight. Neat stacks of firewood framed cottage walls and yards. Cottage gardens lay sleeping beneath the snow.

Folk men, women and their younglings, dressed in warm jackets and cloaks, conducted daily chores—drawing water from wells, stacking wood, filling troughs with feed for the long-legged casish hens, and pulling wheeled carts filled with provisions along the snow-packed paths.

Above the dwelling terrace, northward-ascending orchard terraces were planted with fruit and nut trees. Looking like bare bones sticking up out of the snow, in greening they would be soft and bright with blossoms and young leaves; later their branches would bend under the weight of their fruit. How Alysa yearned to see the orchards flowering once again!

Downslope, the stubble of oil-seed, simmel and other grains and vegetables poked up through the snow of thirty descending field terraces. The fifth terrace down was where her mother had spread her father's ashes; they now lay beneath the snow, waiting to be tilled under when planting commenced. Abso's body, and all who received their final farewell, lived on in the crops that were grown. Alysa smiled, content that one day her ashes would join his and all the others who preceded her. This had always been the Field Folk way.

In barnyards spaced at intervals across the terraces, people tended herds of bleating, wooly udommo, bulky leaprock lambs and other stock.

Farther south, below the last terrace, slept the frozen blue-white lake. Its far shore blended into the lake's cradling hills. Tall foya trees spackled the shore and looked like deep-green shadows laden with snow.

Alysa smiled, aware that soon wintertide would release its grip and surrender to greening; after all, this was the last sun of the wintertide season. A healthy glow had returned to her face. She mourned her father's death during this long wintertide. Though she still missed him—and would forever miss him—brighter thoughts were at last returning.

She forwent the recognition of her seventeenth birth two moons before because she did not feel joyful enough to celebrate it—or to celebrate anything. Perhaps next cycle her family would be ready to acknowledge their birth suns. Perhaps by then her mother would rejoice in living again.

She rounded the curve of the terrace and beheld her destination—the Great Hall. This was where all High Point Gatherings were held and where the crafters labored. The structure sat on the center rim of the dwelling terrace, facing the lake and overlooking the fields and barns. Behind it were several large storage sheds and the homestead Pantry, a structure also of great importance to the homestead.

The Great Hall was built in the same style, stone and logs as were the cottages, but was much larger. Four tall chimneys released curls of smoke into the sky. Closed shutters over tall windows preserved heat given forth by large hearths positioned in each corner of the interior. Unlike a cottage with simple enclosed entryways on the front and back, the Great Hall had entries on the front, left and right sides. They were accessed by stone and sod-packed ramps for ease of loading in raw materials for crafting, and for the removal of finished goods to the Pantry and storage sheds. Between the front and right-side ramp sat many rows of firewood and a covered well.

Alysa trudged up the front ramp recently swept of snow. She pulled open one of the tall, heavy doors. Carvings of Winding Mountains stood out in relief on each door. She entered the hallway, stomped her boots on the coarse mat and shut the door behind her. On one of many pegs along the wall, she hung her cloak. She slipped off her boots and set them down among orderly rows of hundreds. The floor was cold, even through her thick-socked feet. Hopping from foot to foot, she quickly pulled out a pair of woolen slippers from a cubby and slipped them on.

Pushing through another door, she entered the great room, hugging herself to dispel the chill from the hallway. She moved with caution as her eyes adjusted to the dim interior. Many red clay oil lanterns hung from high, hand-hewn support beams that spanned the wide room. All four hearths blazed, giving much-appreciated relief from the cold. Line upon line of dried fruits and vegetables were strung on twine between the walls. Many benches were stacked along the side walls.

In the center of the back wall hung the immense, round Planting Calendar, an imposing, complex carving used by the Folk to plan and track seasonal activities.

Women and older girls worked looms, spun wool, sewed garments, knitted hats and mittens, and fashioned baskets. Soft wool and other materials were mounded beside the craftswomen. In the rear of the room, craftsmen and boys worked hides to fashion boots and slippers. They molded clay lamps, dishes and pots.

Every 'steader contributed to the wellbeing of the clan. Although some of the aged were limited in their ability to work, they did their share. Being productive was everyone's duty. From this principle the 'steaders derived a great sense of pride.

The women gossiped as they worked, regarding Alysa as she entered. Erindi and Malores, girls her age, minded several newborn younglings and wobblies—younglings just learning to walk. The younglings belonged to the craftswomen. It was typical to bring them to the Great Hall while they worked. This gave midling girls with little exposure to newborns much-needed experience in how to care for them in the hope that they would bear their own after they joined.

The girls grinned and waved to Alysa, and she nodded back. She sighed as she spotted her mother sitting apart from the other women. Loralle wove a basket, oblivious to any of the conversations. The women of the homestead were patient. They believed that Loralle was close to regaining her zest for life. Alysa, who knew her mother better than anyone, was not so certain.

As she crossed to one of the hearths to warm her hands, Alysa looked back at Loralle, still in deep despair since Abso's death. She remembered when her mother's skin was a lively mellow-gold; now her color was sallow and dull. Her normally neat, spicenut-colored braid was loose and falling apart. Loralle's green eyes lacked life, as if a flame inside her had gone out. She was thin now, although before Abso's death she was rather plump.

Alysa and her mother shared a strong bond; her mother taught her all the skills she would need to reach her potential as a productive Field Folk woman. At one time, they were able to talk about anything. But in recent moons, they hadn't talked at all. She missed her mother and longed for her return to the way she used to be before Abso died.

Many boys and girls, all with braids trailing down their backs, were seated on fur-covered benches near the opposite hearth. Alysa joined them. They were listening to a story being told by Kendira, the aged Teller. Quiet girls were snuggled in thick shawls of various colors. Some of the older boys whittled with small blades, flicking wood shavings into the hearth and looking up occasionally as Kendira recited a story.

Kendira's age was obvious, not only made apparent by the pure white of her thin, braided hair, but because her color was very dark-gold creased with deep wrinkles. Several long, white whiskers grew from her chin. Wrapped in a shawl that covered a dark-brown smock, Kendira was seated on a cushioned stool. In one aged, swollen-knuckled hand she clutched a walking staff.

Seated among the small faces reflecting firelight was Ellee, Alysa's round-faced, blue-eyed sister, now grown into a fine girl of six cycles. It seemed as though Ellee was recovering well from their father's absence, and Alysa was happy for this. Ellee's aliveness made life bearable. That Alysa resented her before she was born now seemed so foolish!

Alysa sat on a stool and watched in admiration as Kendira plied her skills.

"...and then Father Gord'n came to the aid of the people who were in great confusion. All types of people—young and old, men and women, boys and girls—were gathered together by Father Gord'n just before Cat'clysm!"

The younglings responded with whispers and frightened expressions to this one of many brave stories of Father Gord'n.

Kendira gestured throughout the Telling. She was entrancing, accenting a passage with fervent, dark-gray eyes, her face and body expressing as she explained, in the finest Teller form, yet another feat of Father Gord'n. Though her bones were growing brittle and she walked with a limp, Kendira still showed great skill in Telling and was well respected for her wisdom and patience with the younglings.

"It is so true!" Kendira's engaging voice continued, "Our people were city dwellers and they knew *nothing* about survival in the wilds of Xunar-kun. Father Gord'n was a man of great, great knowledge. He knew *everything* about the seasons and planting and the mountains. And he brought the very first people to Falling Stream, our brother homestead to the south, to be spared from Cat'clysm!"

Kendira paused and, with a shaky hand, lifted a clay mug to her lips. The younglings whispered to each other in wide-eyed wonder. She struck her staff on the floor, startling them. They immediately fell silent, all eyes once again upon her. She leaned forward and looked into their eyes. "He taught us how to tame the wild. How to build. How to fish the lakes. How to plant by the moons. So therefore, we were spared! Over time our numbers increased. He sent our people to dwell in the other directions, to the north, west and east, to settle new homesteads and to build and plant new fields. That's how the five homesteads, including our own High Point, came to be!" She thumped her walking staff on the floor and sat back, signaling the end of the Telling.

The younglings jumped up and clustered around her, each shouting a different question about Father Gord'n. She rose and held up a quieting hand. When they became silent, she explained, "You must be patient! For there are too many wonderful stories about Father Gord'n to be told all at one time!"

With a wave of her hand, the younglings dispersed, running to the center of the room in excitement to retell the story amongst themselves. They shouted, "I want to be Father Gord'n!" "You can't, you're a girl!" Some of the women shushed them, and the younglings played more quietly.

Alysa snatched Ellee as she ran by, and they hugged. "Ho, Thitha!" Ellee lisped, "I love that story!"

"It's my favorite one too, Ellee."

Ellee ran off to play with the other younglings.

Spent from the Telling, Kendira lowered her old body onto her seat. She motioned to Alysa, who wasted not a moment going to her. Alysa gestured reverence by opening her hands palms-up and lowering her gaze to the floor. Such respect was paid to all Folk of rank.

Kendira said, "It's been some time since we've talked, youngling."

Alysa looked away, uneasy, unable to escape Kendira's questioning, dark-gray eyes. "Teller Kendira, it was not my intention to avoid..."

"Come to my cottage after this eve's Gathering. We will talk then," Kendira commanded, squinting intently into Alysa's brown eyes.

Alysa nodded and Kendira waved her off. Alysa backed away palms-up and went to her mother.

"Ho, Mother..." But Loralle was not aware that Alysa was at her side; nor did she hear her greeting. Alysa bent down and kissed her mother on top of her head and stroked her spicenut-colored braid.

Ellee rushed up and hugged her mother, but Loralle did not respond. "Oh, Mother, wasn't that the best ever story about Father Gord'n?" Ellee squatted and picked up a split reed. Her long braid, the same color as her mother's, fell in front of her. She flung it over her back. "I'm nearly old enough to learn baskets, Mother. Will you show me? I can sit right next to you!" Receiving no response from Loralle, Ellee's blue eyes turned sad.

Alysa bent down and placed an arm around Loralle's thin shoulders. She looked into her mother's tired, distant face. Loralle stopped working and stared at her hands. Ellee pouted, and Alysa gathered her with the other arm.

A memory came to Alysa's mind of a happier sun, when they were still a family — when her father was alive. Ellee, then a wobbly, was taking her first steps by herself. The family was playing a game in which Abso hid a small toy in his hand. They were having good fun watching Ellee figure out which hand it was in. Abso was delighted when she picked the correct one. He threw a joyful arm around Loralle.

Alysa recalled her father's words that sun. With pride he remarked, "Ellee is almost as keen as you were at this age, Alysa. Have you been teaching her some of your tricks, Daughter?" They all laughed at his observation. They laughed a lot back then. Her thoughts returned to the not-so-happy present. She said to Ellee, "Soon, Sister. Mother will teach you basket-making soon."

Comforted for the moment, Ellee skipped off to play with her friends.

It was apparent that Loralle was still unable to accept Abso's death. He was her lifelong partner, betrothed almost since infancy. They considered themselves a perfect match. Alysa whispered, "I know how much you miss him, Mother. Five moons just haven't been enough..."

She looked up and saw her clanswomen's sympathetic stares. They looked back to their work, but it was plain that they worried for Loralle. Alysa's throat tightened as her eyes filled with tears. She forced a smile through her fear, kissed her mother on the cheek, and hugged her close. To the women she nodded a silent, "Thank you."

THE HOMESTEAD WAY

Alysa's eyes stung as the frigid air hit her face. She blinked to clear her vision. It was difficult holding in her tears during her visit to the Great Hall. She pulled up her hood as Ellee did, not only to keep warm, but to conceal from anyone else they met the sadness she felt for her mother.

Luckily the only people they encountered as they entered the Pantry behind the Great Hall were a few men who chatted as they gathered provisions. They paid the girls little notice.

The homestead Pantry was a little larger than a cottage. All four walls were lined with floor-to-ceiling shelves which held all types of lighter-weight and portioned items: small sacks of dried grains, beans, meal, fish, nuts, dried fruit and cured meat; tunics, smocks, cloaks, hats, mittens and boots; rugs, baskets and bedding. On the lower shelves were jars, bowls and lattice-front lanterns formed from local red clay. There were shelves holding folds of hides and fur, as well. All these items were necessary for survival or aided comfort in some way. A ladder leaned against the wall so that items on higher shelves could be reached.

On short floor racks rested bulging clay urns with spigots near their bottom front ends and wide, lidded filling funnels on top. Bulk milk, lamp oil, and large quantities of dried grains and beans ready for bagging were contained in these.

A stairway at the rear of the Pantry led to the root cellar. Alysa descended, with Ellee close behind. In the cellar burned a few lamps which illuminated yet more shelves and floor baskets which held root and vine vegetables, cheese and whole fruit. The girls picked up large cloth sacks. They selected small amounts of many items and put them into the sacks.

The men were gone by the time the girls went back upstairs. Alysa said, "What else is on our list?"

Ellee recalled, "Meal, beans, milk, lamp oil..."

"Oh," Alysa said, "I forgot to bring the empty milk jar. Well, we'll just have to borrow another one. Would you get the milk, Little Sister? I'll get the other things."

"Yes, Thitha." Ellee lifted a jar from a shelf, removed the wooden stopper, placed it under the large milk urn's spigot, and turned the handle. Milk streamed into the jar.

Alysa lifted the urn's funnel lid, looked in, and smiled. "Good, there's some cream left!" She removed a small ladle from a hook on the wall, dipped it into the funnel and withdrew a large, soft lump of cream. She dropped it into Ellee's jar and returned the ladle to the hook.

Next, Alysa picked up a small jar of lamp oil and checked the stopper to be certain the wax seal was solid. As she put it into her bag, she remembered, "Oh, a twist of wicking," and reached with an instinctive hand to the place where wicking could usually be found. Finding the supply gone, she dragged the ladder over, climbed it, and put her hand into a basket on a higher shelf. She withdrew a handful of wicking, placed one in her bag and set the others in the empty space.

"Done, Thitha," Ellee said, clutching the stoppered milk jar in her arms.

Both girls were laden with provisions as they left the Pantry. They passed many yards on the way home. Alysa gazed into the distance, thinking how lonely their cottage looked sitting so far across the terrace and not at all close to any of the others.

They passed several people as they walked home through the bright, wintertide light. Evyn, the widowed Miller, passed them on his way to the Pantry. His beard was dusted yellow. He bore a large packbasket of flour on his back. Its hide straps were twisted around his strong hands. His three young daughters trailed behind him like casish chicks.

"Ho, young ones!" he said to the sisters, smiling as he passed. "How is your mother coming along?"

Ellee looked sad.

Alysa hugged her to her side and fibbed, "Very well, Evyn." To elaborate on Loralle's lack of progress would be much too painful.

"That's wonderful, just wonderful!" he said sincerely. "And I hope she continues to feel better with each dawning. Take care of yourselves, girls, and your mother. Come, Daughters!" And they were on their way again.

Alysa knew that Evyn detected her lie. He was close to her parents, so she knew him all her life. She was thankful for his kindness in allowing her to fib. Having lost his wife during the birth of their third daughter, Evyn seemed to be more sensitive to her family's plight than were others.

The sisters passed the gate to Seda's yard. Seda's father and brother carried armloads of wood into their cottage. Seda, now grown into a robust, redheaded young woman, rushed out the door just after her father and brother went in. As she ran down the path to the gate, she gushed, "Ho, Alysa! Ho, Little Sister! Father said he saw you coming up the way. I'm so excited I forgot to throw on my cloak! Moons above, it's cold! Wait, I'll walk with you..."

Alysa and Ellee looked at each other as Seda ran back to the cottage. They shrugged their shoulders and smiled; the news sounded happy.

Seda returned with a cloak hastily thrown around her and walked with the sisters. "Elder Tola came to see my parents last night. You'll never guess what happened!"

Again the sisters looked at each other and shrugged. Alysa said, "Well, tell us!"

Seda grinned, excitement glowing in her blue eyes. "The Councils of High Point and Falling Stream Homesteads have decreed that Aryz and I will be joined!" Alysa halted, staring in surprise and delight. Seda giggled, "Isn't it amazing? Now we can be certain that you and I will join with men from the same homestead. You and I are best friends and Aryz and Orryn are best friends...it's going to be so perfect! After you and Orryn join next leaffall, all four of us will be together!"

Alysa shook her head sadly then managed to brighten. "Yes, I can hardly believe it, either. It's such good fortune, Seda. I'm very happy for you and Aryz. On which Moonsfest did the Councils consent to your joining?"

Dreamily Seda answered, "This coming Greening Moonsfest! I wasn't certain it was going to happen this cycle, but now I know for certain. How I wish we could join tomorrow!"

Seda's burst of glee was contagious. Alysa put her troubled thoughts aside. She wanted to embrace her friend, but her arms were full. Seda saw this and threw her arms around both of them. They giggled.

Alysa said, "I wish you all the happiness a girl — no, a *woman* — could possibly dream of, Seda. I know you and Aryz will be very happy." Then she added with a grin, "And you will, of course, name one of your younglings after me!"

"Of course, silly. You know I will! But I'll reserve your name for just the *right* newborn. Any old newborn will just not do!" They laughed. "But first, there must be a joining." She stopped and pulled Alysa around to face her, continuing seriously. "I would like you — as my best and most cherished friend, and also because I have no sister — to carry Aryz's joining sash for me."

"I would think it an honor, Seda. I will gladly carry the sash!"

The girls embraced again, tears of joy filling their eyes. Seda sniffled, "Got to go. Chores to do." She turned to run back down the path.

"Oh, and see you tonight," Alysa teased, "that is, *if* you can keep your thoughts straight enough to remember to go to Gathering…"

Seda whirled around with a look of astonishment on her face. "Are you joking? I want to be the one to tell the whole of High Point!"

"You haven't told Erindi or Malores or any of the other girls yet?"

"No, you were the first, of course! I'm keeping it secret until tonight…so don't either of you tell anybody else, all right?"

Alysa laughed. "We won't, Seda. See you tonight!"

"See you!" Seda waved and ran home, sliding and giggling down the path. The sisters continued on their way.

Seda's happiness meant a lot to Alysa, particularly since Abso's death. During that terrible time, Alysa confided much in her. Her friend never told her how she should feel about the loss of her father, as some of the others did, offering useless advice such as, "Alysa, you must be strong." "You have to grow up now, Alysa." "The final farewell comes to us all one sun." She thought at the time how easy it seemed for others to say those things; but Seda never did. She just listened, hugged Alysa when she cried, ignored her tantrums, and was simply with her when she needed her to be. Seda was a good and true friend.

Ellee lisped, "I'm happy for Theda; but I'm sad, too."

"Why are you sad, Sister?"

"Because Theda will be gone from High Point. And then you'll be gone. And then I'll be all alone."

"Oh, Ellee..." Alysa stepped in front of her, stopping her short. "Girls leaving is the way of things. You know that! And you will never be alone; Mother will be here."

"Will she?"

"Yes, she will. And just because women leave their homesteads, it doesn't mean they won't ever see their families again. Who knows? Maybe you'll join a man from Falling Stream when you grow up, too. Then all of us girls will be together!"

Ellee sighed.

Alysa gave her an encouraging smile. "We must save such worries for another sun." She cupped her hand to her ear. "Oh...oh...listen!"

"What?" Ellee said, looking around.

"I hear our chores calling..."

"Oh, Thitha...!"

The sisters arrived at their snow-covered cottage and walked across the yard between piles of snow and a few short, stocky nut trees. The casish hens screeched and scattered before them. Alysa pushed the entryway door open.

Suddenly, three small, furry creatures flew at them, touching down for the shortest moment on Alysa's shoulder or on Ellee's head as they escaped the cottage, then sprang away as high and as far as they could—just for fun.

Alysa shouted, "Ho, Tahshi!"

Ellee squealed, "Feelah! Como! You silly little saroos!" They watched the antics of their tan and gray pet saroos as they bounced off the cottage and yard walls, chattering and scampering the casish hens into a frenzy, relieving themselves, and eventually settling into the nut trees. Some nuts stubbornly clung to the branches. Although they hung far out on slender tips, the saroos could easily reach them. They coiled their long, ringed tails around the branches for a tight hold. Tahshi hung upside down in just this way, happily chewing through a hard nut with his tiny sharp teeth.

Their short, rounded, dark ears flicked about as they listened to the noises of the outdoors. Their wide, red eyes focused on their nuts. Occasionally they looked up from their work, paused their chewing and stared in the direction of a sound that neither of the girls were able to hear. The saroos returned to gnawing on their nuts when they decided the sound was of no matter.

The saroos were small enough to carry in a pouch but large enough to keep the cottage clear of crawling insects. After being locked inside all sun, they looked forward to playing outside; but despite their fur, their tolerance to cold was low.

The girls entered the cottage and set their bags of provisions on a bench in the entryway. In the dim sconce-light, they hung their cloaks on pegs and exchanged them for hooded working jackets. They pulled on thick-knitted leggings beneath their skirts and put on heavy mittens.

Alysa gave a handled basket to Ellee. They picked up brooms and opened the door. The saroos bounced back through the doorway, chattering and slapping their paws over their tiny, flat, black noses, apparently complaining about the cold. Alysa laughed and cracked open the inside door. Shivering, the saroos tumbled over each other as they scrambled inside.

The girls went outside. They swept drifted snow from the main path and from the path that allowed access to the firewood, which half a cycle ago their father stacked against the cottage. There was little wood left at this time in the season. Some of the logs were frozen together. Alysa knocked pieces loose with the end of her broom. She arranged them in a short pile as Ellee gathered bits of kindling into the basket.

From the other side of the yard wall, a young man called, "Ho, Alysa! Can I get that for you?"

She looked up, as at first she did not recognize Betram's voice. It seemed deeper than she recalled. She said, "Ho, Betram. Yes, that would be wonderful!"

"Ho, Ellee."

"Ho, Bet."

Since Abso's death, this stocky, black-haired boy two cycles younger than Alysa, and nearly a head taller than she, often stopped by to assist with the heavier work. Bet was an Apprentice Teller, one of Kendira's most promising students. He was nearing the end of his Teller training. It was planned that he would take her place as Major Teller one sun.

Alysa noticed a wisp of dark beard growing on the young man's chin. This was the first time she recalled seeing facial hair on him. She looked into his sharp, brown eyes. They seemed to express a maturity that was not there before. He was growing up, no longer a youngling. He was now a midling, as she was. But seldom did adults refer to them as midlings, as if calling them younglings would keep them so.

Bet entered the yard, hefted the pile of wood, and took it inside. He returned for a second load and returned, ready for another task.

"We must draw water," Alysa said. "The jar's nearly empty."

As it was her ongoing duty, Ellee ran inside to retrieve the bucket, kept indoors to keep the rope and handle from freezing. Betram pushed the square plank cover off the well's low foundation. Alysa stuck in a pole and smashed through the icy skin. Ellee returned with the bucket and lowered it into the water. As she was unable to pull the brimming bucket up by herself, Betram took hold of the rope and helped her haul it to the top. He removed the bucket and set it in the hallway, went back to the well, and slid the cover on.

Alysa said, "Thank you, Bet. We can manage the rest of the chores. You must have plenty to do at Kendira's."

"That I do! Be by tomorrow then." He sauntered down the path.

Continuing their chores, the sisters tidied the wood stack, scattered meal for the hens, and added straw to the hencoop. Alysa found some eggs. "Look, four today!" Ellee held out her mittened hands, and Alysa carefully placed the eggs into them.

Chores finished, the girls were about to enter the cottage. Suddenly a noisy flock of birds passed overhead. The sound was cacophonous, much like many flutes playing different melodies all at once, but joyous nonetheless.

Alysa said, "Look, Ellee, the longpipers are returning. Greening will soon be upon us!"

The migrating flocks of these large, long-bodied birds flew north, where it was thought they spent the warm months in Winding Mountains, and possibly beyond. The birds never landed in the homesteads, even upon the lakes, as far as anyone knew. Their undersides were easily recognizable, having bold, black stripes across creamy-white bellies and under wings; since nobody ever saw them on the ground, how they were patterned on top was a mystery.

Giggling, the girls entered the hallway, warmed once by all the work they did, and warmed a second time by the renewed hope of greening's approach.

Ellee set the eggs on the bench. Alysa tossed her mittens into a basket on the floor and removed her outerwear, which she hung on pegs along the wall. She slipped her feet into slippers and rubbed her hands together to warm them. Ellee fumbled with the toggles on her jacket.

"Need help, Ellee?"

Ellee sniffled, "I can do it myself, Thitha."

"All right. Are you numb anywhere?"

"Just my toes, but not real bad."

"Hurry in, then. Your milk will be waiting. Oh, and it's your turn to bring in the provisions, Sister."

Lugging the bucket in one hand and the milk jar in the other, Alysa entered the dim, cozy warmth of the cottage's main room and pushed the door closed with her foot. She set the milk jar on the floor and emptied the bucket of water into a large clay vessel sitting beside the hearth, which sat in the center of the room. Most of the raised hearth was enclosed, open only toward the front and rear of the room.

All three of the saroos were nestled together in a fur-lined basket on the other side of the hearth. Their peaceful state was a stark contrast to their antics just a short while before. One of the saroos yawned, licked one of its long, dark paws, and snuggled its black nose back into the soft belly of one of the others.

Alysa lifted a few pieces of wood from the pile Betram had stacked and placed them on the embers. The wood blazed, sending sparks up the tapering, sooty stone chimney. She stuck a small piece of kindling in the hearth until it caught fire, and lit three lamps hanging from ceiling beams. Positioned at various places around the room, the lamps' warm light dispersed the shadows.

The light revealed a short outer wall of stone and mortar. On top of the wall, vertical logs formed upper walls twice Alysa's height. Many long, heavy support posts were anchored around the tops of the log walls. The posts angled toward the middle of the room and were fitted into chiseled spaces in the central roof beam.

The chimney pierced the roof to one side of the beam. The roof was covered with layers of a thick type of bark resistant to catching fire from sparks. The bark was fixed to the support posts by wooden pegs and pitch. The roof protected the family from the harshest of storms. Deep snow on the rooftop sheltered them from the wind and helped keep the heat in. Window shutters, concealed beneath thick-woven curtains, helped keep the drafts out.

Alysa brought the milk jar to the large work table which sat on the left side of the room and poured some milk into a clay bowl. The cream spilled out with it. She took a wooden spoon from a drawer beneath the table, scooped out the cream, and rested the spoon on the table.

She placed the bowl of milk near the fire and jumped onto the rocking bench facing the hearth. Not wasting a moment, she pulled the fur blanket off the back and wrapped it around herself. It was a pleasure to just sit for a few moments and warm her toes before beginning the remaining chores.

Placed about the large room were fine Folk-crafted pieces of furniture. Of solid construction, much of what filled the cottage was passed down through the generations. Polished, curve-backed chairs were tucked around the work table. Several woven rugs placed together across the plank floor buffered stocking feet from the cold; the brightly dyed yarns added warmth of their own.

On the right side of the room sat a small loom with warps and wefts of an unfinished rug stretched across the frame. Loralle started it before Abso's death, but as yet did possess the will to finish it.

Sleeping nooks, raised a few steps off the floor and accessed by short ladders, were built into the four corners of the cottage. Each nook was flanked by a pair of curtains that could be drawn across for privacy or for warmth.

Wondering what was keeping her sister, Alysa hollered, "Ho, Ellee! Are you all right? What's taking so long?"

Ellee's muffled lisp came from behind the door. "The string in my hood got all tangled and I'm getting it out!"

"You could bring it in here, Little Sister..."

"Almost...got it..."

Alysa shook her head, snuggled back, and closed her eyes.

This cottage was a little larger than most. Rather than refurbish one of the older ones, Abso built this larger one when he and Loralle joined. Optimism that they would bring many younglings into the world prompted him to build one with four sleeping nooks. Three nooks, after all, turned out to be plenty. Her parents had a nook to themselves, which was, of course, tradition. The girls had their own and were required to share with other relatives only when they visited at Moonsfest, and only if there was need beyond the spare sleeping nook.

Familiar objects hung on the log walls: carvings of leaprock lambs, Alysa's tomoree game board, Ellee's lyre, and a small Planting Calendar. On the mantel above the hearth, a set of white clay jars belonging to Loralle held sweet herbs for refreshing the air and to use as remedies for illness. Abso molded the jars from clay he brought all the way from Yellow Cliffs, the homestead of Loralle's birth. He pressed a type of leaf found in Yellow Cliffs into the clay when it was still damp, which left impressions that he stained dark so the leaf patterns would stand out. He gave the jars to Loralle when they joined. She treasured the gift, as they reminded her of her girlhood home.

The most prized possession in the cottage was a large wooden box centered on the mantel. Abso often took it down to show to the girls, and he never missed a chance to boast about the fine workmanship.

Abso was the Major Trader — one of the best, many said — and he negotiated the box from the Trailmen long cycles ago, before Alysa was born. A relief of a berry branch was carved on the lid, and stains made from wild plants were added to make the design lifelike; the berries looked ripe enough for picking. Abso said it was crafted by a Trailmen. When they examined it together, Alysa remembered her father's comments of wonder, as he always thought himself to be a passable carver. But when he came into possession of the box, he admitted that he was not even close to being as skilled as the one who created it. Alysa found it difficult to imagine that a Painted One was able to carve something that beautiful and often wondered how a savage could be capable of such a glorious creation.

She was about to rise to check on her sister, when Ellee finally entered with the kindling basket. She set it near the hearth then went back to the hallway for the provisions. It took her two trips to bring in the provisions, and a third to fetch the eggs.

Ellee set everything on the table, plopped down on the bench beside Alysa, and flexed and stretched her toes and fingers toward the hearth. Sighing, Ellee remarked, "Oh, this feels so good! I like doing outside chores, 'cause when I come in it's so nice to sit by the fire."

Alysa laughed. "If you like doing outside chores so well, you can do mine, too. I wouldn't mind."

"Oh, Thitha, you're so silly! I don't like coming in from the cold *that* much."

Alysa retrieved the bowl from the hearth and poured the warm milk into two cups. She handed one to Ellee, picked up two pieces of simmel cake from a baking stone on the side of the hearth, and sat on the bench. She handed a piece to Ellee and drew the blanket around them. They snuggled and giggled and sipped and munched.

Alysa said, "When we're done with our snack and your toes are thawed out, would you help me make supper? Then we'll have time before Mother gets home to do needlework. How does that sound?"

"Oh, good! I want to learn the stitch you were doing the other night, on the sash you're giving Orryn at your joining."

Hopefully, Alysa's joining *would* still be taking place as planned. Lucky Seda. Things worked out well for her. Alysa was truly over-joyed that Seda's betrothal to her perfect match a few cycles before was going to become permanent. Aryz recently finished his field learning, and his parents announced their readiness to take Seda into Falling Stream Homestead. They already secured a cottage for the couple near their own.

Alysa returned to the task at hand, the preparation of the evening meal. "Well, little one, what will it be? Stew?"

"Yes, stew!"

"Then we'd better get started so there's time left for needlework." Alysa drained her mug and rose. Ellee emptied hers and licked the last pieces of cake from her fingertips.

Alysa picked up some of the provisions and stepped into the pantry off one side of the dim back hallway. Ellee picked up the rest and followed. They set their cups in the wooden dry sink and put the supplies away. Ellee opened the door to the privy on the opposite side of the hallway, went inside and closed it.

Alysa scanned the pantry shelves that held clay jars, sacks and baskets, just enough to feed a family for a few suns. She removed a wooden bowl from a shelf, picked handfuls of sweetroot and various dried vegetables from baskets, and put them into the bowl. She added a few strips of meat and plucked sprigs of herbs from bundles hanging from pegs on the wall. She poured water from a pitcher into her hands to rinse them.

Carrying two cutting boards, she went to the table and sat down in one of the curved-back chairs. From a drawer in the side of the table, she withdrew a small bundle of fabric tied with a string and unrolled it. Inside were two small antler-handled blades. She removed them and set them on the table. Ellee reentered.

"Hands..." Alysa said.

Ellee returned to the dry sink and rinsed her hands. She then sat beside her big sister. The girls peeled and cut the ingredients, placing the pieces into a clay kettle.

A saroo sleepily climbed out of the basket and made its way to Ellee. It climbed up the outside of her skirt, coiled in her lap, and patiently stared up at her. "Como has come to see me. Here, Como." She gave him a peeling, which he gently took in his tiny, dark fingers and began to nibble.

Ellee hummed a tune that she and her big sister had sung together many times. For a youngling, her voice displayed great skill. Despite her lisp when she talked, each word was clear as she sang the words on the next round:

> "Planter Parsis went to the well.
> What was down there? He couldn't tell.
> He dropped his pail in, down it went.
> When he pulled it up, he breathed a bad scent."

Alysa joined in:

> "Five small spotted stinks jumped on him then,
> And chased him all the way down the glen.
> There's one thing that you can tell,
> He never returned to that stinky well!"

The girls giggled. How they loved that simple, silly song!

Alysa added the last of the vegetables, some tiny dried beans, the cream and three eggs, stirred everything together, and hung the kettle on a hook over the flames. She returned to the table and carefully wiped the blades, rolled them up in the fabric, and put them back in the drawer. She removed the rest of the implements and set them in the dry sink, poured water into her hands to rinse them, and dried them on a towel.

Alysa looked excitedly at Ellee and announced, "Needlework! Wash your hands first…"

Ellee lifted Como out of her lap, rose from the table, and tucked him into the basket with his two friends. She quickly washed her hands, skipped to her front-corner sleeping nook, and went to the bench with a small basket of colored threads and cloth. She was working on an embroidered pillow, a surprise gift she planned to give to her mother at Greening Moonsfest.

Alysa went to her own nook and removed a lidded box from a shelf. She handled it carefully, with reverence. She returned to the bench and sat beside her sister, opened the box, and removed coils of thread and a small pillow stuck with slim bone needles. She withdrew the long sash she would give Orryn to wear at their joining. Nearly finished, she had worked on it for two cycles.

The number and complexity of stitches proved that great effort went into its making. Alysa spun the threads herself and dyed them with flowers, bark and leaves her father brought her from Trade. She even wove the base cloth. The skills she used to make this gift were those all women were expected to master.

Alysa picked out a needle and threaded it.

"How will you know when it's done, Thitha?"

"I guess when it's time for the joining and then there's no more time to work on it."

"You mean you keep putting more and more stitches on, forever and ever, until the joining?"

"Well, I hope it's not going to be forever and ever, Ellee!"

Tradition required joinings to take place just twice each cycle, at either Greening or Leaffall Moonsfest. Orryn's training would be completed by summering. Their joining was set for leaffall. Alysa hoped her mother would be better by then so she could leave without worry.

Alysa focused on helping Ellee. "Which new stitch do you want to learn, Little Sister?"

Ellee pointed to a row of delicate needlework on Alysa's sash. "This one, the one in golden thread. What do you call it?"

"It's grain stalks, end-to-end. See?" Alysa turned the sash so that Ellee could study the pattern with the correct orientation. "It would mean that I wish my husband success in the fields, if he were a planter. The meaning I give to it, because Orryn's going to be a Teller, is to wish him luck in...growing younglings. And I used another stitch—this one—just for Tellers. This one, in the blue thread. It's Winding Mountains, and it stands for the stories of Father Gord'n that Orryn tells. But most of the patterns do have something to do with growing or harvesting."

Ellee regarded the sash their mother gave their father at their joining, which hung on the wall of Loralle's nook. "Is the growing stitch on Fathers sash?"

"No, Ellee. Mother used a different stitch on his; not one used for growing, but one used only for Trader husbands-to-be. I'll show you." She retrieved the sash from her mother's nook. The colors were faded from age. She handled it with great care. Hiding her sadness, she held it so her sister could see. "Look closely. It's a basket stitch. Baskets are used to carry the goods that are traded to the Trailmen. You don't see that one very often because there are so few Traders and because their duty is so very special. Traders don't take as much part in growing or harvesting crops as most everyone else does. So instead of grain stalks, the basket stitch is used as a symbol for their duty."

Ellee nodded. "Is there a stitch for every kind of work people do? Like millers or spinners?"

"No, just for the duties of Traders and Tellers."

"Why?"

"I don't know why, Sister. That's just how it is. Although, I haven't heard of a Law against creating a new stitch..."

Ellee was the only person Alysa allowed to see Orryn's sash. She would carry it at Alysa's joining rite. Ellee took the sash from Alysa's hands and examined the many stitches and colors flowing from one end to the other. With admiration for her big sister, she said, "You must love him a lot, Thitha."

Alysa opened her mouth to respond, but found she had no voice. What Ellee said caught her by surprise, because Ellee did not ordinarily make such comments; but Alysa was perplexed by her inability to answer at once. "Yes," was the only word that rose to her lips.

Alysa carefully returned her father's sash to the wall of her mother's nook and went to her own. She climbed up and sank onto the deep bedding and lay back, disconcerted by her short, hesitant response. She stared up at the ceiling, seeming to look through rather than at it. She wondered why any question should linger in her mind as to how she felt about Orryn. She thought she loved him. She thought she wanted to join with him. Maybe this was the first time she had considered her true feelings.

Orryn was a very gentle, kind young man and also bright. He was one of only a few chosen from this generation to become a Teller. It was a true honor to be picked while still a very young boy by Bakar, the Major Teller of Falling Stream. Weren't Orryn's goodness and position reasons enough to love him and want to join with him? Questions spun through her mind. Didn't she want to dedicate her life to him, as her mother did her father? Bear his younglings gladly?

A girl of seventeen cycles could only imagine what being joined would be like. Most of what she knew she learned by her parents' example—how they behaved toward each other, managed their home, and raised her and her sister. She knew how much her mother loved her father; but Alysa was unsure that she felt as strongly about Orryn. Maybe she would feel that way for him later, once they were joined.

There were stories told by her friends during picnics on summering afternoons in recent cycles; bits and pieces they gleaned from older joined sisters, and sometimes from their mothers, about intimacies between husband and wife. Some facets of loving sounded wonderful—others, quite dreadful.

But how was she to know if she would like being joined to Orryn? The dissolution of betrothals was allowed by the clan, but it was frowned upon. It sometimes happened that a couple would choose to break their betrothal promise, but such occurrences were rare. Betrothal agreements were often made between parents soon after a newborn's birth; finding a new partner at a more advanced age was difficult. Once a couple was joined they were never allowed to part. If she found that she was not happy after she and Orryn were joined—then it would be too late.

She closed her eyes and imagined Orryn stretched out beside her on a cold eve such as this. She could almost feel his arms encircling her bare shoulders as they faced each other. She could see him gazing into her eyes with his, large and dark, and pulling her close...

The image vanished as she gasped and sat upright. Her heart raced and she felt ill, off balance. She knew nothing about shared intimacies. She had no such experience! She quickly made up her mind that it mattered little what she imagined being joined to be like; time would be her teacher. At the same time she thought this, she felt a pang of uncertainty, but she could not locate its source. She could only tell that it did not seem to originate in her mind. This conflict troubled her. She willed the conflict out of her mind and thought, *I will love Orryn, no matter what!*

She descended from her nook, steadied herself and returned to her seat beside Ellee. Ellee handed the sash back to her and said, "I think I can do it, Thitha." And she set to work replicating the stitch on her pillow.

For a long time Alysa contemplated Orryn's sash. She folded it, laid it back in the box, and replaced the lid. She sighed.

Ellee finished a few groupings of the stitch. "There, how's that for my first time?"

Alysa focused on the stitches and encouraged, "Very good, Sister." She rose and went to the hearth and probed the stew with a wooden spoon. One of the saroos lifted its head from the furry clump in the basket on the hearth. "The roots aren't done yet, but it won't be long." She added wood to the fire. "I'll watch for Mother. One of the crafters is seeing her home."

In the front hallway, Alysa removed her shawl from a peg and threw it over her shoulders. Before she could close the door behind her, one of the saroos scampered through. It ran up the outside of her skirt and crawled beneath her shawl, wrapped its tail around her neck and, softly chattering, clung to her shoulder.

"Ho, little Tahshi," Alysa said, reaching up to scratch his ears.

She lit a straw at the sconce and inserted it into a clay lantern's latticework. The wick burst to life. She opened the front door. The sky was dusky-purple. She hung the glowing lantern on the stoop and, shivering, leaned against the doorpost to watch for her mother.

One by one, twinkles of light appeared across the terrace as other welcoming lanterns were hung out. The smoke from many chimneys coiled up, up until dispersed by the high breezes. Alysa's troubled thoughts floated up with the smoke.

THE GATHERING

The interior of the Great Hall was filled with the voices of 'steaders. Their chatter was merry at this first large Gathering since leaffall. Most were too busy with their homestead duties to visit, so an accumulation of wintertide news was being shared. The room was jammed with people of all ages. Most of the four hundred and seventy-eight High Point Folk, including younglings of all ages, were present.

Older boys climbed up to the overhead beams that spanned the width of the Great Hall, gaining the best view of the event. A mother of one of the younger boys scolded him to descend, as she thought he was much too young to be climbing so high. Of course the youngling didn't think so and pouted as his father lifted him down.

Clusters of men were engaged in conversations. Hearty laughter broke out in one of the groups, and one of the men, trying to control his outburst, wiped a tear from his eye. The women and girls talked in quieter groups. Younglings played and chased each other or hid behind their mother's smocks, depending on their age and degree of shyness.

The aroma of simmel cakes baked earlier lent a festive air. Trays were handed around and slices of yellow cake disappeared as each hand took a piece. Steaming cups of fruity drink were passed.

Stacks of slates rested on a long table positioned beneath the large Planting Calendar. Hanging high on the wall, the ornate calendar was the most prominent feature in the Great Hall. Although decorative, its importance was in marking the suns and moons over the course of a cycle. It was the guide by which the Field Folk maintained rhythm with the seasons.

The calendar was divided into quadrants, with the name of each season carved into each. The top quadrant was labeled "greening," followed on the right by "summering," "leaffall" at the bottom, and "wintertide" on the left. The center of the calendar contained the golden sun, called "Tabir-sun" by the Folk. Each of its sixteen rays divided the seasons into moons. Surrounding the sun were star clusters painted in blue. The most prominent clusters visible in the night sky at the time of each moon were painted in the appropriate locations on the calendar. The Roaming Star appeared twice on the calendar, as it passed over two times during the course of a cycle.

Around the circumference beneath the labels, in the marks indicating each sun, were holes; one for each of the three hundred thirty-six suns in the cycle. Early each sun, the peg was advanced to the next hole. A large, red peg marked this sun—the twenty-first sun of the sixteenth moon—the last sun of wintertide.

Once the cups were drained and the cakes were eaten, the bearded Council Elders, each wearing a gray robe worn only at Gatherings, took seats at the long table. Gray-haired, short-bearded Tola, Council Speaker and primary leader of the homestead, picked up a slate. He called the meeting to order.

"Ho! Welcome!" he said in his loud, rasping voice. His patient, aging gray eyes watched as everyone settled into their seats. "It's good to see you all here tonight on the eve of the Gathering Moon, the last moon of wintertide and the first moon of the new cycle, thank Father Gord'n! Did anyone happen to see the longpipers earlier this sun?"

The crowd clapped and cheered.

Tola nodded. "Yes, they are a welcome sight this time of cycle!"

He held up a hand to quiet them and continued, "I doubt that I am alone in thinking that the last two moons after the Roaming Star passes are the longest in the whole cycle!" The gathering laughed and grumbled in agreement. "Please take your seats and we will begin."

The 'steaders unstacked stools and benches stored against the walls and arranged several rows in a semi-circle facing the Council table. Families sat together, wobblies and small younglings climbing into laps. Alysa found seats and placed Ellee between herself and her mother. She noticed that Loralle seemed more alert this eve and remembered that she always very much enjoyed Gatherings. Perhaps this would be a turning point in her mother's recovery.

Kendira limped in, a cold breeze flowing behind her. She hobbled to a hearth and stood before a young man seated on a crowded bench. With her staff she poked him in the arm and glared at him. Without questioning, he understood what she desired. Rubbing his arm where she poked him, he rose and backed away, palms-up, and

45

found a place to stand against the wall. She sat down and clutched her shawl about her.

Soon everyone was settled. Tola continued, "The topics for this eve are: number one, organizing and scheduling the coming season's teams; two, call for an apprentice; three, Moonsfest preparations; and four, an announcement from a very happy family."

Seda, seated with her family, looked at Alysa. They exchanged wide, secret grins.

Tola continued, "Elder Levin will take over this portion of the meeting to enlist workers for the coming season."

Levin, an intense dark man, stood up. His white-streaked beard reached down to his waist. Reading from a slate, he said, "Last harvest's seed is still being separated. We will have a count soon. Planting will commence one moon after Moonsfest. By my calculation, planting will be somewhat earlier this cycle than the last several. The longer growing season will increase the yield. Because we must start early this season, I need workers to organize planting groups well in advance."

Alysa scanned the faces arcing to either side of her. There was never trouble finding people to work the fields. Those who possessed no duties of high responsibility, such as Kendira as homestead historian or Evyn as lead miller, dedicated their lives to the fields. Planting the many types of crops, pruning fruit trees, keeping drainage ditches clear of brush, and maintaining terrace walls and planting tools offered enough variety to keep most Folk feeling useful.

Several hands darted into the air. These same men offered themselves to be field leaders every season. Alysa admired them. Once she was joined and settled at Orryn's homestead, she hoped to find something special in herself to offer the clan. This coming season she would serve in the fields, as usual, doing whatever was needed.

Levin made notations on his slate and concluded, "All those with hands raised, see me following the Gathering and we will arrange a meeting at a time agreed upon by all."

Nodding in approval, Tola signaled another Elder to speak as Levin sat. The four remaining Council Elders bid for assistance in the herding, milling, textile and craft domains. Animated bidding involved the whole gathering, with people jumping up from their seats to be seen and counted into the areas of work that interested them. It was not long before decisions were made as to who would lead the teams.

When the appointments were completed, lively chatter again erupted from the crowd. Tola rose and waited for them to settle then announced, "As you all well know, we have need of a Lesser Trader."

The crowd fell silent, in stark contrast to their previous gaiety. Joyful expressions changed to sad or pensive ones; in general, the folk looked uneasy at mention of this topic.

"Since our Abso's fatal mishap just two suns prior to last Trade, we've yet to find a substitute to work alongside Boshe, recently appointed Major Trader in Abso's stead, and of course, Lesser Trader Panli."

Tola indicated Boshe and Panli, who stood straight and proud against the back wall. Nearly everyone turned to glance at them, many faces expressing awe and curiosity. Boshe's braid was black with streaks of gray; Panli's was a pale color and, despite a bald spot in the back of his head, his braid fell below his waist. As Traders, these two were the only men in the homesteads who possessed no beards. Generally taken on as a lifelong duty, Traders seldom needed replacing.

Tola continued, "We're still looking for one man—even a midling or a man not so young—who's willing to learn a new duty. *And* who is brave enough to face the Painted Ones."

Tola's green eyes passed over the Gathering. Nervous eyes darted away as he searched faces in the crowd. It was never an easy task to find a man willing to face the Trailmen, to extend himself to such an extreme. The obligation of appointing Traders fell to High Point due to the homestead's close proximity to the Trailmen's northern migration route. Perhaps there were men from other homesteads who would be willing to become Trader; but since the Laws required that Folk men dwell at the homesteads of their birth, they could not be considered.

Alysa knew Tola well. He visited their cottage many times; he and her father were boyhood friends and remained close throughout their lives. She was proud of her father and how he served the homestead. He never expressed any dissatisfaction in working with the Trailmen. Although he never stated it, he must have believed it was his duty to tolerate them for the benefit of the clan. She hoped a man would soon step forward. Until then, the clan must again struggle with just two Traders.

"Well," Tola sighed, "I know that some brave man will come forward in time. Let me emphasize that this duty is a most important one. It'll need to be occupied as soon as possible. There's an immediate need to commence training in preparation for Greening Trade." He paused, allowing another moment for someone to come forward in public; but no one did. "All right then. Let's move to the next topic of this Gathering — Greening Moonsfest."

With that statement, the 'steaders began a noisy whispering. The discussion of planting and milder weather to come was exciting enough. But the planning of Moonsfest signaled the certain arrival of the thaw in these frozen mountains.

The crowd quieted as Tola raised his palms. "We need to know who'll remain here for Moonsfest, who'll be visiting other homesteads and can offer use of cottages, and who'll host visiting families. There will, at this time, be five midlings — rather, young men — traveling to other homesteads for their joinings. You and your families have much to be proud of! Please stand, young men, so that we may recognize you one last time before your joining moons arrive...Hovlis, Carpalo. Mirtas...Flendin and Vorta!"

The crowd cheered as the awkward young men rose and tried not to blush at this public display. They nodded to the crowd and immediately sat down.

"In light of the vacancy of these homes due to their sons' joinings, there'll be more sleeping space for visitors. Of course, the betrothed women will host their intendeds and their families; but there are always relatives, friends and prospective husbands' families who need beds. To any who'd like a few suns of company or a chance to make new acquaintances — and, of course, gain the opportunity to determine some joining possibilities — please give your name to Elder Dagg, who's making a list of hosting offers."

Orryn and his mother and father, Bavat and Tach, always stayed at Alysa's cottage when they came to High Point. At those times Alysa shared her bed with Ellee so that Bavat and Tach had a bed, and Orryn, their only offspring, had one to himself.

Several small discussions began around the room as to who planned to go to other homesteads and who wanted to host. Other Moonsfest particulars were discussed: activities were planned, food requirements estimated, and decorating crews formed. There was never a shortage of women to prepare the feast or men to do the heavier chores, as the visitors traditionally lent themselves to the work.

With the preliminary Moonsfest details settled, Tola rose and held up a quieting hand. "I have a surprise to announce. We've an addition to the joinings of our beloved daughters Erindi, Betha, Vivon, Dori and Meriina at the coming Moonsfestivities…"

Squeals of joy erupted from these young women as they jumped out of their seats. Their parents shushed them and urged them to sit, though it was difficult for the excited girls to remain quiet. Everyone looked around, trying to determine who was being added to the group of women already planning to join.

They quieted as Tola held his arms out to Seda and her parents, motioning them to come to the front of the Gathering. They rose and wound their way through the throng of excited faces and joyful whispers to stand beside Tola. He pulled Seda to his side and looked into the anxious crowd. He said to Seda's parents, "Jac, Cara, would you like to make the announcement?"

"May I?" blurted Seda. Giggling and embarrassed, she clapped her hands over her mouth. Tola looked at her parents, who smiled and nodded. Seda blushed and nearly yelled, "The Councils have granted permission for Aryz of Falling Stream and me to join at Greening Moonsfest!"

The Gathering cheered. This brought the number of High Point joinings to six. Seda's face reddened further at the crowd's boisterous approval. Tola spoke words to Seda which were lost in the clamor, and he kissed her on the forehead. Her parents embraced and kissed her, also.

Tola said, "This joyous news brings the Gathering to a close. Those special teams needing to meet must get together before leaving tonight to clarify the calendar. Moonsfest is just a little over two moons distant, so we must get busy with the preparations. Remember that planting commences just one short moon after that. In the name of Father Gord'n, may you be content in all you do!"

Excited talk erupted as the Gathering broke. The boys jumped down from the beams to help the men return benches and stools to order along the walls. Women washed cups and stacked them in cupboards. The other betrothed girls ran to Seda and surrounded her, hugging her, all of them talking at once. As Alysa passed them, she watched but did not join in, feeling happiness for Seda, for her cousin Meriina and the other girls, but not feeling at all like she belonged in a celebration such as this until her own joining season was upon her.

Folk removed their cloaks from hooks in the hallways and began to file out. Wisps of fine snow curled through the open doors. The younglings screamed with delight; the grownups groaned. The talk of greening and Moonsfest made them forget that wintertide was not quite behind them.

Outside, halos of lamplight swung through the swirling snow. One by one, the lights floated off the main way to take their places on stoops. Loralle and Ellee went to Seda's cottage to visit with her family. Alysa assisted Kendira, who was frail on her arm. The Teller's cottage sat a short distance from the Great Hall.

Kendira's furnishings were sparse—just two chairs, a table, a cot placed near the hearth, two oil lamps, and a few fur blankets. A small carved replica of the Planting Calendar hung on the wall. Utensils were laid out on a shelf over the wooden dry sink: a few bowls, clay cups and spoons, and a small blade. The plank floor was bare and cold underfoot. But the hearth was warm.

Alysa did not remove her cape, as she did not plan to stay.

The old woman remarked, "It feels good to my old bones to sit and to sleep by the heat. It bakes the dampness from my sore joints."

She held her gnarled hands near the flames. "Would you like to sit, Alysa?"

"No, thank you. I'm going to Seda's to meet Mother and Ellee for the walk home."

A knock rattled the door and a young boy wrapped in a bulky cloak stuck his head in. "Need anything more tonight, Teller Kendira?" the eager boy asked.

"Why, yes, Fane, thank you. I'll need firewood for morning." The boy withdrew and closed the door. "The neighbor boy is so kind to this old woman." Kendira snickered. "I'm fairly certain that his parents want me to choose him for Teller training, although they have not yet approached me. Not a chance." She tapped her blue-veined temple. "Low memory capacity."

The boy reentered with an armload of wood and piled it next to the hearth. "Think that'll do it?"

"Yes, young Fane. Please thank your mother for the soup tonight. Tell her she's a very, very fine cook."

"Yes, I will, Teller Kendira. Well, g'night," he stammered then added in a rehearsed tone, "and…and thank you for the privilege!" He bowed, backed away palms-up, and closed the door.

Kendira shook her head. "One must have an exceptional memory for detail to be Teller," she confided. "Every Law, every bit of history must be passed on exactly as Father Gord'n recorded it or our whole society will be ruined. If I entrusted the responsibility to that boy, he would befuddle one hundred generations of history!"

Alysa nodded. "That would not be good!"

"The two currently in training, Betram and Thad, are doing quite nicely. There's no need for a third in his generation. Fane is suited for field work, nothing more. Not that I think field work is not valuable, mind you." She paused, an apologetic look at Alysa. "I mean no offense to your preference for field work, youngling. You understand."

"Yes, I understand. I take no offense, since you say you meant none."

"Yes…" Kendira paused; perhaps she did not expect any comment from the girl. "Now I have entrusted you with that bit of information about Fane, and I know you will keep it to yourself. Correct?"

Alysa nodded, astonished that Kendira felt the need to ask.

"Would you like some milk? I have some warming."

"No thank you, I have to leave…"

Kendira stretched to the shelf, took down a mug, and filled it with milk from a jar on the side of hearth. She sat with her back to the flames and said, "Please sit down, youngling. We must talk."

Alysa suppressed a sigh, dropped her hood, loosened her scarf, and sat on the hard chair opposite Kendira.

Kendira asked, "How well do you feel your mother's healing, Alysa?"

"Oh, she seems to be doing quite well…"

Kendira chuckled. "Come, come, youngling. I can see inside people, and I know that Loralle is still not well." With a stern look, she added, "And it's not helpful to lie to me; I can see through any fabrication you may devise to hide the truth. So tell me. How do you perceive your mother's condition?"

Looking past Kendira to the flames, Alysa sat motionless. She resisted answering, but Kendira's demand must be met. More than likely, the wise Teller would always command this power. It seemed as though she could see Alysa's thoughts. The girl wanted to leave the cottage, to run away from the sense of dread growing within her. Instead, she answered in a weak voice, "Mother's made little progress since Father's final farewell." She began to weep. "She cries herself to sleep every night. I hear her sobbing in her bed. Oh, Kendira, I feel so bad for her!"

Kendira cooed, "There, there, youngling. With your help and the help of Father Gord'n, she'll eventually heal. Here, I've something for you to consider."

Alysa dabbed her tears with her scarf.

Kendira set her mug down and placed her hands on Alysa's knees. "I would like to propose that, until your mother has recovered and is capable of taking care of herself and Ellee, you remain here at High Point."

Alysa's stomach clenched. She felt like she was going to vomit.

"Alysa, I think you should stay here, not join with Orryn. I have gone before the Council, and they are in agreement with me."

"What? Why talk of this so soon? Leaffall is more than half a cycle away! There is every hope that Mother will recover by then!"

"Youngling, just as the seasons change and we must plan around them, plans must also be made for every other eventuality."

"But all the other midlings my age are joined, or will be by this time next cycle—Seda, my cousin Meriina, Dori—there won't be any unjoined girls my age left to talk to at High Point!"

"Your mother needs you, Alysa. Nobody on this homestead can do for her what you can. And Ellee needs you. Your poor mother cannot take proper care of Ellee by herself. Think of your mother. Think of Ellee. Think of the homestead. It's what Father Gord'n expects."

Alysa was dumbfounded. Her breathing seemed to stop, and with it, the passage of time. She was stunned that they came to an important conclusion like this without including her in the discussion. Alysa accepted that her mother's needs were real. She felt she owed her mother care in return for what she received her whole life. She loved her mother and sister more than she could express. But did her needs, after all, mean nothing to Kendira, to the Council?

Her stomach churned as she began to recall bits of a conversation she overheard as a youngling. In her memory, late one night before she fell asleep she heard Abso telling Loralle how Kendira contributed to the reversal of a betrothal. It so affected the young couple that they ran off into the forest, never to be seen again. Of course this would never have been publicly discussed. No blame would have fallen to Kendira, as it would have been seen as a shameful error by the couple to have abandoned their homesteads. After that conversation, Alysa sensed sadness in her mother for a time. Perhaps this was the reason.

Was it possible that Kendira was scheming again? If so, her subtle skill in manipulating lives was apparent to Alysa for the first time. How often did Kendira sway her thinking in one direction or another, and to whose benefit? What was the extent of Kendira's will on the entire homestead? The purpose of Teller was to educate people about the past and the Laws, not to hold power over them. She thought, *It is not Kendira's duty to influence the Council! Meddling with people's lives is wrong!*

Spurred by Kendira's betrayal, Alysa's sadness changed to anger. This good friend, always trusted and in whom she confided throughout her life, discarded her opinions and feelings completely.

She jumped up and blurted, "I'll see the Council, ask them to let Orryn live here at High Point after we join and until Mother is well!"

Kendira was taken aback. "Oh, youngling, you know the Laws! A man must remain at his birth homestead. He cannot be away for extended spans of time. And since Orryn's Teller apprenticeship will soon be completed, this rule applies to an even greater extent for him. He's too important to be absent from Falling Stream. Major Teller Bakar is not much younger than I. So unless your mother makes a significant recovery, it will be impossible for you to be joined."

"Then Mother and Ellee can move with us to Falling Stream!"

Kendira laughed. "That, youngling, is inconceivable, and you know it! Loralle joined High Point from Yellow Cliffs and must forever dwell here. And Ellee must remain until her joining sun arrives and she goes to her husband's homestead. It's always been so. There can be no exceptions."

"Why not, Kendira? Why can't exceptions be made when there is good reason?"

Kendira looked incredulous. "Why? Because if allowances are made for you, then *everyone* will expect them! Besides, your reason is not good enough."

"Not *good* enough...? Says *who*?"

Kendira sat back and picked up her mug. The look on her face signaled her withdrawal from the discussion.

Appalled, Alysa backed away. She began the customary gesture of respect but did not complete it. She opened the door and left.

Kendira smiled and drank her milk.

Alysa ran into the snowy air. Without a lamp, the path was dim. She made her way toward the light on Seda's cottage. When she arrived she was still too angry about Kendira's decree to knock on the door. She sat on the icy stoop.

After a while, she noticed that the cold had seeped through her cloak. Shivering, she pulled her hood up and wrapped her scarf around her neck. As she stared through the fine, blowing snow, thoughts spun through her mind. Until this night she revered Kendira as all-wise and caring; but she no longer felt that reverence. Kendira had wronged her!

Perhaps Seda could help with this quandary and offer some advice. Yet Alysa didn't want her troubles to spoil her best friend's joy at this time. Since Alysa's feelings about Orryn were so confused, there was, at least, some relief at not joining with him as soon as was planned. Alysa realized she would not know how to begin this discussion with Seda. Maybe in a few suns, after she had time to sort out her feelings, she would know what to tell her.

The snow swirled ever more harshly around her—but this cold whirlwind was calm compared to the one that ravaged her heart.

A NEW APPRENTICE

A few suns had passed since Kendira thrust the life-changing decree upon Alysa. Since that night—thinking too much and becoming more confused the more she thought—Alysa drifted, unsettled, from one chore to the next. Still not finding a way to talk to Seda, Alysa's duties blurred together these last few suns—cooking, caring for the cottage, stocking the Pantry, spinning fiber in the Great Hall.

This sun she worked in the barns. None of what she did seemed to matter. She took little joy in any of her tasks. Within the lower barn, she emptied a basket of grain into a trough. Hungry leap-rock lambs trotted to the trough and stuck their narrow, large-eyed faces in to munch. They bleated as they crowded each other for position. Their bulky, white-furred bodies surrounded her, and she nudged them aside to get out of their way. She watched her feet to avoid being stepped on by their tiny, hard hooves.

She hung the feed basket on a peg and left the warm barn, which smelled of fresh dung. She followed the well-packed path to a fence rail protruding from the snow and sat on it, watching the onset of evening and its glowing, orange sunset. The snow-covered homestead and terraces above reflected the last rays of warm sunlight.

Countless times her mind reworked the confrontation with Kendira. Each time she felt more frustrated. She always tried to live according to the Laws handed down by Father Gord'n. Why, all of a sudden, did the Laws seem contrary to what she needed for happiness? The Laws ensured the survival and prosperity of the clan. Why, the closer she was to becoming an adult, did she feel less able to accept what was expected of her?

Over and over these questions reeled through her brain. One tenet Kendira had taught with painstaking care over the cycles came to mind: *Let the needs of many overshadow the desires of a single one.*

Alysa replayed the phrase over and over in her thoughts. She found it made no sense. What were *needs*? What were *desires*? Was a need more important than a desire, or were they really the same thing? If dire circumstances were to affect everybody, only then would the same need—the need to survive—exist for all. But if one was alone in their need—or their desire—must it be ignored? *No. Every person's needs were important and should be fulfilled. Each should be able to live life as chosen. She desired—no,* needed—*to choose how she wanted to live!*

Her father's gentle face rose to mind. It seemed as if she saw him at the corner of her vision. Then she thought she heard a whisper which spoke but one word: "Individual." She jumped off the fence and looked around; but there was no one else about.

She shivered, recalling that her father had used that word, "individual." She also recalled hearing him state a few times that he considered himself to be one. But he never explained to her *how* he became an individual. Even though Abso saw himself as one, he obeyed the Laws as far as she knew, and he was very much respected throughout the clan. She thought, *How did he do it? How was he able to be an individual AND live his life in a way that was accepted by the clan?*

She had never spent so much time thinking in all her life! This was the first time she deeply questioned the Laws and the Teller's way of teaching—or quite possibly, manipulating. Nothing Kendira ever told demanded thought by her listeners. The legends were meant to be absorbed and never questioned; the traditions were supposed to be remembered—and lived by. She never heard Kendira utter the word "individual" in any of her Tellings.

Some of the traditions are necessary, Alysa thought. *But others truly need to be changed!* It seemed that again she saw her father's face at the edge of her vision. Suddenly she turned as the boys who milked udommo emerged from the barn. Startled, she jumped back.

Colb, the first boy to reach her, laughed. "Alysa, are you all right?"

Shaking, she nodded, looking all around.

Gripping the carry straps of large clay milk jars slung over their backs, the boys began to climb the terrace walkway. Alysa walked ahead, guiding them by lantern light. Icy stairways linked each ascending stone-walled terrace. The walkways leveled as they crossed the flat terraces, then rose and leveled again until they reached the cottage terrace.

Absorbed in her thoughts, Alysa paid no attention to the boys' banter. She was determined not to let Kendira's injustice prevail. She thought hard about what she could do. Her father was so helpful when she had troubles to work out. How she wished he were here to help her with this dilemma!

But was he really gone? It was thought that those whose final farewell came to them no longer walked upon Xunar-kun, but her father would be alive as long as she or Loralle or Ellee remembered him; and she seemed to be remembering him a lot of late. She resolved to think of him with great joy, no longer with sadness. Her father would forever remain an inspiration to her; that inspiration would replace the sorrow!

But the heavy feeling about Kendira's betrayal still weighed upon her. She seemed unable to let it go. What could she do to lighten this burden? *How can I still my pain AND show Kendira that the Laws cannot keep me from happiness, keep me from becoming – somehow – an individual?*

She sighed, shaking her head, tired of thinking. All of a sudden, the instant she let go of thinking, the answer came, like a bolt of lightning that started in her heart and streaked to her head! She halted her movement up the terrace, forgetting the line of milk-bearers just behind. Colb bumped into her, nearly losing his grip on his jar. He said, "Alysa, what're you doing? Get going, before we all smash into each other and lose the evening milk!"

"Oh, sorry, Colb, sorry…" She resumed her climb up the slippery steps. She started to grin and at the same time shook her head, uncertain: was she dreaming a very silly waking dream, or could her answer really come to pass? *I will ask Council Speaker Tola to give me the vacant Trader duty!* If she obtained the duty, wouldn't that show Kendira that she could not use the Laws to control *everybody?*

Her mind raced, even faster than before, as she thought about how to approach Tola. He often remarked that she resembled her father in many ways. Would he accept her idea to become Trader even though she was a female? He might, because he was desperate to have the third position occupied. Or would he chase her away, laughing at her as if she were a silly little girl?

It was a chance that she must take! She mustered her courage—she would visit him right away to offer her proposal. "Thank you, Father," she whispered, filled with a warm feeling as she gazed into the deepening purple sky. "Tonight you have shown me the way to a new life—the life that's right for me, an individual!"

As she held the lantern high at the top of the last stairway, the light bounced off her hopeful, determined face. She turned and led the boys to the milk shed.

Marli, Tola's wife, answered a knock at the door. She held the front of her thick-woven robe closed. Her gray hair was loose about her shoulders, as she was prepared for sleep. She was surprised to see Alysa so late.

"Ho, Marli. I'm sorry to be a bother, but I need to talk to Speaker Tola."

"I will ask him if he wishes..." the dark woman began.

Tola interrupted and opened the door wide. "Ho, Alysa! Please come in. This is a pleasant surprise. We rarely see each other these suns." His braid was undone. His wavy, gray locks lay over his shoulders. He was not yet wearing his sleep clothing.

"Yes, youngling, come in," Marli echoed. She motioned Alysa into the cozy room and closed the door.

Alysa reverently gestured to Tola and blurted, "Speaker, I'm not here on a social visit. I have an important matter to discuss with you. It's late, I know, but I must talk to you tonight."

"Well," he said, raising the dark, bushy brows above his green eyes. "Let us sit!" He indicated a chair opposite his at the hearthside table, and they sat.

Alysa pushed her cloak off her shoulders and composed herself. As she gathered courage to explain what was on her mind, Marli poured her a steaming mug of sweetleaf, refilled Tola's mug, then retired with needlework to the other side of the room.

"Now, Alysa, what could be so important?" Tola asked, amused, fingering his hair loose from the braid-locks.

"Elder, probably something you've never dreamed of hearing. But before I speak of it, I want you to know that in this matter I am extremely serious. So please try to understand. And please remember whose daughter I am."

"I will keep those things in mind. Proceed," he said, trying his best to hide his amusement. He settled back to listen.

She concentrated her gaze on the steam rising from her mug and said, "I've come to talk about the position for Lesser Trader."

Tola stroked his short, gray beard, but other than that, gave no outward response. He motioned her to continue.

"At last leaffall Trade, there were only two Traders due to Father's final farewell. As we know, it was very difficult for two to accomplish the work of three, particularly because Father was Major Trader. Since no one has shown any interest—I offer myself." She crossed her arms and leaned back in her chair to signal the end of her proposal.

Astonished, he replied, "Well, that is a very unusual offer! But you know there has never been a female Trader in all of history. And you are a youngling…"

"Forgive me, Speaker Tola, but I am a *midling*."

"Yes, you are growing up. I still think of you as a youngling…"

"And you said at the Gathering that a midling man would suffice…"

"That's true, I did, but…"

She sat up straight, tense. Keeping her voice even, she said, "But I feel capable, Tola. I think it would be natural for me to become a Trader."

"You mean because your father was one? What makes you think you could handle the duty?"

"Though I've no experience in trading—what female does?—I do have good knowledge of the stock we trade. I've worked in the granary, so I understand the milling of flours and meals. As for textiles, I know about quality of fiber and workmanship, probably better than any man because I've woven the very fiber that I've spun myself." She continued, her excitement increasing, "And I've worked in just about all the other crafts, and I know value, too."

She bolted from her chair and pulled a fur coverlet from the hearthside bench. "I know the difference between Trailmen furs, what animals they're from, whether a cure is good, and what time of cycle a fur was taken. I know what good bone and antler are, too. Quality Lowlands dye-stuff has a certain color and smell. You know, I do know a lot about tradegoods. Even without having any Trade experience." She replaced the fur and continued, "And you can see that even though I'm young and female, I'm not ignorant!"

Tola laughed. "You are, without a doubt, Abso's daughter! Such courage is very unusual in a woman and a midling, at that; but I do admire this rarity. Please, sit." He paused and drank sweetleaf. "Do you remember the numbers games we played when you were a youngling?"

With respect, and trying not to look anxious, she sat down and sipped her drink. "Yes, I remember. Very well."

"I recollect that you were quite accomplished at figuring. Only rarely were you unable to find the answer. And I always gave you difficult problems to solve. But being able to figure is just a small part of Trade. There is the challenge of communication. You would be required to master tradesign before Greening Trade, a very great task. Many of the sign patterns are complicated. The value exchange procedure is very rapid and hesitation is not well received. In other words, mistakes or misinformation can cause confusion and delays in the process. The Trailmen camp for only a short while and there's not a moment to waste. I don't know, Alysa..."

Struggling to keep her voice even, she said, "Every man who becomes a Trader has to learn. No matter who takes on the duty, he will have to learn tradesign in a very short time. There's no reason I can't."

Tola paused to consider. "I must agree. You'd have no more trouble learning than any of the previous Traders; maybe less. You are bright. But I don't believe intelligence alone is enough. There's more to dealing with the Painted Ones than you know. Even more important than the ability to figure or use tradesign fluently is your attitude toward them."

He leaned closer, serious, and continued. "Trade requires you to meet them face to face. If there is any chance that your stomach would weaken before them, that could create a very serious problem."

She thought for a moment. She looked him squarely in the eyes. "My father dealt with them for many cycles. He never mentioned having any trouble. He never once spoke against them. One time he returned holding a carved box under his arm that was made by a Trailmen...you know the box. We keep it on the mantel among our most special things. I think it was his favorite possession, despite its being fashioned by a Painted One. No, I don't believe he minded trading with the Trailmen. I think he enjoyed it, although he never said so, in those words."

Tola sighed. "You are testimony that the ever dutiful Abso lives on! Please stand, Alysa."

They rose, and the Council Speaker placed his large hands on her shoulders. "Alysa, do you realize that if you become Trader, it'll more than likely delay joining with Orryn even further? It may take some time to find and train another Trader to replace you."

"Yes, I know. First Mother must get well and I must take care of Ellee until she is more—independent. As long as I'm bound to remain at High Point, I want to contribute all I can. Taking my father's place would mean more to me than you could know."

"Well, I cannot ignore your request, Alysa. It's a valid one. I'll make the recommendation at a Council meeting which I'll call tomorrow just for this purpose. I personally am convinced. But I cannot say the others will be."

Alysa looked disappointed.

"Alysa, I'll do all I can in your favor. And not just because you want this so badly. After our talk, I feel you *are* a good choice."

She rose and bowed, backing away palms-up. "Thank you, Elder Tola, for the consideration and for accepting this late visit." She threw her cloak around her shoulders. Her heart pounded in her chest. "May I ask just one more thing of you? Please don't ask Teller Kendira to sit with the Council in this matter."

Tola nodded in acceptance of the request. He assured her, "She is not a Council member. The men of the Council can come to a conclusion without Kendira!"

Two suns passed. Alysa and her mother entered their cottage. Kendira was seated before the hearth! The saroos were sniffing her boots. They sneezed and rubbed their noses. Judging from their squinting eyes and low grumbling chatter, they did not seem at all fond of her. Ellee, who stood at the hearth stirring soup, giggled at their antics.

Alysa took a deep breath. "Kendira...ho! How are you?" But she offered no gesture of reverence.

"Ho, indeed!" Kendira glared at Alysa. "After my trek through the snow I'm quite exhausted, I can assure you!"

Each saroo sneezed one last time and, feeling the cool air that flowed in with Alysa and her mother, the animals scurried to Ellee's nook, climbed up the curtains and under the quilt.

Loralle closed the door. She said softly, "Ellee, did you offer Kendira something to drink?"

Ellee nodded, about to answer, but Kendira spoke over her and said, as if with a sour taste in her mouth, "She has already offered. No thank you. I'll not be staying."

Loralle went to the hearth. As she took yellow dough from a bowl and patted it into flat rounds, she said, "Kendira, if I'm not mistaken, this is the first time you've ever visited our home. Is there some special news?"

Kendira exploded. "Is there some news...? You *do* know what your elder daughter has done!"

Loralle turned to Kendira. "Ah, of course. Her appointment as Trader. Well, I must admit that I did struggle with this, because, as we all know, Trader isn't a traditional role for a woman. When she told me, I didn't know what to think. For two suns I searched for a reason to discourage her. But I truthfully couldn't find a single one and am now well with the decision. Somehow it seems right." She turned back and placed two doughy rounds on the baking stone lying on the embers. The bread sizzled on the hot stone, bubbled and slowly puffed up.

Disbelieving, Kendira raised her fists into the air. Shaking her head in exasperation, she let them drop onto her lap. "Moons above! What's this clan coming to? I can hardly believe that you, Loralle of Yellow Cliffs, one of Father Gord'n's most faithful, can tell me so calmly—even *proudly*—that you accept what *this youngling* has done!" Kendira jabbed a thick-jointed finger at her target.

Alysa sat down at the table. Allowing her mother to continue, she marveled at Loralle's enthusiasm, absent for so many moons. It was too long since even the smallest spark could be seen in her mother's eyes.

Slowly and deliberately, Loralle checked the breads. She picked them up by their edges and flipped them over. She sat on the bench beside Kendira and said, "Do you not remember what Abso was like? It hasn't been long, Kendira, and already the homestead has suffered from his absence. We all admired his dedication and depended on his willingness in the role of Major Trader to do all he could for the benefit of the clan." She reached for Kendira's frail hand. Enclosing it in hers, she continued, "Alysa, though she's a female, can continue where her father left off. It's obvious that she possesses many of his valuable qualities. Gender in this instance makes no difference, Kendira. I see only goodness in this decision. And for the first time in many moons, my heart is light!" Loralle's eyes sparkled. She released Kendira's hand, returned to the hearth, and lifted the crispy breads off the stone.

Kendira looked disappointed. She had preyed on Loralle's sense of duty, hoping she would pressure Alysa into abandoning the idea of becoming a Trader. But Kendira's words did not have the slightest influence. Loralle's mind was made up in favor of her daughter's new role. Alysa remained quiet, watching, smiling.

Kendira opened her mouth to speak, but Loralle turned to her and added, "It seems to me that you did something similar to what Alysa has done."

"What? I'm certain I don't know what you mean."

"You're one of very few women to have achieved Teller. And, correct me if I'm wrong, but wasn't it your own persistence that helped you achieve the duty?"

Taken aback, Kendira said, "Well, yes, I suppose it was…"

"Then can you see that you and my daughter are a lot alike in your…aspirations. I don't know how you, of all people, can condemn her for this."

"But *my* sacrifice was great! I worked for many cycles to achieve my position. I even chose not to join so that I would remain a Teller at High Point. I say that your daughter's appointment came much too easily!"

Loralle went to Kendira and knelt beside her. She looked into her eyes. "Kendira, have you thought that perhaps your sacrifice was enough? Need it always be as difficult for the women who follow?"

Kendira sighed and sat back in her chair. "Perhaps not."

"Then it is time to let go of your anger over this."

At a loss as to how to counter Loralle's reasoning, Kendira gave up. At least she had no more arguments in her at the moment. Her protests mattered little, anyway; though the Council heard the proposal for Alysa's Trader apprenticeship with initial shock and doubt, they trusted Tola's judgment. They decided that Alysa was a good choice and accepted her into Trader apprenticeship. This time, without the support of Loralle and the Council Elders, Kendira would be unable to have her way.

Alysa had succeeded! Her training was set to commence the next sun, and Kendira was unable to prevent it!

THE VISITORS ARRIVE

From the five homesteads, Folk made passage through the greening hills for Moonsfest. Some traveled a great distance. The journey from Green Plateau to High Point, the homesteads furthest from each other, was the most arduous. Often high streams hindered progress and stretched the five-hill jaunt into a three-sun journey, requiring overnight stays at homesteads in between.

From two directions the visitors arrived at High Point. From the west, Folk from Green Plateau and Yellow Cliffs trekked the Upper Path and were met above the Great Hall by their hosts. Valley Ridge and Falling Stream travelers, coming from the south, hiked up the Lower Path, which terminated below the last field terrace bordering the lake. Many of the 'steaders pulled carts the whole way which were filled with goods for Trade that would take place seven suns after Moonsfest.

As they stepped off Lower Path, visitors embraced and clasped hands with their hosts. Travelers were relieved of their packbaskets. The carts were emptied of their jars and baskets for removal to the storage sheds. Old friends and relatives began at once to enjoy the reunion.

The younger Folk still had energy after the long journey. They sprang up the stone stairway linking the terraces, ready to begin play with their cousins. Others lingered—older folk, the very young, and those who just wanted to catch up on news—and formed a chatty crowd in the late afternoon warmth.

Seda and Aryz pushed through the crowd to embrace each other. Pale-haired, muscular Aryz lifted robust Seda off her feet with ease and swung her around. His green eyes danced with delight, and Seda squealed and laughed with glee. She nuzzled her face into his short, light-colored beard, happy once again to be held by her Aryz.

Orryn—a thin young man a head taller than anyone present and with barely a trace of beard—squeezed through the throng. His pleasant face and gray eyes brightened when he spotted Alysa standing beneath a budding tree near the bottom of the stone stairway.

Alysa saw him and marveled at how little his looks had changed since they were small, even though he was now taller than most. His soft, brown braid now fell below his waist. His face still possessed that innocent, light look that Alysa's once had but felt she had lost during the last grueling season. She was glad Orryn maintained that light. Seeing him brought back memories of being little again and of the many happy times they shared together.

He emerged from the crowd and went to her. He dropped his packbasket and hugged her. "Lys, I've missed you! It's so good to see you!"

She hugged him back, realizing how his voice at least was different, huskier. "I've missed you too, Orryn. Wintertide was much too long."

"I'm sorry about your father, Lys. He is greatly missed. People still talk about him."

"Thank you, Orryn. It has been difficult for us…come. We'll settle you and your parents at the cottage."

The couple looked at the thinning crowd and saw Bavat and Tach, Orryn's mother and father, engaged in conversation with Loralle and others. Orryn's parents were younger than Alysa's; Orryn was born soon after they joined, whereas Loralle and Abso waited many cycles before Alysa came to be.

Alysa attracted Loralle's eye and motioned a suggestion to begin the ascent, as the climb up the stairway was a long one. Her mother, sister and Orryn's parents eased away from the crowd—but not before they made plans to get together with several others that eve.

The baggage was shared as the climb began. Alysa relieved Bavat of her packbasket and slung it over her shoulder. She and Orryn lagged behind their parents. Orryn began in a lowered, somewhat strained voice, "Lys, I was very…surprised to hear of the news of your Trader apprenticeship."

She sighed, struggling with the words she had thought about for suns. She knew that she would eventually have to talk to him about this. "Kendira destroyed our joining plans, Orryn. I needed to show her that she does not get to decide how my life is to be. Then I thought of the open Trader position and appealed to Tola. It was as simple as that."

"But how did Tola get the Council Elders to agree to it?"

Taking care not to trip on her skirt, Alysa watched the steps—a good excuse not to look into his eyes. "We were in need of a Trader. The Council decided I was a good choice. Actually, I was the only choice. So they allowed the appointment of a female, just this once."

Orryn grimaced. "I can scarcely believe this has happened! Did you consider how I'd feel about it?"

"Kendira influenced them to delay our joining anyway. I don't see what difference it makes."

"But your seeming attempt at...revenge for what Kendira did may delay it even further!"

"I don't think of it as 'revenge,' Orryn. Well, at first, maybe. But now I look at it as doing something truly valuable for the homesteads. Now you and I *both* get to do something...important."

"Being joined to me would not be important?"

"Of course! It's just that..." Alysa sighed. "Tola said he'd look for a replacement. I believe he'll find someone before long. Perhaps if my first Trade should fail, a man will finally decide to come forward. Not that I'm *hoping* I will fail." She avoided Orryn's hurting eyes and stared across the wide terraces to Winding Mountains and to where the deep forest began.

"Lys, I hope so. I've looked forward to our joining for so long..."

For a time they walked in silence.

It was plain that Orryn was struggling with his next words. "I've tried to imagine...a woman as a Trader. You know...some of the Tellers don't know quite what to think. Some think it's...indecent."

Alysa, already prepared to defend herself, flared. "Indecent? Is that your opinion of me, Orryn? Do you think I'm indecent?"

"No, Lys!" He looked stunned. "I was afraid you'd hear it that way. Maybe that's not the right word. Look at me, almost a Full Teller and not being able to come up with the right word!" He paused and gathered his thoughts. "I do not think you are indecent. I could not. You are my betrothed!"

"I'm sorry, Orryn. I didn't mean to be cross. This is supposed to be a festive time. I don't wish to spoil our few suns together over a disagreement. But I must tell you something that I've been thinking about for a while. Come."

She turned off the walkway and led him far out onto a terrace. Last season's short, brittle simmel stalks crunched underfoot. They set their burdens down, sat on the terrace wall, and let their legs dangle over the edge.

Alysa looked intently into his eyes. "Don't you ever get tired of the traditions, Orryn? Of having one way and only one way to do something? Like work duties or social rules or anything different from what tradition requires of us?"

He wrinkled his brow in thought. "No. I've been trained as a Teller. A Teller's purpose is to preserve history, teach the Laws. To do our best to see that it's followed. That's why I'm having a hard time with your getting the Trader duty. I don't think it's possible for me to think against tradition. I hope you'll eventually see the wisdom of Kendira's ways. I agree with what she did—suggesting to the Elders that our joining be delayed—even though it pains me. I'd probably do the same."

She looked into his bare, boyish face and sighed. "Orryn, if that's how you view this matter, how can you still want to join with such a person as me?"

A painful expression seared his face, as if she had struck him. "We've been betrothed since you were newborn, Lys. I couldn't break a bond as old as that!" He paused, considering what he said and added, "But it's not only our betrothal bond, Lys. We fit, you know?"

She watched the distant line of figures ascend the terraces. Light ripples played upon the lake lying beyond the lowermost fields. She looked toward the distant, shadowy forest edge and shook her head. He did not understand. She wanted to know what he thought as an *individual*, but he responded in the only way that he was able—as one who had spent many cycles in Teller training. She wondered if she would ever be able to make him understand. And did they, after all, really "fit" as he said?

Maybe. And maybe not.

Much remained to be done the next morning in preparation for the eve's festivities. The Great Hall bustled with activity. Men put up long tables in the hall. Noisy boys loaded in firewood, as a clear, cool eve was predicted. Basted casish hens and sections of leaprock lambs pierced through with hardwood skewers lay across the embers in two of the four hearths.

Cakes and breads baked on hearthstones. Baskets of early greens were ready for steaming in pots. The season's first groundberries were heaped in bowls and would be served with a topping of sweet udommo cream. Moonsfest came but twice each cycle, so extra effort was made to create the most sumptuous banquets on these nights.

Alysa and Orryn, along with several other couples, offered to take groups of younglings foraging for flowers to decorate the hall and Joining Circle. Creating the decorations was a tradition the younglings enjoyed very much. Carrying wide, shallow baskets, the couple strolled across a meadow.

The younglings ran ahead, laughing in the bright, chilly sunlight as they sought their fragrant quarry. They combed the fallow fields and forest edges for the first flowers of greening. Stubby six-legged greenwings, clinging to tall grasses to bask in the sunshine, darted into the air and fluttered away on iridescent wings as the younglings disturbed them in their passing.

An excited girl, holding a stem up high from which swayed many tubular blue flowers, ran up to Alysa and Orryn. She squealed, "Look! I found the very first meadowcups of greening!"

"Good, Katti," Alysa said. "Now find a lot, lot more so we'll be able to make the Great Hall and Joining Circle beautiful!" Katti placed the flower in the basket and ran back to her friends.

Alysa and Orryn continued up the terrace. She chose to lead the flower foray, thinking this would be a good time to talk to him. This retreat from the crowded homestead was the first time they were alone since their fruitless conversation the afternoon before. She intended to continue that talk and come to an understanding with him.

The younglings took their clamor up to the next terrace.

"Orryn, I haven't had a chance to ask you, with all the visitors around and news to share, about how your work is going."

"It's going very well, Lys. I'm almost through the training, as you know. I'll be done before this leaffall, as planned. My last big learning task has been given to me." He laughed, "I'll be finished, that is, unless the Major Tellers get together and decide there's something more I need to learn!"

"Does that happen often?"

"No, it doesn't. I think that all Apprentice Tellers fear something more will yet be required of them. But if I lacked any of the necessary training, I'd know by now." Pride tinged his voice. "In just three moons I'll be Lesser Teller of Falling Stream. One sun I will take Bakar's place as Major Teller! When I began, I wasn't certain I'd make it through the first cycle, which was the toughest. That's when the memory is heavily tested to see if capacity exists."

"Of course, you must be interested in that sort of training. That's half the task, isn't it?"

"I didn't think about becoming a Teller when I was very young. I don't think I had any interest when Mother and Father were approached by Falling Stream's Council Elders. But when it was discovered that I had the capacity and was chosen over some other promising youths, I became dedicated to the duty. It's a very high position in the eyes of the Folk."

She stopped walking. "Orryn, that's not what I asked you. What I meant was do you *like* what you do?"

He spun back to her. "Lys, why do you ask such questions? Does it really matter whether I *like* it? It's my duty and I've sworn to do my best!"

She shook her head and closed her eyes to think. She took a deep breath and looked steadily into his gray eyes. "It matters to me what I do, Orryn. Everything in my life has begun to matter. I've been thinking about the Laws and the traditions we live by. We're no longer a lost, starving clan! We have full storage sheds and pantries, time to sing and dance and visit each other a couple of times a cycle. Why do we need to keep so much to tradition? Why *can't* the way we do things change?"

The glee melted from his face.

She continued, "Now we have the time to discover what it is we truly *wish* to become. Now we should be able to *choose* how to live our lives. No, Orryn, I will not be happy as a traditional woman, doing the same things women have done since Cat'clysm! I have great respect for Father Gord'n and how he saved the Field Folk. But I hope you can understand that I need to have a choice in what I feel is a better way, for me."

"And that's why you persuaded them to give you Trader!"

"No, not at first. It was because Kendira spoiled our joining plans. I knew it would upset her if I got the Trader duty. But then the *meaning* that being a Trader would give my life became the other part of the reason…"

"So now that you've got it, are you going to keep it? It's really not necessary now, is it? You did what you had to do. You upset the whole clan, and that's what you really wanted, isn't it?"

"No, Orryn. I did not want to upset the clan! But since I'm being required to stay at High Point, I'm happy to be doing something that interests me, and is important. I can no longer be content just working in the fields or spinning fiber!"

Several younglings ran up with bunches of flowers. Girls carried them in skirt folds. Boys cradled long blooms in their arms. They piled them in the baskets. Ellee was among them. As she ran off with the others to pick more, she began to sing a happy old melody. Each word was high and clear, her lisp absent when she sang. The other younglings joined in as they skipped away:

"On the eve of the moons,
Far from the fray,
He saved us from doom,
And showed us the way.
Father Gord'n the wise!
Father Gord'n the great!"

"Listen to those words, Orryn. That same song has been sung for probably one hundred generations! There are no new songs because there are no new events to sing about. No new legends are being made, because cycle after cycle, nothing different ever happens!"

"Lys," Orryn asked in a firm voice, "do you plan to complete the Trader apprenticeship?"

"Have you been listening, Orryn? Yes! I will be well versed in tradesign by this coming Trade, in seven suns. Boshe and Panli are excellent teachers. And I'm finding tradesign easier to learn than I expected."

"If we were to join at leaffall, then who would take your place as Trader?"

"I told you — there is no one as yet. We'll just have to be prepared to delay the joining again if necessary. Anyway, the Elders have decreed that I can't leave until Mother is well."

Dismayed, Orryn replied, "Do you mean that we may have to wait to join for one whole cycle? I don't want our joining to be delayed any longer than necessary..."

Alysa nodded. She knew she should be sad. It was odd to feel that she was not particularly upset. She turned away from him. "It will work out, Orryn. It will work out."

GREENING MOONSFEST

Leafy, bright-green garlands with arrays of yellow, pink, blue and purple flowers were draped along the walls and down the centers of the tables inside the Great Hall. The floral scent, mixed with cooking aromas, wafted through the hall. Bright lamplight filled the Great Hall and spilled out into the darkness through shutters left open to relieve heat from cooking. Many rows of tables and chairs were set about the perimeter of the room, leaving a large open space in the center.

The path leading from the Great Hall to the Joining Circle, which lay on the next higher terrace, was flanked by blazing lanterns dangling from lamp poles. A few persistent crimson-colored flowerflies still hummed among the garlands that dipped between poles set around the Joining Circle.

The stone floor of the Circle was twenty strides across and was enclosed by a knee-high wall. Entrance to the Circle was gained through an opening on the southern arc of the wall. On the northern arc stood six poles bearing homestead insignia banners. One of the banners represented Aryz and Falling Stream. Two banners identified the men from Yellow Cliffs, two signified Green Plateau, and the remaining banner, Valley Ridge.

Next to births, joinings were the most important of Field Folk rites and further bound the homesteads. Joinings encouraged the generation of new life and assured the immortality of the clan.

The betrothed couples and their parents assembled in the dark at a distance from the Circle. All were dressed in their finest clothing. The brides wore long, fitted gowns of various colors. Women's and girls' hair were fixed into braided coils on top of their heads. Men's wintertide beards were trimmed close, and their braids hung neatly down their backs.

Behind Erindi and her attendants, positioned in the second cluster in the procession, were nervous Seda and her smiling Aryz. They were followed by their parents; behind them, Alysa held Seda's folded joining sash. The group after Seda's was comprised of Betha's attendants. The joining girls dared not speak or even look at each other for fear of giggling during this very solemn event.

When all clusters were finally settled and ready to begin, Tola—positioned at the head of the procession—motioned the three flute players following him to begin the traditional soft, slow melody. All set off toward the Joining Circle, bodies swaying to the solemn rhythm. As the procession flowed toward the Circle, the rest of the clanfolk followed at a respectful distance.

Tola entered the Circle and took his place along the center of the northern arc. A breeze caught the billowing, pale-blue cape he wore only for joinings. In sharp contrast against the dark northern horizon, he held out his arms to the approaching shining faces. He guided the couples and their attendants across the floor to their places below the banners. The Folk quietly crowded around the outside of the Circle to witness the rite.

Seda and Aryz faced Tola but continued to exchange glances of adoration. Alysa, positioned behind Seda and Aryz's parents, re-called how ecstatic Seda was for many moons about the joining. All she talked about was leaving High Point, beginning her new life with Aryz, getting to know new people, and settling down into a daily routine as the wife of a field leader. Alysa thought how lovely Seda looked in the long-sleeved, indigo gown she had sewn. Hundreds of white bone beads Seda had stitched to the gown glittered like stars in a deep-sapphire sky.

Alysa had woven cloth as fine as that in Seda's gown, but hers was pure white. She planned to cover hers with dark-stained beads made from simmel seed, the reverse of Seda's. The girls thought they would be joining at the same time—at leaffall—and that they would have looked well standing beside each other in their beautiful joining gowns. Alas, that was not a possibility now. She tried to imagine how her gown would look when her own joining night arrived; how-ever, this waking dream did not excite her as much as it used to.

She looked at the faces flanking the Joining Circle. Her mother and sister stood near the entrance, and next to them, Orryn's parents and Orryn. Alysa felt a pang of sadness, thinking that her father would not be there to stand with her mother when her own joining sun arrived. She felt sad, along with a growing confusion as to whether she really wanted, after all, to be joined. As her eyes met Orryn's, she avoided them and returned her attention to the ceremony.

Tola glanced over his shoulder, to the north. He held up his palms, and the music ceased. He spoke loud enough for all to hear. "On this eve of Greening Moonsfest, we are here in the name of Father Gord'n to carry out his wish that we go forth and be productive. Couples to be joined will now step forward."

The couples took a step closer to him. He said to each of the young men, "By what name do you live, and why have you come to this Circle this eve?"

Each replied in turn. When Aryz's turn came, he slipped Seda's hands into his and said, "My name is Aryz of Falling Stream. The Councils and our parents have given consent to our joining. I have come to claim Seda of High Point to dwell in my home until our final farewell, as my wife and the mother of our younglings, should we be so blessed."

The remaining young men, in turn, voiced their intentions.

Tola asked, "Parents of these young women, do you wish your daughter to join, though it pains you that she must leave High Point and never again dwell under your roof?"

The girls' parents responded in unison, "Yes, it pleases us to give our daughter so that she may live the life Father Gord'n has planned for her. She has been instructed all her life to do what is right under his Law."

To the men's parents he asked, "Parents of these young men, do you accept this new daughter into your family? To cherish her as one of your own and to allow her to do all she can to benefit your homestead?"

They answered, "With all our strength, we will help her to overcome the loss of her family and the attachment to her birth home, to take her as one of our own, and encourage her to be productive."

"Bring the sashes before us!" Tola rasped.

Alysa and the other sash-bearers stepped forward as the parents moved to the rear of the Joining Circle. The bearers raised the folded sashes above their heads.

Tola continued, "The sash, patiently stitched in anticipation of the joining-to-be, is testimony to a woman's diligence and patience, and to the devotion she holds for the man with whom she is joining."

The sash-bearers lowered the sashes. Seda turned to Alysa, who slipped the sash into Seda's hand. Alysa kissed Seda's cheek and said, "May you forever be *beyond* happy."

Seda smiled and took the sash, allowing its colorful, shimmering length to unfold.

Tola said, "Young women may now say their private vows to their men."

Seda turned to Aryz and grinned. She whispered, "Forever, Aryz, I am yours. Accept my charm of love and prosperity." Seda slid the sash around his waist and knotted it at his side. Aryz's face beamed and he squeezed her hand.

The horizon began to brighten north of Winding Mountains. Tola turned to the skyline and said, "Father Gord'n has given us the moons to ensure us that life will continue; that the cycle of life will always repeat for us. For those joined here tonight, as for those joined in the past, the rising of the moons—one female, one male—shall seal these joinings!"

Flowering trees at the crest of the near-distant hills glowed with pastel light. The branches created a fragmented silhouette as the top of Nanthan-kul rose behind them. The moonlight split into many pieces that melted together as the edge of the moon cleared the trees. The crowd remained motionless as Nanthan-kul rose above Winding Mountains, finally and fully displaying herself.

A second brightening began below Nanthan-kul, spilling a much brighter glow into the sky than even she did. A broader face began its ascent into the paling sky. It was so bright that the stars closest to the horizon began to fade. Donol-kul—easily five times larger than Nanthan-kul—lifted his broad belly above the trees to keep pace with Nanthan-kul's lower left hemisphere.

Everyone cheered. As the two moons rose together, luminous moonsshine cast itself over the joined couples, over the faces of the clanfolk, the fields and orchards, the forests and mountains, with light nearly as bright as the sun. A breeze rushed down from the hills and continued to the lake, where it played across the surface, creating a thousand rippling stars as it reflected the dual lunar spectacle.

"Moonsrise is complete!" Tola rasped above the excitement. He raised his arms as if to embrace all the couples at once. The color of his robe nearly blended with the pale sky. He concluded, "With the joining of the moons, I deem these couples joined. I bless them, and the other couples now joined at our brother homesteads, with the prosperity that is rightfully theirs by the promise of Father Gord'n!"

The couples crowded together in the center of the Joining Circle, congratulating and hugging one another. They melted into the mass of onlookers as the flute players struck up a festive tune and marched down the stairway toward the Great Hall.

Orryn followed Alysa as she squeezed her way through the joyful throng. They hugged Seda, Aryz and the other couples and moved with the crowd down the moonslit path to the Great Hall. The music of the joyful flutes drew everyone into the hall, which was soon filled with high-spirited Folk. The open windows, which were dark with night just a short while before, admitted streaming moonlight. The landscape glowed through every window.

Everyone sat to dine. The musicians finished a tune and set down their instruments to join the guests at the tables. The audience clapped in vigorous appreciation. The musicians bowed.

Several tables away, Alysa found Loralle and Ellee seated with Bavat and Tach. She and Orryn sat with them. Scrutinizing the pillow Ellee gave to her, Loralle declared how proud she was of Ellee for having created such a beautiful gift. The women discussed the perfection of Ellee's needlework.

Loralle said, "How did you make this, young Daughter, without my knowing about it? You and your big sister must have had fun hiding this from me!"

Alysa winked at Ellee, who looked very happy; the gift she had labored upon so diligently made her mother happy!

Bowls and platters holding Moonsfest delicacies began to circulate. Pitchers of mulled berry grog were passed down the long tables. Happy conversation and laughter accompanied the feast, as Folk savored the food and each other's company. The newly joined couples circulated, accepting congratulations and good wishes from the throng.

The younglings finished eating first. As soon as they were able to tease their parents into allowing them to leave the tables, several skipped to the open floor. Ellee was one of the first to join in. They linked hands to form a small circle.

The younglings started to chant, "Dance! Dance! Dance!"

Betram jumped up from his table and dragged two large baskets into the center of the circle. A few men, after downing the dregs of their cups, joined him. One pulled out a gourd rattle and began to shake it. Another took out a reed flute and began a spirited joining tune. Evyn, the third man, pulled out a drum and beat a rapid tempo. The younglings' circle-dance began. Evyn laughed and cheered for his three young daughters who danced with the others.

The giddy, newly joined couples slipped themselves into the dancing circle. Others entered as well, forming another circle around the first. Some went into the center and picked up yet more instruments. Soon the floor was crowded with mirthful people, four circles in motion with a dozen musicians in the center.

Ellee ran from the floor between tunes to ask her mother to dance. Loralle declined. Alysa leaned in and asked, "Why don't you dance, Mother? You're such a beautiful dancer!"

After hesitating, Loralle answered, "The last time I danced was last Moonsfest, with your father. It would not feel right. Please try to understand, Alysa."

"Oh, but I do, my Mother." She smiled and kissed her mother on the forehead. "I'll dance, Ellee!"

They trotted to the floor, Orryn following, and squeezed into the outer circle. A new tune with a difficult rhythm began. Feet moved in a complicated pattern, and the circles moved in opposite, dizzying directions.

They danced in several circle dances, all of them lively. The room had become very warm.

"Orryn, let's go for a walk," Alysa suggested. He nodded.

On their way out, they passed Kendira, seated in her usual place by the hearth. They greeted her, Orryn with the customary full greeting, and Alysa minimally. Kendira acknowledged Orryn and ignored Alysa.

As the two stepped into moonslight, Alysa wrapped herself in her shawl. Orryn pulled up the collar of his tunic and buttoned it. The air was chilly, turning their breath to vapor. They walked up the high orchard terraces, needing no lamp to guide their steps, as the moons had traveled to the sky's zenith.

Looking up at them, Alysa said, "They are breathtaking!"

"Yes, Lys. I agree."

"And how very different they are. Nanthan has such a rough surface; she must have mountains. And Donol is so smooth it looks like he has clouds. How can they look so different?"

Orryn shook his head and sighed. "I don't know..."

They walked for a time without talking. Alysa was relieved to be away from the noisy, crowded hall. As they approached the topmost terrace walkway, a glistening wash of stars was returning along the northern horizon. The sky was darkening again as the moons began their southward descent. Because the air was so clear, it seemed as though the stars were no farther away than the next hill's treetops. The brightest stars pulsed in faint colors of pink, blue and yellow.

A young woman's coy laughter escaped from the dark forest border at the upper edge of the terrace, where a courting couple hid beneath foya trees so dense even the moonsshine could not pierce the shadow. Alysa giggled. Orryn placed his arm around her and held her close to his side as they walked. She considered how this felt; it wasn't as comforting as it used to be.

They moved in silence across the edge of the upper orchard, arrived at the forest border on the other side, and began to descend the walkway.

Alysa halted before an opening between two massive foyas. "Come this way," she said.

"Why? What's in there?" Orryn asked, peering into the dark.

"This is the entry to Gorge Path. I want to show you something."

She melted into the shadows. Her steps stirred up the spicy smell of damp forest floor, which mingled with the delicate scent of greening's blooms and the pungent odor of foyas.

Reluctant, he followed her up the dim path between ancient foyas and broad hardwoods. He watched his footing among thick roots that groped along the soil beneath last leaffall's soft, leafy blanket.

After a short distance, the path began to slope downward and became rockier as they approached the stream. The path wound around large boulders, turning near the sound of rushing water. The moonsshine was again visible and danced upon the speedy mountain runoff as the current rose and fell over boulders in the stream. Alysa paused on a low precipice that overhung the stream. To the right was a cleared area. To the left, many paces from where they were standing, was a path that rose up the side of the gorge. She pointed at the path. "The Tradeground is that way."

He looked at the path and shrugged, as though he did not care. In moonslight the path was clearly visible. It climbed steeply up the hill, growing very narrow. It clung to the gorge's steep walls and turned into the shadows of high, arching trees.

Alysa stepped back onto the path and continued downstream. Her feet trod nimbly along the familiar path. Wary of the swift stream and its many boulders lying just below the narrow path, Orryn followed, grasping branches for safety along the way. They arrived at her secret haven.

"What is this place, Lys?" he asked as he peered downstream and up. Winding Mountains was awash in moonslight but starkly contrasted with the darkening sky and stars surrounding it.

"This is my place." She focused on the water's smeared reflection of the moons and smiled. "The trees, shore and stream I feel are my own. I come here a lot. Just to think and to be alone." She sat down and lay back on a patch of moss. "Seda's the only other who knows about this place. Now that she's leaving, I want you to know."

"But it's so lonely here."

"Oh no, I find it very beautiful and comforting!"

"I think it's dangerous to come out here on the border of Trailmen territory all alone!" He squatted next to her. "Aren't you even a little afraid?"

"This place is not dangerous, Orryn. I've been coming here for as long as I can remember. Even when the Trailmen are camped. But this is the first time I've come at night."

She looked at the overhanging branches. Moonslight caused their buds to glow. As far as she could see, flowering branches burst to spectacular life. "It's even more beautiful at night. Especially on this night. I haven't been here since…for many moons."

Orryn jumped up, startled. "Is this…is this the stream where…"

"They found Father. Yes. Downstream. This is the first time I've been here since leaffall. I've missed it," she confided. She sat upright and pulled her shawl about herself.

"I'm so sorry, Lys." Orryn held out his hand to help her up. "Come, let's leave this place. Let's go back to the celebration."

"No. Not yet."

He sighed, dropped his hand, and leaned against a tree. He stared into the shadows on the opposite shore.

Alysa asked, "You mentioned that you were to meet with Kendira this afternoon. Did you have a good talk?"

He relaxed somewhat. "Yes, oh yes! We talked mainly about my training and what is left to do before I finish." He turned to her, more animated. "She didn't find any more tasks for me to complete, thank Father Gord'n!" And more modestly, "She said all the Tellers are in agreement that my inception sun can be chosen."

Alysa was proud that he accomplished his task. Now that she had one of her own, she hoped he would become as accepting. She questioned him further. "Did you and Kendira discuss my apprenticeship?"

He hesitated and turned his face to the stream. He withdrew a twig from the end of his heavy brown braid. "You would ask that. A little. She said she was—stunned by what you did in revenge."

"Orryn, you do think I should give up the Trader duty, don't you!"

"Alysa, I can understand why you're angry with Kendira. But if you pursued the duty out of spite, then I think you were wrong!"

"Who's *right?* Who's *wrong?* Orryn, whether something is right or wrong depends only on which side you take!" She paused and continued earnestly, "The duty has become important to me, just as yours is to *you*. After I thought about my father's duty as Trader and remembered what he told me about the Trailmen, I felt I could handle it. When I discovered I was tired of the traditional roles we are expected to live, the more excited I became about the idea of becoming a Trader—and remaining one."

"Are you...are you saying that you hope a replacement for you is *not* found?"

Alysa hesitated. She nodded. "At least not for a time. How long, I don't know."

A painful look of realization spread across his face. Fixing his perplexed eyes upon her, he said, "I can hardly believe this is happening! I'm not happy about any of this!" He paced along the shore. He whirled back and said, "This forces me to wonder—what will happen to us, Lys? Everything was planned! Now what'll become of us?" He shook his head and looked downstream through angry, unsettled eyes.

Alysa turned her face away, looked toward Gorge Path and beyond to the high peaks of Winding Mountains. Her determined brown eyes stared at them, unblinking and certain. She sighed and smiled, knowing that her choice was the right one.

SAD FAREWELL

Morning light flooded the interior of Seda's cottage, streaming through the open door and windows. This cottage, in which several of Seda's relatives dwelt, was crowded with furniture, cooking items, extra cots and clothing. Although the cottage was cluttered, it was a clean and happy place. On this sun, the third sun after the joining, Alysa and Seda were the only two in the cottage. As was tradition, the new wives' families stayed away from their cottages on the morning their daughters left for their husbands' homesteads. It was thought this eased the pain of departure for everyone concerned.

Alysa helped her best friend, whose long, red hair was not yet braided, to put the last of her belongings into a packbasket. Dolfi, Seda's saroo, climbed up the basket and poked his wet, black nose inside, intent on keeping track of everything going into it. He continually flicked his short, round ears. He finally jumped into the basket, trying to snuggle into Seda's clothing.

Seda laughed and said, "Dolfi, you can't go, silly..." She lifted him out and set him tenderly on her bed. Dolfi shook his head as if, in rejection, to shake off any interest he may have shown in the girls' activity. He jumped out an open window and disappeared in the yard.

The girls reminisced as they worked. "Do you remember the time," Seda asked, "the one and only time Father let us go fishing with him?"

Alysa laughed. "We tangled the net in the trees. I'll never forget!"

"What do you mean *we* tangled the net? *You* were the one who begged him to let you cast it once. He told you, 'Girls weren't meant to fish,' but you teased him until he gave in. You got it so badly tangled that he just left it there. Don't go blaming that one on me, Alysa of High Point!" They laughed.

Seda climbed into her nook and took a wooden jar and a small covered basket from a cabinet. She sat on the edge of her bed.

Alysa climbed up beside her and recalled, "How about the summering we dried simmel-fronds to smoke because we knew some elders did and we wanted to try it? And your aunt caught us with that pipe and told our fathers. Did we get into trouble for that! Now that one was *your* idea, Seda of High Point!"

They giggled. Seda said, "And the arguments we used to have—remember? We'd get so angry at each other about some silly thing and not speak for a whole sun. Then I'd run to your cottage, or you to mine, and we'd be friends again before nightfall..."

"That's what makes best friends, Seda. Two people who can't let time go by without being together."

"You're right," Seda said, tears shining in her eyes. "What will we do without each other?"

They stared at one another, unblinking, struggling against tears. Alysa hoped to escape sadness this sun; but sadness is inevitable when best friends part. Alysa hugged Seda. Seda threw her arms around Alysa's neck, her hands still clutching the box and basket. For a time the girls wept.

Finally they composed themselves. Alysa wiped her tears. Trying to lighten the mood, she asked, "So have you and Aryz talked about having your firstborn yet?"

Seda's face flushed. She avoided looking directly at her friend and giggled. "Moons, talk about a swift change in conversation!" She giggled. "But yes, we did talk about it last night. We're going to start right away because we want to have as many younglings as we can. A few women have been able to have as many as four! Isn't that amazing!"

Seda climbed down from the nook and placed the items in the basket. She went to the doorway and leaned against the doorpost, watching as visitors, new husbands and their wives gathered, readying for their journey down Lower Path. A youngling who became ill during the night was being pulled to the walkway on a wheeled litter.

"And you, Alysa. What have you and Orryn decided to do?"

She hesitated. "Because of my new duty...we may have to delay our joining even more than we first thought."

Seda turned to look directly at her. Her hair sparked as sunlight streaked through her loose, wavy locks. "What? Is it really necessary to delay it further? I thought Tola was looking for someone!"

"Seda, quite honestly...I've discovered that I like the training. And I'm looking forward to the challenge of trading with the Trailmen. I'm thinking that...maybe I don't want to be replaced."

Seda gasped and stared, bewildered.

Alysa nodded and confessed, "Seda, I must tell you this. I haven't told anyone else and I haven't found the courage to tell Orryn." She hesitated as she gathered strength for what she was about to admit to Seda, and to herself. "I've decided that I do not want to join with Orryn. Ever."

Seda stared back in horror. "Alysa! Explain to me after so many cycles of planning, how can you not? It's been accepted by all the clanfolk since — forever! — that you and he are betrothed! What will Orryn think?"

"I know that he will not be happy. Seda, I'm asking you, my best and closest friend, to understand what it is I must do." Alysa pleaded firmly, "Please try, Seda. I truly want to be a Trader. And concerning joining — I don't believe Orryn is the one. He is my friend, as you are."

"Not the one? Who do you want to join with?"

"There is no one. There may never be."

Stunned, Seda said, "I cannot imagine — would never consider — going though life alone!"

"What would happen to me if I never did join? Would I just dry up and blow away? I don't think so!" Seda pouted. "Seda, with you in my heart, my mother and sister beside me, and the people of my homestead all around — I will never be alone."

Seda sighed and shook her head. She began to braid her hair. "I know you will not mind me saying that you've always been a little...different, Alysa. But I'll worry about you anyway, best friend. And I will miss you terribly!"

"Please don't tell anyone, Seda. I don't want this to get back to Orryn before I've found the courage to tell him myself. I dread it, but I must. I owe him that."

Seda shook her head. "Do you think anybody would believe me if I told them?" Seda secured the end of her braid with a twist of colorful cloth.

Alysa climbed down from the nook. They hugged so that it seemed they would never let go, but finally, they did. They placed the last of Seda's belongings into the packbasket. Alysa picked it up, struggling with its weight, and followed Seda out into the sunshine.

Loralle, Ellee and Orryn's parents were gathered near the terrace stairway leading to Lower Path. Their packbaskets rested on the ground beside them. Alysa looked beyond them and saw Orryn talking to Kendira. He was nearly twice the old woman's height.

Alysa said, "I should get over there so I don't miss the farewell."

Aryz waited at the entry to the yard. The girls walked up to him. He took the basket, easily slung it onto his broad back, and kissed Alysa on the cheek. He tenderly squeezed Seda's hand and left to join the departing group. "Your parents are waiting for us, my beloved."

Seda beamed at him. "I'll be right along, *my* beloved!" She giggled then sobered as she took one last, loving look at her cottage. She turned and gazed at the low lake and over the terraces at the surrounding mountains, her voice on the edge of tears. "I will never forget this view, or how the air smells standing right here in my yard..." She took a long breath and embraced Alysa.

Alysa said, "I hope to see you at Leaffall Moonsfest, my friend." They hugged again.

Seda said, her voice breaking, "I'll get a message to you before then to let you know where we'll be. I do hope it's here!"

"Good life to you both," Alysa said. "Farewell!"

Seda caught up with Aryz, and they gathered with his parents.

Alysa walked over to where her family stood with Bavat and Tach. She hugged them. Orryn came up behind her. As he passed, he paused to kiss her on the forehead then bounced down the stairway. He turned back once and smiled. As his parents and the others followed, he disappeared in the bobbing mass.

Standing with her mother and sister, Alysa watched until, at the bottommost terrace by the lake, Seda stepped to one side of the throng and waved her arm in a broad arc. Then she and the other travelers entered the forest.

Blurred figures toiled at the far end of a dusty field under the sun at zenith. Beneath the orange sky, scattered patches of grain rustled in the furious wind. Dry whirlwinds of air twisted powdery soil into the sky here and there over the field. But there was neither sound of rustling grain nor of wind as it gusted over the fields and through the trees at field's edge. The wind blew an eerie quietness; the air was dull, flat.

The figures, slow and deliberate, toiled in the field, intent on their work. None of them spoke to each other. Not one seemed to sense that another worked nearby.

A small, buff-colored creature grazed at the field's edge; it was a leaprock lamb. It nibbled at soft grasses, mincing each mouthful with tiny teeth, unaware that it was being stalked from within the forest by a fearsome, hideous beast. As the beast crept on two feet toward the lamb, it bent branches from its path. It was slow. It was silent. No one noticed its creeping. It watched through intent, narrow red eyes until, finally, it hovered over the lamb.

With deftness inconsistent with its bulk, the beast howled, breaking the dull silence, and thrust its twisted ugly maw onto the lamb's back. The beast clenched its slathering jaws for a tight hold. The lamb squealed in helpless pain.

A woman with hair of fire and a face that lacked any features ran across the field, pelting the beast with stones; but the beast didn't seem to notice. Registering only mild annoyance, it turned and glared at her with its red eyes, while the lamb bleated, frantic, flailing in the beast's mouth. The beast turned and loped into the underbrush.

The woman opened her mouth wide and emitted a whining scream that grew louder and louder. She clutched her head of fire between her hands and watched as the beast made its way deeper into the trees. The woman began to follow but halted as roots erupted beneath her, coiling about her feet, ankles and calves, winding around and binding her legs, crisscrossing her skirt as they encircled her body. They wrapped tight about her waist, making it impossible for her to move, to follow after the stolen lamb. She pulled at the roots to free herself, but her hands were too weak to break them.

A powerful, broad-antlered firestag bounded across the field, kicking clouds of dry soil high into the air as it leapt. With head poised for battle, the firestag plunged into the forest on the track of the beast. Its antlers clashed against saplings, splintering them as it dove onward.

The firestag's antlers impacted the beast's back, driving deep into its body and knocking it to the ground. The beast dropped the lamb and began to howl in a half-strangled scream that pierced the depths of the forest.

"Alysa. Come, wake up," Loralle urged as she gently roused her daughter from unsound sleep.

Curls of incense smoke wafted through the air. The burning herb was thought to purify the air and drive illness away.

Tahshi sleepily crawled out from beneath the quilt and scratched a dark ear with his hind foot. He climbed backwards down the quilt and made for the saroos' basket near the hearth.

Loralle felt Alysa's forehead and face. "Alysa, do you hear me?"

"Mother?" The girl's voice was hoarse. Her breathing was rapid, and she was winded when she finally awoke. Beads of perspiration on her face reflected the dim lamplight. She tried to look around but shut her eyes tight. "Oh, that hurts!"

"Your fever has finally broken." Loralle pulled the fur blanket off Alysa. She was soaking wet. "I'll have to put dry bedding on. And we must change your sleeping-smock."

"What happened, Mother?"

"You had bad dreaming. I tried to wake you for the longest time! Come."

With great effort and with her mother's help, Alysa sat up, holding her aching head. She lifted her arms but held her eyes shut as Loralle removed her smock and pulled a dry one over her head. Loralle worked the damp bedding from beneath her.

"My head hurts, Mother."

"I'll be done before you know it. There's been an illness. Many other Folk have fallen to it during the last few suns."

Alysa was dizzy. She squeezed her eyes shut. "I don't remember the dream, Mother. But I feel scared. Did I say anything in my dreaming?"

"You cried out several times before I was able to wake you. You thrashed around so, I thought you'd fall out of bed!" Loralle slipped a fresh sheet beneath her daughter, tucked it in, and threw the blanket over top of her. "There, it's done already."

Alysa opened her eyes and looked around for as long as she could bear. She saw that her sister was gone. "Where's Ellee?"

"She's at Evyn's. We're trying to keep the ill apart from the healthy to keep the illness from spreading. It'll soon be time for planting, and we can't have half the field teams in bed."

Loralle took some herb leaves from one of the white clay jars on the mantle, crushed them with her fingers, and sprinkled them into a bowl of water. She dipped a cloth into the water, wrung it out, and pressed it to Alysa's face.

"That feels good, Mother. May I have a drink?" Alysa ran her tongue over her parched lips.

"I have some broth…"

"No, I can't eat anything. My stomach's churning."

"Your stomach will be able to take broth. You need it for strength, Daughter."

Loralle returned with a mug and helped Alysa sit up. Alysa's shaky hands took the mug, and she slurped the broth until half was gone, squeezing her eyes shut as she drank. She handed the mug back to her mother.

"No, no, you must finish it."

Reluctant but obeying, she finished the broth. Loralle took the mug and helped Alysa rest her head back on the pillow.

"How long did I sleep, Mother?"

"Since afternoon of last sun. It's morning again."

"Oh, I thought it was night. It's so dark."

"I closed the shutters and curtains. It's supposed to help if the ill are kept in darkness. I would also have pulled your nook curtains, but I wanted to be able to see you."

Loralle took Alysa's hand and caressed it. "Do you need to go to the privy, my Daughter?"

Alysa shook her head. The idea of walking anywhere was not possible to think about!

"Would you like to talk a bit to help pass time?"

"I don't want to keep you from your duties, Mother."

"You're my only concern, Alysa, and I'll stay with you until you're well."

Alysa clapped her hands over her eyes and said, "All right. Maybe talking will help. How long does an illness last?"

"Well, let me see; this one has occurred two times that I recall — usually five or six suns. You've had it for three."

"I hope it passes before Trade. I don't want to miss it." Alysa bolted upright, looked at her mother, winced, and slumped down again, covering her eyes. "Are Boshe and Panli ill, too? If they are, there will be no Trade!"

"Don't worry, Alysa. They're much older than you and have small risk of becoming ill. This illness ignores those who have been struck with it before." She paused and regarded her daughter. "I don't think, after all, that talking is going to help you. Just be still. Rest."

Alysa obeyed. After she was arranged under the covers again, she said, "Mother, I have something to tell you about Orryn and me."

Loralle smiled and stroked Alysa's cheek. "I know, Daughter. I watched as he left. You didn't part as the typical betrothed who will not be seeing each other again for moons. You no longer want him, do you?"

"You've grown close to Orryn and his family over the cycles. I don't wish to disgrace you, Mother, or Bavat or Tach. But what you perceive is true; I no longer want to join with him. But this truly has nothing to do with *him*."

"Daughter, do not think me so shallow! And Bavat and Tach will take no offense; they'll be saddened, but we'll always remain friends.

We were friends before you and Orryn were born. Bavat and I are both of Yellow Cliffs, remember. It's important for you to be true to what you want in life. This is important for Orryn, as well. He will find another."

"I've been wondering something, Mother. Did you ever want anything different?"

"What do you mean, Daughter?"

"When you were a girl, did you ever think about doing anything other than joining and raising a family?"

Loralle smiled. "Ah, I see. I don't recall ever wanting anything else in my life other than being a crafter and a mother. But that doesn't mean that you or Ellee or any other woman shouldn't desire a different life. I'm beginning to think that maybe it's time for things to change."

Alysa squinted and smiled a feeble smile. "Thank you, Mother. You are truly marvelous."

"No, no. You are, my Daughter. I do realize how you've struggled with all the changes in our lives these last many moons. I did not expect any of these outcomes in our lives, including those that go against tradition. But things do change, whether we want them to or not. So I've begun to see things in a different way. My strength is returning because of what you've accomplished all on your own. I'll always miss your father, always treasure the life we lived together. But since his final farewell, it's as if I've been gone, too. I apologize for that. I will make it up to you, and to Ellee."

"I adore you, Mother."

Loralle kissed Alysa's hand and placed it under the covers. She smoothed her daughter's damp, tangled hair and said, "Somehow, I will make it up to you."

GREENING TRADE

By lamplight preparations for Trade were being discussed within Boshe's cottage. Boshe, Panli and Alysa sat at a table. Slates bearing fieldscript symbols were stacked on the table and in a vacant chair. Alysa set the last slate on the pile.

Boshe, the elder of the two beardless men, said, "It sounds to me like we're ready for Trade. All of the baskets in the storage sheds are labeled?"

Alysa replied, "Yes. The helpers worked very hard to get everything ready."

"Everything's loaded into carts?"

Alysa nodded.

"You did an excellent job organizing the tradegoods," Boshe said, "in particular because the homesteads produced an overabundance this cycle." His keen, blue eyes danced. The gray streaks in his dark hair shone in the lamplight.

Alysa said, "For my first time organizing the tradegoods, it went well, Boshe. I'm glad to have done it. It's exciting to see the abundance we have to offer. The Great Hall is half-filled with carts!"

The balding Panli asked, "Did you find anything interesting about any of the goods?"

Alysa paused and said, "The item that stands out in my mind is the Yellow Cliffs pottery. One of the young potters created a new motif. While it's not one of our traditional patterns, it is unusual."

Panli asked, "Do you think it should be included among the tradegoods? That would not be expected."

Boshe considered this. "It's worth trying. We'll just have to see how the Trailmen react. We can always retract the items if they object to them."

Alysa nodded and added, "Green Plateau produced some of the deepest green wovens I've ever seen. It's very good cloth. The Trailmen will no doubt trade more than usual for it."

Panli scribbled notes on a slate. He asked, "I wonder if they'll have any Before Cat'clysm items from the Lowlands this time? If they do, maybe they'll trade those for some of our holdbacks. Do we have any good holdbacks that the Trailmen may be willing to give more than usual for?"

Alysa replied, "We have the usual pieces of clothing. You know, we could use the new pots as holdbacks. Then if they don't like them, we won't be obligated to retract them."

"That's a good idea," Boshe said.

Alysa continued, "I have a good amount of fine cloth that I wove wintertide before last. I was intending to make...a smock. But I no longer have need of it. We could use that as a holdback and end up with something valuable in return."

"It sounds like you've traded before, Alysa!" Panli said with a hearty laugh.

"Well, Father brought a few stories home from Trade, along with some odd B.C. trinkets!"

Boshe said, "Whatever you get for your cloth, Alysa, you may keep for yourself."

Alysa nodded. "Thank you!"

Boshe sighed. "Alysa, I want you to know that I did enjoy serving under your father. And we did have some very productive times."

"I appreciate your saying that, Boshe," she said. "You know, I've wondered why Father became a Trader; I never did ask him. I don't know whether everyone has the same reason, and I couldn't guess what his was. Why did you become one, Boshe?"

Boshe leaned his large frame back in the chair, hands behind his head as he pondered the question. "I'll confess something to you. It wasn't enough for me, tending the fields and herding udommo. A life of planting, harvesting and crafting is enough for most Folk. But that work never gave me enough—was not satisfying. I guess that's the right word."

Alysa nodded. "Yes! That's exactly what I've come to think!"

He continued, "Trading with the Trailmen, coming into contact with those fierce Painted Ones—now *that* seemed like it would add a little risk to living! Although it's a thrill that few people look for. So when the opportunity came, I gladly took it. Even after seventeen cycles, I've never regretted my decision."

"It's a challenge," offered Panli, "and the prestige of doing a dangerous and unpopular duty drew me to it. When I was a boy, I never missed an opportunity to carry goods to the Tradeground. I could hardly wait until I was old enough for the Council to consider me for Trader. People do hold us in high esteem for dealing with the savages, you know. My wife told me that was one reason she was attracted to me. With five cycles behind me, I know that I chose the right duty!"

Alysa asked, "Panli, why do you say being a Trader is 'dangerous'? And where is the 'risk', Boshe?"

Boshe advised, "Ah, you never know what a Trailman will do. Those Painted Ones cannot be trusted! One must constantly be on guard."

"Has a Folk Trader ever been...attacked by a Trailmen?" she asked.

The men looked at each other, shrugged, shook their heads.

"Then there's nothing for me to fear. Unless you think there will be trouble when they find that the Folk have a female Trader."

"We don't know," Boshe said. "Panli and I've speculated, but there's obviously nothing in the history that kept the Council from making the decision they did. The Trailmen will soon see that you're worthy. I'm certain that Trade will proceed smoothly."

"I have no doubt!" Alysa said.

Boshe slid his chair back and rose. He decreed, "I do believe that we are ready for Trade. The light will come early enough tomorrow, so we had best get our sleep. See you two at sunrise!"

Drops of dew slipped from tips of leaves and dripped through branches. Their sporadic *pat-patter-pat* broke the quiet of dawn at the Tradeground. Far below in the gorge, the silent stream rushed over rocks, high with melting run-off from Winding Mountains. A plateau of mist hid the lower reaches of the mountains.

Several paces from the Tradeground, a wide, ancient bridge spanned the gorge. Some of its rusty metal girders had fallen away or lay against each other at odd angles. Sections of the floor had given out, and through these openings the stream could be seen. Many very coarse, dark vines were wound around the girders. Some held tight to fallen pieces of the structure and suspended them beneath the bridge. The Folk never crossed the bridge—or the stream at any point—which led into Trailmen territory.

Boshe dismissed the bearers, who made haste back down Gorge Path. In silence, he, Panli and Alysa organized many baskets containing the tradegoods beneath a large canopy. The baskets were of three kinds. The first was made of loose-woven splints that held cloth and other lightweight articles. The second was a tight-coiled, insect-resistant grass basket containing meal, dried vegetables, fruits, nuts and small bags of cheese. And the third was a heavier woven type of basket that held root vegetables, pottery, lamp oil, boots, rugs and other heavy, bulky items.

The Folk Traders left the canopy and laid out three thick mats. Boshe sat in the middle and Panli to his left. Boshe directed Alysa to sit on his right. She sat down cross-legged, as did the men, and tucked the edge of her long skirt under her legs.

As they awaited the Trailmen, she smiled to herself as she realized, *I'm sitting next to the exact spot where Father used to sit!* She closed her eyes and felt that, for a moment, he was sitting beside her. She sensed something—a warm feeling that rose up in her when she was around people she loved. She tried to define what she was feeling. Could it be that she sensed—her father's presence?

She opened her eyes and to the side of her vision she almost thought she saw him, instead of Boshe, grinning at her! No matter that he was not. She closed her eyes again and smiled, relishing the illusion, allowing it to linger.

"They're coming!" Boshe whispered.

Alysa startled from her thoughts.

He pointed across the gorge. The Folk drew deep breaths in anticipation and sat up alert, watching. A line of figures appeared along the rim of the gorge. Men and younglings of various ages bore bundles upon their backs or atop close-shorn heads. They were dressed in green and brown hide tunics and breeches. Some wore bulky fur vests.

Alysa studied them and with surprise whispered, "Boshe, are some of the bearers…girls?"

Boshe whispered, "I don't know. I've never been able to tell for certain. Quiet now…"

The Trailmen crossed the old bridge, well aware of the holes in the floor and weaving a path around them. They entered the small clearing that had been the Tradeground for a hundred generations. From this point on, neither Folk nor Trailmen would utter a word.

The Trailmen's eyes revealed nothing more than mild curiosity when they rested on Alysa's seated form.

Panli and Boshe had prepared Alysa as to the Trailmen's appearance and mannerisms. But one thing she did not expect to witness was the grace and silence with which these people trod. She marveled at how, even though last leaffall's litter was thick on the ground and fallen twigs were scattered everywhere, it seemed that each booted foot was set down without disturbing a single leaf. Although scores of feet passed over them, each leaf seemed to remain as it had fallen, each twig unbroken. Even the delicate red-capped fungi poking up through the leaves went unscathed as they passed.

The bearers set down many bundles opposite the Folk goods. The Trailmen Traders organized their goods as their bearers re-crossed the bridge and melted into the trees.

To Alysa, the Trailmen did not look, at this first meeting, much different than her own people, other than in their style of hair and clothing. But they did appear to be thinner and stronger than most Folk. Their faces lacked expression. Teachers Boshe and Panli taught her that this was a Trade technique which would take time for her to master. But their faces were not harsh or mean as she always imagined. They were every bit as comely as were her people.

Her stomach tightened. Her breath became shallow, and she noticed that her hands were shaking; but she could not tell whether this was due to anticipation or anxiety. She laid her hands in her lap in an effort to conceal this.

The Trailmen unrolled fur mats and spread them on the ground barely two paces opposite the Folk. They settled on their mats, the eldest in the center facing Boshe.

Alysa noticed the bright tattooed patterns that started on the tops of their ears and spread down the backs of their necks. Alysa thought, *So this is what has earned them the name 'Painted Ones'!* The paintings were striking. The designs were different on each of the three men. Some of the paintings looked like animals, others like scenery, and some appeared to be symbols of some sort. She wondered what they meant.

The eldest Trailman seemed to have the most numerous patterns on his deep-golden skin. When he turned his head, Alysa could see that the colors fanned out broadly from the back of his neck and seemed to stretch across his shoulders. She wondered if the patterns continued down his body; but she couldn't tell, of course, because his clothing covered his torso.

As was tradition, Traders did not wear beards. It was thought, at least by the Folk, that a barefaced Trader presented himself as open and honest.

Alysa looked into each Trailman's eyes and they reciprocated, a show of mutual respect. After that, her shaking began to subside.

Boshe and his Trailman counterpart held palms forward in the customary greeting.

Alysa's musings ended as Boshe signed with both hands: *Good – See – You – Men – Of – Trails. – Trust – Travel – From – Lowlands – Safe – For – Tribe?*

The Trailman acknowledged, *Travel – Good. – Lost – Not – One – This – Time.* He eyed the large number of baskets beneath the canopy. *Expect – Your – Wintertide – Passed – Well!* A sharp clap of his palms accented the phrase.

Boshe signed, *Good – Surplus – From – Harvest. – Grain – Crop – Large – This – Trade.*

The Trailman leader said, *Trapped – Many – Animals. – Collected – Many – Hides. – Wish – To – See?*

Boshe nodded. The formalities over, Trade began. Alysa relaxed somewhat as Trade got underway. At the bidding of their leader, the younger two Trailmen retrieved a large bundle of furs stacked skin-side out and placed it between the two groups. They untied its twisted hide bindings and unfolded the bundle, revealing plush furs of varied hues. They were very thick, as the animals were taken during wintertide.

This – Is – Sample – Of – Harvest, added the eldest Trailman.

Each Folk picked up a fur to assess tanning quality and suppleness. The fur remained attached to the thick skins when pulled, and excess fat and sinew were thoroughly scraped off. These were two signs of good tanning.

Panli took out his small blade and drew it across the edge of a fur and scrutinized the cut. He signed, *Excellent – Work!* and clapped his palms. All three Folk were in agreement that the tanning was good. Though none of them smiled at the compliment, the Trailmen's faces could not completely mask their pride.

Boshe signaled Alysa and Panli and they withdrew to the canopy. They shared the load of a coiled basket and carried it to the Traders. They removed the lid, and Panli poured small dippers of meal into each Trailmen's palm. They smelled, tasted and nodded.

More – Dried – Foods? asked the gray-haired Trailman elder.

Will – Trade – Dried – Fruit – Vegetables – For – Furs, Boshe gestured.

Have – Eleven – Bundles – Fur. How – Many – Baskets – Grain?

Boshe looked at Alysa for the tally. She signed, *Forty – Baskets – Grain.* Then she added, *You – Can – See – Very – Fine – Quality.*

Boshe glanced at her sharply. He reached in front of her and held out his hand to silence her. She realized too late what she did wrong. It was Boshe's job to ensure smooth and concise trading and to conduct the official bartering. Panli and Alysa, as Lesser Traders, were on hand to provide information and to assist their elder when necessary. More important, they were there to learn.

I – Am – Not – Without – Eyes! the Trailman exclaimed, glancing hard at Alysa. It seemed that no permanent offense was taken, as he remained seated.

Boshe motioned, urging him to continue. The Trailman signed, *Lowland – Greatclaw – Very – Difficult – Hunt – Kill. – Will – Trade – One – For – Ten – Baskets – Grain.*

Boshe hesitated. The Trailmen were taking an advantage allowed under the laws of Trade, which meant their next bid must be accepted as the result of Alysa's signing out of turn. The black and white-spotted greatclaw furs were very large and rare, but they were not worth as much as the Folk were now obligated to trade for just one.

Trade – Fair, Boshe signed, his face neutral, hiding his disappointment.

Good! clapped the Trailman elder. The other two lesser Trailmen grinned at their leader's savvy.

The bartering continued through the morning and into afternoon without pause. Boshe managed to secure antler for tool making, carved bone toggle-buttons and beads, and many small blades with antler handles. He traded cheese for sacks of cured marshdoe meat. For Folk textiles the Trailmen exchanged sacks of smoked Lowlands shimmerfish, which were much larger than those caught in the mountain lakes and streams.

Finally, after trading many other items, only one basket and one bundle on either side remained. These were the special holdbacks that each saved for the close of Trade. Trading of holdbacks was the time allotted for the younger Traders to practice without risking the loss of important goods.

Have – Rare – BC – Goods, the Trailman leader motioned. A bulky blanket was unrolled before the Folk, revealing several objects contained therein. The Trailmen arranged their artifacts from the Lowlands: a small, shiny disc; a spouted vessel made of a lightweight material similar to glass and bearing the remnants of a broken handle; a rusted metal cup with a raised design below the rim; a thick book in oldenscript; a pink slipper fashioned from a smooth, shiny substance; and a gleaming metal pendant on a hide string. In the center of the pendant was fixed a blue stone. When the light hit the stone just right, many tiny stars glimmered within it.

How Alysa desired to hang this last item from her neck! She intended to obtain it.

Boshe sat back and observed as Panli and Alysa rose and retrieved the Folk's remaining basket. Panli withdrew some finished items, which he and Alysa spread out before the Trailmen—a colorful, embroidered woolen vest; several blouses in Trailmen style; heavy woolen mitts; and an exquisite shawl. The Trailmen had difficulty containing their excitement when they saw the new style of pottery the Folk set before them.

From the onset, Panli bid for the pendant. He picked up the vest and signed, *I – Trade – Handsome – Vest – For – Blue – Stone.*

Boshe sat back and grinned at Panli's too-obvious interest. The Trailman sitting opposite Panli shook his head and signed, *Not – Even – For – All – You – Offer – Here!* Panli pointed to both the vest and shawl and with persuasive gesturing said, *Good – Gifts – For – Wife!*

The Trailman signed, *Will – Trade – For – Any – Other – Object. – Not – Enough – For – Stone!*

Panli looked at Boshe, whose amused nod advised him to concede. Panli lost his chance to obtain the stone and demonstrated his concession by picking up a few less appealing articles.

It was Alysa's turn. She picked up several objects and scrutinized them. The material the slipper was made from was intriguing but she thought, *What good is only one slipper?* The book and its strange symbols engrossed her as she fanned its thick, waxy pages. She marveled, *It's amazing that these mysterious markings meant something at one time!* But even though it was interesting, the book was of no practical use. She placed it back on the cloth. Her hand swept over other objects. She pointed to the shiny disc.

What – Use – Is – This? she asked.

The young Trailman opposite her looked at his leader, then back at Alysa. He shrugged. *Do – Not – Know. – Found – In – Ancient – Dwelling.*

She held up a clay pot and he nodded. She exchanged the pot for the disc. They continued to barter until all the Folk goods were gone and the only remaining Trailmen offering was the stone pendant.

Trade appeared to be finished and the Trailmen relaxed, the stone still in their possession.

Have – One – Last – Item – To – Trade, Alysa added.

The Trailmen looked mildly perplexed. There was nothing left on the Folk side to trade. Alysa reached under her vest and produced a thick fold of cloth, fine textured and as white as snow.

This – I – Offer – In – Exchange. She handed the cloth to the Trailman opposite her. He unfolded it and passed it to the others. They were awed by its brightness and fine-woven texture. All three rubbed the smooth cloth between their fingers.

White – As – The – Moons, she pointed out.

The elder shook his head, gathered the cloth and handed it back to her. *Trade – Over!* he signed with a sharp clap.

Alysa was crushed after all that difficult work for nothing! She even ended up with the useless slipper. She held what she thought was a very good trade object for last so her chance to get the stone would be better. But she failed, after all, to obtain the most beautiful object she ever saw.

The Trailman sitting across from her picked up the pendant, wound the hide string around it, and placed it into a pouch hanging from his neck.

Everyone rose, Alysa the last and most reluctant to end Trade.

Boshe and the other leader gestured to each other simultaneously, *Good – Trade! – Meet – After – Leaffall – Moons!*

Trailmen and Folk began to close lids and tie bundles to make their goods ready for removal. The Trailmen departed to summon their bearers.

Once they were out of hearing range, Alysa spoke to Boshe while Panli rolled up the sitting mats. "Boshe, I feel foolish for disrupting Trade from the start. Not only once did I err, but twice!"

"Don't let it trouble you," he chuckled. "We did extremely well, overall. You should be proud of yourself for the bartering you did!"

Panli added, "We'll take home a bounty of unusual B.C. items. We'll store them in the shed behind the Pantry with the rest. Who knows; perhaps some sun we will find a use for them."

"Well, Trade did work out well, I suppose."

Panli laughed and added, "You did better than I did!"

Boshe rested his hands on Alysa's shoulders and turned her to him. "Listen to me, midling. I know for certain that you do possess a gift for barter. I've never seen anyone do so well at first Trade, on either side. You were calm, showed confidence, and you were very quick to reply when asked questions. Your signing was without error. Your father would be very proud!"

Alysa knew this, somehow, and managed a smile.

Boshe continued, "So don't be so hard on yourself. Just remember next time not to talk so much. You must remember that if they see value in something, they don't have to be told—only shown. You tried a little too hard, that's all."

"I see. All right, Boshe. Thank you. I'll remember." She looked toward the Gorge Trail. "Should I summon the bearers?"

Boshe bent backwards to work the stiffness from his back. "Yes, that's one among the many 'privileges' of being Lesser Trader! Panli and I will ready the bundles. Watch your footing on that rocky path. There's no hurry. Plenty of time before nightfall to get back to High Point."

Alysa started down the path, her dejection already subsiding due to her companions' encouraging words. The mists had long evaporated from the hills and the afternoon sun warmed the air.

She reached a point midway downpath where rays of sunshine no longer touched the ground. The sun was walking its own path toward the horizon. A breeze surged through the gorge and caught loose strands of her hair, whipping them across her face. The breeze tugged at her skirt, which she drew up a bit to ease her steps. Soon she reached the level of the shadow-dappled stream. The path widened, became less stony, and melted into the shore. The air became less breezy.

She paused to free a stone that found its way into her slipper. She was glad after a long sun of silence to hear the voice of the noisy, plunging stream. She emptied her slipper and continued along the path. The bearers waited around the bend, beyond the precipice overhanging the stream. She could see the line of carts lined up and ready to receive the traded goods as they were brought down.

Suddenly, a young Trailman stepped in front of her, stopping her short. He was taller than she. His face was bare and angular. His dark-streaked hair was sweaty and was littered with leaves and pieces of bark. His body was lean and strong. He wore a brown hide tunic and breeches.

She took two surprised steps back and looked past him, hoping the bearers would be in sight. She opened her mouth to call out then, thinking better of it, closed it.

The Trailman smiled and spoke, oddly pronouncing some of the words. "I heard that a woman was with the Fielders this sun. I wanted to see for myself. I never foresaw that would happen. But it is true!"

Alysa was taken aback by his talk even more than by his sudden appearance. *His talk!* A Trailmen spoke to her with his *voice* — and she understood! Aghast, she asked, "What — what do you want?"

"I was curious and just wished to look at you. Our Traders say you were ruthless in your trade methods." He smiled. "Not only are you the first female Trader anyone can recollect, but your ability was also an unforeseen circumstance, to be certain. Admirable qualities among the Trailmen are persistence and cunning. I was curious and wanted to look upon you myself."

Uneasy, she shifted from foot to foot, prepared to run. Fear welled up in her. She looked past him to where she knew the bearers waited. She whispered, "We shouldn't be talking!"

"Do not worry. I certainly do not plan on telling anyone that I spoke to a Fielder. They would think me mad!" He chuckled. "And I think that your tribe would think the same of you."

She paused, not certain how to reply.

"But although they say you were a challenging Trader, you were denied this." He reached into a pouch and withdrew the pendant she had so much desired. He dangled the blue star-filled stone before her eyes. "I would like to test your ability. What do you offer in return?"

She stared at the gleaming object. "Nothing. I don't want it any longer," she lied. But it was true that she desired to distance herself from him. She feared that continued talk with the Trailmen would cause great harm if they were discovered.

"They say you traded all your tribe had left except for a piece of purest white cloth, unlike any a Trailmen has ever seen. And that you kept it hidden until the very last. Now you say you do not desire this?"

In an attempt to cover her fear, she said, "I'm no longer interested in the object!" She pushed past him and continued at a fast pace.

He called after her. "I must tell you this. I would not have uttered a word if I were not certain that we had met before."

She balked at the statement. She turned around, propped her fists on her hips, and looked at him with the fiercest glare she could muster.

"Right I am!" he laughed. "You are the one, all right. I am called Szaren. But I see by your expression that you do not remember me. Below on this stream, many cycles past, I came upon a girl crying like a newborn."

Ellee's birth sun, and the encounter with the strange boy who had crept up on her, tumbled back into her memory. She was traumatized by that meeting and had managed to keep it hidden even from herself—until now. She glared into his pale-blue eyes. "I was not crying!" she insisted, bitter.

"I remember how angry you were. You still are an angry girl! My memory is better than yours, I can see. I also recall a voice calling over the stream. A-sa, Ya-sis, Yissa..."

"Alysa!" she snapped.

"Yissa, then. And I was very surprised to see that we spoke the same tongue."

"Our speech is not the same," she whispered, wishing she could shout the words. "And it's 'Alysa'!"

"We can talk, same enough, Yissa." Irritation colored his voice as he pursued, "Do you want to trade or not? This is the only time Szaren will ask!"

"No! I want nothing more to do with it. Or with you—Szaren!" She hurried along the path, shaking with fear, leaving behind the young man and the dangling stone.

107

He grimaced, watched her disappear around the bend, shrugged his shoulders, and pouched the object. With little effort, he leapt into the shadows of the bordering trees.

At the temporary campsite where men and boys had spent an anxious sun, they awaited the summons of the Traders. Alysa stumbled into the group of bearers, still shaken by the Trailman encounter. Their faces beamed with relief. This season's Trade was over, once the traded goods up top were retrieved and they had returned to the safety and familiarity of the homestead.

As Alysa led the bearers back up Gorge Path, she often peered into the undergrowth or into treetops. She was relieved that Szaren was nowhere to be seen. She was grateful to have worked with the Trailmen in the capacity of Trader and so could justify enduring limited contact with them. But she would not be able to tolerate anything more; and she knew for certain that the Folk would not condone it.

She hoped to never again have the misfortune of speaking face to face with a Trailman!

THE STORM

Hot sunshine washed over the terrace as Alysa and many other 'steaders bent over knee-high simmel stalks. The tender green fronds swayed in the light breeze. Still feeling an attachment to the fields, and to those who labored with her, she managed to spend time on the terraces even though she was now a Trader and was no longer obligated to do so. She liked spending time in the fields, as the ashes of those who passed before her nourished the crops, completing the cycle of life. She felt close to her father here. Someday her ashes would join his and contribute to the harvest.

She removed her wide, straw bonnet and wiped her dripping brow with the back of her hand. She fanned her face with the bonnet. Her arms were a mellow gold color, the result of wearing sleeveless blouses in the fields and orchards.

This field team, as well as many others scattered about the terraces, thinned crowded simmel seedlings. With great care the workers scooped the plants out of the ground with long, narrow forks carved from wood, which left the roots intact. They placed the young plants into short, rectangular baskets filled with damp soil. The seedlings would be replanted on sparser sections of the terraces.

Alysa reflected on the good news that arrived a few suns before: Seda would not be coming to High Point for Leaffall Moonsfest as they planned, nor would she be traveling to any of the other homesteads. She was with unborn! Some women had difficulty carrying their unborn to birth; Loralle delivered but two offspring for this reason. Alysa was Loralle's fifth attempt, and she was confined to bed until Alysa's birth. Ellee arrived much later, after several subsequent pregnancies were lost.

Seda was much more robust than Loralle and less likely to have difficulty. But since this was her first time carrying unborn, she wanted to avoid putting its life at risk by traveling. For this reason, Alysa was very happy to visit Falling Stream for Moonsfest and spare her best friend the worry. Her mother expressed interest in going, too. Ellee had rarely been taken to visit the other homesteads, so this journey would give her the opportunity. They decided to make the journey together, as a family.

It occurred to Alysa that an advantage in leaving High Point for Moonsfest would be to distance her from the reminder that she was supposed to have joined with Orryn at that time. The change in scenery would be good for all three of them!

She straightened and arched her spine. She waved a persistent buzzfly from her face. Her throat was parched, so she took up her basket and walked to the edge of the terrace. She set it down with an accumulation of other plant-filled baskets in the shade of a spreading, large-leafed tree.

A basket containing a newborn hung from a shady branch. She looked in at the napping youngling and for a moment watched his peaceful, little face. She smiled and adjusted the thin blanket that covered him.

A water bucket hung from another branch. Alysa lifted a dipper and gulped water, allowing some to drizzle down her chest and dampen her lightweight brown blouse. She poured some into her palm and patted her face and neck.

She sat down, stretched her legs, and flopped back on the cool grass. She thought about the upcoming visit to Falling Stream. Though she felt sad about it, she would confess to Orryn her decision not to join with him. Then releasing him from the betrothal pact their parents made long ago, he would be free to join with another. Though thinking of this caused her stomach to tighten, she would not be truly at ease until she made a break of their betrothal. She owed Orryn the truth.

Others from the team approached the resting place. Their chatter ended her thoughts of the coming Moonsfest. The sun was beginning to sink. All were weary from the hot work. But even though the sun was hard, the workers were cheerful. Their convivial chatter and banter made her smile as she lay listening. Her people were fine folk, despite their sometimes stuck-in-the-muck attitude. Although she had come to think of herself as an individual with her own needs and desires, she knew that she would always be devoted to her people and the goodness of their ways.

Leaffall Trade arrived. The trek up the ridge to the Tradeground was unusually cold for this early in the season, the wind quite blustery. Even the harvest planners did not foresee this weather in signs of sky, insect or leaf. Though the severity of the impending weather could not be predicted, it was determined that a storm was on the way and that it would arrive the next morning. Fortunately, the remainder of the harvest was gathered in.

The Folk Traders and tradegood bearers were wrapped in heavy cloaks, fur-lined boots, and knit caps. Chill gusts of wind whisked down the gorge, threatening to wrench lids from baskets and hoods from heads.

As they hiked, Alysa thought back to the journey she made to Falling Stream just half a moon ago; it was a much warmer sun than this one. She and Orryn spent time alone. They walked in the warm, colorful fields and orchards of leaffall and visited the high waterfalls near the homestead.

As she promised herself, she was honest with him. She explained, "I don't know how else to tell you, Orryn. You're one of the very best friends I've ever had. I'm the one who is changing, and you've done nothing to spark this. I simply no longer desire to join, as I think we have become too different in what we want in life."

Orryn replied sadly, "I feared it would come to this, Lys. Although I was holding onto hope, I already decided to let you go if you chose to live the other way. I understand that you must do—whatever it is that you must do. But you'll always be in my thoughts."

"And you in mine, Orryn. We will always be the closest of friends, as I feel we were meant to be."

"If you change your mind, Lys…" he added with resigned sadness. "There has never been any other for me."

She took his gentle face in her hands and said, "Good Orryn, the perfect woman for you will come your way. She just hasn't quite made it to you yet. I *know* this!"

They spent time remembering all the little adventures and secrets they shared as they grew up. Those memories would always be with them. Orryn took her to the shrine of Father Gord'n. It was a number of cycles since she was last inside the old cottage with its back wall built into the hill. She was a little girl the last time she was there.

Visitors were welcome inside; but no one was allowed to touch what long ago were Father Gord'n's personal effects—cooking utensils, game boards, bed clothing, tall shelves loaded with ancient books he was known to have actually read. There were slates and paper journals of fieldscript open on the table. Even the hearth was kept fueled as if he had stepped out for a moment on some homestead duty. Nonnee, an older woman of Falling Stream, kept this cottage and the flowered yard so well kept, it gave a sense that Father Gord'n was near, although his life on Xunar-kun ended three thousand cycles before. Standing in the cottage gave Alysa an odd feeling.

Alysa had difficulty finding Seda in the crowd when she first arrived. But as she greeted and spoke to others, she did finally come upon Seda who looked rosy and plump as could be and very healthy nearly halfway through her time with unborn. She and Seda were overjoyed to be together again!

Aryz barely left Seda's side throughout Moonsfest, having become quite the serious father-to-be; but the young women did manage to spend a few moments alone, to talk and feel like the girls they once were.

And what a change Loralle achieved! For the first time since Abso's death one cycle ago, she allowed herself to truly enjoy the celebration and reunion with old friends. She danced and sang and made merry like the still vital woman she was. Alysa couldn't help but notice that her mother danced quite a number of times with Evyn, Miller of High Point.

Kendira also made the journey, transported the whole way in a cart pulled by poor Apprentice Teller Betram. He did not look altogether pleased that she assigned him the task. Kendira had nothing but harsh criticism for the bumpy ride on the stony path over which Betram had little control.

Alysa did not attempt to speak to Kendira on the trek; they communicated little since the previous greening. After the joining ceremony, Kendira stood behind her as they waited to enter the Great Hall. "Alysa, do you still hate me?" Kendira asked in a small voice.

Alysa spoke over her shoulder. "Kendira, I don't hate you. But I must be honest and say that I dislike some of the things you do."

"I understand," Kendira seemed to sympathize. "You are a very bright young woman of some eighteen cycles. Is that correct?"

"I will be eighteen in a few moons, during wintertide."

"You are still at an age when you see life in the short distance. I must look at life in the far distance. I have good reasons for doing things that on the surface may not be apparent to others, particularly to the young. So it's natural that you and I will collide at times. Especially since — if you will excuse my being so blunt — since you have such a tenacious will. But I do the things that I must."

Alysa faced her. "Kendira, I must be honest with you. Some of the things we are expected to do in the name of Father Gord'n seem unnecessary — even backward."

Kendira sighed and said, "You see what I mean? We'll never agree on everything." She smiled a stiff smile. "But let's remain friends. It makes no sense to quarrel because we disagree on a few things. What do you think?"

Alysa mulled the offer and nodded. "You're right, Kendira. We should remain open."

"Good!" Kendira said. "By the way, I've been meaning to congratulate you on how well you did at your first Trade. You made some marvelous decisions, I heard. Even though I have known you since your birth, I misjudged your talents. Carry on, with my blessing."

Alysa was suspicious of Kendira's compliment and remained so as she climbed to the Tradeground this sun. A huge blast of wind returned her to the task at hand. The weather at the Tradeground was no milder than that on Gorge Path. As the same six Traders settled cross-legged on their mats, tiny prisms of intermittent snow lighted on cloaks, capes and fur mats and then melted. Trade was carried out at its usual pace, the best possible trade remaining the goal of both sides. From time to time a worried eye glanced at the dim, flat sky.

As Trade continued, the flurries grew heavier and the snow began to stick. Trade ended early. Panli left for the bearers while Alysa and Boshe packed the traded goods. The last Trailmen Trader crossed the bridge in haste as the increasing wind grabbed his cape, nearly blowing him over the edge.

"Boshe," Alysa said, "they were in such a hurry, they didn't even offer any B.C. goods this time!"

"They rarely speak of their travels, but I understand that they could get trapped in the pass that gives them access to the south if the snow gets too deep. That could mean death to them."

"They have plenty of food now, and they must have shelters of some sort since they usually remain here for several suns. Don't you think, Boshe?"

"I doubt they would have enough to eat, even after Trade, for the whole wintertide."

"Do you think this will be a true wintertide storm? It's too early, isn't it?"

"Alysa, I wish I could answer that question, but I cannot. I leave the weather to the Planters!"

The canopy was packed the by the time Panli arrived with the bearers. Boshe commanded them to pick up the baskets and bundles and quickly led the bearers down the path.

"It's getting slippery," Panli said. "We must be very careful going down. And we must leave now!" He pointed to the northeast, where thick, dark clouds were fast coming upon them.

"Go!" Alysa said, "I'm right behind you!"

Panli hurried the last of the bearers down the path and yelled to them, "Some very big wind may be coming upon us! Grab onto anything along the wall that you can. Vines, roots, grab something to steady you!"

Alysa picked up her packbasket but decided to carry it by the strap rather than sling it onto her back and risk being blown over the edge of the gorge. She wrapped her scarf around her hooded head and left the clearing.

Panli turned back and called up to her. "Hurry, girl, get below the wind!"

"Just behind you!" she yelled, running to the path.

A heavy rush of wind brought a dark cloud of blowing, confused snow upon the ridge. Without warning, the air became a gray-white curtain that she could not see through. She halted, unable to determine which way to go. The footprints in the snow made by the others, visible just a moment before were wiped away by the blast of snow all about her. In horror she remembered that the edge of the gorge was only steps away. She dropped her basket.

"Which way, Boshe!" she yelled. But her words were swallowed up by the rampaging storm. Her only option to escape falling into the gorge was to reach the higher side of the ridge. With her right foot she reached out, tapping, stepping, reaching, tapping.

The ground began to rise underfoot, so she knew she was moving upslope. With the next step, her foot bumped into something. She reached out and grabbed hold of a sapling and pulled herself a few paces up the slope. One sapling, one vine at a time, she drew herself higher. She dared not look behind for fear of losing her balance in the disorienting storm and sliding into the gorge.

As she climbed, the fury of the storm grew. Fear crowded her mind as the fierce cold began to seep through her clothing. She thought, *Where am I getting myself to? How will I survive even one night up here?*

Her arms began to ache from climbing. Her foot got caught in some rocks. Pain shot through her ankle as she struggled to dislodge it. Limping and unaware that she reached the top, she pitched herself over the summit. She tripped and tumbled down the other side of the ridge, bumping her head and body on rocks and trees. She sprawled at the base of a tree that caused an abrupt end to her fall.

Several inches of snow were heaped upon her by the time she gathered enough wits to drag herself to her feet. The pain in her body was intolerable. Being lost in a blizzard was trouble enough; now she was hurting and her vision was blurred. Stunned and bruised, she wandered through the forest. She did not know in which direction to go, though a voice within her said, *Keep moving or you will die!*

She had no idea how long she dragged herself through the storm. The sky grew darker. She began to fear the worst as the pain increased and her body weakened. But the Folk girl was not alone. Another figure trudged along the snowy ridge, a dark shadow on her trail.

Leaning against a tree, she panted, exhausted. She wiped moisture from the back of her neck with a cold-numbed hand, wondering how she could be sweating when she felt so cold. She peered at her hand through foggy eyes and tried to make sense of the red smear on her fingers. When she realized that it was not sweat but blood trickling down her back, in despair she let her hands drop, and she slid to the ground. She began to weep in pain and fear.

She lifted her head and saw a figure gliding toward her. It was Abso! He knelt before her and smiled. It took all her strength to raise her arms to him. He extended his to her. "Father!" she cried. The image of Abso evaporated and was replaced by the figure of a horrible beast! Its body was covered with fur, and it glared at her from narrow eyes set deep in the thick, gray skin of its face.

Suddenly, another creature much smaller than the first and running on four legs came up close. Its wide-set, bright-yellow eyes scrutinized her. It thrust its long snout into her hair and touched her face with its icy nose.

It backed away, opened its mouth to bare sharp teeth, and emitted a deep snarl. The little beast sat back on its haunches and held up a large, three-toed paw as if to keep a distance between itself and the girl.

Alysa wanted to scream, but instead she listed sideways, semiconscious. The larger beast caught her. It lifted her to her feet, slung her over its shoulder, and plodded away into the darkening forest.

RESCUED

After Szaren had walked only a short distance, he decided it would be impossible to reach Ridge Camp. It was growing darker, and the storm gave no sign of easing its furor. Alysa was not heavy, but her added weight and the deepening snow made the going very tiring. The moisture from Szaren's labored breathing began to freeze to his hide mask.

Drongo, Szaren's peltee and constant companion, walked behind him in the trail he broke. Drongo's curly, black and white fur-covered body was only as high as Szaren's knees when standing on all fours. The peltee continually moved her long, narrow face and keen, bright-yellow eyes over the landscape as though she could see through the snow-laden air and deepening snow.

The peltee rose up on her hind legs to look behind, ahead, and up into the trees. She pricked up her long, soft ears until they stood firm and tall. She stared into the blizzard, at full attention. She flicked snow from between the webs of her large front toes and shook her body to remove snow that accumulated on her head and broad back. She turned her pink nose to the sky, sniffing the air, and sneezed when she drew a large snowflake into her nostrils.

Szaren rested his burden on the ground beneath the branches of a snow-laden foya tree. Here, Alysa would be protected from exposure to the frigid wind while he searched for a place to build a shelter.

There were several large, fallen trees nearby. He found two spaced a few strides apart. Working quickly, he reached beneath his cape and unsheathed the long blade hanging from his belt. He moved about the trees cutting down many low-hanging foya boughs and dragged them to the logs. Trudging around in the space between the logs, he shoved aside what snow he could and tamped down what remained.

Drongo ran back and forth between Szaren and Alysa, staying aware of her master's activity and, at the same time, keeping a wary eye on Alysa. The peltee's curiosity pulled her attention to the smell

117

of the strange girl. Drongo sniffed her from head to toe, jumping back and snarling when Alysa twitched in her semi-conscious state.

Szaren pushed his hood back, untied his cape, and removed it. The cold wind tore at his short, dark-streaked hair, which prompted him to pull up the collar of his fur vest. He quickly spread the cape fur-side up on the ground.

With no time to lose, he went to Alysa and squatted behind her, pushed her limp body forward, and thrust his arms under hers. He crossed his arms over her chest and dragged her from beneath the foya tree. Drongo snapped at Alysa's feet.

"Hold, Drongo!" Szaren commanded. The peltee instantly stopped snapping and backed off. With care, Szaren settled Alysa on one side of the cape. Drongo paced as Szaren bridged the logs with branches and boughs and heaped them with snow to form a roof. He stacked boughs at one end of the shelter and shoved snow against them. He crawled through the remaining opening and called, "Drongo, hup!"

Drongo scampered into the shelter. Szaren drew branches against the entry to close them in. Lying on his stomach, he watched the storm. Drongo lay next to him, listening, panting and licking her wet nose from time to time with her black tongue.

For only a short while the whirling snow was visible through spaces between the branches. It took little time for the storm to bury the shelter. The howl of the storm faded as the snow grew deeper.

Szaren slid himself to the rear of the dim shelter, cut a thin branch hanging from the crude roof, and in several places poked it through the wall near their heads to make openings for fresh air.

The edge of the hide mask that was earlier frozen to his moustache and half-grown wintertide beard was thawed; he removed it and rubbed and dried his face. His tattooed ears were numb, and he rubbed some of the cold out of them as well.

He untied a large pouch at his side and laid it near his head. The pouch contained cured meat, nuts and dried fruit. Trailmen were always certain to carry at least three suns' sustenance when they set out from camp.

From the side of the shelter he scooped out a handful of snow and let it melt in his palm. He parted Alysa's lips, dribbled some into her mouth, and the rest into his. She could live without eating for a few suns, but Szaren knew she would survive only if she received adequate water.

Alysa remained motionless. Her breathing was irregular. In the growing darkness, Szaren searched for her hands. Drongo took interest in what Szaren was doing and moved to Alysa's other side. The peltee growled.

Szaren warned, "Drongo..."

She whined, sat down and cocked her head, watching her master closely.

The girl wore no mitts to protect her hands, or else lost them along the way; her hands were ice cold. Szaren held them and breathed on them and worked her fingers until some warmth returned. He removed her scarf, pulled her hood back, and wiped her cold, wet face. He felt her scalp and found the wounds. One cut on the back of her head was severe; there were several other bumps and small cuts that were no longer bleeding.

Drongo sniffed the scent of Alysa's blood and lightly whined.

Reaching beneath his heavy vest, Szaren tore strips from his shirt. He folded one strip into a thick bandage and placed it on Alysa's still-bleeding wound. He wrapped another strip around her head to secure the bandage.

In his search for further injuries, he found several warm, swollen places on her arms, ribs and legs; but luckily these appeared to be bruises only, not broken bones. He removed her boots and wet woolen stockings and discovered substantial swelling in her left foot. Massaging her frigid feet and toes for a while brought some warmth to them. He wrung out the wet stockings and put them back on her feet, knowing that within a short time her body's warmth would dry them.

It seemed that Fielders knew very little about survival; perhaps there was no need, as it was known that they preferred to live in large, stationary dwellings with many people around for comfort. But alone, without existing shelter, they were paralyzed. This Fielder demonstrated that very deficiency. Alysa would not have lived through the night if that morning Szaren was away from camp as the Trailmen packers returned from leaving the goods at the Trade-ground. Word went around that the persistent girl had returned. A few speculated as to what surprise she was hiding away to try to wrangle the best trade this time!

Wanting to catch another glimpse of this strange girl, it was indeed fortunate for Alysa that Szaren was crossing the bridge when she disappeared in the squall. Tracking her was easy, even if the snow in the air prevented him from seeing more than a few paces ahead. Drongo helped guide him around the holes in the bridge. But the peltee's attempts to track Alysa by smell were lost to the wind. Fortunately for Alysa, she left many signs that Szaren was able to track—broken branches, disrupted patches of leaves, and smears of blood.

Before this sun, Szaren rarely gave thought to Fielders. Having very little favorable knowledge of them, he never desired to know more. But he sensed something different about this one. He guessed that it was her persistence and intelligence, valued Trailmen traits not thought to be possessed by any Fielder.

Of main concern for them was to rest this night and stay warm. He moved closer to her and folded the cape around them. He called, "Hup, Drongo!" The peltee quickly maneuvered her body beneath Szaren's head and lay down on her side. He rested his head on her thick curly fur and draped his arm around Alysa's middle.

Drongo carefully sniffed Alysa's head and, as if finally accepting her presence, slowly stuck her snout into the girl's hair. The peltee sighed and settled to sleep.

Szaren hoped that Alysa would live, that she would be brought back to life; and he hoped the storm would last only a short while. Exhausted, listening to Alysa's labored breathing, and feeling the soft peltee's heartbeat against his face, he was soon asleep.

Dense clouds parted. Sunlight dappled sections of forest buried in snow. A few flurries still powdered Winding Mountains. At times rays of sunshine highlighted the distant falling snow, gossamer against dark and more distant clouds.

Sitting at the entrance he kicked open earlier in the morning, Szaren wove snowshoes from flexible branches as if he had done this many times before. Small, gray-blue birds emerged from their own shelters and snapped up wind-blown wildflower seeds from the snow's surface. They fluffed their feathers for warmth and hopped along tops of drifts level with leaffall's dried blooms.

At a distance from the shelter, Drongo relieved herself and sauntered back up the new path that Szaren had broken. Szaren gave her a strip of meat and chewed a piece himself.

He was thankful that his tribe left Winding Mountains before the storm struck. Up there, storms were many times harsher than at these lower points along the trail. He closed his eyes to concentrate on the sound of the breeze in the trees. Swirling, directionless, the breeze tugged at his hair and ruffled the fur of his vest. He sensed some moisture returning to the air, even though it was still very cold. He felt that the winds would shift back to their seasonal pattern and that warmth would soon return.

For two suns the unrelenting blizzard forced quiet time upon him. He contemplated why the girl was still consumed by the sleep of the wounded. Sometimes she mumbled and was much more restless last night than she had been the night before. He thought that perhaps she was trying to wake but was unable. Maybe her body was trying to heal itself by remaining asleep. Or perhaps she would never awaken.

Even though he wondered what his tribesmen would think when he brought the girl in—if she even survived the trek back to camp—he would not have felt right about letting her wander off into the storm, knowing for certain that she would be dead before the sun was down. Alysa proved herself to be more resilient than he imagined any Fielder to be. Therefore, her recovery was now of concern to him. She was still alive, so there was still hope. The Healer would know how to bring the girl back to life. It was urgent that he get her back to Ridge Camp.

While he used his trail knowledge to help her, he also did more. Much of his time the past two suns was spent in contemplation for his tribe, for himself, and for the girl. He contemplated the welfare of his tribe, because this storm would delay crossing the pass and gathering with the rest of his people for wintertide. For himself he contemplated living — he needed to survive, to help his tribe prosper and one sun take his place as Elder, as is promised to the most worthy of his lineage; and for Alysa he imagined a good outcome, because although she was ignorant to the ways of the wild, she had courage.

He thought about this sun's journey. The trek would be taxing and dangerous. Which would be the best and quickest trail to take back? Which would spare them from the danger of avalanche on this steeper side of the ridge? He rose, reached his fisted hand to the sky and spoke, in a very humbled manner, to someone unseen:

"For every drop of blood spared,
a host of thanks to you.
For every mouth fed,
a host of thanks to you.
For every morning bloom,
a host of thanks to you."

He lowered his arm and spread his fingers over his heart. He stared in silence across the ridge where dark clouds were breaking up over the distant mountains, his summering home, now formidable in its frozen state. A gusty breeze swirled snow about him.

The return to camp would take the entire sun. Though within easy walking distance in typical leaffall weather, these conditions would hinder travel. With hunter's luck, they would reach Ridge Camp before dark. He knew that he could easily survive another night; but Alysa would die for certain if she spent a third without the Healer's care.

He pulled Alysa by the legs from the snow-covered shelter. Drongo clamped her teeth onto Alysa's cloak and also pulled. Szaren rested her on a drag-litter which he constructed from saplings, tight-meshed for good support and strength over the variable terrain. He pulled her cloak snugly around her and bound her with bark strips at the chest, knees and calves. He tucked her hands inside opposite sleeves and bound her forearms together to keep her hands from freezing. He wrapped her scarf around her hood and face.

From the shelter he pulled his cape, shook ice from its underside, and flung it around his shoulders. He placed the hide mask on his face and pulled up his hood. He stepped into the snowshoe bindings, plodded to the front of the litter, grasped its handles and began the long, dangerous trek back to camp. Drongo followed behind, continually looking around and listening, ever vigilant.

THE HEALER

Alysa was unable to determine whether she lay on her back or stomach, or whether she was upside-down or right-side-up as she floated in the cold, silent, starlit darkness. Her bare arms were stretched straight out from her sides, or so it seemed; she was unable to turn her head either left or right. Neither was she able to move her eyes. Her bare legs stretched straight from her hips, and at the lower edge of her vision she was able to see only the tips of her bare toes. The rest of her felt naked as well, and her pale, unbound hair floated about her shoulders.

As she drifted deeper into darkness, her body slowly rotated. She recognized a bright group of stars that her father had called the Hunter. A dark sphere—a world with mostly brown land and yellow-green water—appeared below that star pattern she knew since she was a youngling.

Each time her body turned and she faced the brown world, it looked smaller, farther away. As the Hunter's pulse dimmed, so did interest in her memories, which grew fainter with each turn. It mattered little that she no longer could recall her name.

The speed at which she drifted into the dark seemed to increase. As the discomfort of being cold, naked and alone in the darkness began to lessen, her curiosity about what was happening faded. The absence of light had grown so complete that she could no longer discern the tips of her toes. She began to feel very peaceful. Her eyelids grew heavy. The darkness overcame her, enfolding her in its shroud.

Out of the darkness her father appeared. She was overjoyed to see him and thought, *I'm coming, Father!* Abso smiled and shook his head. Looking at her as he always did with that spark in his eyes, he placed his hands on her shoulders. He gently shoved her out of the darkness and back among the stars. Alysa struggled to yell, *No, Father, let me come to you!* But she could muster no voice. He vanished.

Suddenly, and from nowhere, hands—hundreds of disembodied hands—were around her. Startled, she struggled to understand what was happening. The hands gently stroked and tugged at her body. They grasped her feet, arms and head. The hands, now feeling warm, halted her drift away from the brown world and began to draw her back to it. The girl strained to resist but found herself powerless against the hands. She was being dragged from the peace that lay within the beckoning darkness, and away from her father!

As the hands continued to guide her out of the darkness, the world grew closer. Soon it loomed before her and she saw that it was not completely brown; there was snow at the top and bottom of the world. Scattered splashes of green and blue appeared on its face. Swirling clouds sped through the atmosphere. The hands drew her toward a large patch of green. Even more hands appeared, pulling on locks of loose hair and at her flesh. Sometimes this caused her pain. There seemed to be no portion of her form that escaped their hold!

The hands began to laugh and sent a reverberating echo into the stars. Some spoke muffled words. She tried to scream at them, enraged at their relentless touch, at their insistence in dragging her from the peaceful darkness — and from her father. But her effort to resist proved wasted.

Hovering above the large patch of green, the many hands propelled her into it. They released her, dumping her onto the world. She began to tumble and her body fell faster, faster toward the expanding green. Her ears rang with the rush of wind and laughter. She recognized the shapes of mountains, forests, lakes and streams as she sped toward them.

At last she was able to move her hands and arms. She pressed her palms hard against her head to stop the ringing, but it grew louder still. As she fell into the forest, her legs and arms flailed in a last desperate attempt to stop her fall.

Black nothingness filled Alysa's eyes. A softness supported her back as she sensed the weight of her body. The ringing in her head subsided as her hearing returned. The crackling of fire was the first sound she recognized. She rolled her head in the direction of the sound, but the flicker of light she expected to see was absent. She panicked, thinking she had been blinded.

Shakily raising her hands to her eyes, her fingertips rested on soft cloth wrappings. She could feel the orbs of her eyes beneath the cloth and was relieved to find that they were still there. She startled and raised her head from the pillow as firm but gentle hands removed her fingers from her face and placed them under the fur blanket.

The owner of the strong, gentle hands moved away, and a pair of lighter hands caressed her forehead. A voice said, "You must be still, midling."

"Who...who are you?" Alysa asked in a soft, hoarse voice. "Where am I? Am I at High Point?"

"I am Obala, the Healer," the owner of the hands said.

Alysa realized that the hands and voice belonged to an aged woman.

"And at High Point you are not," Obala continued. "You are at the Ridge Camp of the Trailmen."

"Where?" Alysa asked in disbelief. "How..."

"First you must rest," Obala persuaded, "We will talk when you are well enough. Then I will tell you anything you wish to know."

Alysa tensed her body as she discovered that another of her senses—pain—had returned. Her foot, arms, legs and right side ached when she tried to move. Her head hurt the most, on the outside from bumps and cuts and on the inside from the pounding that resulted when she tried to lift it.

An object was placed against her cracked lips. "There now," Obala said, her soothing voice coming from the hearth where Alysa heard the sound of stirring in a clay pot. "My assistant will help you partake of some broth."

Another healer was encouraging Alysa to sip the broth through a bone straw. Rich, warm broth streamed through the straw as she sucked. She drained the contents of the vessel and began to feel drowsy.

"Ah, the broth flavored with healing herbs will work wonders on your wounded frame, midling," Obala assured her. "You will sleep again. In two suns I will remove the bandages. But for now, worry not. You will mend safely here."

Resistance was impossible. Alysa was too weak and in too much pain to object. She wished more than anything to be back home, in her own bed; but since she was too injured to travel anyway, she had no choice but to remain.

As sleep began to overtake her, she tried to recall what happened. The last thing she remembered was losing her footing on the ridge and plummeting through the trees. *It is indeed fortunate that I found my way to this camp,* she thought. *I might have been lost forever in that storm!*

Tingling warmth crept into her hands and feet. She felt safe as she lay beneath the warm blanket. She fell asleep to the sound of the crackling fire, the rhythm of Obala's slow stirring, and the soft breathing of Obala's assistant at her side.

Dreams flooded Alysa's sleep over the next suns, at times causing great restlessness. Often caught in the grip of a nightmare, she drew in deep breaths in an attempt to wake herself. The giggling of younglings assaulted her, and the raucous laughter of grownups seemed to surround her at times. They touched her, sometimes causing pain to her aching body. Then the strong, gentle hands returned. They chased all those hurtful hands from her side and caressed her cheek.

Still half asleep as the last bandages were removed, Alysa's eyes remained closed. A remnant of dried blood was patted from her head wound. An herb-dampened cloth caressed her face, wiping away two suns of sleep-sand from her eyes. The sweet-pungent smell of the damp cloth kindly assaulted her nose. The attention was soothing and assured her that her bad dreams had ceased. The ministering ended as footsteps carried the gentle hands away from her side.

Obala's lilting voice encouraged, "Midling, it is time to eat and bathe. Can you hear me, Yissa?"

Alysa blinked. At first her vision was unclear, but after a few moments her eyes were able to focus on the dim ceiling. There was a hole in the peak of a high, conical roof made from many hides sewn together. Smoke curled up through the opening into the night sky.

With great effort, Alysa rolled onto her side and propped herself up on an elbow. She looked in the direction of Obala, whose short, brown and gray-streaked hair caught the firelight. Obala squatted in the center of the round hut where she stirred a steaming pot over the open hearthring. She was wearing the hide tunic and trousers typical of the Trailmen.

Not certain that the youthful-looking person seated before the fire was the one who belonged to the aged voice that spoke just a moment before, Alysa asked, "O...Obala?"

Keeping to her stirring, Obala smiled and looked up. "Yes, Yissa?"

"How do you know my name?"

"Ah, well," Obala smiled, "word gets around, Yissa."

"My right name is 'Alysa'."

"Ah, my apologies — A-yissa."

Confused, and still a little dazed, Alysa squinted around the room and saw that it was dug into the ground. She guessed the hut to be about twenty paces across. The low walls were made of stacked stones. The hide roof was supported by slender poles pegged into place around the top of the wall. Three steps led up to a door flap.

Alysa asked, "How long have I been here?"

"Two suns, Yissa."

"Oh, moons above!" She tried to raise herself up, but the pain throughout her body was great. She moaned and dropped back onto the cot.

"Take your time, midling," Obala advised. "Mending takes time."

The smell of the cooking food caused Alysa's stomach to growl. Finally, one at a time she dragged her legs from beneath the blanket and sat on the edge of the narrow cot. With her weak hands, she worked the hem of her Folk-made sleeping-smock down over her knees and hugged herself for warmth against the cool air.

Alysa saw that Obala also had painted skin. A leafy vine bearing flowers with long, yellow petals began at the top of one ear and trailed down her neck toward her shoulder.

Obala turned toward Alysa and rose. "Good!" she rejoiced as she approached her. "I am pleased to see that you are ready to once again join the living!" The other side of Obala's neck was painted with a detailed forest scene. One of the trees curved over the top of her ear.

Though she was of very small stature, Obala's composure conveyed great strength. She seemed content with the repairs she had done on Alysa as she examined her. "The wounds are healing very well, Yissa. You have come a long way, a very long way, indeed! Are you hungry?"

Alysa rubbed her throat. "Yes, but I'd like something to drink first. My throat's scratchy and sore."

"Of course. Here, I have just the thing. I was about to offer it to you." Obala handed her a wooden mug.

Alysa admired the ornate carving of the deep-red wood. She took a sip of the thick, sweet liquid and downed the whole mug. "It's much better now!"

"I thought that would help. Now would you like to eat?"

"What you're cooking smells very good. May I have some of that?"

"You may have all that you desire," Obala answered. Her lively blue eyes conveyed joy. "It is wonderful to see you healed!"

"Almost healed." Alysa winced as she put weight on her injured foot.

"The worst for you is over, Yissa."

Alysa looked up, trying to hide her annoyance by the repeated mispronunciation of her name.

Obala sensed the girl's irritation and said, "I apologize again for my error, A-yissa. I have been calling you 'Yissa' for three suns, and your name is strange to us Trailmen. It will take some time for me to learn your correct name."

Alysa reconsidered and smiled. "It's really of no matter, Obala. I'm very thankful for what you've done for me. You may call me 'Yissa' if you like."

Obala nodded. "Whatever you wish. Now, about your condition. I must tell you that you had quite a bad fall, possibly several. But now look at you, on your feet!" She wrapped the fur blanket around Alysa's shoulders and squatted down. She signaled the girl to raise her right foot, onto which she placed a thick fur slipper. Alysa winced when her hurting left foot received the other.

"Come, I will help you to sup," Obala said. She offered a shoulder to lean upon and assisted Alysa across the floor covered with many short-haired furs. She helped the girl lower herself onto a pillow near the hearthring.

Obala removed a wide, oval board leaning against the low wall, unfolded short legs tucked beneath, pegged them into position, and placed the table before Alysa.

"I have cooked hoptail stew," Obala smiled. "Do you like hoptail stew, Yissa?"

"I don't know. I've never eaten any."

"No? Then this will be a treat! It is my favorite meal and certainly far tastier and more filling than plain broth."

"Where's your helper? Will she be back?" Alysa wanted to meet the woman who belonged to the other caring hands.

"My helper has gone to other duties now that you are back. Eat, midling," Obala urged. "Eat and become your old, strong self again!"

Obala placed a mug of water, a small Folk-crafted basket containing rolls, and a wooden bowl before the girl. Steam rose from the bowl, which was also carved in an ornate fashion.

Alysa took a warm, dark roll from the basket and broke it into pieces. She dipped a piece into the stew and tasted it. With haste she continued to eat until the bowl was empty, she had devoured a third roll and had downed two mugs of water.

The whole time, Obala watched with satisfaction. When Alysa stopped eating, Obala asked, "Would you like more?"

"I'd very much like some more. But I think my stomach would burst! Thank you, Obala. It was the best stew I've ever eaten!"

Obala smiled. "I am glad that it pleased you. Well, then! How would you like to have a bath?"

"A bath? But the streams and lakes are too cold his time of season..."

"Ah, but we are not restricted by the seasons in regard to bathing, midling!" Obala chuckled. She removed the eating utensils, refolded the table, and placed it back against the wall. From beneath the cot she removed a rolled animal hide and a bundle of thick, arm-length poles. Not far from where Alysa sat, Obala pulled up a rug to expose an area of dirt floor not much wider than two paces. The floor was punched with a circular pattern of six holes, and into each she inserted a pole. The hide had six pockets spaced evenly around its perimeter, which she placed on the tip of each pole. A circular, knee-height container took shape as she smoothed the baggy hide within the support of poles.

Alysa said, "I see now what you're doing; you're making a bath right here in the hut!"

Obala smiled. Steam wafted from the container as she filled it with several hot kettles of water and enough cold to temper the heat.

A perplexed look crossed Alysa's face. "But I have a question, Obala. Where does the water go when the bathing is finished?"

"You are an inquisitive girl, are you not! But it is good that you ask questions. That means that you are again able to think clearly!" She pointed to a stone-filled hole a couple of paces from the bath. "I will simply lift a pocket off the nearest pole and let it down so the water runs into the hollow. The water will sink down into the stones. Then the hide will be hung up to dry."

"That is so clever!"

"Now please remove, midling," Obala urged, pointing to Alysa's sleeping-smock.

Obala steadied the girl as she stood, removed her garb, stepped into the bath and lowered herself into the water.

Alysa exclaimed, "Oh, oh, OH! That is good..." She eased herself fully into the warm bath.

Obala picked up a small clay jar and poured green liquid into the water. "This sweet oil will clear your wounds and soothe your bruises. If you wash some into your hair, the oil will leave it soft and shiny."

The water sloshed up to Alysa's collarbone. She smiled. "My skin is tingling!" She sighed and relaxed into the bath. She sank down to her chin. The heat penetrated to her bones.

What a wonderful idea, this hide bath! It could be set up quickly and was plenty big for full bathing. This was much better than scrubbing with a cloth and bowl of water like she normally did during the cold seasons.

"Now you should have drink, plenty of drink," Obala advised.

"I'd like some, please," Alysa said.

Obala handed her a mug. She held it under her nose with both hands and sniffed the steam, delightfully surprised.

Pleased, Obala nodded. "Berrybark. My favorite!" She fastened the toggles of her fur jacket and picked up the eating utensils that Alysa had used. "Do you think you can get back into bed by yourself?"

Alysa nodded.

"I shall say goodnight then. You will find scrubbing and drying cloths in the basket beside the bath. There is more warm drink on the hearth, and another helping of stew in the pot. There is a covered pot for the purpose of elimination on the other side of the hut."

"You're leaving? But I thought you lived here. Isn't there another folding cot hidden somewhere?" Alysa peered around the hut, trying to see detail in the shadows.

"I remained only while you needed me. You will be fine on your own this night. If there was more light in here, you would see that along the walls and hanging from ceiling poles are bows and quivers, spears, weapon-making tools and many other things that I have no use for. All my life I have been a Healer. In my hut, which I share with my mate Trabo—you know him as our Chief Trader—I keep bundles of dried herbs and items necessary to my skill. No, this is not my hut. This is used by Szaren. He is, of course, staying at another hut while you are here."

Alysa recalled the unexpected and uneasy meeting Trade before last. "But why, Obala?"

"Why what, midling?"

"Why did he let me stay here?"

"A quiet place was needed to keep you. And since he brought you in..."

"*He* brought me? But I thought..." She paused, unable to recall the events that brought her here.

"Szaren found you in the storm. He sheltered you for two suns while you were in the sleep of the wounded. Then he brought you here."

"I didn't know. I'm truly grateful to him," she said, stunned by the revelation. "I'll thank him when I see him."

Obala smiled. "I will come back in the morning and bring suitable clothing, a meal, and herbal drinks that will further aid your healing. Good night, Yissa. Enjoy your bath." Obala bounced up the steps and disappeared through the door flap.

Alysa thought it beyond reason that Szaren did so much for her, a Field Folk, particularly after her less-than-pleasant treatment of him after her first Trade. She never would have expected such kind caring from this clan—or rather, tribe—to one who was of no kin to them. What would she do if faced with the same situation as Szaren? Would she help a Trailman in need, even risk her life to do so, as he must have?

She could summon no answer. She thought this tribe must harbor as many secrets as did this room!

She sank back into the water, still feeling considerable soreness but knowing that she was on the mend. She felt even more peaceful—and safe—because Obala demonstrated much warmth, and Szaren, extraordinary generosity.

As her head became clearer, her thoughts turned to Boshe, Panli and the bearers. She hoped they had reached the homestead safely. She thought of everyone in the homestead and hoped the storm did not create a difficult time for them. She thought of her mother and sister and hoped they did not worry for her too desperately.

She closed her eyes, and in thinking warm thoughts of them, knew they were well.

THE TRAILMEN'S WAY

Two suns later, the last of the snow had melted from the roof of Szaren's hut, and only drips remained as the light-colored hide dried in the bright sunshine. The sunlight penetrated the roof and illuminated the interior of the hut with a yellow glow.

Alysa tugged at the Trailman-style clothing that Obala had given her. At first she thought she had put it on wrong because it was so uncomfortable. The heavy, green woolen trousers hugged her hips and thighs, and the belt gathered the loose tunic into a great bulk around her waist. However awkward it felt, the clothing was very warm. She assumed that the Trailmen used the thick Folk-woven cloth to make bed coverings and cloaks, as her clan did. But fashioning it into tunics and trousers was practical in a setting like this. The hide roofs kept out the weather but allowed much heat to escape.

Obala also brought news on the condition of the mountain pass the Trailmen must cross to reach the Lowlands. A scout reported that a small avalanche was blocking it. But if the sun continued to shine as brightly as it had since the blizzard ended, and if the air returned to its seasonal warmth, in three suns the route should be clear enough to allow passage.

Taking into consideration Alysa's still-healing condition, Obala suggested that she remain in camp until the Trailmen departed for the Lowlands. The Healer assured Alysa that in a few more suns she would be nearly as good as new. She agreed to stay. She had no choice, anyway. The path back to High Point would yet be too dangerous for travel.

Alysa sat near the hearthring to braid her hair. She startled when she heard loud sniffing and snorting along the bottom of the hide roof where it met the stone foundation. She realized that the sound and short shadows belonged to curious peltees. The sun before, Obala chased Drongo away when she attempted to enter Szaren's hut. Alysa had yet to gain a clear look at the odd creatures. Peltees were unknown to the Folk, and it was all right with her if they kept their distance!

Many footsteps sloshed up to join the peltees. The footsteps stopped at the door flap. Young voices whispered at the opening. Alysa looked up, expecting someone to enter. Instead, a few small hands parted the flap. Little golden faces peeked through the opening. Sunlight bounced off their hide helmets. When they saw the stranger staring back, they ran away in excited shrieking and chatter, the peltees yelping behind them as they ran off.

Alysa laughed. Younglings would be younglings, no matter where they were grown. It was unlikely that any of them had ever seen a Folk. At high sun she would be sitting at the same table at which the Trailmen ate. Although she had never in her wildest imagination anticipated such an event, she looked forward to it all the same, particularly since being rescued by Szaren and receiving Obala's kind care.

She tied her braid with a hide strip, rose and hobbled to the cot. She tugged at the trousers and tunic again in an attempt to arrange them more comfortably. She sighed. "Maybe this attire just takes some getting used to."

"It is very becoming on you, Yissa." Alysa startled. Obala smiled from the doorway, standing just inside the flap. "Your young woman's form is more obvious than under a smock. Once you have worn our clothing for a few suns, you may prefer it to Fielder style."

Alysa shrugged, doubting that she would ever feel right in Trailmen's clothing. "Is it time for my first try at walking?"

Obala produced a walking staff from behind the flap. Still smiling, she held it out. The Healer said she would bring a staff, but Alysa expected one that would simply aid her in walking. This one was fashioned from two entwining red briarwood branches. It looked like it took much effort to create.

Staring at it in awe, the girl took it and set the end on the floor. With her hand resting on the knob, she leaned on it. The staff held her steady, and it was exactly the right height. She exclaimed, "Oh, how wonderful...!"

The curved knob on the top was smooth and rubbed with oil. It fit in her palm like it was made for her. She picked up the staff to look at it closely, and in turning it noticed that it gave the appearance of either spiraling up or down as she turned it one way then the other.

In a short span of wood between the knob and where the shaft began to twine, her fingers found a small design—a recessed carving of a firestag's head above Winding Mountains.

"What does this design mean?" Alysa asked.

"That is the carver's symbol. Everyone has their own. We take great pride in each object we create and so add our symbols to everything we make."

"Do you carve, too?"

"I have done a bit in my time."

"This staff must've taken a long time to make!"

"Due to the storm, we have had much spare time. It is best to be productive while it passes."

"Who made this? I would like to thank the carver."

Obala hesitated. "We must leave, midling. We have a long walk, considering your foot. And the lodge is at the other end of camp."

Alysa laid the walking staff on her cot and pulled on a fur jacket. Obala produced a pair of short, heavy boots. She placed one on Alysa's well foot but let Alysa dress the still-swollen one. Alysa picked up the stick and Obala helped her up the steps. They emerged into the high sun's brightness.

Alysa paused and held a hand over her eyes, squinting against the sunlight. What an unexpected sight! Perhaps as many as one hundred round huts populated the clearing. Smoke curled from each hide rooftop. The huts were not scattered throughout the forest as she expected; instead, they were nestled together in small groups along a central muddy trail. The trail sloped up through the melting snow toward a very wide, low-roofed hut.

Alysa grew up with the belief that the Trailmen were little more than animals, so she was surprised to see such order in their lives. They were every bit as organized and settled, in their own way, as were the Folk.

Her attention was drawn to the sound of younglings playing at the forest edge. Dressed in hides of various dark colors, boys and girls climbed trees and swung upside-down from high branches. The peltees on the ground beneath them jumped and yipped, excited by the younglings' exuberance.

They saw the old Healer helping the stranger up the slippery path and dropped from their lofty perches. Screaming in excitement, they ran toward them. The peltees followed, now alert to Alysa. They pounced toward her, snarling, their long ears standing tall in excitement.

Alysa hid behind Obala as all the creatures — younglings and peltees — ran up. The curious peltees wasted no time and came right up to the strange girl, sniffing her feet and legs. Alysa was afraid that the snarling peltees might bite her.

Obala laughed at the excited mob and urged Alysa along the trail. The peltees got their fill of the girl's scent and became less interested in her, much to her relief. The pale-golden, rosy-cheeked younglings accompanied them, their curious faces stealing glances at Alysa as they danced ahead, jostling back and forth over rivulets of melting snow.

"Younglings!" Obala warned when they ran too close to Alysa or to her staff. "Do not be so rude. Be off, or I will call for your parents!"

Again shrieking in excitement, the younglings and their pets ran back to their forest to play.

Obala said, "The Traders and bearers are the only ones who have seen any of your tribe until Szaren brought you in. And that brings to mind something I must mention. All now know that our tribes share the same tongue. There will be many who will not speak to you. But take no offense. It shocked the tribe, me as well, when we found out. You see, we knew nothing of this similarity. For nearly three thousand cycles we believed our tribe to be unique. So we have harbored a sense of importance above yours. But now possibilities exist regarding our ancestry. And although we have no knowledge from whence the possibilities spring, it disturbs many. Personally, I find this to be fascinating."

Alysa said, "My...tribe...will be as surprised as yours to know of our ability to speak to each other. The Field Folk hold the same idea that we are somehow — better than the Trailmen."

"The Trailmen's purpose has always been to search for truth, for the purity in thought which the Forever One expects of us. Therefore, we will eventually find the answer as to why we can speak to each other, and make it fit our purpose."

"Did you say, 'forever one'? What is forever one?"

"You do not know who the Forever One is?" Obala was surprised.

Alysa shook her head. "Please, tell me."

"Well...the Forever One provides everything to us—the forest and the animals we hunt. The moons and the lakes. The Lowlands and its people with whom we share kinship. And the Field Folk, without whom we would have a more difficult time surviving." She fanned her arm across the sky. "The Forever One gave us Xunar-kun!"

"The Forever One sounds like Father Gord'n."

"Father Gord'n? Now who would that be?"

"He was a very great man. A brilliant man who saved our ancestors from the Cat'clysm. He gave us everything."

"You say he *was* a man? Do you mean he is dead?" Obala asked, skepticism in her voice, "How can you attribute the great accomplishment of *everything*—the making of the lakes and the spinning of the moons—to a man now dead? The Forever One and your Father...who?"

"Gord'n..."

"Yes, this Father Gord'n cannot be compared!" She said, somewhat indignant, "The Forever One will *never* die!"

"That's what the Field Folk are taught, Obala," Alysa countered respectfully.

"I am sorry, Yissa. I meant no disrespect to what you have been taught. Younglings have no control over that. But it is hard for me to understand such Fielder notions."

Alysa paused in thought. "Father Gord'n himself left books of his accomplishments for all to read and know. Do you think he would mislead my...tribe?"

"Yissa, men have done much more serious damage in this world, the Cat'clysm being the worst."

"Oh!" Alysa said. "Do you know about the Cat'clysm? I don't know much about that. Our Tellings begin from the time after we arrived in the mountains. We know very little from the time before."

Surprised, Obala said, "Have you never been out of these mountains? You would learn much by what you would see!"

"What would I see?" Alysa asked, eager.

"There is not enough time for detail," Obala advised. "We are almost to the lodge, and it is much too serious a topic to discuss among new acquaintances. Perhaps one day you will be able to see for yourself."

As Alysa and Obala approached the low lodge's entrance, men, women and their young began to leave their huts. Alysa stopped and looked back. Some carried baskets, and some were laden with armloads of firewood. Others carried slings made from fur on their backs; tiny faces peeked out of openings in the slings. Alysa had never seen babies carried that way. When the Folk took newborns into the fields, they placed them in baskets and set them nearby or hung them from tree branches. She thought how clever this device was, in that parents' hands were left free to work while enabling them to keep their newborns close.

As she and Obala drew closer to the lodge, she noticed many colorful paintings upon its low-sloping hide roof. She was able to see some of the detail in the paintings closest to the entrance. There were scenes in different seasons set in the mountains, by streams and waterfalls. Paintings of hunts depicted unrecognizable animals. There was artwork showing people going about family life in camp, and of hearthrings and star clusters at night.

A motif she easily recognized was that of two moons rising above three peaks. This was very similar to the motif of Winding Mountains of which the Field Folk were fond.

Alysa admired the artwork and was impressed with the Trailmen's skills. "The paintings—they are beautiful!"

Obala smiled. "We take great pride in our work."

They arrived at the lodge's entrance. Alysa's initial impression as they walked up to the lodge was that it was no taller than a man. But when Obala lifted a door flap and guided her down a deep stone stairwell, this misconception was dispelled. The stairwell dropped into a wide, circular room much deeper than Szaren's hut. A large hearthring glowed red in the center of the room. A lofty ceiling made from countless hides stretched across arcing support poles. There was another entrance at the back of the lodge toward which Obala escorted Alysa. They sat near the back entrance on a fur-cushioned stone bench built into the foundation's tall, curving wall.

Trailmen of all ages began to fill the interior. Those who carried baskets set them on long tables near the front entrance and removed their contents. Bread, steaming bowls and platters of meat were placed on the table. The food was then covered with cloth blankets.

Two young peltees tried to enter, but their masters sharply commanded them to wait outside with those who knew better. Peltees were rarely allowed indoors.

Several younglings carried firewood and distributed it over the embers in the hearthring. Flames sprang up. With long poles they pushed open flaps in the ceiling to allow the smoke to escape.

Alysa noticed that every single person—men, women and younglings, including the tiniest of newborns—bore tattoos. During her first Trade, it seemed like the eldest Trailman possessed the most extensive patterns. She saw that the paintings on the wobblies did not yet cover the tops of their ears. She knew she had guessed correctly; the number of tattoos on a Trailmen had something to do with their age. She was intrigued by this odd tradition and desired to learn more.

As they entered the lodge, each person found a place to sit on the benches projecting from the walls. The room grew lively with chatter. Alysa recognized the faces of the three men she traded with. Even though she never spoke to them, she felt comforted that at least not every face in the lodge was strange to her. Trabo sat down beside Obala and clapped his hand firmly on her thigh. He nodded cordially to Alysa. She nodded back and smiled nervously.

Animated talk ceased when a woman appeared on the stairway. All eyes were on this woman, whose short, bright hair curled around her dark-golden face and feathered out over the tops of her tattooed ears. Her sharp, gray eyes surveyed the room before she continued down the steps. Her brown fur cape nearly touched the ground. Beneath the cape she wore the same dark-green tunic and trousers as did the others.

She descended the stairway and glided down the lodge past Alysa and Obala. Holding her cape away from her taut body, the woman sat in an effortless, cross-legged position on Alysa's other side.

Obala rose and stood before the woman. She respectfully addressed her in a voice loud enough for all to hear. "Elder Islean, this charge of mine is called 'Yissa'. She is a Fielder of the High Point Homestead, which lies beyond Rocky Stream. She is of the tribe with which we trade." Of course the whole camp had heard of Alysa's presence, so no one seemed surprised by the introduction.

The bright-haired woman turned her face to Alysa and regarded her. It was difficult to guess Islean's age. Her hair was either white or very blonde, and although her skin was very dark, there were no age wrinkles around her sparkling eyes or anywhere else on her face. The paintings that began on her ears and trailed down her neck were many and very complex. Patterns on the backs of her hands flowed over the tops of her fingers. They may have trailed up her arms as well, but her long sleeves prevented Alysa's being able to discern this.

The woman spoke loudly, yet her voice was smooth and resonant. "Yissa, I am Islean, Chief Elder of the Winding Mountains Trailmen gathered here. Obala tells me you have survived great injury and have, quite miraculously, escaped death."

Alysa mustered courage to speak before Islean and all the other strange faces. She never spoke in front of a large group. The only words she could think of—words of true gratitude—rose to her lips. "I owe my life to you and your people, Elder Islean. I thank you and them heartily."

A low murmur grew within the lodge.

Islean smiled. "My, you do speak our tongue rather well, Yissa." She looked to the gathering. "Does she not?" She turned back to Alysa. "We would be pleased if you would take part in our festivities. On this sun you may be as one of us!"

"I am happy to be a part," Alysa said.

Islean addressed her kinsmen. "Do we have any contests this sun?"

Two young men with half-grown beards rose, one of whom was seated across from Alysa. They reached beneath the benches and picked up heavy poles a little longer than the men were tall. The poles were ornately decorated with sinuous patterns carved along their length. The men walked to the center of the floor. They bowed to Islean and to each other.

Islean gave a high-pitched whistle, and they lowered their poles to waist level. They began to circle, keenly watching each other. One pole-bearer struck his opponent's, and a jostling fight ensued as each blocked a descending blow or attempted to break through the other's defense.

Alysa asked in a horrified whisper, "Obala, what are they doing with those poles? Are they going to—to kill each other?"

The old woman chuckled, "Of course not, midling! And the poles are called 'battlerods'."

"But why do they fight? Are they angry at each other?"

"They are merely testing their skill," Obala answered, her eyes intently following the contestants. "The worst that could happen is for one to be rapped on the head with a battlerod."

"Qohrlat! Throw him, boy!" Trabo encouraged. He bounced on the bench and slapped his thigh.

The audience cheered.

Alysa asked, "But why do they test their skills like this, Obala?"

"They must soon do this before the whole tribe. In addition to demonstrating their battle skills, this is also the way to win a mate."

"Isn't this rather—savage?" Alysa asked.

Obala looked at her sharply. Her brown eyes grew intense. "Ah, but the strongest are the ones who will pair and bear young. Only the strong can survive in this world. It is the way of life!" She returned her attention to the fight.

Alysa thought this practice unfair and the contest violent. She leaned back against the wall and covered her eyes.

Islean placed a hand on Alysa's arm and leaned close. She said in a quiet voice, "This way is different from yours. Your tribe arranges joinings."

"Yes," Alysa answered as she peeked between her fingers, "but how did you know?"

Islean said, "Our way is noble, Yissa. Please try to understand. I wish your stay to be informative as well as pleasant."

The contenders moved in Alysa's direction. One swung his battlerod at the other's legs. His target sprang over the hearthring, tumbled and fell, just missing her. His motion ended as his body rolled against the bench. The young man looked up at her with his pale-blue eyes. Although he wore a half-grown beard, Alysa recognized Szaren. She opened her mouth as if to speak, but before she could utter a word, he was on his feet again, battling his opponent.

"He got up in time—Szaren is still in the contest!" Obala cheered, obviously favoring him.

Alysa was not aware that Szaren was in the lodge. Why did he not speak to her? He gave much aid to her, yet he stayed away from the hut where she mended. And so far he gave her no opportunity to thank him. She watched the contest with increased attention and began to chant with the others, though in a subdued manner.

For some time the men ducked and jumped over each other's battlerods as they swung, both of them very agile, seemingly untouchable.

Finally, Qohrlat fell as his rod was struck from his hands and careened across the floor. Szaren extended a hand and pulled him to his feet. The spectators jumped from the benches and cheered for both of the fine, young contestants. The two winded men ran up and stood before Islean. She nodded to Szaren and he whirled to face the crowd, who cheered for him.

"The champion," Islean's voice rang above the crowd, her flashing gray eyes full of pride, "once again, has won the right!"

Alysa looked to Obala for explanation. Obala said, "Many have fought for her, but Szaren has kept his right to pair with Haraht, also one who is of worthy lineage. They have been close since they were very young. She usually travels the Far Reach Mountains route with her parents. Szaren and Haraht will pair within a cycle or two, unless another challenger defeats him. Which is not likely."

Szaren glanced at Alysa as he passed on his way back to his seat on the opposite bench. He beamed with pride in his accomplishment as kinsmen clapped him on the back in congratulation.

"Does she want to—pair with him?" Alysa asked.

"Ah, yes!" Obala replied. "She has fought as well to retain her right to him. Szaren is a cunning hunter and warrior. Almost any woman would want him. He is Islean's own nephew and shows great promise as a future Elder. Does he not resemble her?"

"But why do you need fighting and warriors? There are no enemies!" Alysa protested.

Attentive to Alysa's claim, Islean cautioned, "One may come to us one sun, Yissa. That is why we maintain the warrior's way. If any should threaten, the Trailmen will be ready."

A tall, lanky young woman halfway down the lodge jumped to her feet. Her wild shock of black, light-tipped hair stuck out in unruly directions. The back of her tattooed neck bore bold symbols of spears, arrows, and what appeared to be bolts of lightning.

With darting eyes as dark as her hair, the woman looked down the row of seated faces. She met the green eyes of a light-haired woman of like age and stature and smiled at her. The woman grinned back and jumped up. They ran up to Islean.

Obala said, "Ah, another contest!"

Islean whistled and the women tackled each other. With a sweep of a foot, the black-haired one knocked the other to the floor. The crowd cheered. Szaren sat upright, intent on the contest.

Alysa drew in a deep breath, staring in disbelief. Obala looked at her, as if more entertained by Alysa's reaction than by the contest unfolding before them. Obala laughed. "Not accustomed to watching women in fight-play, are you, midling?"

Entwined, the women rolled across the floor, just missing the hearthring.

Alysa covered her eyes and leaned back. She mumbled, "I don't understand why women would want to do this!"

Obala patted her on the thigh and chuckled.

The women tumbled and rolled across the floor. They untangled from each other and jumped to their feet. Each leapt into the air to avoid the sweeping feet of her opponent.

The dark-haired woman grabbed up one of the battlerods the men had used and swung it at the other woman, who was quick to jump out of the way. Laughing, she also picked up a rod and they struck at and blocked each other for some time.

At last, the dark-haired woman shoved the other to the floor with the rod, threw it aside, and straddled her. She pinned her shoulders to the floor. The crowd cheered, "Haraht!"

Laughing at the woman beneath her, and holding her down longer than Alysa thought reasonable, Haraht glanced up to be certain that all eyes were upon her. Only then did she sit back and wipe her hands through her wild, light-tipped hair. She jumped up and pulled her opponent to her feet. Both of them laughing, they approached Islean.

Alysa peeked through her fingers. Seeing the fight had ended, she dropped her hands, a look of shock plain on her face.

Islean said, "Haraht! Kailee! You were both magnificent!" She instructed the young women to turn to the crowd. They breathed hard, sweating from their effort. The spectators cheered again and several commentaries on the battles began.

Islean turned and said above the din, "What a treat those contests were! Now let the feasting commence!"

As Haraht passed Alysa, she looked at her sidelong, haughty. Then she turned and smiled proudly at Szaren. He rose, clapped Haraht on the back and followed her.

Alysa whispered to Obala, "And Szaren is betrothed to *her?*"

"Yes, midling, at least as things now stand."

Alysa shook her head. Obala rose and gestured for her to follow. The girl limped behind.

As people moved toward the long table, most avoided eye contact with Alysa. But she did see some curious glances. She thought, *I have never felt more like an insect!*

The blanket was removed from the food, and the smells wafted into the air. Alysa was hungry, so she filled a bowl with the foreign concoctions. She was certain that the food must contain many ingredients grown by the Folk, but she didn't recognize any, with the exception of yellow bread that resembled simmel cake.

Suddenly she missed home terribly. She was never away from her clanfolk long enough for anyone to miss her and was alone only when she chose to be. It was not enjoyable being away from home when it was not her choice.

She picked up a piece of bread and placed it on top of the food in her bowl. She turned, bumping into Szaren. The bread fell to the floor and she stared at it sadly. He placed a fresh piece in her bowl.

"Szaren, you're always helping me," she said. "But you haven't given me a chance to thank you properly for my life, and I would like to…"

"You did thank me earlier, Yissa, when you thanked the tribe. That was enough. Besides, I would have done it for anyone." He turned away and moved back into the crowd.

She sighed and hobbled back to her seat. She tasted her food.

Obala, her bowl already half empty, watched Alysa's reaction. "Well? Do you like it?"

"It's good, but I like your hoptail stew better."

"Well, my stew is hard to outdo! But that you are willing to try other foods is good."

Alysa was quiet for a few moments, thinking while she ate. She shook her head and turned to Obala. "Szaren told me he would have done for anyone what he did for me."

"I would describe him as a very…inwardly proud but outwardly modest young man," Obala informed her. "He needs no thanks for what he gives freely. That is how Islean raised him. It is the Trailmen's way."

"Islean raised him? What of Szaren's parents?"

"Alas, they died when he was very young. As well as aunt and mentor, Islean has been mother and father to him. Not an easy task for either of them, as she never paired or birthed young of her own; but he has turned out well."

Islean made her way back down the lodge and sat beside Alysa to eat.

Alysa said, "The Folk place orphaned younglings with families, often with couples who have not been able to bear young. But never with unjoined or unpaired people as far as I know."

Islean interjected, "It would take time to digest all the facets of another society, a different way of life, Yissa. Our tribes are moons apart. Yours has many ways that I cannot understand, the same as you cannot understand ours."

"How do you know about the ways of the Field Folk, Islean?"

Islean looked into the crowd and shouted, "Are there any dancers here this sun?"

Several men and women rested their bowls on their seats and jumped to the center of the floor. Two women and one man dragged finely crafted wooden drums from beneath a bench. They sat down and placed the drums of different heights and widths between their knees. They struck the taut drumming hides with their hands. The tones of the drums varied, which added richness to the rhythm. The beat was uncoordinated at first, but it was not long before the drummers settled into a rhythm that was challenging to both them and the dancers. The drumming sound filled the lodge.

The dancers' wild kicks and spinning turns resembled some of the fighting motions displayed earlier. But it was joyful, and as others finished eating, they joined in with contagious gaiety until the floor was alive with fierce, spirited bodies. Obala hurried to empty her bowl and rose to join them, demonstrating that she was quite limber for her age.

Islean spoke to Alysa, who listened closely to hear her words above the drumming. "It is most unusual for a Trader to be female."

"Yes, it is, Elder Islean."

"I do not mention this because we object to female Traders. Quite the contrary. Trailmen of the female gender, if they are capable and ambitious, can attain any position, the same as males. That is how I earned my place as Elder."

"That was a surprise to me. The Folk have no female Elders."

"Yes. This I am aware of. The only reason the Trailmen do not have female Traders is because it has, until now with your becoming one, not been accepted by the Folk. Perhaps the Trailmen will now train female Traders." Islean paused. "I am myself curious about something. I know that Fielder women are allowed to gain few positions. If I may ask, how did you manage to obtain Trader?"

"Quite honestly? They were desperate. They couldn't find a willing man, so I offered. I already had some skills and was familiar with the Trade process. It also helped that I was favored by the Council Speaker."

"I have noticed that you are quite a diplomat. Answer me something. Our Traders told me the bright-haired Trader that came for many cycles has been absent the last two Trades. Where is he now? Did he go to another homestead?"

Alysa saddened as she explained, "You mean Abso, my father." She paused. "He had a mishap. Just before Leaffall Trade last cycle, he had his...final farewell."

Islean's jaw set and her gray eyes misted. She set her bowl down on the bench and looked at the floor. "You mean he has died. I am sorry. Please forgive my intrusion, Yissa." Islean rose, leapt up the back stairway, and pushed through the door flap.

Alysa was bewildered by Islean's quick departure, but her attention was drawn back to the joyous drumming and wild dancing.

During the afternoon following Alysa's introduction at the lodge, Obala escorted her around Ridge Camp as a demonstration to the tribe that Alysa's presence was legitimate. The next two suns proved to be a time of great learning for her. With the diminishing snow and the healing taking place in her foot, she became better able to maneuver the grounds by herself and was able to witness the daily activities of the Trailmen.

Some peltees began to accompany her. Alysa became quite familiar with several of them and could count on them to come to her when she left her hut. She learned their names, and Obala taught her how to call, "Hup!" combined with simple handsigns to get them to obey a command.

She felt a special attachment to Drongo, Szaren's peltee, when Obala mentioned that the creature dwelt in the shelter with them during the blizzard. However, Szaren was himself scarce during the remainder of Alysa's stay. Neither did she see any sign of Haraht. The peltee kept company with Alysa as she observed families tending to their duties and as she watched young boys and girls being taught fighting skills such as swinging a battlerod or throwing a spear. These warring activities were attended to with a sense of great enjoyment. The young took to them with wild, unafraid abandon.

Alysa was careful to conceal her laughter, however, when they were instructed to shoot arrows while hanging upside down from tree branches. How ridiculous Alysa thought this particular skill to be, even more so than the other fighting skills they were being taught. It seemed that the time spent in these activities would have been better applied to a more practical use. As she witnessed hunting parties returning with the carcasses of a large variety of game animals, it was apparent that the skill of archery was at least worthwhile. But the use of battlerods and spears still seemed to be a pointless activity.

Evening was her favorite time, after the meal and before the tribe retired to their huts to sleep. They gathered around hearthrings and told fascinating stories of hunts and treks north and south, and east to more distant mountains that Alysa never heard of. She could not imagine what other mountains looked like. But that was of no matter, as she would never consider leaving her own Winding Mountains.

She listened to the tales from outside the glow of hearthring light, as she was not comfortable sitting among the Trailmen and still felt that her presence was not entirely welcome. She wondered why they had no Tellers. Perhaps this was a good thing, in that everybody could tell the stories and they would not be limited in the number of tales that could be told—neither would their content be restrained. Many of the stories seemed boastful. Sometimes the Trailmen would challenge each other about the accuracy of details. This was how she learned about the purpose of their tattoos.

One of the many challenges this night revolved around an event that took place many cycles before any of the young ones present were born. Qohrlat, Szaren's young opponent in the fight-play of two suns before, was telling a tale about the redirection of a trail route into Far Reach Mountains.

Qohrlat said, "My older sister, Taria, now dwells with the Far Reach Mountains tribe since her pairing. She told me that soon after she arrived, a landslide wiped out a very long stretch of trail." He pointed in the apparent direction of Far Reach Mountains. "Upon their return to the Lowlands at migration, they had to find another route out of the mountains. She told me that she and Pratte, her mate, were very instrumental in finding the new trail."

Ferran, one of the older men, shook his head. "That is false, midling. A tale of your sister's error."

Insulted, Qohrlat glared at Ferran.

"Now hold, midling, and learn." Ferran rose and loudly declared to the others. "It amazes me how the tales can be so altered to suit someone else's needs. I remember Taria's Pratte when he was but a youngling. I see him often; he still has that thick tuft of red hair that wants to stand on end, does he not?"

Everyone that knew Pratte agreed and laughed.

"That landslide occurred when Pratte was but a youngling. That was when I and others made the new trail. Taria and Pratte were not involved. It was many cycles after that before Taria even came to dwell with the Far Reach tribe as Pratte's mate."

Qohrlat jumped to his feet and contested, "But my sister would not lie about such a matter!"

Ferran faced him and continued more gently, "I am certain that Taria did not intentionally lie. Or it could be that your young ears misheard her."

"So you accuse either her or me of lying!"

"Ah, well," Ferran chuckled. "Let us put this discussion to an end, young Qohrlat."

Ferran unbuttoned his vest and removed it. The others, understanding the gravity of the disrobing, mumbled to one another. He tossed the vest on his log seat and pulled his tunic over his head. His bare upper torso was stocky and muscular. Alysa half-covered her eyes, unaccustomed as the Folk were to public disrobing.

He turned around slowly so that all could view his broad back. Alysa gasped when she saw the intricate patterns that covered his whole back and shoulders. He said, "You know that the truth of our lives is depicted on our person. I am a Painter myself so am keenly aware of the truth of the representations. It so happens that I spent that cycle with the Far Reach tribe so that I could learn to accurately paint those lands on the skins of Far Reach tribesmen. About midway down my back, you will see the painting of that very landslide. That slide was the most important event of that cycle. What number is written within the painting?"

Someone examined the tattoo closely and said, "Twenty-eight."

"Yes. I was in my twenty-eighth cycle when that landslide happened. That would make Taria at that time perhaps…eight cycles old? She would have been a little too young for pairing with Pratte at that time, would you not say, Qohrlat?"

Defeated, nodding in agreement, Qohrlat sat down. Ferran pulled on his tunic, went to him and roughed his hair. Everybody, including Qohrlat, laughed.

Alysa learned two things that eve. First, when there was a disagreement the Trailmen would arrive at a point where all could agree on the truth. Any matter would be settled fairly and with humor before moving on to the next. And second, the paintings on their bodies were used to keep track of the Trailmen's history and of each person's place in it. The paintings described who each individual was.

Now that she finally understood what the paintings were for, her curiosity made her wonder how they got there. Although she could not imagine how they were created, neither was she bold enough to ask.

She was beginning to see the Trailmen in a very different light. Their ways were not "wrong" as she was taught; they were just different.

HOMECOMING

The morning hike back to High Point took Alysa a long time due to her injured foot. The melting snow turned the trail between Ridge Camp and the bridge to muck. Springs gurgled from the ground where there were none several suns before. Rivulets spilled over the edge of the high gorge, crashing onto the boulders below and splitting into showering arrays that melted into the swollen stream.

Birds of all colors were busy as they flitted, joyfully singing, about the trees; the rising sun turned their feathers translucent as it shone through them. They also perched in the treetops, the first boughs to be clear of snow, and preened their feathers. They seemed to appreciate the return of the fairer, more seasonable weather.

Alysa stared at the entrance to the wide bridge. With one hand she steadied herself using her walking staff. In the other she held her bundle of Trailmen's clothing, which was rolled up and tied with a length of hide. The bridge was long. She uneasily surveyed its hard stone-like floor and estimated that it was perhaps one hundred paces long. Never having crossed the bridge before—and because it was pierced through with many holes—she must be very careful where she placed her feet. Some of the holes were large enough for a person to fall completely through. Others were small, but a leg could easily be broken if a foot stepped into one of them.

She looked over the edge at the boulders and rushing stream far below. Her stomach felt queasy. Her breath became short. But she had no choice other than to cross the bridge if she wanted to get home.

She slipped her hand under the rope of her bundle and slid it up to her elbow. She used that hand to hold her skirt up high enough so she would be able to see her feet and avoid the holes. After taking a deep breath and letting it out, she carefully stepped onto the floor, tapping along with her walking staff. Although most of the snow had melted from the bridge, it was still slippery in places. When she moved past open holes, she avoided looking down at the stream, which she quickly learned made her feel dizzy. She did her best to keep her eyes fixed on the other end of the bridge and, at the same time, not step into a hole.

After weaving around the many holes, she finally reached the other end of the bridge. She let out a big sigh of relief and looked back at her crooked path of wet footprints.

When she turned to continue, she saw many footprints in the slushy remains of snow. Most of them crisscrossed the Tradeground; many ran close to the edge of the gorge. None of them went up the slope that she had climbed to avoid falling into the gorge.

As she slowly made her way down the soggy Gorge Path, she was often forced to wade through puddles that collected from water seeping from the rock walls. The puddles flowed over the edge of the path into the gorge.

To keep her mind off her sore foot, she thought about the Trailmen and all she learned these last few suns about their ways. Most of what the Folk taught about them had proven false; just stories. The Trailmen possessed a complex, intelligent way of living and a most interesting view of — what did they call it? — the Forever One.

After a long, slow hike down Gorge Path and the adjoining path that led to her cottage, she entered High Point. Seven suns had passed since she was lost in the storm. Hearth smoke hung low over the homestead. The aroma of breakfast cooking was the best thing she ever smelled! Figures walking along the main path at the far side of the cottage terrace did not notice her as she emerged from the trees and struggled across the meadow through the slushy snow.

As she entered the yard, the cottage door flew open and Ellee ran out. "Thitha!" She flung her arms around her big sister. Tahshi, Como and Feelah scampered out behind Ellee. Before she knew it, Alysa was covered with welcome-home excitement.

Ellee cried out in delight, "Mother, Mother! You were right! Thitha is home!"

Alysa stooped and wrapped her arms around her little sister. She winced when Ellee returned her affection with a big squeeze to the midriff, but she gave Ellee's cheek a big kiss anyway before releasing her.

154

Loralle's bright, welcoming face appeared in the doorway. Happy tears glistened in her eyes. She laughed. Her soft voice urged, "Ellee, don't make your sister stand out in the chill!" Loralle approached Alysa and embraced her. "Ho, my lovely daughter! We have been expecting you. Come, have breakfast with us." Noticing Alysa's limp, she helped her inside.

The saroos leapt off Alysa's cloak and scampered around the mushy yard as the family entered the cottage.

"I'm so glad you're home!" Ellee said. "Where were you, Thitha? We were so worried! How did you hurt your leg?"

As Alysa hung her cloak in the hallway and removed her muddy boots, she pondered where to begin. She limped to her nook and placed on it her memento of her adventure—the bundle of dark-green Trailmen clothing. She leaned on her walking staff and tapped over to the table. Tired from her hike down Gorge Path, she plopped down across from Ellee. Her mother spooned hot simmel into a bowl.

Glancing around the room, Alysa's happy eyes rested upon the familiar objects of home. She noticed that her mother had resumed work on the rug stretched across the loom; it was nearly completed. Alysa smiled and sighed. "It's wonderful to be home, to be back with the people I most care for. And who care for me!"

Loralle smiled as she placed steaming bowls before her daughters. Alysa reached for her mother and pulled her close. She wrapped her arms around her middle and hugged her tight.

Loralle chuckled. "There, there, Daughter. Everything is right now. You are back with us. Now eat."

Alysa released her and turned to the bowl. She ate a spoonful of the yellow mush flavored with sweet spicenut powder, tasting it as if for the first time. She smiled and gobbled another spoonful.

Ellee squirmed in her seat, not at all interested in breakfast. "Come on, Thitha! Tell us! Where've you been?"

Loralle nestled to Ellee's side. "Yes, it's time to hear your story, Big Sister."

Alysa toyed with her simmel as they listened to her adventure. She told as much as she could recall about the terrible storm and her rescue by what turned out to be the most caring of people. She described the camp and the round huts, the Healers and the bathing hide, their short hair and paintings, and about the younglings swinging from trees.

Ellee's eyes grew large as the moons when her sister recounted the contest between the men in the lodge, and she grinned when it was revealed that Alysa's daring rescuer had won; but both Loralle and Ellee were astonished by the description of the fighting women. Alysa was still amazed that she witnessed that event.

"The Trailmen customs are so strange," Alysa said, "and their clothing!" indicating the bundle on her bed. "I'm bewildered by many of their ways; but it was still fascinating to dwell among them for those suns, among people that are different. I'm almost glad the storm happened!"

"It was indeed a remarkable adventure, Daughter. But *we* are not glad it happened! We're very happy that you're home at last, and safe. The whole homestead will be overjoyed to see you!"

Loralle rose and put on her shawl. "Ellee and I are spinning yarn at the Great Hall this morning. We must also visit the Pantry for provisions. You must come with us so everyone can see that you are home and well. Boshe's been beyond himself with grief! It's plain that he felt responsible, despite all of our urging for him to feel otherwise."

"All right," Alysa said. "I want to see Tola and Kendira, too. I've so much to tell them!" Alysa rose, limped into the entryway and wrapped herself in a shawl. "But now *I* have a question, Mother. Ellee said you knew I'd be coming home. How did you know?"

Loralle looked thoughtful. She brushed loose hair off Alysa's face and said, "I'm a mother. I sensed that you were well." A happy grin stretched across her face. "A runner came from Falling Stream on Council business. He brought a bit of news with him that also gave me hope. Seda gave birth to a female four suns ago!"

"Oh, how wonderful!" Alysa rejoiced. "Was it a good birth?"

"It was reported that Seda is doing very well. However, I don't think Aryz was truly prepared for fatherhood. It seems he doesn't know quite what to do with himself!"

Alysa laughed. "All anybody has to do is give him a chore to keep him busy and he'll be fine!" Then she silently calculated. "But it's too soon for the birth. Is the newborn well?"

"She is fine. Very tiny, but healthy. We hear she has red hair, too, like her mother!"

"I can hardly wait to hold her!" Alysa said. "Have they named her yet?"

Ellee gushed, "Her name's 'Thureena'!"

"Sureena? Oh, such a precious name for a precious newborn," Alysa mused. "Maybe the next one will be named after me..."

Loralle laughed. "We will remain hopeful that they have a second. And a third! Now, let's go to the Great Hall and see who's about, shall we?"

Alysa hugged her mother.

Ellee examined the Trailmen staff upon which Alysa leaned and said, "I'm going to show that to the boys who think they're such great carvers. They haven't made anything as pretty as this!"

"All right, Ellee," Alysa laughed. "As long as I'm sitting down before you take it from me!"

One by one the 'steaders saw that Alysa had returned. Soon a crowd began to gather around her family as they crossed the terrace. The 'steaders were all very happy that she was safe; at the same time, they were most curious about where she was and how she survived the storm. Question after question was hurled at her until, finally, she covered her ears to close out the din and said, "If I must tell the story again, I'll do it gladly; but to all at once!"

The 'steaders followed her into the Great Hall; soon it seemed the entire homestead was crowded inside and engaged in merry chatter. They urged Alysa to step onto a table to allow all to see. She balked because of her hurt foot, so two men lifted her to the table's surface.

Once again, she told the story. This was the first time she ever spoke before the homestead. She never imagined anyone caring to hear her speak. But every wondering eye was fixed upon her. As if she were telling one of the old stories, the people listened, entranced. The story tumbled from her lips, the same one she told at the cottage, but in more detail.

Boshe and Panli burst through the door. Tears of relief filled Boshe's eyes. Panli Tradesigned, *Glad – See – You – Are – Well!* He took Boshe by the arm and guided him to stand against the wall.

The Councilmen bore expressions ranging from curiosity, to objection, to fear. Tola leaned against the back wall, watching the crowd's reactions. Kendira presented a passive face, but she wrung her hands so hard her knuckles were white.

During the Telling, the thought came to Alysa why all were so curious about her adventure: she was unique! No other Folk shared the same experience. None of them had spoken to a Trailmen, let alone live at their camp. So she included as many details about them as she could remember so they would know how different their ways were from their own, and also how truly unthreatening they were.

Alysa concluded, "…and when my foot's better I'll show you that wild dance of theirs!"

People began to murmur to one another. "Isn't it a wonder!" "She's the first Folk to ever cross the bridge!" And some who appeared stunned, "They didn't kill her! I can't believe it!"

Tola stepped through the throng and grasped her hand. "Alysa, we welcome you home. Your coming back is a blessing to us!" Turning to the crowd, he rasped above the din, "Everyone must go back to their duties. Please disperse!" As the Folk obeyed, Tola helped Alysa down from the table. "We're overjoyed that you are back!"

Boshe hurried to Alysa and wrapped his large arms around her. "This has been the longest seven suns of my life! It's a miracle of Father Gord'n that you're alive! When the snow cleared for a moment, all that remained on the edge of the gorge was your packbasket. I feared that you'd fallen in. But when we searched among the rocks below, we were relieved you were not there. Yet I was still fearful you'd been whisked away by the stream!"

"I'm grateful for your concern, Boshe. But I'm afraid that you're stuck with me!" she jested, trying to ease his pained expression.

Panli teased, "It's good the Trailmen found you, Alysa. We would've had to find and train yet another new Trader!"

The reunion was interrupted as the dour Kendira forced herself between the men and Alysa. Boshe and Panli—aware of Kendira's immediate desire to speak to the girl—left them.

"It's good to see you're well," Kendira said in a measured tone. "Would you care to hobble with me to my cottage?"

Alysa hesitated. "If you wish. One moment." Alysa called to Loralle as she and Ellee situated themselves with the other women among baskets heaped with wool. "I'll be back in a bit to help, Mother."

Loralle nodded. "Take your time, Daughter. I'm certain that you two have much to discuss."

"I'll wager we do," Kendira said in a soft voice, her wrinkled eyes narrowing.

Kendira sat near her cottage hearth and urged, "So, tell me more, Alysa, about the Trailmen's ways."

"Kendira, there is so much more that I didn't tell the people, because I don't understand myself."

"Try to explain to me. Maybe I can help."

Alysa sat down as she formed her thoughts into words. She ran her hands along the walking staff's curves and said, "I learned so much about them the last few suns. Do you know of the 'Forever One', Kendira?"

"No—not much. But tell me what you've learned."

"Well, the Trailmen believe in someone—or rather, something—like Father Gord'n—but not like Father Gord'n. They believe that the Forever One isn't a living creature, but also isn't dead. And he—or it—is present everywhere at the same time. And it's responsible for events that happen to us." Frustrated, she added, "It's confusing trying to explain, but it makes perfect sense when the Trailmen speak of it."

"How can the Forever One be known if it has not lived?" Kendira challenged.

"That's what confuses me. I don't know, Kendira. I certainly won't be able to make the Folk understand."

"Oh, I think you should not try. *Our* way is the right way. Confusing your own people would be wrong."

"But I have a question for you, Kendira. Why do the Field Folk still so highly revere...a dead man? And so many, many cycles after his final farewell?"

Kendira retorted, "Father Gord'n gave us all we have! Most important, he gave us a way of life. Something to strive for. And security. Because we still live according to the Laws he handed down, he is not dead!"

"Kendira, I meant no disrespect to Father Gord'n..."

"These foreign notions are not good!" The old woman scowled. "I can see trouble coming for our whole clan if you repeat that nonsense!"

Alysa had still more questions. "Kendira, answer me honestly. How come the Folk and Trailmen speak the same tongue? How come we look like them, other than the way we dress, wear our hair, and don't paint our bodies? How can we be so much alike when we aren't related to or have never known them?"

"I cannot answer your questions."

"Cannot — or will not?"

"You speak blasphemy, girl!"

"The Trailmen seek the truth, Kendira. Don't the Folk also strive for truth?"

"Our way is the one true way! It is written in the texts!"

"Whatever the truth may be, Kendira, I think that we should at least change the way we think of the Trailmen. And change the Tellings so that the Folk learn what they're really like."

Kendira rose to refill her mug. Her body became rigid as she faced away. "We owe them nothing, despite what they did for you. And that includes changing our opinion of them. The current teachings will stand!"

"Kendira, since a woman is Chief Elder of the group I stayed with, and many more of the Trailmen's leaders are women, doesn't that say much about a woman's capacity to do what we consider to be men's work?"

"Just because they allow this, it does not make it right. They do many things we would not be proud of. You should cease in such meanderings of thought, youngling!"

"They think the Field Folk are foolish for having no warrior knowledge. And because we never leave these mountains. And because we rarely spend time alone."

"It sounds to me like you admire their ways too keenly, Alysa!"

"I think questioning our ways is good, if there may be a *better* way."

"Change would destroy our society!" Kendira quipped. "Would you find satisfaction in that, foolish girl?"

Alysa shrank in response to what seemed an unwarranted reaction. After all, she was trying to be forthright about what she learned. She sat up tall and said, "Shouldn't the truth be especially important to you, Kendira, as a Teller of the history? Do you not want to pass down the truth?"

Kendira bent very near to Alysa's face and spat, "Do you want to know the *truth*, youngling? Well, I'll tell you a little-known truth. The Council hoped to keep this secret forever hidden. But since you are insistent on knowing the truth…" She hesitated. "Your father had no simple mishap. He was murdered!"

Murdered! It was a word seldom spoken, a concept that had always been difficult for Alysa or any other Field Folk to grasp. She stared at Kendira in disbelief. "Who would've done that to Father? We have no enemies! There'd be no reason for anyone to kill such a gentle, caring man!"

"Use your head, Alysa. He was found along the stream bordering the Trailmen's territory. And he had not been alone. Footprints other than his were found in the soft mud around his body. And a staff, a tall winding staff—yes, very similar to the one you are holding—was found beneath him. Which can mean only one thing. He was murdered by the Trailmen!"

Though Alysa wanted what Kendira said to be false, she found it difficult to refuse the possibility. It was long thought that the Trailmen were an aggressive, territorial people; but the side of them she witnessed at their camp, the generosity and respect for life they demonstrated, clashed with what the Folk believed about them. And Kendira's account of the Trailmen was a drastic departure from what Alysa experienced. Could it be that they displayed only good behavior while she was at their camp? If so, what advantage would that have been to the Trailmen?

"I'm going to talk to Tola about this!" Alysa protested.

"Youngling, it was Tola who figured out the details of your father's murder. He will tell you no different." Kendira paused and continued in a gentler voice. "Why do you think he treated you so special after Abso died? He coddled you and your family. He supported you in every way he could to try to make up for what happened to you, including allowing you to become a Trader!" She paused then asked, "*Now* how do you feel about your Trailmen?"

A wicked smile spread across Kendira's face as Alysa rose and hopped on her sound foot to the door.

"I don't believe you, Kendira. I'm going to talk to Mother!"

"Yes, do that, youngling, and you'll ruin the progress she's made. You'll revive her pain. Do that, and she will forever remember Abso with great shame!"

But of course Kendira was right! Alysa wanted no additional conflict to harm her mother and sister. "Why didn't Tola tell us? Why, Kendira?" she pleaded, tears sliding down her cheeks.

"And accomplish what? We could never hope to replace your father. It would be unsound to cut off Trade in revenge, which would be the Folk's chosen recourse if they knew what really happened. Revenge is a word only whispered, certainly not practiced in our clan. Father Gord'n taught us that a civilized society does not engage in revenge. So forget about becoming friends with the Trailmen. We must never try to be. Leave the savages to themselves!"

Alysa shut Kendira's door behind her. After her tears cleared enough so she could see the path, she limped back to the cottage as quickly as she was able. She felt like throwing the Trailmen staff aside but knew that without it she would only re-injure her foot.

There was such confusion in her mind that she had a difficult time keeping her thoughts straight. She could not accept that the Trailmen carried out the atrocity Kendira described. But she dared not question Tola or risk reopening a wound that was beginning to heal. Her mother and Ellee had made such great progress.

The correct resolution would be to question Islean. But the Trailmen would have crossed the pass half a sun ago on their way to congregate with their tribe in the Lowlands. They would have left behind the circular pits of the huts, the folding things and hide roofs stacked within until their return next greening. Besides, Alysa's hurt foot would not allow her to follow. Even if she were able, she had only a remote chance of finding their trail. Testimony to their passage would be scoured away by melting snow or buried in oozing mud.

Alysa knew that she was no longer only of the Field Folk. A part of her reached out to the Trailmen's kindness and to the practicality of many of their ways. But she was now confused as to their true nature and the part they played in her father's death.

Unfortunately, there would be no chance to confront them until next Trade.

THE M'RAUDA THREAT

Alysa brooded throughout the long wintertide, keeping Kendira's dark knowledge to herself and trying her best not to let it darken her mood. If anyone tried to engage her in talk of the Trailmen, she changed the course of conversation. After her foot healed, she hid the twining walking staff beneath her sleeping nook. Out of sight, it would no longer inspire unwanted Trailmen thoughts or conversation. She went to her place by the stream and threw the bundle of Trailmen clothing into the water and watched it float out of her life. Not thinking or talking about the Trailmen at all was her best strategy — until the time came when she could approach Islean.

Greening Trade finally arrived and proceeded as usual. Field Folk and Trailmen played their traditional roles, Tradesigning as always, although they were well aware that they spoke the same tongue. Alysa performed her appointed role, too, although she was restless throughout Trade. She easily recognized the Trailman Traders, after having spent much time at their camp. Trabo was the Chief Trader and was paired with Obala; Moronda was the next eldest, and Folie was the youngest.

Her brown eyes connected with theirs; she thought it foolish to conduct Trade in the old way. She tried, to no avail, to persuade Boshe and Panli to learn the Trailmen's names and to speak instead of sign. But she gave up, having come to understand all too keenly that changing her people's ways was not something that would be easily accomplished — if ever.

Time seemed to lengthen as she waited for the sun to pass, particularly during the afternoon. She was often distracted by the light breeze playing among young leaves in the treetops and by insects fluttering and diving on new wings. More than once, Boshe looked at her, perplexed, after her preoccupation caused pauses in the process.

After a sun that seemed as long as a season, the exchange of goods ended. Alysa brought no holdbacks to offer this time. Neither did she have an interest in acquiring any of the Trailmen's oddities laid out before them. Folk and Trailmen both seemed daunted by her indifference to this chance to participate in what was the only truly fun part of Trade.

As Trade ended, Alysa announced, "I wish to see Elder Islean." The Traders, who had begun to pack their goods, halted their work. Uneasy, they looked at one another, but none of them spoke. Boshe excitedly motioned her to be quiet, to no avail. "I need to speak to Elder Islean. It's urgent."

Trabo turned and walked toward the bridge. Alysa followed him, and in silence they crossed the gorge, weaving around the open holes in the bridge's floor. Her companions and the other Trailmen watched after them as they crossed. Too shocked to move, Boshe still held the objects he began to pack when Alysa first voiced her wish.

Trabo led her into the newly sprouted forest cover. Soon they came to the green glade with its neat conical huts spread across the space. Several peltees ran up to them, snarling at first when they saw Alysa. They sniffed her and nuzzled their heads into her hands as they remembered her.

"Ho, my peltee friends!" She vigorously patted their thick, curly fur as they gathered around her.

Trabo led her to Islean's hut. He poked his head through the flap, spoke a few words, returned to Alysa and addressed her. "Islean will see you."

"Thank you, Trabo."

Trabo nodded. "Hup!" he said to the peltees as he firmly pointed away from the hut. They yelped and scampered off.

Alysa walked down the few steps into the hut. Slender wood shavings flicked from Islean's blade and flamed in the hearthring as she carved a design into a thick, peeled branch that lay across her lap. Her pale hair glistened in the firelight. Her strong, calm features were defined by light and shadow as she carved. Her brightly tattooed fingers worked quickly. She looked up and smiled, then returned her eyes to her work. "I did not expect to see you again, Yissa. But I am delighted!"

Stern, Alysa replied, "I would've been back the very sun I left if I'd been able, and if you hadn't also left for the Lowlands."

"Did your people winter well?"

"My people wintered just fine. But I spent the whole season desperately awaiting your return!"

"How so?" Islean asked, raising her bright eyes to the girl and setting her work aside. "Please, sit."

Alysa stiffly sat on a cushion across from her. Without hesitating, she said, "The very morning I got home, I learned something that caused me enough pain to last all wintertide. I've waited half a cycle to understand how it can be true."

"Now whatever could that be, Yissa?" Islean asked, concerned.

Alysa struggled with the words. She swallowed hard, containing her tears. "I spent a few often confused but very wonderful suns among your people. I can't understand how you could have done it!"

"What did I do?" Islean asked.

"Your people...they murdered my father!"

Islean's gray eyes revealed rising anger. She summoned enough control to ask, "What would cause you to claim such, Yissa?"

"I learned of a secret kept from my family and from all but the Elders of my clan. If my people knew what happened to Father, the Folk would likely choose to end Trade. But we need Trade. So it was kept secret that he was found murdered. By the Trailmen."

"Nonsense! We are not murderers. And you know that in your heart, Yissa, do you not?"

"Islean, I want to believe you. Please give me a reason to believe!"

"Where did you hear of this?"

Her voice strained, Alysa said, "The Teller of High Point told me. When I asked her to start teaching the truth about you."

"Ah!" Islean jumped up from her cushion. "Kendira, the *true* leader of your homestead! Is she still causing trouble? Resorting to lying now, is she."

"You know Kendira?" Alysa asked, bewildered. "But...how?"

"I know of her, which is just as good—or bad—as knowing her!" Islean continued, her voice much quieter, "It is time for you to hear something. Do you remember at leaffall when you told me about your father's death? I left the lodge directly after. I ran to the forest to be alone. To wail in grief! It was a cycle since he came to Trade. It occurred to me that he may have died, but I did not want it to be so."

"You knew my father? How can that be?"

"I did not know how to approach this topic when you were last here. I thought it best to not mention it. But I can see that it is time. So know that what *I* say is the truth and Kendira's words false."

Alysa nodded and listened carefully.

"We were meeting after every Trade. Just your father and I, for several cycles. To discuss ways to bring the tribes together."

"The Trailmen want to bring us — together?"

"Not the Trailmen. I," she sighed. "Now that Abso is dead, I am alone in the cause."

"How did you and my father meet?"

"I will tell you about that sun many cycles ago." Islean sat down and leaned toward Alysa. She spoke quietly. "I went for a hike one afternoon farther downstream than usual. It was in a small clearing on a sunny knoll that I first saw him lying on a patch of ewegrass. He stared up into the sky, just thinking, it appeared. I was curious about who this man was and did not wish to startle him. So like the breeze, I whispered, 'By what name are you called, stranger?' He seemed to be expecting me! He said that for many cycles he waited during our migration times, at the edge of our territory, hoping to meet one of us. Since that sun, we met secretly after Trade."

"Do you know my mother?" Alysa asked.

"Only through your father. He felt that the sun, moons and stars revolved around her. And his daughters. I wanted to know her, but we discussed that and felt it best that our friendship remain secret, to protect her."

"What did you talk about?" Alysa asked.

"Mostly what it would be like if our tribes were to have more contact, share more of ourselves. You see, our first meeting was by chance. But it so happened that our desires for the future of our people were similar. We talked about ways to truly bond our people, beyond the reason of the twice-cycle tradition. But since the laws of both tribes were so strict about our separation, we never did determine a way to convince our stubborn tribes that each needs to recognize the valuable qualities of the other; strengths that, if melded, could make both of our tribes even stronger."

Islean shifted, brought her knees up and wrapped her arms around them. "We managed to prevent anyone from finding out. Even if any of my tribe *did* discover us, they would have demonstrated nothing more than posturing toward him, although I may well have had to resign my position as Elder. If any of my tribe did happen upon Abso alone in the forest, they would have done him no harm. The Trailmen are not prone to violence; we only practice defense skills that may be needed to protect the tribe at some time to come. If we were discovered talking to each other, it certainly would have shocked my tribe. It would have thrust us into turmoil for a time, much as eventually happened by your coming to us. We have now begun to work through the conflict in our beliefs and the mystery of our ancestry. And the contradiction of our oldest legends. It will be a slow process."

Islean paused and smiled. "So you see, Yissa, there was no motive for anyone to harm Abso; first, because our friendship was never discovered. And second, because the Trailmen are not a violent people. Kendira created this deception purely to manipulate you. To help you despise us."

Alysa began to weep, partly from relief of the secret pain she harbored for so long and partly for the vindication of the Trailmen. "I know that you speak the truth, Elder Islean. Please forgive me. I'm ashamed for accusing your people of such a terrible deed. At the same time, I'm happy to learn of my father's desire to bring the tribes closer together."

"You are, of course, forgiven, Yissa," the gracious woman said. "And I am very glad that I was able to tell you about your father and me. But from this sun forward, please beware of Kendira. I would tread lightly in any further dealings with her." Islean returned to her cross-legged position and picked up her carving.

"I believe that I have, at long last, learned my lesson about her, Islean. Thank you." Alysa breathed a deep sigh, dabbed her eyes, and sat up straight, much relieved by Islean's tale.

Islean nodded and smiled. "Do not be hard on yourself for having fallen for her lies, Yissa. Being deceived is easy when the deceiver is so very clever and the victim is innocent to such tactics."

"Yes, Islean, I understand." Alysa looked at the Elder's carving. "May I look at your work?" Islean handed it to her. "This is lovely, Islean. What's it going to be?"

"A hanging for my Lowlands hut. Then again, I may give it away. It does not matter where it resides. The best part is in the making."

"It looks so real and looks like…berries?"

"Yes."

"I've seen this pattern before…"

Islean smiled. "Yes, you very well may have."

"My father's box!"

Islean nodded.

Alysa smiled. "Now I'll treasure it all the more!" Alysa rose and handed the carving back. "I must get back to the Tradeground. They'll think I got lost again." She laughed. "Thank you once again, Islean. Safe travels for your tribe."

"And may your fields grow plenty this season." As an afterthought, Islean added, "Ah! Perhaps after all it is good that you sought me out. I have some news from the Lowlands that you may wish to pass on to your Elders." Alysa listened attentively. "A band of nomads called 'M'raudas', perhaps as many as three hundred in number, were recently seen to the west of the Lowlands territory. We believe it is of little importance, but your tribe may wish to be more vigilant as far as your herds are concerned. The M'raudas may be scavenging for food, and tame animals would be easy quarry."

Fearful, Alysa asked, "Who are the 'M'raudas'? And where do they come from?"

Islean shrugged. "Nobody knows their origin. They are different from our tribes and the next thing to animals. They stand upright and use weapons to an extent. But they are not thought of as a threat to people. Just be watchful of your herds."

"Weapons? To me the M'raudas don't sound like a trivial matter! Thank you for the information, Islean. I will tell my Elders."

"The next time we meet, Yissa, I hope it is for a more pleasant purpose."

Alysa's apologetic smile and nod assured Islean that she hoped for the same. As Alysa left the hut, the slanted sunlight blinded her and she walked into the path of four passing figures.

She recognized Obala's soft voice. "Yissa, what a surprise to see you! How nice. Your foot has apparently healed well."

"Yes, Obala, thanks to you…" Then she recognized barefaced Szaren. He carried a bow and quiver. The young black-haired woman, Haraht, stood beside him. With them was Kailee, Haraht's opponent in the fight-play. Alysa was at once repulsed by the small, furry animals dangling from Haraht's belt. They reminded her of saroos.

Drongo ran up to Alysa, rose up on her hind legs, and nuzzled Alysa's hand. She stoked Drongo's curly black and white fur.

Obala said, indicating her companions, "Of course, you already know Szaren."

"Ho, Szaren," said Alysa, delighted to see him.

"Yissa," Szaren replied, avoiding looking into her eyes.

Obala continued, "And this is Haraht, Szaren's betrothed; and Kailee, Haraht's companion."

Alysa and Haraht inspected one another. Cropped hair on a woman was another Trailmen fashion, along with trousers, that held little appeal for Alysa.

Haraht's eyes swept Alysa from head to toe. In a dry tone she asked Szaren, "This is the one that was swallowed in the storm?"

Haraht well knew about Alysa. She had been in the camp then.

Szaren shifted his feet. "Yes."

"And have you come for more pampering?" Haraht quipped.

"No. I'm quite well, thank you," Alysa said, disappointed by the remark. "I came to see Islean." So this was the woman for whom Szaren had fought to maintain the joining right! How could a man love a woman who hunts and fights? A shiver ran up Alysa's spine when her eyes again roamed over the dead animals and the long blade hanging from Haraht's belt.

"We are going to skin out the hoptails we snared," Haraht said with a sly smile. "Would you like to help?"

"No," Alysa replied. "My companions are waiting for me at the Tradeground."

"Ah, that is right," Haraht sniped. "I remember now that Fielder women never clean game; they barter for it after the nasty work is done."

Szaren intervened, "Haraht will be with the Winding Mountains tribe again this season. She will be learning the trails and the running of the streams..."

"So that I will make a fine mate to Szaren," Haraht added. Kailee laughed and Haraht joined her, their hearty outburst biting to Alysa's ears.

Alysa decided this to be as much of an introduction to the rude huntress as she needed. "Have a good summering," she said in a flat voice to Szaren. She began to walk back to the gorge beyond the trees. In a softer, respectful tone, she turned back to Obala and said, "It was good to see you again, Healer Obala."

Obala smiled and nodded, and she and Kailee continued on their way. Haraht waited for Szaren. He stood between her and Alysa, watching Alysa as she walked away. Drongo began to follow her.

"Hup, Drongo!" Szaren called. The peltee came to him, and Szaren turned to follow Haraht.

Alysa faced the Council Elders who sat at the long table beneath the Planting Calendar at the rear of the Great Hall. She said, her voice bordering on anger, "I don't understand why you don't believe them!" She stomped her foot, and her shawl slipped onto the floor. "I have a feeling they could come to harm us!"

"Listen to me, Alysa," Tola said, calm and attempting to keep order in the proceedings. "The M'raudas haven't been seen for—I don't know how many generations. Their time has long passed. They no longer exist, youngling."

"The Trailmen wouldn't lie!" Alysa maintained.

"They may simply be mistaken," Levin said. "A few seasons back, a runner came upon a longtooth on the trail between Yellow Cliffs and Green Plateau. As usual, the skittish thing ran off as soon as it saw the runner. A longtooth can walk upright for short distances. Maybe that's what they saw."

Elder Dagg chided, "You think your new-found *friends* care what happens to the Folk, anyway?"

"They care about life, no matter whose it is!" she insisted.

Tola asked, "Do you know what the M'raudas were, Alysa?"

She shook her head.

"I know a bit of before-Cat'clysm history which is not in the usual teachings. It is part of the information reserved for Elders. I'll tell you, in confidence, so that you may understand. The M'raudas' ancestors, unlike ours, were trapped in the cities at Cat'clysm. Many were blinded and scorched by the brilliant heat and light of war. Many were struck down by an invisible death brought upon those who tarried. Their skins were blackened by the fierce, stinging flies that left no living being unharmed. Those who were still alive after they left the City were left to roam upon Xunar-kun with no purpose, no plan."

Levin added, "It's said that many of their offspring died at birth, and those that didn't die were born stupid and with misshapen bodies."

Dagg added, "The last few that were seen were ill and dying. There were so few then that I cannot understand how there can be any more left. Certainly not the three hundred the Trailmen claim. I agree with Tola that they gave you incorrect information."

Alysa bowed her head and rubbed her temples. "We don't know how to defend ourselves if they or any other enemy should come to our hills. We should be prepared!"

"It's our belief," Tola replied, "that we are the only peoples left on this world. There are no others to harm us. Alysa, would you rather maintain the views of your own people, or more readily adopt those of the Painted Ones?"

"I think we should ask them, while they're still camped here, to show us how to raise a hoe to an attacker if need be."

The Council, each member aghast, sat motionless, mouths gaping. Tola rose and said, with controlled anger, "I declare this meeting over. Alysa, please remain."

She stared out the window at the placid scene of Folk carrying out daily activities. She wrestled with the desire to tell Tola about Kendira's brutal lie in the circumstances surrounding Abso's supposed 'murder'. But she thought better of burdening him with one more bit of contention. *She* knew the truth. As of this moment, that was all that mattered.

After the others left, Tola went to her. He picked up her shawl and placed it around her shoulders. "I'm sorry to have to tell you this, Alysa. But I must say that if you continue to upset the homestead with your Trailmen talk, we shall forbid you to be present at any more Gatherings! Many Folk think you exaggerated the kindness that was shown you when you were found in the storm. Or that you even made up the stories. But they didn't care because you provided them with fanciful entertainment. Others were upset and confused when you tried to convince them how benevolent the Trailmen are. Many took your words as truth and have since been questioning. I've had all I can do to maintain order. Now I don't know how much clearer I can be in saying this: we can have no more of your reckless interference with the workings of the clan!"

Alysa whirled around and faced him. "I thought you would believe me, Tola. Out of everyone—I hoped you would see the truth. But I was wrong, Speaker. You want to know no more than the others, the blind, bound-up bunch that rules this homestead!"

Sad, Tola shook his head and turned his back to her. "That is all I have to say, youngling. Please leave."

As Alysa swept across the terrace, her furious gait subsided. Her anger was being replaced with feelings of deep fear. But she could not define the origin of the fear. She also wrestled with the possibility that Tola was right. Perhaps there *was* no reason to fear.

But deep within her, she thought she heard her father's loving voice—for so long absent—whisper, *You are right, Daughter. There is reason to fear!*

THE SECRET OF FATHER GORD'N

A little more than eight moons later, after the passing of a long, hot summering, the Folk were in the process of clearing the fields of spent stalks and debris in preparation for wintertide's approach.

Leaffall Trade, just eight suns before, was uneventful. It was carried out in the traditional way, complete with tradesign and the typical detachment expressed by Traders on both sides. Alysa made no demand of Trabo to see Islean this time. She played her part and focused on the best Trade possible.

It was late, long after the Folk went to bed. Alysa and her family were tucked into their nooks, peacefully sleeping. The saroos were coiled at the bottom of Ellee's bed. Ears twitched and tails flicked, as in their dreams they may have been chasing each other around the yard or pestering the casish hens.

Pounding on the door roused Alysa and Loralle from sleep.

Alysa yawned and said, "I'll see who it is, Mother." Weary from a hard sun of helping in the fields, she dragged herself from her nook and opened the door. Her unbraided hair was disheveled.

Orryn was before her, out of breath, holding the stump of a torch. Shallow light flickered on the ground around him and on his haggard face. He looked old, tired, unlike the boy she knew. His face and hands were scratched and bruised, his braid thick with brambles from his nighttime journey from Falling Stream.

He spoke with difficulty. "Lys. I have very sad news."

Loralle climbed down from her bed. She pulled the curtains of Ellee's nook so the sound of their voices would not wake her. The saroos were now half awake and chattered anxiously. Perhaps they were annoyed that they were startled from slumber; or perhaps their senses told them something was amiss.

Loralle rushed to the door with a grave knowing on her face. The last time someone came to the door looking upset like that, it was to tell her of Abso's death.

Orryn was sweating and leaned against the doorway, recovering his breath. Alysa cast the torch on the ground and helped him inside.

177

Loralle lit a lamp and urged him to sit. She brought him a mug of water, from which he took several gulps. She refilled the mug.

Ellee sleepily peeked through the curtains. "What's happening? Why is Orryn...?"

Loralle went to Ellee, shushed her and helped her back under the covers. Loralle stroked her hair. The saroos, now plainly annoyed and sputtering, crawled under the quilt. Ellee promptly fell back to sleep.

Orryn caught his breath. "Something terrible has happened! This morning Seda worked in the field, gathering and tying dried stalks. As she always does, she left Sureena playing on a blanket near the edge of the field, not far from where she worked. Seda looked to her often and Sureena was perfectly content. The wee one has yet to stand by herself. But when next Seda looked up, Sureena had vanished! At first it was thought she finally found her legs and wandered off. But when they looked for her—across the fields, in the brush, even into the edge of the forest—they found no sign of her! A youngling newly on her feet would not be able to wander far..."

Loralle sat at the table and calmly said, "Someone must have taken her for a walk. Then later took her back home, perhaps after you left Falling Stream?"

"No," he said. "We checked every cottage, thinking that one of the younglings may have taken her to play with. We talked to *everyone* at the homestead."

"Were there any animal tracks?" Alysa asked, afraid of the answer.

"No tracks. There were only our own footprints. Although..." Orryn furrowed his brow. "The fields have been cool and damp, and no one has worked barefoot for several suns. Yet there were fresh, bare footprints near Sureena's blanket. The footprints went into the forest and back. I thought at the time they belonged to someone who left the field to search—but those tracks could have come *from within* the forest—and they could have carried Sureena *back into* the forest! Oh, but had we thought of that then! Instead we wasted time running around the homestead when we should've been following those footprints!" Remorseful, he slumped in the chair and dropped his head into his hands. "I must tell them of this possibility. I'd better get to the meeting the Elders are having."

Alysa stooped beside him and reasoned, "I think you're too upset to think clearly, Orryn. Who would take a youngling? It's a foolish idea that anyone would…" She thought for a moment and then jumped up. "Oh, no it isn't! I just remembered something!" She grabbed her shawl and asked, "Where are they meeting, Orryn?"

"At Speaker Tola's. Aryz is there, and this situation is so dire that Council Speaker Poolan and Elder Yiul from Falling Stream came, too. We came to the closest homestead to seek help, advice, *some* way to find Sureena."

"I think—rather, I'm *afraid* that I think I know the answer. Come!" Alysa dragged him from the chair. Not taking time to braid her hair, she threw her shawl around her sleeping-smock and lit a lantern.

They left the cottage and ran down the path. The lantern sent swaying light ahead and long, chaotic shadows behind. When they opened Tola's door, they beheld a silent, perplexed group of men. All of High Point's Elders were there, plus Falling Stream Elders Poolan and Yiul and, of course, Aryz. The sight of this number of Elders gathered in one small cottage caused Alysa's breath to catch. In formal greeting to this gathering, she and Orryn bent forward, palms-up, and straightened.

Alysa greeted fatigued Aryz with an embrace. "Aryz, I'm so sorry," she said. She faced Tola. "Elder Tola, may I speak?"

Tola looked from her to Orryn, then to the other Elders who responded with various expressions of indecision. Tola said, "Orryn of Falling Stream would like to speak."

Orryn looked at Alysa, questioning, because she was the one with the request.

Elder Poolan conferred briefly with Elder Yiul, and he said, rubbing his fingers over his damp, gritty forehead, "If you have information that you feel may be of use in this situation, Orryn, you may proceed…"

Orryn opened his mouth as if to speak, but looked blank and shook his head. He looked at Alysa. She blurted, "The M'raudas are here! They're in the homestead territories. A M'rauda took Sureena!"

A few tired, cynical groans emerged from the group. Levin rolled his eyes and said, "Oh, moons above, girl, not that again!"

Alysa said, "But it's true. This is real. There is danger!"

"Wait!" said Poolan, motioning for silence. "What do you mean, 'M'raudas'?" He looked back and forth between Tola and Alysa for explanation.

Alysa said, "The M'raudas. Once people, now beasts. They were recently seen in the Lowlands."

"Who's been in the Lowlands to see anything?" Poolan asked.

"The Trailmen," Alysa said, biting her lower lip. The room fell silent.

"Alysa," Levin said, "we don't care to hear any more Trailmen talk!"

Poolan said, "Trailmen? What's this about the Trailmen?"

Tola added, "We're tired, Alysa. Please leave. Poolan, ignore the girl."

But Alysa persisted, explaining how it was very possible for the M'raudas to be in the mountains. She related the facts as Islean told her and that she relayed to the High Point Council. She ended with, "None of what I've said has been fabricated. I'll leave now, but I challenge you to find a better reason for Sureena's disappearance!"

She hugged Aryz and looked with hope into his eyes. She looked back one last time at the group of men who bore expressions of varying degrees of incredulity. She and Orryn left. He carried the lantern in one hand and rested the other on Alysa's shoulder as they walked back to the cottage, the only one with a lighted doorpost. Both were drained from worry and frustration.

Orryn paused and struck a half-hearted Teller pose. Alysa stopped to watch, a questioning look on her face. He said, "Fear not failure of the field as much as failure of the heart." He dropped the pose, and they continued.

"I haven't heard that one before. Did you make it up, Orryn?"

"No. It's an ancient saying. It seemed fitting to say it out loud."

"It says what I'm feeling right now," she said, her voice cracking. "My heart's breaking. I'm powerless to help my friends and afraid of what the M'raudas may do to Sureena."

"What would you do if you could, Lys?"

She considered his question. "Find them before they steal any more younglings."

"And when you've found them? Then what?"

"I suppose they'd have to be run off."

"What if they resisted?"

"Then they'd have to be…killed!" she said with resolve.

"You make it sound like an easy task."

"I'd ask the Trailmen to help chase them from our hills. I think they might. But I'd never get the Council to consider an alliance. They want as little as possible to do with them. There seems to be no solution," she said with resignation.

Orryn's next thoughts caused him pain. He stammered when he spoke. "There may be…a way."

Alysa stared at his tired features, barely visible in the early dawn. "What do you mean?"

They reached Alysa's cottage and entered the yard. He took her hand and urged her to sit on a bench set against the low stone wall. His gray eyes looked around nervously. He sighed and continued, "What I'm about to tell you—I have revealed to no one else. Tellers take a strict oath to keep certain ancient knowledge secret. I'm about to break that oath for you, Lys. I'll tell you because you believe you can help the clan. Maybe there's something in what I've learned that will help us figure out what to do."

Alysa's curiosity was aroused by his decision to break his Teller oath. She listened with care as he released his thoughts and allowed his words to pour forth.

He said, "One of a Teller's abilities is to read the script of Father Gord'n."

Disappointed by this "revelation" of which all were well aware, she said, "That's the big secret? We all read fieldscript, Orryn!"

"Everyone reads fieldscript, that's right. But I'm talking about *oldenscript*. Before fieldscript came to be, many of Father Gord'n's early books were written in oldenscript. Oldenscript is taught only to Tellers. It's much more difficult to read and write than fieldscript. So we're the only ones who learn it. Passing on the teachings of oldenscript among Tellers keeps the meaning of the ancient texts alive."

"Are there enough oldenscript books in Father Gord'n's cottage to make learning it that important?"

"There are just a few on the shelves, but…"

She leaned forward, cutting him off, "Then why's any discussion about oldenscript necessary? Orryn, what're you trying to say?"

"Lys, please! Listen! Just listen…"

She sat back and folded her arms across her chest.

He continued, "One sun a few cycles ago, I stopped to get a book from Father Gord'n's cottage. There was one I hadn't read before on a high shelf on the back wall that faces the hill. When I reached for the book, my sleeve caught on something on the side of the shelf. When I pulled my arm back…" He paused, watching his hand. "When I lowered my arm, a lever on the side of the shelf caught on my sleeve and came down with it. Before I knew it, the wall was trembling. Like a door, the wall swung open."

He rose and began to pace up and down the path, taking great care to recall each detail with the most precise words. "By the time the wall stopped moving, there was an opening wide enough to walk through. Curious, of course, I looked inside. I saw a flicker of light. I stepped behind the wall. A dim lamp burned on a table. I lengthened the wick and found myself in a large room. There—in stacks on the floor, on shelves and hanging from the ceiling—were the most incredible things! There were many more journals and books, ancient books. Maps of the mountains. Odd-looking Planting Calendars. And many of the most wondrous images scattered around."

"By 'images', do you mean drawings?"

"No, not drawings. But exact likenesses, on thin, metal-like squares, some maybe one pace wide, others small enough to fit in the palm of my hand. Here, I'll explain." He picked a flower and held the stem between his fingers. "If you compared this flower to the image of it…" He raised his other hand and opened it palm-side up, "…the same colors and details as in this flower would stand up from the metal square resting on my palm. As you turned the metal square bearing the image of the flower, you would see all the way around it. Almost as if the flower in the image was real. Do you understand?" Alysa shook her head. "I was afraid of that. I don't know how to explain an image without showing you one. But even though I can't show you one, I can still *tell* you what I've learned."

Excited now, he assumed formal Teller stance, happy to at long last be telling someone of his wondrous discoveries. "There are many, many images of the City."

Drawn into the Telling by Orryn's great skill, Alysa gasped, "The City? Oh!"

Orryn held up his hand to quiet her and continued, "The City was a magnificent place! Many people lived there. Families thrived and enjoyed a wealth of celebrations and abundance. Vast, fertile farmlands spread as far as the eye could see. There were many religions and people who dressed in a variety of ways. They spoke many tongues, not just one. There were many entrances and exits to the City over high-arcing bridges so that people could easily come and go. They traveled in fast land and air machines. A great sea bordered the far edge of the City. The people lacked for nothing." His face saddened as he added, "There are also images that look as though they were obtained just after the City was destroyed. They are frightening, of broken buildings and burning..."

He continued, changing his mood from one of horror to one of wonder. He gestured in broad circles, as if he were drawing the images in the air, trying to represent them as best he could for Alysa, to help her see what he saw. "There are some dark images, most of them black with small colored circles floating inside them. In one image, an oldenscript title reads 'Planets of Tabir-sun System'. Beneath one of the circles are the words 'Xunar-kun,' and smaller circles on either side read 'Donol-kul' and 'Nanthan-kul'. There are many more circles and names on this image, I'm guessing of other nearby worlds, and still more images with closer views of those worlds. And views of our world! They show Xunar-kun *covered* in green and blue—forests and water! There are images of star clusters, too, and faces of men. They must be—there's no way these could *not* be—images of the Ancient Ones! Some perhaps even of Father Gord'n!"

Lost in his own Telling, Orryn stopped gesturing like a Teller. He just talked. "There are so many objects in that room—machines, I guess—made of metal and having so many pieces that I couldn't begin to guess their use. Even though the images and other objects may be of little use, I have learned much from some of the journals and texts. I've read journals written in Father Gord'n's own hand! His personal writings tell of his wife, younglings and great-younglings, things he loved about City Infinity, journeys he made all over Xunar-kun, before Cat'clysm, and the things he did to rebuild our society when we became—the Field Folk.

"I would've liked to have studied the journals more thoroughly, kept them with me so that I could truly understand them. But I haven't dared remove them, because someone else goes into the room, probably Major Teller Bakar. And if he hasn't shown me the room, which he hasn't, then I'm not supposed to know about it. So late at night I go there to study. I've learned things that I thought I'd never tell anyone. And I'm convinced that wherever those images and machines came from—they were obtained before Cat'clysm! There is so, so much more to tell, more than I could tell in a cycle!" Orryn was out of breath, spent from his revelation.

Alysa was overwhelmed. She did not seem to notice the sun's first warming rays as they peeked over the mountains. How had Orryn kept all the knowledge locked within for so long? She understood little of what he told her, but she knew that his Telling was truthful and that he believed what he told with his whole heart. "Orryn, that's truly remarkable knowledge! But I don't understand what it has to do with Sureena…"

"There's something else, Lys." She listened, bewildered. "Father Gord'n had a brother, who was also a leader that commanded great respect. The brothers did not get along. They had different ideas about how the people should live—so over time, the people separated…"

Alysa took a deep breath. "…Folk…and Trailmen?" Orryn nod-ded. "Now everything makes sense! Orryn, can you get one of the journals and some images to show the Council?"

Orryn winced. "Why? You're not going to tell them, are you?"

"Only if I have to." Orryn looked fearful. "Orryn, we're not taught that Father Gord'n had a brother! I think that his having had one, particularly one that may have led the first Trailmen, is some-thing to wonder about, don't you? If we're of the same Ancients, doesn't that give us enough reason to approach the Trailmen?"

Orryn began to pace. "But even if I did bring one of the texts be-fore the Council, they can't read oldenscript. And I'm certain that Kendira and none of the other Tellers would allow me to read it to them."

"Then we don't need a journal. You can tell them what you told me."

He looked at the rising sun, his expression ill. Alysa went to him and placed her palms on either side of his fair, tired face. "Orryn, don't you know that you've done something courageous and won-derful?"

"I'll never achieve Full Teller…"

"Do you feel you were wrong to tell me? You seemed glad to let someone else know."

"You deserved to know because you were so forlorn. I couldn't have kept it from you and felt right about it."

"Then you were right to tell me, good Orryn. Remember that an-cient saying you spoke earlier, 'Fear not failure of the field…"

"…as much as failure of the heart.'" He nodded, at last finding something to smile about. "Father Gord'n wrote that down; they were his brother's words. Father Gord'n used them as an example of his brother's weakness. Father Gord'n didn't believe there was a place for 'heart' in survival. Just hard work. When I first read those words, they stirred up conflict inside me. But over time, I've grown to feel the saying fitting. My heart does feel good, even renewed, that I told you the true history. But I don't know if I'd be able to tell any-one else…"

185

THE TRUTH BE KNOWN

Early the next morning, Nilt, a runner from Falling Stream, burst through the door of the Great Hall where several crafters labored. Loralle and Ellee were among them. The Elders were gathered at the long table beneath the Planting Calendar, engaged in a quiet discussion. They looked up, surprised by the intrusion.

Bent over, resting his hands on his knees, Nilt tried to catch his breath. He yelled, "Elder Poolan! Two more younglings have vanished!" Nilt collapsed on the floor.

The crafters rushed to give him aid. One of them said, "Moons above, *more* are missing?"

Loralle said, "They've not yet found Sureena, and you say that two more are gone?"

They raised Nilt to sitting.

Loralle knelt beside him and looked into his face. She shouted, "Someone bring water!" She felt his face and unhooked the top toggles of his tunic. "Moons, it doesn't look like he took time to stop to refresh himself…"

The Elders ran up to Nilt. Tola commanded the crafters, "Leave! All leave now!"

Loralle said, "No…wait…!"

The Elders pushed the crafters out the door. Loralle grabbed terrified Ellee by the hand, and they ran down the ramp. Loralle turned back and demanded, "Tell us what's happening to the younglings!"

The Elders slammed the large doors shut.

At first the crafters were stunned. Then they began to wonder if their own younglings were safe. They scattered to their cottages, calling their younglings' names across the terraces as they raced home. Loralle and Ellee ran toward their cottage.

Inside the Great Hall, the Elders hurried back to Tola and Nilt. Tola said, "Bring him some water! Now try again, Nilt. What's happened?"

"Two more younglings. Missing. One from Valley Ridge. One from Green Plateau. A terrible beast, on two feet, was seen carrying one of them away!"

At a loss, Tola shook his head and said, "Help us, Father Gord'n..."

A short while later, Speaker Tola, Orryn, Aryz, the Elders from Falling Stream, and three other Elders from High Point gathered outside the Great Hall. They were readying to depart, to be part of a collective Council meeting to be held at Falling Stream the next morning.

Aryz had stayed the remainder of the night before with Cara and Jac, Seda's parents, and told them of Sureena's disappearance. Of course, Cara and Jac were not able to contain their sadness and visited several of the neighbors to tell them of the tragedy.

In the midst of their chores, the Folk were rapidly learning of the younglings' abductions and ran to the departing group of men. Loralle had retrieved Alysa from the cottage. In dismay, the growing crowd demanded answers to their questions. A mother clutched her tiny son. Her frightened voice called out above all the others, "What must we do to protect our younglings, Speaker? Must we hide them indoors until they're too large to be carried off?" Her fearful voice spoke for others as they voiced the same concern.

All eyes focused on Tola, awaiting his response. He said, "We don't know as yet what we'll do. That's the purpose of the meeting at Falling Stream. But I'm certain the decision will be to keep our younglings close until the trouble passes."

A man yelled, "What is to become of the ones already taken?"

Tola answered, "There's no plan as yet. We'll discuss that when the Councils meet."

Alysa stepped into the center of the mass and said, "You know as well as I that nothing will be done to save them. Those younglings are as good as lost. The M'raudas have them now!"

Tola grabbed her by the wrists and pulled her to him. Angry, he pleaded, "What're you saying? You don't have rational answers for the people, so be still!"

Loralle gasped and stepped forward. "Alysa...no!"

Tola threw up a hand to stop Loralle from coming any closer. She halted, tears springing to her eyes.

Alysa turned to her and said quietly, "Mother, everything will be all right. Please." She looked into her mother's eyes and gestured for her to retreat. Loralle nodded anxiously and stepped back with the other women.

Alysa took a deep breath and turned back to Tola. She said in a firm, loud voice, "Elder, I'm not afraid of what you or Kendira or anyone else thinks of me. It's time for everyone to hear what Orryn has learned. It is the truth. It is their right. It is also their legacy!"

She motioned to Orryn, who stood at the back of the departing group of men. Reluctant, he moved forward as confused, inconsolable 'steaders watched.

She said, "Will you please, *please* tell them, Orryn? You know the history. The *true* history."

He faced her. "I don't think I can. I don't know if the words will come."

"Tell them exactly what you've learned. They'll understand," she assured him. "Orryn, you have the skill and you have the knowledge! It's for the sake of who knows how many younglings. Please, for the younglings—for *your* younglings, Orryn. The younglings you will be teaching!"

He closed his eyes in thought, collecting his composure, and nodded. He walked in a circle, motioning with his arms spread wide for the 'steaders to move back, to make space in the center.

Council Speaker Poolan stepped forward, cautioning his Teller from Falling Stream. "Orryn. Orryn, what Telling are you planning to do here?" Poolan clenched his hands at his sides, doing his best to maintain the calm demeanor appropriate to Elders before gatherings.

Orryn swept his hand over Poolan, and he reluctantly stepped back into the group. Orryn assumed Teller posture, the intense attitude he perfected in his training. Like younglings, the observers were drawn into his Telling. This was to be their first hearing of true ancient history.

In a commanding voice, Orryn revealed the name of the ruined city from which they had come—it was called 'City Infinity'. It was a gleaming structure of stone and metal and glass. There were many connecting tunnels and even more dwelling space *beneath* the wondrous city. It covered such a large span of land that it took three suns to walk the length of it. It was thought that City Infinity would last forever.

Orryn was magnificent. His voice drew such vivid pictures in their minds of the horror of a world at war, that hands covered eyes to block out the fire-filled sight and covered ears to halt the deafening sounds of the ultimate war between kings. He did his best to explain the flying machines and how they battled far above Xunarkun. He explained that the mysterious Veiled Slayer, unleashed by the war, was part of the reason that so few younglings were born, even unto three thousand cycles afterward. He told how the deformed M'raudas came to be, that they yet existed and came to threaten the Folk, raiding their fields and yards to rob them of their cherished younglings.

Even the Elders became enraptured, drawn into the Telling, so much so that it seemed they forgot, at least for the moment, that Orryn was going against Teller tradition by telling unsanctioned stories.

Orryn described the reason for the minimal relationship that existed for so long between Field Folk and Trailmen. He revealed the secret that Father Gord'n had a brother named Willim, who was unmentioned and unnamed in all of Field Folk history, and who was a partner in the salvation of people from Cat'clysm.

Willim had a different philosophy of living and survival; he earned equal respect with Gord'n among the people. The brothers struggled for leadership. Willim led many into the high mountains and adopted the tribal name 'Trailmen'. But Willim's name faded over time because he did not claim an eternal place for himself in the Trailmen's history; the Forever One was the name that always stood above all others.

From the same city, of the same blood were the Field Folk and Trailmen — brothers divided, as were Father Gord'n and Brother Willim.

One by one, the listeners sank to the ground. Confused, some wept, afraid, yet desiring to hear more.

"Rubbish!" Kendira puffed, interrupting the Telling. Arriving too late to stop it, she hurried as best she could through the field of distraught Folk. The angry old woman pulled hard on a man's sleeve and said, "Get up! Get hold of yourself!" Instead, he crumpled to the ground. Kendira continued and stood a breath away from Orryn. Her chin came only to the middle of his chest, but she raised her face and screeched, "How dare you blaspheme so wickedly? You will be punished for this!"

Orryn said, "Do what you will, Kendira. I couldn't have spent my whole life *wishing* I had done what I just did. The people had to know."

Tola turned to Alysa. "You put him up to this. What do you think you have gained? These people are so overwrought, they're as useless as heaps of wet straw!"

"They are relieved, Elder," Alysa answered.

Poolan said, "Relieved? They're stricken with grief!"

Alysa countered, "There's only one way to defeat the M'raudas. We must ask the Trailmen for help!"

"Again I say rubbish!" Kendira retorted as she pushed herself in between Alysa and Tola. She held up a fist and shrieked at Alysa, "Silence!"

No longer able to stand in the background, Loralle rushed to Alysa's side, prepared to shield her from Kendira. Kendira held her ground but so did Loralle, finding sudden strength to do so.

Alysa said loud enough for all to hear, "Kendira, your lies caused me to detest the Trailmen for a time. But I've learned the truth about them and the truth about you. I can be silent no longer."

Tola said, "What are you talking about, girl? What lies?"

"I was told that my father was murdered by the Trailmen."

Loralle gasped, horrified.

"Nonsense!" Tola retorted.

"Then how did it happen, Tola? Tell me, was there a tall, winding staff found with him?"

"Girl, this is not the time..."

Kendira sputtered an unintelligible protest.

"Tola, I need to know. We *all* need to know!"

Several others in the crowd spoke up, demanding an answer. Loralle fought back tears, but some did manage to escape and slid down her cheek.

Tola sighed, "No, there was not."

"How did you find him?"

He shook his head. "It was very clear that the embankment gave way...he fell into the stream...and received a blow to his head! Now, why did you need to hear a recounting at *this* moment?"

"Because I was told he was murdered. I wanted to hear the truth."

Tola's jaw set. "Where did you get that impossible, preposterous notion?"

Alysa pointed at Kendira who was suddenly speechless, tangled in her own deceit.

Tola said, "What?" He shook his head and frowned. "There was never, has never been such conjecture! Kendira..."

Loralle rested her head on Alysa's shoulder and began to sob. Alysa held her and said, "Speaker Tola, Speaker Poolan, we have no time to waste. The Trailmen can teach us how to get the younglings back. We can consider them savages no longer. They're our brothers and sisters. Our own Folk! Brothers can help brothers. Sisters can help sisters!"

Orryn said, "It's true that I broke a Teller oath, but I know it was the right thing to do, as what I told *is* true! I expect to be punished for this. Shouldn't Teller Kendira be punished as well for leading Alysa to believe that the Trailmen murdered her father?"

Poolan said to Orryn with scorn, "I don't see how anything that Teller Kendira may have said has anything to do with our current troubles!"

Orryn said, standing up to Poolan, "It has a lot to do with them, Elder! We can now see how lies maintained throughout the ages have continued to cause the separation of Folk and Trailmen. As a result, this has caused the Folk to be weak!" He glared at Kendira, the guilt plain on her face.

Tola turned to the Elders, who shook their heads. "The Council refuses to accept what you've told, boy. I am aghast—no, ashamed of your blasphemy!"

Orryn countered, "If Major Teller Bakar was here, he'd tell you that what I told is true!"

Poolan laughed, incredulous. "Do you think so? I do not. When we get back to Falling Stream, we'll recommend to Bakar, and to the rest of the Council, that you be stripped of your Teller duty!"

Kendira recovered and spat, "I would request that they both be forever banished from the clan, if the Laws permitted!" Beyond words, an angry Kendira pointed a gnarled finger at Orryn's nose and cast a sidelong glance at Alysa. Loralle, her green eyes still wet with tears, raised her head and glared at Kendira.

Nearly yelling, Tola turned to Kendira. "Enough! Kendira, that is quite enough. I believe that you and I have some talking to do upon my return."

Kendira shrank back and Tola guided her away from the others. He motioned to one man who was still standing. He came to Tola and, at his instruction, scooped Kendira into his arms and carried her toward her cottage.

Orryn said, "I tried, Lys. I failed, and I'm sorry." He turned and sadly hurried down the terrace stairway.

Poolan, at a loss for words, cast an apologetic look at Tola. Dismayed, he and Elder Yiul turned and followed Orryn. The High Point Elders, with the exception of Tola, joined them. Tola remained, thinking, shaking his head and obviously trying to make sense of all that just happened.

Alysa called, "Orryn, you did not fail! Wait and see!" She felt so bad for him and all she brought upon him. Tears flowed down her face. She whispered to her mother, "It'll take time for the Folk to truly understand that Father Gord'n misled them. And that the Elders and Tellers that followed kept his lies alive."

Loralle nodded and held Alysa close.

"Mother, we have not been told the truth for over three thousand cycles. Do you know how that makes me feel?"

"Yes. Lost. Very confused. It is plain that everyone else feels the same. It'll probably get worse."

"But now the people will have no choice but to believe that all Orryn told is true!"

"I hope they choose to do so, Daughter."

Saddened, Tola approached Alysa. "Since I was instrumental in seeing your appointment as Trader, I'm stripping you of the duty. I hold you responsible for instigating this blasphemy! You're forbidden to trade again or approach the Trailmen in any capacity. A watchful eye will be kept on you, and on your family, to make certain you never breach the Laws again!"

New tears sprang to Loralle's eyes, and she held Alysa tighter. A new fear shadowed her face.

Disbelieving, Alysa shook her head. "My family? Why? No...!" Her mouth dropped open, trying to understand the ramifications of Tola's threat. What did he mean, "Keep a watchful eye?" Did he mean that he or someone else would follow them around to be certain they would not talk of anything that may inspire further questioning? That Tola was able to conceptualize such punishment as *keep a watchful eye* stunned her!

Distraught, Tola stomped down the stairway after the other Elders. Alysa, standing in the middle of the crowd, watched as he descended. She finally found her voice and yelled, "Elder! We *cannot* get the younglings back all by ourselves!"

Tola did not turn back.

Confused, the 'steaders picked themselves up and began to walk away. Some shook their heads, others wept. Some glared at Alysa. None of them seemed to know what to think or what to do next.

Empty of any further words, tears rolled down Alysa's face. Sad but defiant, she thought, *Then on my own I will seek the Trailmen. I am not afraid!*

ON HER OWN

Alysa could bear it no longer. Thoughts of what transpired the sun before kept her awake all night. Neither had Loralle slept. They both rose well before dawn and debated about whether or not Alysa should leave, given Tola's threat.

Loralle said, "I don't fear Tola or any of the Elders, Alysa. We'll survive any criticism that results. I believe that you should go before it's too late and the younglings are lost forever. I'll make excuses for you until you're so far into your journey that no one will attempt to follow."

Alysa knew her mother was right, that she should seek out the Trailmen; her anxiety was relieved when she heard Loralle's words of encouragement. They hastily gathered a supply of food and clothing and stuffed them into a packbasket.

"I have no idea," Loralle said, "what kind of terrain or weather you'll come upon. I have no trail knowledge to give you. But I can tell you this: you must *think* while you are traveling; always stop to think when you are unsure or frightened or lonely…and come home to us! I'll worry for you, Daughter, in hope that my worrying keeps you safe."

Alysa kissed her sister lightly so as not to wake her and patted the sleeping saroos. She hugged her mother tight for a long moment.

Wearing her cloak and field boots, Alysa slung the basket onto her back and sneaked out of the cottage as faint sunlight appeared on the horizon. Loralle watched after her and leaned out the door to be certain that nobody was around to see her leave.

Alysa held little hope that the Trailmen would still be at Ridge Camp. Her fear came true. By the time she arrived, they had left—probably just the sun before.

She removed her packbasket and sat down on a log flanking a smoldering hearthring. She gathered her cloak and skirt and bunched them in her lap to keep them from getting wet in the dewy morning grass. The last time she was at this hearthring, she witnessed the debate between Qohrlat and Ferran and learned about the

Trailmen's tattoos. That was an amazing time for her. She smiled at the memory. Now she struggled with what she should do. Returning to the homestead was not an option. That would mean she had conceded any hope of getting Sureena and the other younglings back. Yet she was having difficulty going forward, fearing what she did not know, and with good reason: she possessed no wilderness survival skills.

The sun was rising above the trees. Overnight, snow had fallen on the highest peaks of Winding Mountains. If she was going to reach the Lowlands Camp before winter was upon her, the moment to leave was now.

She rose and lifted the packbasket onto her back and faced in the direction the Trailmen had indicated many times when speaking of the Lowlands. She searched the ground for any sign of their passing. She found none. She struck out, hoping she would find the right trail.

Alysa stared in disbelief at the endless landscape that lay below. She expected the Lowlands to begin just the other side of the pass; but she discovered yet another range of mountains to be crossed. It took all morning to climb this pass. Daunted, she wondered, *How long will it take to reach the Lowlands? How far is the Trailmen camp?*

She sat down in the middle of the stony trail to catch her breath. She stared at the endless range of hills crisscrossed by streams, wondering in which direction the Trailmen went. Dark cloud formations hovered above the faraway landscape. Lightning from the clouds pelted the hills.

The packbasket that Loralle filled with cheese, fruit, nuts and bread rested beside Alysa. She looked at it and wondered, *Will this food take me the whole way? What if it doesn't? What if I starve to death, never to see my family again, and they never know what became of me?*

She shook her head at this impossible task, overwhelmed by the unexpected, rugged vastness that spread before her. She dragged herself to her feet, brushed loose hair from her face, and sighed. There was no question. She would have to go home.

She picked up the packbasket and turned to go back; as she did so, she tripped over something, perhaps her own feet, and stumbled — or was she pushed? — a few steps farther along the trail. She whirled around and thought for an instant that she saw someone standing there! But there was no one. She was indeed alone, and so far from home. But the lasting sensation on her back was that someone's firm but gentle hands pushed her, causing her to lurch forward. She was reminded of her father, who often held his hand at her back, encouraging her to take her first unaided steps or to try a new skill he had just taught her. *Was* it just her imagination? Or did he give her a push, urging her to go on?

For an instant she thought she saw him standing back up the trail, smiling that warm smile she remembered so well, the one that always brought a sparkle to his eye. Then it seemed as if he was motioning her to continue down the trail.

She nodded, picked up the basket, turned again toward the unknown, and let her being submit to whatever lay ahead. She looked back once and thought she saw him holding his hand high, a sign of farewell. She half-waved back thinking, *Why would I imagine him saying farewell?* Then he vanished. Shaking her head, she did not know what to think. Feeling tight fear in her stomach, all she knew was: *I must go on!*

She slung the packbasket over her shoulder and picked her way down the pass. She held her cloak close, but this did not prevent thorny bushes reaching out from between rocks to snag her clothing as she walked.

Her mother had advised, "The air will be cold at night and you'll have no shelter. Wear the heavy stockings I put in the basket. Bundle yourself well with your cloak. And pull your hood up when you sleep!"

Thickening brush and rock swallowed a lonesome Alysa at the bottom of the pass. The urge to turn and go back to all that was familiar was nearly overwhelming. The fear this impossible journey imparted was great. But she knew that she had no choice but to complete this task!

Nanthan-kul's fullness rose over the hills behind her. Her light would show the ground for as long as Alysa cared to walk, so she decided to travel as far as her body was able. Once she progressed farther into the journey, she hoped the temptation to turn back to what was familiar would cease.

Without looking behind, the girl moved as swiftly as the terrain allowed toward the far mountain range, up hill, down hill, up hill more times than she cared to count. She jumped over streams when they were narrow enough. After a while they began to widen, and she simply waded across.

Many hills and streams had passed underfoot. Alysa's boots were soaking wet and her feet were sore. She stopped sometime during the night and sat beside a gurgling spring. She set the packbasket down and removed her boots. She rubbed her aching feet and stuck them into the spring. The water was very cold and stung at first, but soon a slight numbness began to ease the ache.

There were so many twists and turns that sun that one hill looked like another. When she looked behind, she had no idea from which way she had come. She lost sight of the pass; the only recognizable landmark was now hidden behind other hills. She doubted that she could find her way home if she tried. Worse still, she was not certain that her direction was correct.

Nanthan-kul was sinking behind the hills up ahead. Those hills loomed larger than when she first laid eyes on them. They were growing dark, their contour cutting an outline against the sky. As the moon finally rested behind the hills, countless stars blazed overhead.

She gazed at the sky. The stars pulsed through the clear leaffall air. Her father taught her that whole groups of stars were in different places in the sky during the cycle but that the same ones always stayed together. He said the stars could be used like maps when people were required to travel in darkness. Clusters of stars had names, and he had pointed many of them out to her. But she never memorized their movements through the cycle, as she had little interest in the stars or in traveling at night. The Planting Calendar kept track of star positions throughout the cycle, and one only had to refer to it to find out when certain clusters were overhead.

She took a small rug out of the packbasket, spread it over the moss, and sat down. She rubbed her feet dry and put on the heavy socks her mother packed. She took some food and a narrow-necked jar of water from the basket and scrutinized the stars as she fed her hunger and slaked her thirst.

Her mother's advice was to *think!* So she thought as she ate. The Trailmen traveled this way only twice each cycle. If the hundreds of look-alike hills and streams confused them as much as they did her, then they must have some way to find direction. And they must be guided at least partly by the stars, the only landmark that stayed put. But which stars would they use? If she chose to follow the wrong ones, she would never find the Lowlands. She must choose the right stars!

As a mass they meant nothing to her. But as she concentrated on one cluster, she recognized the shape of one her father had called the Grazing Udommo. Another cluster nearly circular in formation was called the Joining Circle. And the one hovering directly over the dark mountains he called the Hunter, although the traditional Folk name for it was the Planter. He told her that he thought it looked like a figure drawing back a bow, not lifting a hoe. She studied it and was able to clearly see the shape of a bow. As she studied the entire span of stars, she tried to think, think, *think!* Which would have guided the Trailmen this time of cycle? The Hunter seemed to brighten as she looked from one cluster to another.

Her thoughts were pulled back to an eve at Ridge Camp following the storm, which now seemed so long ago. She recalled a tale that Obala had told. Within the story she mentioned traveling through Hunter Pass. Alysa realized that Obala must have been referring to the Hunter—the star cluster. Now she was certain that she had chosen the right stars to use as a guide!

How did her father know the name of that star cluster? Perhaps in one of the conversations he had with Islean, she revealed the Trailmen name for that cluster, and that was how he came to call it by the same name. If she saw Islean again, she would ask her if she and Abso ever talked about the stars. Alysa sighed and thought, *How I would have enjoyed being a part of their conversations!*

Alysa's mind was engaged, excited. Yet her body was exhausted from this sun's journey. She finished eating and took another drink from the jar, draining it. But no worry, as there was plenty of water right in front of her, and she could refill the jug in the morning.

She pulled her hood up and lay down, bunching her shawl to use as a pillow. She drew up her legs and tucked her skirt around her feet. The shape of that round-topped mountain framed against the sky etched itself in her mind.

Comforted that she had found the way — and certain that she was no longer lost in the wilderness — Alysa was soon asleep.

The next morning was alive with animal chatter. Several tiny water birds must have assumed the sleeping figure to be a part of the landscape and, unafraid, they splashed in the clear spring. A few paces away, a family of small, spotted rodents scoured their faces with quick little paws.

Alysa yawned and rubbed her eyes while stretching her legs from beneath her skirt. The birds bolted into the sky, a shower of water trailing behind them. A swishtail that was floating just below the surface of the water startled, rose to the top, and paddled with large, webbed feet across the water. It dove down into a mossy hiding place, leaving behind a swath of bubbles. The spotted family, softly growling at the intrusion, ambled off into the brush.

The girl sat up and looked around. Stiff from sleeping on the ground, she groaned and gently stretched her neck and arms. The mountain that she memorized glowed blue and pink in the morning light. It appeared closer than it did last night. She planned to head straight for that mountain after she ate.

She reached for the packbasket. To her dismay, the whole bottom was torn open. The food was gone, and everything else was scattered about. "Moons above! What happened?" she said, examining the hole. She muttered, "Well, I guess something else had my breakfast! And all my other meals, too. Looks like wildberries from here on!"

Her few pieces of spare clothing were strung along the edge of the spring. After she picked it up, one sock was still missing; but she had no intention of wasting time looking for it under every bush and boulder. It was fortunate that she found her small blade nearby. She stuck it into her waistband.

She lay the clothing on the rug and rolled it up. She filled the jar with spring water and plugged it with the wooden stopper. Her boots were still wet, but she had no choice but to put them on. She picked up her belongings and set her eyes on the mountain.

As she walked around the spring and up the hill, she made a brief stop to pick a handful of dark-purple wildberries. They hung from a tall bush that had already lost its leaves to leaffall.

Little sleep came to Alysa the second night. Animal noises that she could not identify caused her to spend the night shivering inside a tiny cave in fear of becoming supper for a prowling greatclaw. She argued with herself that it was foolish to be afraid of what probably would not happen. But on the other hand, what did she really know of the dangers of the wild?

During the third night, Nanthan-kul and the landscape seemed to have plotted to keep her awake. Rocks and moonlight cast creeping shadows. Each time she lifted her heavy eyelids, the sizes and shapes of the shadows changed, growing, shifting, supplying her imagination with reasons to fight sleep. Had somebody—or something—been following her? Waiting for her to drift off to sleep? All she could see in her shallow dreams, when she slept at all, were endless rocks and streams and unknown shadows. To make things worse, her stomach was beginning to bother her. She was ill all night and more than once nearly vomited.

On the fourth afternoon, she reached the summit of the pass to which the Hunter guided her, and which she now called "Hunter Pass." She rested in the shade of a rocky overhang, picking burrs from her skirt and braid. Her clothing was very tattered and torn. Her cloak rested beside her, as the sun was warm.

It was a difficult climb up Hunter Pass. The stomach upset that started the night before had turned to cramps, which often washed through her, causing her to double over. Each time the pain and nausea came, she had to rest until it passed.

Another wave passed through her and she moaned. "Oh, stomach, please be well! I can't bear much more of this!" She liked to think that all those times spent at her place along the stream counted for something and that she had gained knowledge by being close to the forest, by catching creatures in the stream and watching the animals. But that was a naive belief. She knew nothing about sheltering and feeding herself. All she found to eat were wildberries, and she was so tired of wildberries!

There were probably many suitable foods right at her feet. If she had learned plant lore as her father often urged, she would have more strength. These mountains would have long passed by, and she would be that much closer to the Trailmen.

A cool breeze refreshed her sweaty, hot face. It blew from up ahead where thick, white clouds washed across the sky. Some of them looked so heavy with rain that they would burst at any moment. But almost any weather was better than snow!

She walked across the blunt top of the mountain, turned and looked behind. Only the very tips of Winding Mountains were visible. She knew that once she descended this pass, she would lose that last remaining glimpse of home.

Feeling a great sense of loss and an equal urgency to continue, she forced her steps along the winding trail that threaded around rocky outcrops and scattered boulders.

When her eyes next met the horizon, she was relieved to see no more mountains, even in the distance. The land sloped far down from where she stood and flattened. The many streams she crossed suns before cascaded from deep crevasses and emptied onto the land below, collecting into hundreds of small lakes. Between the lakes, pale-green and golden grasses waved as far as she could see. Through the hazy air it looked as though stands of trees darkened the farthest edge of this land. That must be the Lowlands, at last!

The sight of all that water reminded her that she was very thirsty, having emptied her water jar much earlier. Finding water would be no trouble in this land; but would she find any food? This didn't look like wildberry country. It looked much too wet for them, thank the moons, and she needed something better than wildberries to fill her still-aching stomach! *There must be fish in those lakes,* she thought. Though she had never cleaned a fish, she did watch her father kill and clean them. She didn't like the idea that she would have to do this, but she was so hungry that she would eat one raw if she could catch one!

With renewed hope she hiked down the slope. This side was slippery with moss and lichen, so she took care with her footing.

She arrived at the bottom and approached the lakes. The surroundings grew lush. Soft grasses with wispy, drying fronds brushed against her legs and cushioned her steps. Songbirds and insects flew out of the grass as she walked. She came to a clear pool surrounded by reeds and large-leafed water plants. She set down her belongings and knelt, bent over the water and blew on it to clear windblown seeds from the surface. She drank several long, sweet sips and splashed her face, neck, arms and chest. This water felt cool, but not all that cool for as hot as she was. She delighted in the thought that perhaps it was warm enough to bathe in!

She looked across the maze of small lakes. Interconnected grassy rises of land a few strides wide separated them. The rises looked more like a series of short dams such as those the 'steaders built for irrigation. Alysa wondered if the Trailmen built them as a way to traverse this watery land. If so, this task would have been quite an undertaking. Yet they did not look as orderly or measured as people would build them; the rises were of random widths, and angles were often rounded or uneven.

As she walked across the rises, she looked into the shallows of the lakes. Before dusk arrived she must find something solid to eat. She passed several lakes and came to one in which a great *splash!* sounded out in the middle. It startled her. She crept to the edge of the lake and saw several shiny streaks dart out of the dim, gray depth into the shallows. She thought these to be fish escaping from whatever made the splash. Large bubbles churned up from the depth; then the water became still again. She raised her eyebrows and shook her head. Not understanding what caused the bubbles, it was not likely that she would be bathing in *that* particular lake!

The girl was again growing weak from hunger. She squatted down to think. *How can I catch a fish?* She had no net, which is what the men of her homestead used. She could take her shawl apart and use the yarn to make one, but she knew that it would take a long time to do so. She didn't have time. Also, she had never made a net, so that idea was definitely not a good one.

Perhaps she could make something else? She looked around at the abundant reeds, smiled and nodded. She took out her blade and cut several tall, heavy reeds. Her shaky fingers fashioned a deep, narrow basket like one used to store raw wool. She braided a long reed tether and fastened it near the rim. She searched through the grass and collected several insects, which she put into the basket. After all, the fish would need a reason to swim into her trap!

Sitting on the shore and well hidden by the grass, she flung the basket into the clear water. It floated to the bottom not far from shore and lay on its side, as she intended. She watched to see if any fish would swim into it. She waited. She waited longer. Her stomach grumbled without pause. Doubt was growing that her trap was going to catch anything. She pleaded, "Fish, come to me! Come and be my dinner, please?"

Finally, several shimmering fish swam near the basket. They seemed to barely move at all as they sucked mud in and blew it out, sifting tiny pieces of food from the soft mucky bottom. Finally, one approached the basket and poked its head through the opening.

"Not yet," Alysa quietly cautioned herself, squeezing the end of the tether with both hands. "Wait, wait…" Very slowly the fish entered the basket. "Now!" *Snap!* She pulled so hard on the tether that the basket flew out of the water onto shore.

"Ha! It worked!" She stepped to the basket and pranced around it, giggling. She could hardly believe that she caught a fish without a net, in a way that probably no one ever did before! Was she happier that she caught a fish and had something to eat, or that she caught it in a way she thought up herself?

In haste she emptied the fat fish out of the basket and squatted down before it. It was about as long as her forearm. It moved its tiny fins and flipped its long, feathery tail as if trying to swim through the air. It began to roll over and over, apparently trying to get back into the water.

Alysa lurched to pick it up. It snapped its large mouth at her, revealing several rows of tiny, sharp teeth. She quickly pulled her hands back. Its large, pale-colored eyes sitting atop slender tubicles blinked and stared at her.

"I'm sorry, fish, but I *must* eat you! It's for the younglings!"

She grabbed hold of it with two hands and wrinkled her nose at the cold, slimy feel of it. It did not have scales, so at least it would be easier to clean. She reached out and broke a large leaf from a water plant. Wrestling with the flopping fish, she wrapped the leaf around it so she could hold onto it. She shut her eyes, recalling what to do next.

Abso had taught her, "If there's a favor you can do a fish that you intend to eat, you must first kill it before cleaning it."

She held it with one hand and placed the point of her blade on top of its head, just as she saw her father do. She closed her eyes—and did what she must to end its life and spare it further pain. She set the blade down and closed her eyes. "Thank you, fish, for giving me life." She looked at it and sighed. Fish was supposed to be eaten cooked; but even if she had had no blade to clean it with, her hunger would have forced her to eat it scales and all!

Her hunger was not decreasing, so she proceeded to clean it. Working as quickly as she could, she tried not to think about what she was doing. She cut it open and cleaned it and portioned the flesh into small chunks, which she placed on a large leaf.

Plugging her nose for the first bite, she was prepared for the worst. But she was surprised to find that it tasted as good as it did. After a few careful bites, she ate ravenously. The sweet, white fish meat tasted good, and there was plenty to fill her empty stomach. The cramps finally ceased.

When she finished eating, she tossed the bones aside and squatted on the shore to wash her hands and fill the water jar. She returned to her belongings and picked them up, then continued on to find a place to sleep.

At dusk, as Nanthan-kul lifted herself above the horizon, the tired but no longer starving traveler found a somewhat higher, dry place between lakes. She set her belongings on the ground and gathered a bed of grass, much like a nest. She unrolled her rug and placed it on the grass, folded her shawl and plumped it for her pillow. Because the air was beginning to cool down as night drew near, she put on her cloak.

As she removed her braid-tie and loosened her hair, she looked around, listening to birdsong as they settled to sleep in the tall grass. They must have felt safe here. Even without a fire, she too felt safe; this land was much friendlier than the harsh hills she crossed the suns before. Here there were no thorn bushes to grab at her, no sharp stones to bruise the bottoms of her feet.

Exhausted, she rested her body on the rug and her head on her shawl-pillow. She pulled her cloak about her and drew her feet underneath. The surrounding grasses bent over her nest and, like the walls she was accustomed to, gave her a feeling of comfort that eluded her the last few nights. The soft fronds on top of the grass bobbed in the light breeze.

Mist rose from the lakes, concealing gentle ripples that would otherwise have reflected pieces of Nanthan-kul's small, bright face. The mist overflowed onto the banks in the dim light, merging into one large, low cloud over the land.

Alysa watched the stars in the Hunter pulse until the mist consumed them. Her eyes closed, and she smiled as she fell asleep, dreaming of the amazing capture of the fish!

LURE OF THE LOWLANDS

Light, warm rain wet the grasses early in the morning. From the sky came the sound of familiar squawking and fluting, waking Alysa. Though at first disoriented and sleepy-eyed, she rose from her warm nest and crept through the wet grass to the edge of the small lake. Several longpipers settled upon the water. A few paddled into the reeds on the opposite shore.

So this was where they landed during their migration! Although everyone knew they were mostly white underneath, for the first time someone would know how they were colored on top. She studied them so that she could tell everyone if — no, *when* — she got back home what they looked like: they were black from beak to tips of curling tail feathers, except for the very tops of their heads, which were speckled with bright-yellow spots. Out of all her discoveries so far on this journey, Alysa thought this one was the best!

And the same lake that gave her dinner last night was about to provide her with breakfast this morning. She knew that birds laid eggs — the casish hens did every sun — so these must, too. She thought, *How good a fresh egg or two would taste!*

She removed her cloak, rolled up a good length of her tattered skirt, and tucked it into her waistband. She took off her boots and stockings and, with as much stealth as she was able, sneaked along the lake's edge. She came closer to the reeds in which the birds floated and preened their feathers. She jumped out of hiding and charged into the reeds. The large birds flailed their wings to escape, a useless tactic among the dense water plants. They dove under and resurfaced in the safety of open water, where they hissed their indignation.

Wading up to her knees, Alysa reached a nest, dismayed to find only a few scraps of shell. The others held the same disappointment. The eggs she expected to find had hatched, the nestlings long ago flown away.

She turned to leave the water, tripped on some roots and fell backwards, full into the lake. The large birds rose up out of the water and in a noisy flurry paddled or flew to the other side of the lake. She stood up in the waist-deep water. Her long, dripping hair formed a curtain in front of her face, which she flung back.

"Cold!" she yelled. She wiped water from her eyes and spluttered, "I guess I got my bath after all!"

She tried to move to the shore and found that her foot was still caught among the roots. She reached underwater to dislodge it and heard a bubbling sound behind her. When she turned and saw a swath of large bubbles coming her way, she pulled on the roots as hard as she could and freed her foot.

As quickly as she was able in her heavy, wet skirt, she charged out of the water and turned around to see what was behind her. But nothing surfaced, and the bubbling ceased.

"What in the moons was *that*?"

She shook her head and retreated to her little camp, wringing out her hair and skirt and watching the still-scolding birds. She thought that if she could lay her hands on one of those, it would make a good meal. If she had a fire. Of course she would also need fire to cook the eggs if she found any. *There must be ways to create fire,* she thought. But there was never a need for the Folk to learn how. If a cottage hearth's flame was allowed to go out, which was seldom, all that was necessary to start a new one was to obtain embers from a neighbor.

Anyway, the longpipers would be impossible to catch since she alerted them. And she doubted they would fall for the basket trick! By now, all of the fish in this lake knew she was there, so she would stop at another along the way and try her luck again.

In the early-morning chill, she shivered and threw her cloak around her shoulders. She rolled up her belongings in the rug, boots included, and picked up the fishing basket.

Orienting herself for her continuing trek, she wove her way over the spongy rises of land between lakes until the sun was nearly overhead, her hair and clothing were dry, and her stomach began to growl. Then she stopped to fish.

Alysa sat in the warm sunshine near a small lake finishing the last bites of her second catch of the sun. This land had become monotonous, with lakes upon lakes divided by narrow rises of land. The trees on the horizon were closer, however, so at least she could see her progress.

Then she saw the bubbles again, bursting on the surface of the water. Several bubble-trails rose from the depths and crossed the water to the opposite shore. Five yellow, scaly round-headed creatures, much larger than rockhoppers, crawled out of the water not more than thirty paces distant.

Alysa set her leaf-plate aside and lay down on the ground to watch. The tailless, six-legged creatures crawled to a point on one of the rises where water had broken through and was spilling into a lower lake. The creatures sat on their haunches and stared at the flow of water. They each raised a four-toed, webbed front foot to gesture to each other. Their gurgling speech varied in pitch and intensity. Their orange eyes blinked, narrowed and enlarged at different points in their squabbling, adding an expressive quality to the dialog that Alysa thought humorous. They seemed to be discussing the problem of the spilling water. With startling speed, they dove back into the lake.

Had they seen her? Were they heading to where she lay? Her heart raced. But the creatures resurfaced at the location of the break and crawled back onto land. They spat large mouthfuls of mud onto the break, balanced on their front legs, and with their four back feet patted the mud into place. They continued the process of diving into the lake and returning with mouthfuls of mud until the flow of water ceased.

Relaxed that she was in no danger, Alysa thought, *So this is how all these rises of land and lakes came to be! They were not built by the Trailmen!*

The creatures finished their task and examined their work. With odd, cackling laughter and excited, flashing eyes, they were in apparent agreement that their work was done. They dove into the neighboring lake and vanished, perhaps on their way to another dam in need of repair.

Marveling at what she just witnessed and giggling to herself, Alysa finished eating, gathered her things and set out again. By the time she reached the tree line that was on the horizon that morning, the sun was beginning to descend. She was as tired of raw fish as she had become of wildberries!

The scenery was changing again. The lakes were becoming fewer and farther apart. Small, well-defined streams flowed from the lakes and joined to form one wide stream that raced across the land. Trees were more numerous, and the flowers of leaffall bloomed everywhere. Grove after grove of colorful trees warmed the scenery.

The ground was drier and harder here. The dark, crumbly rock beneath her feet was very odd, indeed. It stretched in a band that looked to be twenty strides across for as far as she could see, both to her left and right. Trees and grasses pierced the dark, cracked surface in many places. Where the stream flowed over it, a section of the rock was torn away, its crumbling, dark mass heaved to one side.

Deciding to change direction to explore the curious rock, she walked eastward, away from the stream. She wondered what kind of rock would let trees push up through its surface. In some places huge slabs were forced upward. The dark rock seemed to flow on forever. Before long its novelty wore off, and she left the dark path on her southward course.

A few paces from the edge of the rock, a sparkle of sunlight from within a mass of vegetation caught her eye. She went to the greenery and pushed a section aside. Something bulky lay beneath the plants. The thing was oval-shaped and several paces long. It was no taller than she, and pieces broke off when she touched it; when she looked at her hand, rusty powder streaked it. She pulled away more of the greenery and took a few steps back to look at her find.

"It's a machine of some kind!" She laughed and shook her head. Metal was very scarce and precious to her people. It was ironic that this huge piece sat out in the weather cycle after cycle, turning to dust, and that there were probably many more wasting away throughout this land.

She ran her fingers up the rough form. It curved toward the top and became smooth. She found that part of the machine was made from something other than metal. The smooth areas were covered with moss. She wiped some away and was surprised to find the largest piece of glass she had ever seen. She wiped more of the moss away to expose a larger area of glass. As sunlight reached into the machine's interior, it bounced off objects inside. She peered into it.

"Moons above!" she exclaimed, jumping back. She tripped on the overgrowth and fell hard on her buttocks. Then she realized that the hollow eyes staring back at her from inside were the bones of dead people! She looked at the machine and the black path and realized that she must have uncovered one of the land-traveling machines Orryn told about.

When she finally stopped shaking, she was far away from the machine and the dark path. Then the idea occurred to her that those poor people were not given a proper final farewell. *All* those lost in the Cat'clysm had not! This saddened her.

She returned to the stream and stared at the water, still thinking of the grotesque, grinning expressions, feeling bad for them, but hoping she would come upon no others. Hungry again, she sat down on the shore. She looked around, uneasy in these surroundings, and tossed in the fishing basket. Almost at once the current snatched it, tearing the tether from the rim. The basket bobbed halfway out of the water, collapsed and sank.

She cried, "Oh, Father, what do I do now?" She looked around, but Abso was nowhere to be seen. "Father, I so need your help..." Dazed and holding the limp tether in her hand, she dragged herself up from the shore and plodded off. Entirely unsure in which direction to go, she simply wandered, hoping she was still heading south.

The tall trees, growing fewer, were being replaced by shorter, scrubbier ones that seemed to be everywhere. They were thick and impossible to see through. There were narrow paths between them, barely wide enough to squeeze through. Every time she did push through one of the "paths", it seemed as though her clothing became snagged and torn by thorns—and too many times, they caught her skin.

She emerged from a scrubby grove into a meadow of red and gold flowers that spread as far as she could see. Far off, to what she presumed was east, were sharp mountains shaded in purple and pink. She did not know these mountains; but she was so hungry and exhausted that it did not really matter. Standing in the middle of the meadow, she turned her weary head to look back to what seemed to be north. She wondered if she could find her way back to the land filled with lakes. At least there was something to eat there!

A thin, black cloud was on the horizon behind her. It was not a typical-looking cloud. It quickly shifted shape, dipping and rising over the land, moving left and right as if on a whim. It moved in her direction. Marveling at this sight, she thought it odd for a cloud to move so fast; she decided that her eyes must not be working right.

Turning to continue, she heard a far-off humming that grew louder with each step she took. She looked back at the cloud and saw that it was nearly upon her. And the cloud was not black, but crimson. Then she realized that it was not a cloud at all. It was an enormous swarm of flowerflies! Except for her cloak, she dropped her belongings and ran. She had never seen so many flowerflies in one place! Suddenly, the crimson cloud dipped to the ground, surrounding her.

There must have been millions of them! Soon every bloom in sight was crawling with flowerflies. Thousands joined to form a small, humming whirlwind around her. They crowded to her so closely she could barely breathe, but she dared not try to swat them away; she knew from having been stung more than once that this would only make them angry. Several lighted upon her.

"Oh...oh!" she yelled as they stung her. She flung her cloak about her and dropped to the ground below the level of the blooms. Pulling her hood up and drawing her feet under her cloak, she hoped she would be safe from any further stings.

It was apparent that the flowerflies were settling for the night. She would not be able to move from this spot until they flew off. Hopefully they would be gone by morning. The stings ached. If she were not so exhausted, she would have wept. This was going to be a long night! She was less certain than ever that she would find the Trailmen—or that she would survive at all.

Beyond a stand of scrubby trees and tufts of tall, arcing grasses, a hearthring blazed in the darkness. Firelight flickered off figures surrounding the flames. Game cooked on skewers. Firelight glinted off blades as hands sliced off pieces of roasted meat.

A melody was being plucked on fine strands of twisted hide strung across the length of a wooden strum. Animated faces boasted about their latest adventure. Boisterous talk, laughter, music and fresh-cooked game were the Trailmen's rewards following a successful hunt.

Jesh, a tall young man, jumped up, continuing an argument already in motion. His light hair took on an orange cast in the firelight. His light-brown eyes reflected the flames. His thin moustache followed the outline of his upper lip as it turned down angrily while he proclaimed, "You will never admit to the firestag I brought in this sun as being the biggest you have ever seen, will you, Rainur!"

The men and women seated around the fire grinned, watching and waiting, seeming to already know the outcome of this dispute. Rainur, a strong, older bald man, continued to chew his mouthful of food. He swallowed, slowly rose and stared up into the taller Jesh's young face.

Rainur's blue eyes danced. "I cannot agree that it was the biggest, because…" Rainur grinned, glancing at the circle of faces, "…because I speared the biggest one anyone has ever seen. Yours is, I will agree, the largest of any that hang over there this night. But it is by far much smaller from nose to tail than one I speared last season. I am certain that all here will agree."

Everyone nodded and commented in Rainur's favor. Jesh whined, "Rainur, you knew they would side with you! They always do!" Jesh stomped his foot. Everyone burst into laughter.

Rainur pointed a stern finger at him. "You have much to learn, young Jesh—about judgment, hunting, and about the people you hunt with. You know as well as I that we would admit it if your firestag was the largest. You should save your boasting until you are tain you have got the biggest or best of anything!"

The hunters laughed and shook their fists to proclaim an end to the bickering, granting Rainur final say in the matter. The musician rapidly strummed a chord to accent the end of the argument. The two men clasped each other's shoulders, the younger Jesh bowing his head in surrender to Rainur and finally smiling as the rough play ended. Rainur messed Jesh's pale hair and playfully pushed him away.

Suddenly, a ghastly figure appeared where firelight met darkness. Peltees that were resting quietly beside their masters jumped to their feet and, with ears pricked and backs raised, charged toward the figure.

Alysa, with eyes glazed, face and arms filthy and scratched, cloak and skirt tattered, took a few feeble steps into the light. She fell several paces from the hearthring. She struggled to rise as the Trailmen, in almost perfect unison, unsheathed their long blades. Alysa opened her mouth, attempting to speak.

"Hold!" Rainur commanded as the hunters surrounded her. "It brandishes no blade, so put yours away!"

The peltees snarled and sniffed her. Some recognized her from Ridge Camp and began to whimper in confusion. The peltees who were not familiar with her smell looked to their masters for direction.

Jesh called to his peltee, "Vonni! Hold, boy!" The peltee came to Jesh's side, and Jesh stooped to grip its curly, brown and tan-colored fur. Vonni's brown ears went limp and drooped along his head. The others also ordered their peltees away from the haggard girl.

Rainur moved closer to her. "What manner of creature are you?"

It took great effort, but Alysa's ragged voice whispered, "Islean...Szaren...Islean..." She collapsed again and lay motionless.

THE TRIBAL DECISION

The next morning, Rainur and Marteen, his mate, led Alysa over a long, rolling trail that passed through tall grasses, reddish soil, scrubby trees and the merry chirping of birds. The morning was bright. Alysa looked north, but Winding Mountains was nowhere in sight. Instead, other mountains which she did not recognize dominated the view.

Cleaned up and looking somewhat rested, she was once again dressed in Trailmen's garb—dark-green tunic and breeches topped by a hide vest; this time it did not take as long for her to feel comfortable to the fit of the clothing.

As they walked, Rainur noticed her staring at the mountains and, having the desire for conversation on any topic just to break the quiet, he said, "They are called 'Staghorn Mountains'. That is where I was born and where Marteen and I spend summering."

Alysa said, "They're very different from Winding Mountains."

"Yes," Marteen added, "they are not as cold as Winding Mountains at wintertide!"

"That is true," Rainur agreed.

"They are colored oddly," Alysa added. "Purple and pink."

"They are very green during summering," Marteen said.

The three returned to silence, as Alysa's worry was deep and the Trailmen seemed to sense that she was not interested in conversation.

Rainur had taken Alysa into his hut the night before, since he was the one who spoke for her safety when she fell into the hunting party. Marteen was an Elder of the tribe and joined the hike to the Lowlands Camp so she could learn why Alysa had come. But Alysa declined to speak about her purpose to anyone other than Islean. Rainur and Marteen respected this and did not press her for information. They were intrigued that it was possible to speak to a Fielder. The news that their charge had stayed at Ridge Camp the cycle before was not widely spoken of by those who were there; they still denied any claim to kinship.

They emerged from the scrub into a large, green clearing filled with many small groups of huts—the Lowlands Camp. There were smoldering hearthrings scattered around the perimeter. In the center was a lodge much like the one at Ridge Camp; this one possessed a similar low hide roof, but was much wider.

As they crossed camp, they passed many Trailmen. Several stopped to stare at this stranger with the long braid. A few nodded with looks of curious recognition.

Finally, they came to Islean's hut located half-way to the lodge. At the doorway Rainur held a hand to stay Alysa. Elder Marteen entered alone.

From inside Islean called, "Please enter, young Yissa!"

Alysa entered with Rainur close behind and she said, "Ho, Elder Islean…" and halted in surprise when she saw Islean stretched out face-down on her cot. She was wearing breeches but was unclothed from the waist up. Ferran knelt at her side.

Alysa gasped and covered her mouth when she witnessed the extent of the tattoos on Islean's back. The paintings started at the tops of her ears, flowed down her neck and the whole length and width of her back, across her shoulders and down her arms, ending at her fingertips.

A smile flashed across Islean's face. She encouraged, "All is well, midling. Ferran is adding a new painting. Our way of painting ourselves must be so foreign to you; but the Fielder way of *not* painting yourselves with your individual histories, of remaining naked of description, perplexes us. We cannot understand how you can know each other! But come, sit. I gather that we have much to talk about, given your journey." She patted a cushion an arm's length away.

Marteen and Rainur watched. Although Marteen still looked curious, she nodded to Islean, satisfied that Alysa was indeed welcome here, and left the hut. Rainur scratched his bald head, shook it in wonder, and turned to leave. Alysa noticed that the tattoo on the back of his neck was broken, the painting nearly obscured by deep scars that disappeared beneath his tunic.

Alysa called after them, "Thank you, Elder Marteen! Thank you, Rainur!" She returned her focus to Islean and watched as Ferran, with a fine-pointed bone needle, pricked a design onto Islean's lower back. He looked up and nodded at Alysa. He returned to his work, but glanced up at her often as he repeatedly dipped the needle into tiny bowls of pigment and carefully poked the color into Islean's skin. With each prick, tiny dots of blood rose to the skin's surface, which he frequently dabbed with a cloth so that he could see his work. As Ferran stippled, Islean winced only very slightly.

The Elder's gray eyes scrutinized Alysa's scraped and bruised face and hands. She asked, "Did Obala see to you?"

"Yes. She was so kind to come to Rainur's hut. She looked me over and applied her healing salves." Alysa looked at her scratched hands. "She also gave me this green drink that did not taste good at all!" Alysa grimaced at the memory of it.

Islean laughed. "Ah, that would be the rejuvenation liquid that some request after migration. Obala, and all Healers, keep the recipe a secret unto themselves. But vile as it tastes, it does work, as you can attest."

"Why didn't she give me any during my healing at Ridge Camp?"

"That would be because the ingredients are not available near Winding Mountains. The plants are found only in the Lowlands and to the south. Now, did you have plenty to eat, Yissa? Enough rest?"

Alysa nodded. "And I thank the tribe for yet another set of clothing!"

"It is a marvel that you found Lowlands Camp. Had you arrived but one sun later, I would have already left with a hunting party headed south. I am very happy that you made it; but I can only assume that it must be a very urgent matter that has brought a Fielder so far from home!"

"I don't know how or where to begin," Alysa confessed. "There's so much to tell of what I've learned about the origins of our tribes..." It was Alysa's turn to try to describe, as well as Orryn had, the true history of their peoples. But Alysa's eyes rested on Ferran, and she hesitated.

Islean noticed Alysa's discomfort and said, "Ah, you may speak of anything you wish with Ferran present. He has, trust me, Yissa, heard everything, all kinds of secrets in his work as a Painter and in helping people select the best details of their history to portray." Ferran nodded and laughed. Islean continued, "The Painters know more history than the rest of the tribe counted together. You can be assured that he will keep to himself anything that is said here. Please, Yissa. Proceed."

Islean paid close attention as Alysa related Orryn's learnings. Islean asked many questions—questions she had held inside for many cycles, and for which she thought she would never find answers. She speculated for most of her long life about the Trailmen's true origins. On the other hand, although Islean was not at all a fearful person, she did wonder what could happen when the information was revealed. The tribe's identity was very strong and they were very satisfied with who they were—a people separate from the Folk. Ferran often nodded his head in understanding, as if he also harbored the same questions as Islean and also feared the outcome.

Alysa answered Islean's questions, recalling from Orryn's Telling as much as she could. But it seemed like the longer they talked, the more Alysa's own questions arose for which she had no answer. She said, "Perhaps at some point in time ahead, the secrets in Father Gord'n's cottage will all be deciphered. Then we'll have answers to all of our questions."

Islean paused and nodded, thoughts connecting. "The distrust the tribes have maintained for each other these three thousand cycles has long perplexed me. Now I understand what happened and how both our early leaders hardened the people against one another!" Tears welled up in Islean's eyes. Sensing her tension, Ferran stopped working. Islean asked, "Yissa, did you undertake this journey just so you could tell me the new tales? Not that I am ungrateful for the good news that there is now proof that you and I and our tribes are of the same people. My heart rejoices to know this is true! But could you not have waited until our return at greening?"

"Islean, it must seem like I'm out of my head for setting off all alone to find you. I'm certain that by now my tribe believes that I—a foolish girl who left against their order and who possesses no wilderness skills—has lost her mind for having left. I must appear as just a stupid girl to the Trailmen, as well…"

Islean grabbed Alysa's hand. "Now hold, young woman. It does not matter if a person is male or female, young or old. It is who they are in their depths and the strength of commitment to their passion that is of importance. Always keep that at the front of your mind!"

Alysa nodded, partly understanding. She took a breath. "I journeyed to the Lowlands not so much to tell you the tale of our kinship, but to tell you of the M'raudas."

Islean laughed. "M'raudas? What of the M'raudas?"

Farran was also amused and shook his head. He dabbed the blood off Islean's back one last time, dipped his finger into a tiny clay pot, and spread a light salve on the new painting. He began to gather his materials.

Alysa did not laugh. "They've made their way into the mountains and have been stealing our younglings! Five were missing when I left High Point; there may be more by now." Avoiding Islean's eyes, she continued, "And you know the Folk. They wouldn't raise a hoe in defense, let alone chase after those beasts and reclaim our younglings!"

At the news of the missing younglings, the Trailmen's expressions turned dour. Islean motioned for her tunic, which Farran handed to her. She sat up, facing away from them, and pulled it over her head. She turned to Alysa and said, "Yissa, has anyone witnessed the M'raudas?"

"Yes. One was seen as it ran back into the forest carrying a youngling. But there must be more, because the younglings disappeared quickly and from different homesteads." Straining to speak evenly, Alysa imagined little Sureena being slobbered upon by one of the creatures, blanking an even worse scenario from her mind. "I left because—and I know it's very bold of me to ask this of you…"

Alysa paused to muster courage, more courage, it seemed, than it took to cross that first mountain pass. "The Folk would never try to stop the M'raudas. The Elders would sooner wait for them to leave the mountains. But I cannot stand by and watch them steal as many younglings as they please! I know that many others of my tribe feel the same as I but feel powerless. Islean, the Folk need help from the Trailmen. We need you to help us rid our homesteads of the M'raudas!"

Islean considered the plea. "Why are the M'raudas stealing younglings? Certainly they need not go to all that trouble to obtain food..."

"Food?" Alysa was horrified.

"It is well known that they hunt and catch game. Occasionally animal carcasses are found on the outer edges of our territory at what are believed to be M'rauda kill sites. The mountains have plenty of game. They do not raid your herds?"

Close to tears, Alysa shook her head. "Not that I've heard."

"So why are they doing this? For what purpose?" Islean thought and shook her head. "This certainly is a sad mystery. Well, I am very willing to help my newfound kin; but I cannot say that my tribe will be. The Trailmen are not sympathetic to the Field Folk. They have so little to do with your tribe, of course. And they may not believe the news you brought, as it is so very odd. So out of place. They may feel the story to be a mere contrivance. I do not believe that it is yet time to tell them of our kinship. Ferran?"

Ferran shook his head in agreement.

"But then again..." Islean continued, heartened, "even though it would mean returning to Winding Mountains so soon, they might just welcome a chance to drive the beasts into the ground! The tribe will have to be called back together and the rest of the Elders involved. There will probably be much dispute. As for helping the Folk, I cannot answer what their reaction will be. But this I promise you, Yissa. I will do what I can to encourage this."

Islean embraced Alysa, who breathed a great sigh of relief, thinking this was the end of her long, perilous journey and that rescue would be coming to her people.

Islean warned, "It is far from over, midling. We may be embarking on the most dangerous venture that you—and the Trailmen—have ever undertaken. Regarding the M'raudas, it would be foolish to underestimate their strength—and their number."

Islean rose. "I wish to show you this." She turned around and raised her tunic, exposing the new tattoo on her lower back.

Ferran fixed his pouch to his belt and nodded. He smiled, pleased with his work.

Alysa looked closer at the new painting. Islean's dark skin was a little raw, but the subject of the painting was clear enough, as the pigments were bright. It was a scene with two figures, one standing on either side of a stream with a bridge behind them and Winding Mountains in the background. Represented very accurately were Alysa on the Trailmen's side of the stream and on the Folk side, her father. Alysa held back tears. "Beautifully done, Ferran!"

Ferran, containing his pride, nodded to them and swiftly left the hut.

Islean said, "The painting is in honor of both you and your father, Yissa. It expresses how strongly I desire to include my association with you in my individual history."

"I'm honored, Islean, to be remembered so. My father would be honored as well!"

Islean let the back of her tunic down and embraced Alysa. Islean closed her eyes and said, "I am certain that he is, midling."

The interior of the lodge was much larger than the one at Ridge Camp. Alysa was seated on a bench resting against a wall halfway around the structure, marveling at the size of it and feeling so small. She sat alone in its vastness, wondering how the Trailmen were able to put a roof over such a large span using materials as light and as simple as poles and hides.

Earlier, Rainur had brought her here to wait. She was not certain what was going to happen tonight, but she knew that she was the reason for the gathering. She watched as many Trailmen and women entered the lodge. As they steadily streamed in, their number quickly grew. Uneasy conversations were in progress.

"Why the likes of her is allowed into our camp is what I want to know!" one irate young woman mumbled to a small group, casting a sidelong glance at Alysa. They spoke rudely, as if she could not understand what they were saying.

Qohrlat's brown eyes flashed, emphasizing an important detail. He said, "I was there. The long-haired one came back from the dead last cycle at Ridge Camp. Szaren brought her in."

Jontif, a tall, irate man with stiff gray hair added, "But an explanation why she has followed us to the Lowlands is what I am most curious to hear. A good explanation!"

"Did you know that not only this one, but that all Fielders speak our tongue?" a young woman mused. "That is what Folie told me. I think it is strange that for all this time we did not know."

Jontif crossed his strong arms and retorted, "Well, I think it is a shame that they have learned our tongue and have found where we live. Now they can bother us whenever they choose!"

They also speculated as to the urgency of the meeting about to take place. They knew that it must be of importance, as all the hunters were told to roll and stack the hides they collected without first tanning them. And they were to bring back all the game for storing in the caves south of the Lowlands Camp. All they knew for certain was that tonight's event had something to do with the Fielder in their presence.

The tribal Elders, scouts and hunting leaders were summoned that afternoon. Some were hunting at a distance from the Lowlands Camp on their way to the outer wintertide camps. Half arrived in time for the gathering that eve.

Islean entered with other stern, prominent-looking tribesmen, swept Alysa off the bench, and took her with them to the back of the lodge. As they sat on cushions, many more Trailmen entered and settled on the floor; bench space was becoming scarce. The discussions ceased as Islean raised her hand to speak. "It pleases me to see that so many of you could be here this night. Thank you for responding so quickly. We will get right to it. What we are here to discuss does involve, as I am certain you have reasoned, this Fielder, Yissa of

Winding Mountains. She has traveled far from her home to find us and request aid in a most unusual matter."

Someone from the crowd commented, "The Fielders have always gotten by quite well on their own!"

Islean continued, "Something is happening near our own Winding Mountains that we cannot ignore. The M'raudas are wreaking havoc among Yissa's people. They are stealing younglings from their very fields. Yissa has come to ask us for help in dealing with them."

Jontif jumped up from the bench. His green eyes flashed as he asked, "Why do the Fielders not deal with the M'raudas themselves, Elder Islean?"

"Come, come, Jontif! You know Fielders do not possess the skills necessary..."

Elder Marteen was seated beside Islean. Her brown eyes were lively. She said, "It seems to me, and I mean no disrespect to our guest, that the Fielders lack many skills which would help them survive better. They would not need to ask us for such favors if they could defend themselves."

Islean countered, "Do you think the Trailmen should learn to plant and harvest grain? Or fashion pottery? When we already have the Fielders to do that for us? The Fielders have never had an enemy to combat so have had no need for defense. We ourselves have had no confrontations with M'raudas in recent generations."

Many of the Trailmen, including Marteen, nodded, considering.

"So why have the M'raudas not taken any of *our* younglings?" Jontif wondered. "It must be because they know we are capable of tracking down and killing them quick!" The crowd reacted in loud agreement. He continued, "Things should be left as they are, to run their natural way. If the Fielders are not strong enough to protect themselves, then that is their concern. That is their end!"

Islean jumped to her feet. "So if something more powerful, more deadly than we anticipate comes upon us and causes our demise — then *that* is the natural way of things!" The crowd was stunned, suddenly quiet. She continued with rising fervor. "None of us knows what life ahead holds. We do not know *everything* about what lies beyond our territory, do we? We must take every action to prepare our way, to ensure that the existence of the Trailmen continues. What is happening — please, hold your judgment and try to see life ahead — is that Fielder younglings, once they are grown, become planters, harvesters and crafters. The future providers of many items which we must have in order to survive...are disappearing! Younglings who were meant to grow and bear younglings themselves will not be. As a result, there will be that much less food available to us. That much less fabric woven to fashion the wintertide clothing that is so essential to us. The Folk will have less of *everything* to trade."

Islean scanned the room as this revelation sunk in. Her eyes connected with others as they considered the consequences. The Trailmen listened, alert. She continued with broad gestures so that those in the back would feel the impact of her speech. "We have thought all along that our survival was done on our own. For as far back as the Trailmen remember, we have believed the Fielders to be weak. But they are strong in those skills that we lack. In the end, it is younglings — ours *and* theirs — who will ensure the survival of the Trailmen!"

The Trailmen murmured to one another. Some nodded. Others shook their heads.

Alysa, watching angry and undecided faces and fearful of the crowd's decision, was cheered when Szaren bounded into the lodge. Following close behind were Haraht and Kailee. They halted just inside the entryway, blocked by those who crowded the floor. Szaren scanned the lodge with his keen, pale-blue eyes. He spoke quietly to a woman who stood nearby, evidently catching up on what he had missed.

Suspicious, Jontif continued, "Something is not right. How is it that this Fielder came to you? How did she know the location of the Lowlands Camp?" The crowd reacted to his statement, demanding an answer.

Rainur, who was watching and listening but had not yet offered any comment, rose and proclaimed, "She stumbled upon my hunting group, Jontif." The crowd fell silent. Rainur crossed his large arms, mirroring Jontif, and focused his calm blue eyes on him. "I took her to Elder Marteen's and my dwelling for healing. It is quite obvious, if you would but notice the scratches and bruises on her hands, arms and face—and if you saw how torn her clothing was—that she did not know the trail. It looks like she walked through every prickle-bush and patch of smartgrass she could find!"

The Trailmen seemed to agree that she did look a mess, and they broke into hearty laughter. Alysa found enough humor in how she must have looked the eve before to manage a light laugh.

Serious, Jontif's green eyes widened and he protested, "But that still does not explain how she was able to find us…"

"Jontif!" Szaren interrupted. "Have you ever had an impossible task to do?" The crowd parted for Szaren as he advanced. He surveyed their faces. "One for which you had to use every bit of strength left in your being to complete?"

"Why, of course!" Jontif answered.

Szaren continued, "Did you wonder at the time of your task from where you were gaining that strength?"

"No, I just did what had to be done."

"There is your answer!" Szaren indicated Alysa. "This Fielder did the same as you have done. Her task was to bring aid to her people. She would have died doing so, not stopping until she gave all she had. Which it would seem she did." He turned around, surveying the group. "She is a very brave young woman, even by Trailmen standards. So you see, Jontif, there is no reason for suspicion."

Jontif considered the appeal. Nodding, he seemed to accept Szaren's reasoning and turned back into the crowd. Changing Jontif's thinking would be a boon to Islean's efforts. Held in high regard by the people, and always secure in his beliefs, Jontif's opinion often helped settle the minds of others. And agreement was required amongst all Trailmen before action was decided on matters of this stature.

Elder Marteen said, "So it would seem that this situation does warrant remedy. However, this is the wrong time of cycle to undertake a journey back to the Winding Mountains. What would happen if we became trapped there by the snows?"

Anxious, Alysa answered, "We have more food stored than the Folk could eat in two cycles. If you became caught in the mountains, you could stay with us. I am certain that my tribe would allow this, if you helped us."

Some Trailmen groaned and many laughed at the notion of spending wintertide with the Folk. Alysa blushed, as this was a genuine offer, the best she could think of under the circumstances.

The Elders conferred. After some debate, some scratching of heads and, finally, nods of consensus, Islean turned to the crowd. "The Elders believe that there is merit in lending aid to the Fielders, despite some uncertainties. But it is up to you. If you think that the effort and risk involved are not worthwhile, then we will talk no more of this. If you would rather chance coming upon the M'raudas at greening, camped upon our own mountainsides—then we can just as well wait. So who would join us?"

Nearly every Trailmen nodded, though a few still looked unconvinced.

Marteen said, "Since it looks like most are in agreement, the tribe shall be called back together. On this night, runners will be dispatched to the outer camps to urge that the others come back tomorrow. There is little time before the snows of wintertide will be upon us."

Alysa exhaled a big sigh. The Trailmen began to plan for the journey back to the mountains. Alysa closed her eyes and bowed her head, finally feeling hope.

FABLED CITY

The lodge had cleared, with the exception of Alysa and the Elders, who settled on activities that needed attention early the next sun in order to allow the swiftest return to Winding Mountains. They would take only the provisions necessary to sustain them during that time and, of course, all the weapons they could carry. Alysa marveled at their ability to manage the swift organization of such a large task. When the discussions ended, the Trailmen left the lodge.

Islean escorted Alysa across camp. The soft melody of a strum floated through the air. Islean glanced at a glowing hearthring on the perimeter and said, "Ah, it looks as though some of us have not yet finished discussing the task ahead. But that is good. Discussion gets all the ideas out. And the anxieties. Or perhaps they are just telling tales. We Trailmen do enjoy our tales."

"I'd like to hear more of them," Alysa said. "The tales I heard at Ridge Camp were fascinating!"

"I think it would be all right if you joined them. They seem, in general, accepting of you."

"Tell me, Islean. Will I have to go through a time of acceptance every time I meet a new Trailman?"

"Most likely, midling." She smiled at Alysa and winked.

Alysa left Islean's side and walked toward the hearthring. As she drew closer she slowed her approach, as she was unaccompanied and felt a sudden awkwardness.

Though it was late, several Trailmen and their peltees tarried at the flames, reluctant to say goodnight until they shared just one more tale in the starlit darkness. Szaren was speaking. Standing behind him in the shadows, Alysa listened. But she could not understand what he said, as the breeze carried most of his words in a different direction. As he finished, the group burst into laughter. Szaren must have told a humorous tale; but she wondered: if she had heard the story, would she have understood its humor? There was still so much to learn about them.

The group around the hearthring bade each other goodnight and left Szaren and Drongo alone. Szaren squatted by the fire and poked the embers with a stick. Drongo lay stretched out, her stomach facing the hearthring's warmth. Alysa backed away quietly. Without turning around, Szaren said, "Come, Yissa. Do not be timid."

Drongo jumped to her feet and stared into the dark. She trotted over to Alysa and sniffed her.

Surprised, and a little embarrassed because she tried to sneak away, Alysa went to the hearthring, accompanied by Drongo. She stopped within its dim circle of light and spoke the first words that came to mind. "Did you just tell a tale?"

"Yes," Szaren said. He rose and faced her.

"Would you tell me one?"

"Do your people not have any tales of their own?"

"I've heard Father Gord'n stories my whole life. But they're very different from the tales your people tell. Those that I've heard, anyway."

"Well, I am by no means ready for sleep. I will gladly tell you a tale."

Alysa sat on a log opposite him. The night air was chilly. She buttoned her vest and stretched her boots toward the embers.

Szaren asked, "What kind of tale would you like? A tale of migration? A hunting tale?"

The machine with the dead people inside came to her mind. "Tell me about—the City."

"Ah, the City! In the Sleeping Lands. How much do you know of the City?"

"I really know little about it. There are no tales of it in the homesteads. Only of the escape from it."

"Well then! I tell you, the City is a place everyone should see."

"You've seen it?"

"Yes, many times. But from a great distance. One of the hunting trails runs near the Sleeping Lands. I have never been inside the City—no one can go inside."

"Is it far?"

"It is about a fast three-sun walk there and back."

"I wish I could see it. I'd like to see where our people came from."

"*Our* people?"

"My people. That's what I meant," she said uneasily.

"We could go there."

"But we're going back to Winding Mountains..."

"It will be four suns before all those who will make the journey and supplies can be gathered. We cannot leave anyway without adequate preparation. So there is time enough for a quick journey to the City."

"But wouldn't that keep you from your tasks?"

"There are plenty to help and many more will be coming in. I will not be missed. The City is something you should see."

"I don't know..." she said, anxious.

"Yissa, there is nothing that you can do to move preparations along any more quickly. This may be your only opportunity."

"And Haraht? What will she think?"

Szaren paused, perplexed. "What about Haraht?" He looked at Alysa and laughed. "It is true that Haraht has been my life-long friend, and I hers. It is expected that we will pair. But until then, I am a free man!"

Szaren may have thought her question humorous, but Alysa saw Haraht in action. So in her mind, fear of reprisal was justified. She shook her head, unconvinced.

"Yissa, she will do no harm to you. She has never objected to my having female friends. Why should she object to friends going on a short journey? Ah, I will take my chances!"

Friends? "Friends" was what he called them. Szaren's voice echoed inside Alysa's head as she lay back on her cot in Islean's hut. She no longer cared that he mispronounced her name, even if he did so to irritate her when they first met. They had at last, despite the misunderstandings, become friends; and it was so long since she was among friends—Seda, Orryn, Boshe; her mother, Ellee—all were so far away. Islean, Obala and Szaren all demonstrated that they were her friends. And Szaren, although he might be inviting Haraht's wrath, offered to take her to see the City.

As she drifted into sleep, the faces of her family and friends, all whom she missed and loved, passed through her thoughts. But the face that most often floated through her dreams was that belonging to Szaren.

Three figures with packslings, hunting gear and water bladders slung over their shoulders followed a southwestern route over the increasingly sparse, stony landscape. Two of the figures were Trailmen: Szaren and his taller, life-long companion, Jesh. Alysa was the third. Far ahead, the men's peltees tracked animal scent.

Not long into the journey to the City, Alysa discovered that the narrow trouser legs of the Trailmen garb whisked effortlessly through the scrubby brambles dominating this land. This style of clothing would have served her far better on the journey to the Lowlands than did her traditional Folk clothing!

At first the pace her companions set was difficult. She had trouble keeping up with them, and they were generally several paces ahead. She wondered why traversing the rough ground seemed so effortless for them, so she studied the way they walked. Finally she understood; first, they walked with very light steps. They did not leave a foot on the ground for long. Next, it seemed that they anticipated exactly where they would place their next steps. She tried this theory. By the end of the afternoon, she was able to keep up with them and still have enough breath to converse as they walked.

She noted the stony, dry surroundings; this land was so very different from anything she had encountered thus far. She said, "This land seems dead, Szaren. Why does anybody bother coming this way to hunt?"

Szaren waved his tall walking staff over the surroundings. "Oh, but this land is not dead! We are not even close to the Sleeping Lands. Why do you think that, Yissa?"

"Just look around," she gestured. "All I see are bushes and rocks, not much grass."

"Ah, you see very little then," Jesh said. "That is a big difference between the Trailmen and Fielders. You are unlearned, Yissa. Now I understand why you nearly starved in just five suns!" He plucked a fat stem of grass and pulled it between his large front teeth. "When you are in a harsher land such as this, you can die from thirst. But if you chew on these stems, you lessen the chance."

Like a youngling imitating a parent, Alysa picked a stem and chewed it. She raised her eyebrows. "Not bad."

Szaren said, "There is a fruit that grows under the lowest leaves of this bush." He put his hand into some stubby growth and withdrew a firm, yellow berry. "This little fruit can be found at any time of cycle. It stays on the stem through wintertide. All throughout this land, there are many, many plants with parts that are good for eating. Berries, nuts, roots. Animals abound here because of them."

"But how do you know there are animals?" Alysa asked. "It's so stony here. The ground is so hard. I don't see any tracks."

Szaren said, "My mother was a great tracker. She taught me when I was very young that there are animals everywhere. Even if you do not see their tracks, they leave many other signs in their passing." He looked at the ground and stooped beside a bush. He plucked a tiny green feather from a branch and blew it into the air. "See? That is from a blackcap. And right there between those stones are hoptail droppings."

Jesh pointed to a short bush. Its branches were cut off at an angle. "See this? This is a highbush, or it would be if it were not the firestag's favorite food. When left alone to grow, this bush rises well above a man's head."

Alysa looked around. "Firestags? Here? Not many are seen around the homesteads."

Szaren said, "I think the Trailmen have taught them to stay away from people!"

Alysa said, "Do all the plants have names?"

"Of course they have names!" Jesh said, laughing.

Into evening they played a naming game. By the time they tired of it, Alysa could identify many edible as well as healing plants by sight and smell.

The sky was deep purple when they stopped for the night. The nightchirpers were beginning to sing. Szaren led Alysa and Jesh into a dense stand of trees. The peltees circled the area with ears pricked high and noses to the ground, searching for possible danger. They disappeared into the thick undergrowth.

Szaren walked up to a tall, dark structure covered with vines. He called, "Hup!" and the peltees reappeared. They slowly poked their sniffing noses through a doorway with a heavy metal door frozen half-way open. Deciding the structure to be clear of danger, the peltees ran inside. Szaren followed, then Jesh. Wary of this odd place, but more so of what might be behind in the darkness, Alysa followed.

The large, open room was clear of vines or brush. The floor, however, was covered with soft grass. The peltees ran sniffing around the room. When they finished a complete once-around of the room, they ran out another open doorway on the opposite side of the room. They playfully yipped as they ran into the overgrowth.

Alysa cocked her head and looked around. "What is this place?" she wondered, touching the wall and running her fingertips along an orderly section of black hexagonal blocks.

Szaren answered, "This is an ancient dwelling."

She walked around the shadowy interior. There were six adjoining walls made of the same black blocks. At one time there was a roof, and also a second level. An ancient hearth sat in the center of the room. Its chimney, which had long ago pierced a ceiling and a roof, jutted into the open sky. There were two window openings in each wall, one low and one much higher.

Alysa asked, "But how is it that the walls are still together after all this time? Do the Trailmen tend to them? And how is it that the stones are all shaped alike?"

Jesh said, "This shelter was built by a method we do not understand. We have been camping in dwellings like these for many generations. Repair to the walls has never been necessary, although we do find a need to cut the vines back and pull brush out from time to time."

Szaren removed the water bladder from his shoulder and poured some into his mouth. He handed it to Jesh, who also drank. Szaren added, "The remains of the roof rest many paces from here, but it is not known as to how it got there. There are many more of these shelters nearer the City."

The men dropped their packslings near the hearth but held onto their bows, quivers and water bladders. Szaren said, "We will find food. We will retrace our steps to where we saw signs of brush fowl. Would you make a fire while we are gone, Yissa?"

She shrugged her shoulders. "Well, I can gather wood…" She dropped her pack and followed them outside.

The men called, "Hup!" to their peltees, and the four ran out into the trees.

Alysa spent some time collecting sticks, staying as close to the structure as possible and often peering into the darkness. She delivered armloads to the hearth, returning a few times to gather plenty for the night. She heard many animal squeaks and howls, some near and some far, all unknown. She made the least noise possible so as not to attract any curious creatures!

As quickly as she was able, she finished her chore of filling the hearth with wood and piling up beside it what she thought was enough to last the night. On the grassy floor before the hearth, she unrolled their sleeping mats and blankets. The whole time, she kept a fretful vigil for her companions' return, listening carefully to the many strange, sometimes unnerving animal sounds coming from outside.

Suddenly, the peltees bounded inside. She did not hear them coming and was startled when they entered. The men appeared carrying four large, white birds. "Oh, how wonderful!" she said.

"Yes," Jesh smiled. "These are good ones."

Her nervousness relieved, she walked over to the hearth. "All we need now is a flame."

Szaren and Jesh set the birds outside and returned. Szaren said, "Ah, you have never had to make a fire, Yissa." He nodded and smiled. "But you did find a lot of wood!"

Jesh laughed, "Yes, enough for two, maybe three overnights!"

Alysa shrugged and laughed at what appeared, after all, to be quite a lot of wood.

"Then let us make fire," Szaren said.

She studied Szaren's process. She learned that making fire was an essential skill and longed to understand how to do this. Szaren searched the ground and collected a few handfuls of dried grass. He leaned over the hearth and placed the grass inside, broke some slender branches, and laid them in several rows on top of the grass. He took two small, yellow stones from his pouch and, holding them close to the grass, struck their rough surfaces together several times. Sparks jumped into the grass. He blew on it softly, and the sparks leapt into a flame that quickly spread through the kindling.

She shook her head, marveling at how easy making fire seemed to be after all. Eager, she held out her hand. Szaren placed the stones in her palm. She looked at the rough, yellow stones and noticed the tiny pockmarks left from many strikes. She asked, "How did you come by these stones, Szaren? Where can I get my own?" She handed them back to him.

Jesh took a small pouch from his belt and handed it to her. "You may have mine."

Alysa took the pouch, surprised. "Oh! But don't you need these?"

"Firestones can be found most anywhere. I will find more."

"Thank you, Jesh! Will you teach me to use them?"

Jesh nodded, "Of course!"

Alysa smiled at the thought that she would be able to make fire herself. What a valuable new skill! She would never again have to be without fire for cooking or for comfort, as she had been on the long, dark trek to the Lowlands! Pleased, she tied the pouch to her belt.

The men set their gear down near the doorway, and all three went outside to clean the birds.

Alysa was glad to finally be able to contribute something to this trek, as she had cleaned many casish hens. She was proud that she had her own blade to work with, even though it was much smaller than were the men's. But she did her part, and that was what mattered.

It was not long before the task was finished. The peltees took great interest in the activity, sniffing and scattering the feathers around.

Szaren said, "We will wash the birds, our hands and blades inside."

"Where?" Alysa said. "Is there a well in there?"

"No, but there is a place in the wall from which water flows. All we will need."

Szaren picked up two birds and walked inside. Fixed to a wall at waist height was a heavy metal knob, and below it, a down-curving spout. He pulled on the knob. Immediately a flow of water began. It flowed out of the spout, into a metal grate which was nearly concealed by the grass, and sank into the ground. He set one bird down while he washed the other.

Alysa was fascinated by this water source. "Where does it come from?"

"Apparently from within the wall!" Szaren laughed.

"But water comes from the ground, from wells...springs or streams..."

Jesh brought in the remaining birds to wash them. Overhearing, he said, "It must come from somewhere underground, as there are no streams close by; and then it comes in through the walls. All we know is that it has always been here."

"That is a true wonder, isn't it?" Alysa marveled.

Szaren nodded. "There. They are clean. You may wash your hands, Yissa. Push in the knob to halt the water."

Alysa held her hands under the spout and rinsed them. The water was very cold. She pulled the knob in and out several times to stop and start the flow. "How clever!" she said. She splashed water on her face and neck, pulled up her sleeves and rinsed her arms. She cupped her hands and took a drink. "How sweet it is!" She drank another handful and pushed the knob in one last time. She flicked water from her hands and went to the hearth, where the men ske-wered the birds with branches and laid them over the flames.

Firelight danced on the walls of the dwelling as the fowl roasted and the friends relaxed on their bedding. The tales that Szaren and Jesh told while the game cooked captured Alysa's imagination. They exchanged sagas of the greatest hunting and fighting leaders; of pair-ing rites, feasting and dancing in the bare, brilliant light on the Eves of Moonsrise just before their migrations north and south. They told of encounters with ferocious greatclaws.

Alysa said, "I don't know of anyone who has seen a live great-claw. All the Folk have seen of them are the black and white-spotted furs you trade to us. Has a Trailmen ever been killed by a great-claw?"

Szaren answered, "Not in recent cycles. But there have been some nearly killed."

"Oh!" Alysa answered. "Have I met anyone that happened to?"

Szaren and Jesh looked at one another.

Jesh said, "Yes. Rainur would be one."

Alysa recalled the scars that stretched down Rainur's neck and distorted his tattoos. She said, "Of course. He was attacked from be-hind."

"Yes, but how did you know?" asked Szaren. "Ah, the scars. That was a terrible time for us. He nearly died. But it was a good lesson for the young ones!"

Alysa said, "How did it happen?"

Jesh said, "It was at the end of a marshdoe hunt. When was it, Szaren? You tell it, as I was off on a different hunt at the time."

Szaren paused. "Let me think. I was but twelve cycles old. It was during wintertide, and our group was not too far from the Lowlands Camp. Our hunting group split up, some of us to clean the captured game, others to track a marshdoe that was injured by an arrow and had to be tracked. Rainur found a heavy blood trail, so it was thought that the marshdoe did not go far. Rainur and his peltee Shambli followed the blood, which led them down a narrow rocky trail. Shambli heard something and ran ahead. It met eye-to-eye with a dreaded greatclaw!"

"How frightening!" Alysa said.

"The beast found the dead marshdoe and was already feeding on it. Shambli made a howling fuss! As Rainur came upon them, Shambli positioned himself between him and the greatclaw. But the greatclaw swiped at the peltee with one of its huge paws—killing him with one blow!"

Alysa gasped and said, "Oh, how terrible for the brave peltee!"

Excited and having heard the tale many times, Jesh jumped to his feet. "Rainur began to back away. A greatclaw may leave a hunter alone if he or she steadily looks into its huge, black eyes in a threatening manner. As Rainur was doing just that, he stumbled over the stones and fell backward. He jumped up and ran back up the trail. It seems that having a marshdoe to eat was not enough to distract the greatclaw. It bounded after Rainur, and as he reached the top of the trail, it jumped on his back and tore into him with sharp claws as long as our fingers!"

Alysa exclaimed, "Oh, no!" She covered her eyes.

Szaren added, "Hunter's luck was with Rainur that sun. Others in the group—Jontif and Rainur's mate Marteen—were following to help him carry the marshdoe. They heard the attack. Rainur never called out, but the screams of the greatclaw brought them quick…"

"Good!" Alysa said, uncovering her eyes.

Jesh said, "They speared the ferocious beast and killed it. It took all the strength they had, working together, to force it off Rainur."

Szaren added, "Although he was badly torn, Rainur never entered the sleep of the wounded. He yelled an order to his companions, which I recall to this day: 'Bring back what is left of the marshdoe—*and* the greatclaw's hide!'"

Jesh said, "That is how dedicated a hunter Rainur is."

Alysa sat back and shook her head. She could see the event clearly. Now she understood what Rainur had survived. The scars distorting his paintings became a part of his tale. Never had a serious attack like that happened to anyone in the homesteads—that is, until the M'raudas appeared.

Szaren added, "After that, he never did find another peltee to bond with."

After several more hunting tales, the birds were cooked, ready to eat. The companions concentrated on replenishing their strength. They had eaten only light meals since high sun. The men shared their fowl with the peltees. The roasted birds tasted so good that Alysa wanted to eat a whole one by herself! But she also shared with the peltees, and they nibbled the juicy, dark meat carefully from her fingertips.

The three cleaned up after their meal, throwing the bones out a window opening. The peltees rushed out into the dark.

Looking up into the clear, starlit darkness, Jesh said, "It is going to get cold."

Szaren agreed. They filled the hearth with wood, rinsed their hands and faces in the mysterious water, and settled onto their sleeping mats.

Alysa asked, "Jesh, are you of the Winding Mountains tribe? I don't recall seeing you there."

"My family is of Far Reach Mountains. Szaren and I see each other during wintertide when we are congregated largely in the Lowlands. We have been friends all our lives. Our families have partnered on many hunts. My father was a great warrior. Szaren's father was a warrior, and an Elder."

"Yes, he was," added Szaren. "Jesh and I have much in common."

"Please, tell me more about your family, Szaren," Alysa said. "What were your parents' names?"

"My father was called Efram. My mother was Callia." Szaren smiled; fond memories of them, no doubt. "Here, I will show you." He unbuttoned his vest and removed his tunic. He turned his lean, strong torso so that Alysa was able to view his back.

She looked away at first. Then she reminded herself that this was common among the Trailmen. She saw how comfortable Islean was baring her back to Painter Ferran, Rainur and Marteen. She decided that it was proper for her to look. She thought how pleasant Szaren's bare chest looked and could not help noticing his muscular back and arms.

His paintings trailed down his neck and one-third of the way down his back. His shoulders and arms were not tattooed, as he was still a young man and had not yet done enough living. Alysa could make out images of animals and hunting gear, scenery and people's faces. There were also many other smaller symbols.

Szaren said, "Do you see the man and woman, just at the level of my shoulders?" Alysa nodded. "Those are my parents."

"But I don't see any other people in your paintings. Brothers? Sisters?"

"No. I was their single offspring. They might have had others, but they died when I was still very young."

"That's sad," she said. "I've also lost a parent; my father. How did your parents die? I mean if you don't mind telling."

Szaren continued, "I do not mind. It was very long ago. This is how it happened. There is a number within that level of my painting, number eight. On my eighth greening migration to Winding Mountains, my parents went ahead of the tribe to track animal sign. As I said, Mother was a tracker. Father always accompanied her on her treks. As they walked through a valley below the mountain, an avalanche came down. Later that sun, we came upon the avalanche blocking the route and took a higher trail around it. My parents never did arrive at camp, so we suspected they perished under the snow. Later in the season, after the avalanche melted, they were found. Islean, my father's sister, raised me after they died. She was also given my father's duty as Elder."

"I'm sorry, Szaren."

He rose and removed a cloth from his pack. He went to the water, pulled the knob and wet the cloth. He returned and wiped his head and upper torso with it. "Things happen that we cannot influence. Good things happen also by a twist of events. But we perceive good and bad differently. Good things are taken more easily. Often, at a later time, good things come out of the bad. But one must *look* for the good in the bad."

Alysa considered his words. Jesh nodded.

Szaren laid the wet cloth over the edge of the hearth to dry. He reached into his pack, removed a clean tunic and put it on. "Islean has been a wonderful parent. We have had many adventures togeth-er. Jesh is a true brother. The Trailmen are all brothers and sisters. We do not let each other fall." He smiled. "What matters most to the Trailmen is that each sun we give all we can, live life as best we can. That is how my parents lived, so they lived well. Besides, the dead are never truly gone. Their essences live on."

Intrigued, Alysa asked, "What do you mean, 'essences live on'? What is 'essence'?"

Startled, Jesh said, "You do not know what essence is? How can this be!"

Szaren raised his hand. "Jesh, we have explained many things to Yissa this sun; this is but one more." Jesh nodded. Pausing to think, Szaren took a deep breath and exhaled. "I will try my best to explain. Essence is our...source of life. Our essence—or maybe a word you would better understand is 'root'—is who we are, behind our faces, underneath the skills we have, beyond the place we find ourselves in life. Our essence, or root, reaches down deeper than we or anyone else can see. A spark rises from our essence and gives us life. The Trailmen, the Folk, we are each born with an essence."

"But where is it?" Alysa asked. "It must have a beginning place."

Szaren pressed his fingers to his chest over his heart. "Our es-sence begins here. You cannot see it, but you can feel it if you try. It feels very warm and it—moves."

Alysa touched her fingers to her chest, paused and shook her head.

"It may take time to learn how to feel it, but once you do, you will never forget! So I need to explain how our essences, the roots of who we are, live on after our bodies die." He took another deep breath and exhaled. "We believe that this life that we are now living, now seeing, is but one level of life. There are many others, and the essences of my parents now dwell in one of those. Not too far away, but different. That is why we do not grieve too harshly when one of us dies."

Alysa was silent, not certain what to think. Her father remained alive in her memory. What Szaren said made sense to her mind and to her heart and lessened her pain of loss. Could it be that her memory was the "level" on which her father's essence dwelt? Or perhaps when she thought she saw him, she was actually seeing his essence? Either possibility was of great comfort to her. She now felt closer than ever to him since his death. And she no longer believed that a final farewell was "final" at all.

She smiled and lay back on her mat. She could see the image of roots twining down through her body and into—somewhere, some indescribable, vast place; she could understand that way of thinking of essence. She again touched her fingers to her chest, knowing how much her father would have enjoyed this adventure.

Sparks burst from the top of the chimney into the dark sky. How odd they looked, seeming to rise up out of nowhere. At the same time she thought how right this whole journey to City Infinity felt, with its surprises and revelations. She pressed her whole hand to her chest, closed her eyes, and sighed.

Szaren and Jesh continued to converse. She heard none of the usual Trailmen boasting from either of them. They talked as do the closest of friends, as she and Seda did—relaxed and open. If she gave them a questioning look, they explained what they were talking about.

They were so different from her, yet—a sameness existed. She so longed to tell these men, her brothers, all she told Islean about their kinship. But something told her to wait, that the right moment was yet to come.

As they continued to talk, Szaren retrieved his hunting gear and sat back on his mat. He picked up his bow, examined the twisted hide bowstring, took a cloth out of a pocket sewn to the side of his quiver, and began to rub the bow with it. Alysa noticed a symbol carved along the curve of the bow. Curious, she sat up to look more closely.

"Szaren, the same person who carved your staff carved my walking staff. Look, it's the firestag's head over Winding Mountains. Isn't that the same symbol that's on your back?"

Szaren remained silent, but Jesh said, "Yes, Szaren's symbol."

Alysa asked, "You carved my staff, Szaren? Why didn't you tell me? Or why didn't Obala when I asked her? I wanted to thank the carver, but she never did say who it was!"

Szaren's face reddened.

Jesh quipped, "I swear on a greatclaw's paw, this is the first time I have seen you with nothing to say! What would Haraht think?"

Szaren retorted, "It does not matter what Haraht thinks! Can I not give something to somebody without Haraht's permission?"

"Well, your pairing moons are approaching. After the Eve of Moonsrise at greening, you will need her permission for everything!" Jesh laughed. "When Haraht found out that Szaren not only saved you and gave up his hut, but cared for you alongside Obala until you were out of danger, she flew into a most dreadful rage! You should have seen..."

"Jesh!" Szaren roared.

Alysa could barely believe it. She knelt before Szaren and reached for his hands. He yielded them to her. She studied them, turned them over, caressed his palms and fingers. She placed them on either side of her face and closed her eyes. It was true; these were the hands, no woman's at all, that had bathed her wounds, fed her broth, and coaxed her back to life!

She looked into Szaren's eyes. Firelight sparked within their pale-blue centers. Alysa threw her arms around his middle. "Now I can thank the one who did so much for me! I know you're humble. I know you're proud and don't need my thanks. But I thank you all the same!"

Szaren, hesitating at first, wrapped his arms around her. After a long embrace, they released. They stared at each other. Szaren awkwardly began to talk about what Alysa could expect on the next sun's trek.

Jesh, keeping to himself any further comment he may have had, grinned and stretched out on his mat. He pulled his blanket around himself and watched the flames. Listening to his companions' excited talk, the crackling fire, and the constant song of the nightchirpers, he was soon asleep.

At mid-morning of the next sun, the travelers walked across soggy, green land that began a gradual dip to the south. Springs gurgled to the surface and collected in hollows which drained down the slope between slimy stones and pale, struggling vegetation.

They followed a yellow spring around an outcropping of rock. Jesh, in the lead, pointed through the haze and said, "We must go no further. Hup, Vonni! Drongo!" The peltees, who were surging ahead, halted.

The vegetation grew sparser and sparser downslope until the land turned brown. A great expanse of sunken land curved like a vast bowl into the distance.

Jesh said, "The Sleeping Lands. It means death to go there."

Szaren pointed to the far-off center of the depression. Murky green-brown water collected into a sick, shallow sea, and from it a mass of fractured shapes rose high into the sky, piercing the haze. "That is the City. The City of the Ancient Ones."

Alysa lowered herself onto a broad rock, stunned by the broken mass of what was once home to a great civilization. She was at a loss for words. Finally she said, "City Infinity? It's not what I expected. I didn't imagine it to be so vast!"

It was plain that many shattered roads dipping into the water-filled depression once led into the City. Their broken paths could be traced to bridges, twisted and tipped at odd angles into the murk. The City's gray skeleton reminded her of the bones that had grinned back at her from inside the land-traveling machine.

She stared in wonder, trying to imagine what the giant structures looked like before they were laid waste, before the dwelling spaces and roads and tunnels beneath the City collapsed and sank into the depression. Perhaps one sun she would see the images of the City that Orryn told her about, before it was ruined. Then she would know what it looked like when it was whole and alive.

"Our people must've worked very hard to build that great city," she said. "Our people must've been very keen, very clever. But not keen enough to prevent it from being ruined."

Szaren said, "Again you have said 'our people', Yissa. I do not think you said it this time in error."

She bit her lip, wondering if this was the time for them to hear. She hoped it was. "Would you both be willing to listen to a tale that we Field Folk have just heard? A tale of the Ancient Ones and City Infinity?"

Curious, the men looked at each other, nodded, and urged her to proceed. She rose and motioned for them to sit. They did so, attentive, waiting to hear their first Field Folk tale.

Alysa held as close to Teller fashion as she was able. She told them all the details she could remember: about the texts and maps and other mysterious things Orryn discovered in Father Gord'n's secret room; about two brothers who fought and separated themselves and their followers from each other; to the conclusion that they were all brothers and sisters and must shun each another no longer.

When Alysa's Telling was done, Szaren and Jesh stared at City Infinity. By high sun, the haze had melted and the City stood doubled, mirrored in the murky sea. It seemed to loom closer as the air became clearer. A warm, foul-smelling breeze flowed upslope from the stagnant water.

Szaren said, "You told us true, Yissa. I am seeing the City in a different way. It was just a territory marker before. It meant that hunting parties should keep to another direction because no game lives there. It meant that if anyone dared drink the water, or cross over onto the Sleeping Lands, that they would be smitten by the Veiled Slayer and would die in a short while. Now it means much more."

"Now it is a very sad place to my eyes," Jesh said. "But many cycles ahead, the land will be green and the City—it may live once again. Where we are sitting was once dead like down there. The green reaches downslope a little farther each cycle."

"At some time to come," Alysa said, wistful, "our people may very well rebuild and again live within City Infinity's walls."

246

"Our people..." Szaren echoed, taking Alysa's hand in his.

Jesh said, "We must make certain the others know of our kinship before we begin the journey back to Winding Mountains. I think it will mean much to them if they know." He glanced west of the City, rose and pointed at a watery whirlwind that sprang up from the depression. The funnel of water began to make a thunderous hum as it grew larger and began to spin in their direction. It sucked at the surface of the water, growing darker as it churned up debris from beneath. The peltees were agitated and began to circle around their masters, waiting for their command. Jesh shook his head. "There it goes again…"

"What is that?" Alysa asked. "I've never seen anything like it!"

"Whirlwater," Jesh replied. "Seems like one rises up every time we pass by here."

"Where do they come from?"

"They seem to come from nowhere. But we had best not get caught in it!"

Szaren asked, "Do you think it could climb up this slope?"

"I do not know," Jesh replied, "but I would not like to be standing here if it should end its course right over us and let go of its poisoned water!"

Szaren nodded, and he and Alysa rose. Jesh stood between them and placed his hands on their shoulders, urging them back up the slope. The peltees were relieved that their masters were at last leaving and ran ahead. Alysa had a difficult time releasing her gaze upon City Infinity. It was such a wondrous sight!

Up ahead, she noticed a dark, wide strip of ground and recognized it to be a road, possibly part of the same one she saw suns before. She walked up to it, the men following. They scanned the length of broken path and saw that downslope it disappeared beneath the moss, reappeared once more, and sank into the murky water. She said, "Their machines rode atop that dark path."

A realization came over Szaren's face. "Of course! That makes sense. They were not created for walking upon, as we have used them. We have always thought they were much too broad for simply walking upon, but we did not know about the machines. How did you come to know this?"

"Through the ancient knowledge that was revealed to my tribe. And I had a recent encounter of my own with one of the machines." She again thought of the bones in the machine and shuddered. She began to tell the tale but decided to save the horrific story for another time. Enough had already been revealed, and she was still digesting the recent knowledge of history.

Upslope and to one side of the path, a smooth, rectangular stone a few paces wide and three times taller than they rose from the ground. It was covered in red slime, with only part of an inscription visible on its face. Alysa picked up a handful of moss and wiped off the slime as high as she could reach. She stepped back and stood between the men. They gazed at it in wonder. Words in oldenscript and a carved design in the middle of the stone were revealed. The carving was in the likeness of Winding Mountains at moonsrise. They could not decipher the script, but this was obviously a direction marker, planted beside the dark path to point the way to Winding Mountains.

Alysa shook her head and tears filled her eyes as she fully realized, in her heart, the connection between the Field Folk, the Trailmen, and City Infinity.

Jesh pointed at the still-advancing whirlwater as the air about them began to churn. The peltees were already many strides ahead of them. Alysa and her companions turned in silence and began the trek back to the Lowlands Camp. The next challenge in their adventure was about to begin.

ALLIANCE

Nanthan-kul cast her soft light upon the dark forest. Tiny glimmers, reflections of her light, perched for an instant upon ripples in Rocky Stream, were swallowed by the dark water pushing ever downward, then rose again to ride the crest of new ripples. It mattered little that the night was cold and that frost glinted on the soft needles of foya trees and crept along the edges of curling leaves. Alysa was home, in her mountains, and the spicy scent of fallen leaves and musty soil brought her much happiness.

From below, lantern lights rose up Gorge Path on their way to the Tradeground. Their reflections bounced on the surface of the stream as a line of figures made its way up the path. As they ascended, the reflections faded.

The Folk—after two suns of anxious deliberation—finally agreed to meet with the Trailmen. Alysa, acting as messenger, delivered the Trailmen's ultimatum to the Folk that afternoon: if by that eve the Folk failed to meet with them to discuss the M'rauda problem, the Trailmen would break camp and go back to the Lowlands.

Standing in torch light in the center of the Tradeground, Trailmen Elders and leaders awaited the arrival of leaders from the homesteads. Alysa watched at the top of the path, holding a lantern as a beacon. She was pensive. She took a great risk to bring the Trailmen here, and she hoped the Folk would do nothing to anger them. The strain from the trial they might be facing together could, unless each individual made great effort, forever break the slender thread that bound them.

Tola was the first Folk Alysa welcomed to the Tradeground. His frosty breath labored as he paused to wait for the others. Tola greeted her with a conciliatory smile and placed a hand on her shoulder, pulling her into a hug. Alysa hugged him back, accepting his silent apology. She recognized Elders from Valley Ridge and Green Plateau as they stepped to the top, followed by Boshe and Evyn. Orryn—who was reinstated as Apprentice Teller—and Aryz were also there.

Szaren, Jesh and Jontif were clustered with the large Trailmen contingent.

Betram and Thad arrived at the top. With hands linked, they carried someone between them—Kendira! Alysa clapped an agonized hand over her eyes. If anyone was lethal to the purpose of this gathering, it would be the aged Teller. Kendira's apprentices panted as they set her on her feet.

Warm fingertips gently pulled Alysa's hand from her face. Loralle stood before her. She smiled and winked and followed close behind Kendira as she hobbled into the clearing. Loralle's gesture assured her daughter that she would be mindful of Kendira and that Alysa should not suffer anxiety over her.

Soon all were assembled on traditional sides of the Tradeground, their faces revealed in lantern and torch light. Islean, Rainur and Marteen faced Tola, Poolan and Boshe.

The peltees sniffed and snarled among the Folk, who looked very uncomfortable with the creatures running about. Never before had they seen such aggressive little beasts. Rainur detected the Folks' unease, yelled "Hup!" to the animals, and pointed at the bridge. The peltees bounded over the gorge and disappeared in the trees.

Tola began a formal discussion. "I'm Council Speaker Tola of High Point. We have come to ask you—to aid us," he rasped.

"What kind of help do you seek?" Islean asked, her posture stern.

Poolan said, "Nine of our younglings have now been taken. The homesteads have debated at length, and we've decided that we want them back—even at the loss of our lives. We are prepared to do battle, if you'll show us how."

Rainur asked, "Are you certain that the younglings are yet alive?"

"No, we don't know that they are," Tola answered, eyes weary. "But we have hope."

"We agree on that matter, which is good," Islean said. "We all have hope and from hope we shall draw strength. And we must learn to cooperate as we have not for thousands of cycles. We must bring to the fore all of our skills and knowledge so that we can defeat the enemy. Do you understand what battle entails? Have you adequate people for battle?"

Tola said, "Although as a peaceful people we cannot say that we understand battle, all of the homesteads have dedicated men to the cause. The pain we've suffered is great. And although we lack the Trailmen lust for battle, we all wish for an end to this madness..."

Jontif lurched forward and interrupted with hot words. "Lust for battle! That is an insult!"

Islean raised her hand to hold Jontif.

"You're right," Tola said. "I apologize for my poor choice of words. We can only wonder what the circumstances were that kindled such great distance between Folk and Trailmen so many cycles ago. This must be put behind us so that we can meld our efforts. It'll take time, I fear, to adjust to..."

"To this unrighteous, unsound partnership with the Trailmen!" Kendira interjected as she hobbled between the leaders.

"No, Kendira," Loralle said, stepping forward and taking hold of Kendira's arm. "To the long overdue learning of our kinship."

No comment on either side was made in favor of Kendira's statement or in objection to Loralle's. Kendira's disappointment was sharp as Loralle turned her from the Elders and guided her away. It was clear that she would contend to her last breath that the relationship was wrongful. But it was also apparent that her fight was one she would suffer to carry on alone.

Nervous, Tola looked at Islean, who appeared undaunted by Kendira's words. Islean said, "There is no need to apologize for her. She is of one mind—her own; and she bears allegiance mainly to herself. But the Trailmen are not without fault." She glanced hard at Jontif. "Some who came on this journey are still not entirely convinced. But we will eventually win that battle, too."

"Will you then teach us, Islean, so that we can defeat the M'raudas?" Poolan asked.

"We will gladly teach you, and more. We will fight side by side. At the Ridge Camp are three hundred and sixty-four archers, battle-rod bearers, spearmen and scouts. They are always at the ready for battle."

Islean added, "The Folk may even wish to continue to hone the fighting skills you will learn, in case another enemy comes to harm you."

"Other enemy?" Boshe asked, tradesigning out of habit.

Marteen said, "You have not ranged as far upon this world as have we. It is a very large place. Over time we may be visited by others, friendly or fiendish, who have left their own territories in search of fresh land or conquests."

The Folk were awed by this conception. They never considered others might want to gain hold of their land or people. They had lived in their own isolated world for so long!

Islean continued, "We shall come to High Point early tomorrow to make plans and begin training. The sooner we begin, the sooner the trouble will be past and we can return to the Lowlands."

She extended her strong, narrow hand to Tola. He clasped it and said, "Tomorrow a woodworking team will be dispatched to place a new floor on the bridge. There are going to be many footsteps traveling across it."

Islean smiled and nodded.

Boshe reached across to Jontif and introduced himself. Marteen clasped Poolan on the shoulder. Relaxed and relieved by the behavior of their leaders, the others took up the gesture.

The first step succeeded! Alysa took a deep, relieved breath and beamed at Szaren. They lingered as Folk took to the path and Trailmen crossed the gorge. Finally they said goodnight and parted, each following the people who reared them, who gave them life.

Several large slates were propped up on a Great Hall table. Chalk markings were drawn on one of the slates. Lines representing streams, lakes and other landmarks of the homesteads indicated that this was a map. Circles represented the locations of the five homesteads.

Many men-Folk, Trailmen and Trailwomen were seated on benches arranged in rows. They listened attentively to Rainur as he pointed to various features on the map. Szaren sat to the side, listening and thinking.

Rainur said, "The locations of Yellow Cliffs and High Point provide important information. They are the only homesteads that have not been raided for younglings. Can anyone tell me why?"

A young Trailman jumped up, certain he had the answer. At the same time, young Betram—seated in the back row between Boshe and Panli—popped up from his seat, begging to be called upon. Rainur shook his head and motioned Betram to sit. The young Trailman answered, "Because they are too high in the plateau to attempt a theft."

"You are partly correct," Rainur said, "but why?"

Again Betram begged to answer and Rainur passed him over.

"It is too far back to their camp," Haraht said. "Their camp must be somewhere to the south, in the direction of the Short Mountains which lay below Field Folk territory."

Betram dropped to his seat, apparently having the same answer and again disappointed that he was not called upon. Boshe patted him on the shoulder to console him.

"Well, Haraht," said Rainur. "It seems the M'raudas have not covered their trail well enough to escape your keen eyes, have they!"

Haraht smiled proudly.

Rainur drew a series of lines from the locations of the three affected homesteads. They intersected at a point to the south. "These lines, drawn in the order of the nine thefts, point to the most likely area of the M'rauda camp."

All nodded in understanding and excitement.

Szaren continued, "We must decide as precisely as possible where the M'rauda camp is so scouts can be sent to see if they are still there. Is there a Folk here familiar with the territory below the southern homesteads?"

Orryn rose. "Once I hiked very far southwest of Falling Stream. I was gone for at least half a sun, and I crossed much territory."

The Trailmen burst into laughter, as their idea of "very far" was much different from Orryn's.

Szaren smiled and held up a quieting hand. He urged Orryn to continue. "Can you show us on the map, Orryn?"

Seeming pleased that Szaren thought his contribution worthwhile, Orryn picked up a piece of chalk. He marked an "X" on the map. "There's a steep ridge with thick trees about here. The stream flows below it. That might be a good place for them to camp."

Szaren asked, "What is the terrain like there, Orryn? That will be important to know. Can you describe it in more detail?"

Orryn nodded and spoke as he drew a profile of the ridge and its details on a blank slate. In a delivery very close to Teller style he said, "There's a high, wide ridge right here, straight down from Falling Stream. Below the ridge, the land drops at about this angle. At the top, the ridge is bordered by thick trees, both foyas and leafy types. The trees grow sparser farther down, where there are many stony outcrops. Then the edge of the land drops off into the stream, which is quite far down."

"How far down?" Szaren asked.

Orryn thought. "Far enough to kill a man—or M'rauda."

"That was an excellent accounting of the ridge," Szaren praised. "You are a keen observer, Orryn of Falling Stream!"

Szaren clapped Orryn firmly on the shoulder. Orryn looked into his eyes, nodded and smiled.

"This," Rainur said, tapping Orryn's mark on the slate, "is where the scouts will search this night."

Two suns later, stacks of spears, arrows and battlerods lay in various stages of completion in the front area of the Great Hall. In the back, many rows of benches faced the Planting Calendar upon which were seated Folk and Trailmen. The scouts—Orryn, Aryz, Haraht, Kailee, Jontif and Jesh—faced the gathering. Elders Tola, Poolan, Islean, Marteen, Levin and many others of rank stood to the side to learn what, if anything, the scouts had found.

Alysa, pensive and wishing to stay out of sight, peeked through a doorway to watch.

Tola said, "First, I want to thank the brave scouts who traveled to Falling Stream to evaluate the M'rauda situation. What have you to report?"

Aryz rose from the bench. "Orryn led us to the place he described. There is no doubt that the M'raudas are camped there."

Trailmen and Folk reacted differently: the Trailmen shouted and thrust their fists into the air; the Folk nodded, determined.

The commotion settled and Aryz continued. "But since we watched from higher up the ridge, we were able to see only the M'raudas' hearthrings in the dark. At times we caught glimpses of ragged, limping figures passing between us and the flames. They were too far away to see any detail, but at least we know they're there for certain. And we did hear..." Aryz's voice began to break.

Orryn wiped the corner of his eye. The Trailmen scouts, including Haraht, glanced at each other and lowered their eyes to the floor, evidently touched by what they had heard but trying to conceal their sorrow.

Jontif rose, motioning Aryz to sit, and continued. "We heard something that tore at our hearts. We remained still for a long while hidden above the camp, listening to the weak yet definite sound of— crying younglings. We desired to raid the camp then and there! But of course, we were too few."

Folk and Trailmen began to weep at the thought of the younglings in misery. But at the same time, the news that the M'raudas were still in the area and the younglings were alive bolstered hope that they would be brought home.

Catching a glimpse of Alysa as she peeked through the doorway, Poolan leaned to Tola and whispered, "We have a public forgiving of two midlings to do!" With tears welled up in his eyes, Tola nodded.

Jesh turned the conversation back to the matter at hand. With optimism he said, "We gathered much knowledge about the area, such as the distance from the camp to the ridge, the location of game trails that will allow access to the M'rauda camp, terrain conditions and so on."

Islean stepped forward and said, "Then it was a good decision to keep High Point as our base camp. If we were training for battle at Falling Stream, the activity could well alert the M'raudas to our plans. What say we then?"

She looked to the Elders and battle leaders to confer. They congregated and talked quietly for some time. It was agreed that in two more suns there would be enough weapons made, and the men-Folk would be ready for battle.

Alysa was overjoyed to hear that the younglings were found — and that they were still alive. She left the Great Hall, happy in her heart to learn this.

The leaders faced the gathering. Tola announced, "The final decision has been made. We'll finish our preparations for the battle at — 'M'rauda Ridge'."

THE BATTLES WITHIN

The next morning, one hundred and seventy-three Folk-men were learning to defend themselves with battlerod and spear. Many needed constant encouragement to force their Trailmen "opponents" into positions of defeat. Elder Marteen and Rainur drilled a group on a lower terrace. Marteen said, "If I were an ugly, stinking M'rauda, would I wait for you to make the decision whether or not you are going to put a spear into me? No! You must not—and I want none of you to forget this—you *must not* hesitate, or you will end up dead on the ground!"

Rainur added, "You will be of no use in this cause if you cannot understand the purpose of the drill. Now try again, Orryn. Rush me! And this time do not hold back!"

Rainur and Marteen chuckled as Orryn wiped his sweaty palms on his trousers. Rainur said, "Do you think I will not counter you, Orryn? I will, and do not think otherwise! You must become used to rushing at a living being, and countering its attack, as well. I understand that you find this difficult, but you must do it!"

Marteen added, "Another thing to keep in mind at all times is that you must approach your opponent from the higher side of the slope. From the higher position you will always have the advantage. If you find yourself downslope of an attacker, be certain to maneuver yourself above it as quickly as possible!"

They practiced with spear and rod until the Trailmen determined the Folk competent to perform the maneuvers at will. Then Folk and Trailmen sparred together until they were exhausted.

The Folk also trained with the peltees, as the creatures must be able to respond to commands from whomever they were closest to. This was how they worked with the Trailmen during hunts, and such cooperation would also be required of them in battle. It was necessary for the Folk to understand what the peltees were capable of. The Folk must first learn to trust the snarling, sharp-toothed creatures. Neither was it a simple task for the peltees, as the Folks' scents and mannerisms were much different from those of their Trailmen masters. In the beginning of the training, obeying the Folks' commands was confusing to the peltees.

As they continued to work together, it became much easier for both Folk and peltee. The Folk gradually lost their fear of them, and the peltees learned on command to joyfully leap upon makeshift "M'raudas" — poles set into the ground and wrapped in shocks of spent grain stalks.

Evyn was one of the most successful new "masters", and Trekkar, a peltee considered to be one of the strongest and wisest, seemed to have bonded with him. Trekkar had lost his aged master the cycle before and had not as yet adopted a new one until, apparently, Evyn.

As the warriors worked with the peltees, the high-sun meal was being prepared in the Great Hall. Many clay kettles hung in the hearths, and bread baked in the ovens. Hundreds worked in the Great Hall, finishing weapons for the raid planned the morning after next. Points were whittled on the ends of slender, peeled saplings and then heated in fire to harden them for use as spears. Sharpened antler tines were inserted into the ends of plain, unadorned battle-rods. Trailmen, expert in the art of arrow-making, worked beside the Folk and filled barrels with finished arrows.

Alysa, Loralle and many other women, mainly Folk, sat at long tables fashioning Trailmen-style clothing from dark-green cloth. There was an absence of younglings. Their mothers did not think weapon-making to be a suitable activity for their younglings to be around. Ellee was at home, put in charge of cooking the evening meal while her mother and big sister worked in the Great Hall.

Standing before Folk students seated in the back of the Great Hall, Haraht — with Kailee close at hand — spoke to the warriors. Haraht said, "Real fighting is little like fight play. It will be bloody and dirty, and for many Folk, it will no doubt be frightening. But you must overcome any fear that arises. Carefully heed my words: battling through your fear will be the *only* way you will survive!"

Looking into the eyes of as many Folk as she could, Haraht watched for reactions. They expressed some looks of doubt, but most of the faces looked back at her with resolve. "The killing is nothing you will be proud of. We do it because we must, to take back what has been stolen. You must keep the thought of staying alive in your minds, and you must think of nothing else! When it is over, then you can be proud of winning."

The Folk cheered at these words, heartened that they would, indeed, accomplish their task.

Haraht's knowledge of battle was daunting to Alysa, as what the warrior-huntress knew seemed extensive for one so young. Alysa admired the words of encouragement Haraht spoke to the warriors-in-training.

"We have advantages over the M'raudas. For one, they will not be expecting us. The surprise attack will catch them unaware. Surely many of them will perish before they manage to pick up their weapons!" The Folk nodded and murmured words of relief. "Another advantage is that there are a good number of us, so we will surround them on three sides and not allow any to escape." More optimistic murmurs rose from the group. "The thing most in our favor is that we are organized. They are sickly creatures and probably possess weak defensive skills. That is why they have avoided us Trailmen."

Alysa thought, *What a courageous woman, this Haraht!* It was no wonder Szaren was drawn to her. She was almost a mirror of him—strong, capable, sure. As Alysa looked up from her work, Szaren entered and crossed to Haraht.

Loralle, sitting beside Alysa, reacted to her daughter's affectionate gaze as she watched Szaren. "I do approve of him, you know."

"Approve of him for what, Mother?" Alysa asked, blushing and returning her eyes to her work.

"I've watched you together while you converse about various matters. I see how well you mesh."

"We are friends, Mother."

"You are more than friends. A mother can tell."

Alysa sighed and smiled. There was no fooling Loralle, who had grown more keen and alive than ever and skilled in understanding the moods and sensitivities of others. Loralle found great joy in lending help to smooth the many small, inevitable conflicts between Folk and Trailmen. Every chance she found, Loralle asked Trailwomen about their ways and passed on explanations to the Folk. Both tribe and clan were curious about—and growing more accepting of—each other.

As Haraht and Kailee excused their students, Szaren went to Alysa. Haraht watched after him and glared at Alysa. He said, "The battle leaders are gathering here to finish the planning. You may want to stay and listen."

"No, I don't wish to stay. I don't need to know exactly how the battle's going to happen. Besides, Mother and I told Obala that we'd help the healers finish readying the healing supplies. We must make more bandages and…"

"All right," Szaren said. He leaned closer and talked softly. "Since I have now missed an opportunity to escort you home after the meeting, may I come to your cottage later?" He glanced at Loralle. She subdued a smile and kept her eyes on her work.

Alysa glanced at her mother, aware that she was just pretending not to hear the conversation. "Do come by if you like. Ellee has been anxious to ask you about your carvings, anyway."

Szaren laughed and rocked back on his heels. "Ah, I see, I see. Then I will be by after the meeting." He politely nodded to Loralle and joined the gathering group of leaders.

Haraht opened a space for him to enter the group. She glared one last time at Alysa. Alysa did not notice this, however, as she had already turned to leave.

Loralle looked sidelong at Alysa as they walked together to the barn. She clicked her tongue and lightly scolded her. "Alysa of High Point! Szaren has no desire to talk with Ellee and surely he wishes to play no tamoree with me! You should've invited him to sup…"

"Mother, please. We're just friends. Come, we must help Obala."

Loralle nodded a knowing smile but pressed her daughter no further.

Loralle and Ellee snuggled in their nooks, sound asleep. The hearth embers glowed. The front door was partway open. Nanthan-kul's light spilled inside, spreading a soft glow across the late-evening floor.

Outside, the stars were bright on the horizon. Alysa and Szaren sat on the stoop, leaning against the doorposts in awkward silence. In the high-angled moonlight, they listened to nightchirper song—in part for the music's beauty, in part to avoid voicing what was on their minds. They watched the moon's reflection on the calm lake. An occasional breeze caused its reflection to ripple. All of the cottages were dark. It seemed as if Alysa and Szaren were the only ones still awake.

Earlier the air was quite warm; but as the evening was turning cold, Alysa drew her shawl closer about her shoulders. She reached behind and pulled the door closed.

Drongo, after a long sun of carrying out battle commands, lay sound asleep beside Szaren. Szaren twirled his fingers in her soft, curly fur. Tahshi snuggled across the back of Alysa's neck, beneath her shawl. The creatures spent the first part of the evening getting used to each other; Drongo and the other peltees were taught that the saroos living in the homestead were not game animals. It took some firm training by their masters to teach them this, but the peltees did eventually make their peace, and the saroos finally stopped sneezing when peltees stuck their wet noses in their faces.

Finally, Alysa turned to Szaren and broke the silence. "I've...I've been feeling odd around you."

"Yes, I know."

"Do you wonder why, Szaren?"

"I know why. It is because of Haraht."

"No, Szaren, it's not because of Haraht. Well, it's partly because of her and who she is to you; but it's mostly because of you. I don't know what you think of me."

He laughed. "Oh, come now! How can you not? Do you not know how brave I think you are? How resourceful you are? How strong you are in here?" He tapped his chest over his heart.

Alysa nodded and sighed.

Szaren thought and added, "Ah, but you do not wonder how I *think* about you. You want to know how I *feel* about you, do you not?" Alysa nodded. He continued, "Ah, feelings. They are more difficult to describe than mere thoughts. But I will try." He rose and placed his hands on his hips. He left the stoop and paced a few steps into the yard, turned, came back and stopped. He started to speak a few times, halting each time to gather his thoughts, using his hands to aid in forming the words. "Moons, this is more difficult than I thought it would be!" Finally the words came. "Since I have gotten to know you—I have been having doubts that I want to pair with Haraht. There!"

Alysa nodded. "I feel like I'm in the middle of that, and I guess I don't know what to think."

Szaren said, "But I am in conflict, as I have fought for and won her. That sealed my promise to her, and to the tribe."

Alysa rose and stared at the moon. "I've discovered that sometimes we have to break promises to find the right path. Sometimes we have to leave promises behind. I've had to do so. For how can we know that an old promise is going to fit us in the suns to come? I've struggled with this. This kind of thinking goes entirely against my tradition."

Szaren agreed, "Yes, it is the same for us Trailmen; it is not good to break promises."

Alysa continued, "But on the other side of this, we can't force ourselves to live a lie. I think that if an old promise threatens to prevent us from pursuing what we come to know to be our true purpose...or if it keeps us from that thing that may bring to us our deepest happiness—then we must find a way to reconcile that."

"That makes some sense to me. But I will have to ponder that. I must see if I can find an allowance in our betrothal tradition."

Alysa looked at him. "Szaren, tell me. What's been traditional about anything we've been through this last moon? Or this last cycle for that matter?"

He pulled her to him and lightly, though passionately, kissed her. She gasped and pulled away. Stunned, she raised a hand to her mouth.

"Yissa, I apologize! What you said overwhelmed me with a sudden sense of...freedom. And *knowing*. But all the same, I should not have done that. It was wrong."

"No...it wasn't..."

"Yes, I believe that it was..." He sprinted off and jumped the yard wall. "Hup, Drongo!" The peltee groaned, slowly rose and trotted after him. She jumped over the wall, caught up to him, and peltee and master hastened toward Gorge Path. They disappeared in the shadows of the trees.

"Wait...!" Alysa said, too late. Again touching her fingers to her lips, she entered the cottage.

MISGIVINGS

The outer cottage door flung open, waking Alysa from sound sleep. Loralle pulled back the curtains and peeked out of her nook. As sleepy Ellee slid from her bed, the door was torn from its hinges and thrown to the floor, splitting into pieces. Suddenly fully awake, afraid, Ellee backed away from the doorway.

A stench too horrible to describe flowed in from the dark hallway. The sound of ragged, raspy breathing sent chills up Alysa's spine. Though she couldn't see it, she knew that a beast waited just outside in the darkness. Unable to move, her heart pounded, filling her ears.

Ellee tried to scream when the beast staggered into the room. It paused on the fragmented door, scanning the space from amber, over-large eyes, drool matting the fur on its chest. Then it spotted Ellee.

Terrified, Ellee stretched one hand to Loralle, who gripped her youngling's fingers and pulled her to her. The beast grabbed Ellee's other hand and yanked her to itself. Loralle screamed, pleading with the beast to spare her daughter. It pulled hard, and Ellee cried out. Loralle lost her grip—forfeiting her daughter to the beast—lost her balance, and fell to the floor. She tried to rise but was too weak with fear. Kicking and screaming, Ellee tried to free herself from the beast as it dragged her from the cottage.

All across the homestead, the same assault was taking place at the other cottages. The beasts had torn every youngling they could find from their beds and were dragging them into the forest. Folk and Trailmen ran with weapons poised in an effort to stop them, but their arrows and spears fell with either too little force to stop them, or missed their marks completely.

Szaren ran with spear ready but was knocked down. The beast that sent him to the ground lifted up its large, filthy foot and placed it on his head, poised to crush it.

Ellee's screams and those of the other younglings filled the homestead.

Their terror echoed in Alysa's head as she awoke and sat upright in bed, gasping for air. The door closed and Loralle entered, lugging a bucket of water. Ellee sat on her bed braiding her hair and smiled at her sister. The saroos joyfully tumbled and chased each other across the floor, full of pre-dawn vigor.

Alysa focused on the calm scene and inhaled the fresh air that followed Loralle inside. Alysa wiped the sleep-sand from her eyes, groaned, flopped back onto the bed, and pulled the quilt over her head.

"It's time, Daughter," Loralle said. "Hurry and dress. Everyone's gathering for breakfast at the Great Hall. The warriors must be south of Falling Stream by mid-afternoon so they're in position before sunrise tomorrow. I'm leaving now so that I can be of help to the cooks."

Loralle left. Alysa climbed down from her nook, rolling her head and rubbing her neck.

"Did you sleep bad, Thitha?" Ellee asked.

Alysa made an effort to laugh. "I guess so! My neck has a big knot to show for it, too."

They dressed and finished their hair. Alysa waited as Ellee patted and kissed each saroo and closed them in the cottage. The sisters left for the Great Hall.

On the way, Ellee pointed to a figure standing on a higher terrace. The stark figure made a silhouette against the dawn's fragile light. Ellee asked, "Is that...Orryn?"

Alysa studied the figure. "Yes, I believe it is..."

Orryn practiced with a spear, confident, playing at rushing an imaginary opponent. Again and again he yelled and thrust and swung around, fearless, as if he were fighting a whole army of M'raudas. Alysa shook her head and smiled, then realized the agony she would feel if he should come to harm.

Outside the Great Hall, the peltees ate their breakfast—leftover stew from the night before.

Alysa recalled the dream as soon as they entered. She worried for Szaren's life for the first time. After spending much effort in bringing this battle about, she was now beginning to regret it. Not only was Szaren's life at stake; hundreds would be in the forest the next morn.

Many could die. Last-moment doubts began to rise up in her. What she set in motion — was it, after all, a good thing?

She clutched Ellee to her and said, "Over these next two suns I want you to listen to Mother. You're to do as she tells you. And stay inside, do you hear? Don't leave her for a single moment!"

"Thitha...are you all right?"

"Yes. I'm afraid for you, that's all."

"I promise..."

Although some of the Folk warriors were taken into cottages to sleep, many stayed in the Great Hall the last few nights. The cots were now stacked against the walls, tables and benches set up in their place for the morning meal.

Alysa and Ellee joined the line that filed past kettles of steaming food. They filled bowls with hot simmel. A few conversations were being conducted in lowered voices. All seemed to be concentrating on the event that lay ahead. If it were not for their manner of hair, Alysa would have been unable to tell which of the warriors were Trailmen and which were Folk, dressed as they were in the same dark-green tunic and breeches.

She and Ellee sat at a table half filled with quiet warriors. Szaren slid himself and his bowl from the other end of the table and sat across from them.

Alysa avoided looking into his eyes. She said, "Oh. I didn't see you."

"I know. But I saw you come in. Yissa, I want to..."

"It's all right. There's no need to...can we just forget about it?"

Szaren nodded and stirred his simmel.

Alysa looked nervous. She could not eat and felt like she might vomit.

Szaren said, "You do not look well."

She began to tell him about the dream but thought better of it. He needed no doubts added to this sun's burden. "I...no, I'm all right."

"You are worried, are you not?"

"No," she lied, stirring the simmel for which she had no appetite.

"Yes she is, Szaren," Ellee said.

He reached across the table and took Alysa's hand. "You must rise above worry. Fear can paralyze thinking. It can render one defenseless."

"You're right. It's just that..." and Alysa whispered almost inaudibly, "I don't want to lose you. I know I shouldn't say that. I'm so confused..."

"I will come back, have no doubt," Szaren assured her.

"And I will come back, too," Haraht added, "to take my place at Szaren's side." She slapped her bowl on the table and crowded in next to him.

Alysa wondered why he allowed Haraht to believe he still desired to be betrothed to her. Was Szaren deceiving Haraht, or fooling both of them? His silence, his seeming acceptance of Haraht's continued proclamations, kindled doubts in Alysa's mind about how he honestly felt. Did last night's conversation — and kiss — mean anything to him? Alysa finished breakfast in silence, though Szaren tried to appeal to her through reassuring glances.

She rose and took her and Ellee's bowls to the sink at the back corner of the Great Hall where utensils were piled for washing. She returned to the table and, avoiding eye contact with Szaren, motioned Ellee to follow. They went to Loralle and helped her and the other women collect dirty dishes.

In silence, the warriors filed out of the Great Hall. Trailmen and Folk walked together through the early morning light, descending the terrace walkway leading to the barn where the weapons were stored. Peltees found their masters and walked beside them.

On her way to her duties in the barn, Alysa trailed not far behind the warriors. Szaren and Haraht stopped up ahead and were talking. Alysa slowed her pace. Haraht faced Szaren and raised her fist, but did not strike him. Trailmen following close behind took a wide path around them. Drongo looked confused and sat down at a distance to wait. After a moment of agitated conversation, Haraht pushed Szaren hard, nearly sending him to the ground. Then she turned and stomped off at a swift pace down the terrace.

Resigned, Szaren shook his head and continued to the barn. Alysa wondered what happened. Was Haraht's behavior a display of

pre-battle nervousness? Was she bolstering her bravery in preparation to fight? Haraht was one of the most difficult of Trailmen to
understand.

All the way to the barn, Alysa continued to wonder what took
place between them. But once inside, she was jolted out of those
thoughts. She slowed as she passed orderly rows of weapons stacked
in racks along the walls. Her stomach tightened; her throat became
dry. She hoped for a quick end to the battle and that none of her
brothers and sisters would be harmed.

She climbed the stairs to the loft where the healing supplies were
gathered, trying her best to calm her stomach and focus on her duties. She went to a window and pushed the shutters open. She gazed
upon the field of warriors spread across the terrace and was touched
by what she saw.

Islean, Loralle, Obala and Tola walked among them, stopping to
offer last-moment encouragement and blessings. Trailmen husbands
and wives held hands as they awaited the command to assemble.
Wives and younglings of Folk men clung to them during the last
moments; battle-dressed sons held their mothers. Evyn's daughters
crowded around him, dragging on his clothing as if to pull him back
up to their home. Rainur escorted Betram from the field, knowing
that the youngling was not yet ready for battle. Betram looked de-
jected as Rainur ordered him back up to the cottages. Panli rocked
his wife in his arms and dabbed her tears with his braid. Boshe stood
beside his Trade companion but turned to talk to a Trailmen warrior,
allowing Panli and his wife one last private moment.

Then Alysa noticed something unexpected. Several Folk men and
Trailwomen were holding hands or embracing. It may have been the
desperate duty approaching that caused the reaching out of their
hearts. Or perhaps they had discovered enough similarities between
them and ceased to define each other's differences as shortcomings!
She smiled and felt, for the first time, that she was not alone in her
good feelings for the Trailmen.

Her eyes passed over many she had known her whole life. Would
this be the last she would see of Orryn, Boshe, Evyn or Aryz? Would

she ever see Szaren again? The thought of this was almost more than she could bear.

She again placed a hand on her stomach and discovered that it was not her stomach, after all, that was upset; a little higher, around her heart, was where the unease was located. A warm, wild fluttering — a feeling she never experienced before — rose up within her. The fluttering, she realized, was her essence speaking to her, at last making itself known!

She closed her eyes and took several deep breaths, and the fluttering became calmer. Her whole body became warm and seemed to relax. She thought of the walking staff Szaren made for her after her injury and how the branches twined together as one. That was how she saw Szaren and herself, their essences intertwined, as roots grown together.

Again she searched the faces spread across the field, at last finding Szaren. He was standing alone. Haraht was not anywhere near him. Alysa searched for her and found her standing with Kailee on the other side of the field. As Alysa focused on Szaren, it seemed as though her essence leapt from her chest, reaching out to his. She was about to run down the stairway, to go to him, when Rainur's large, gruff voice called out, "All to weapons!"

Her heart sank. It was too late. She would have to let Szaren go off without speaking to him one last time. She watched as reluctant family members let go of their Folk warriors.

The clanking of weapons being taken in hand as warriors entered and left the barn ended the still of morning. If she ran downstairs, she knew she could not find him in the throng, would only be in the way. She waited at the top of the stairs, watching below, hoping to catch one last look at him as he passed through the barn. He did not pass through her view, though, and soon all the warriors had returned to the field, weapons in hand.

Several healers who would be helping tend the wounded at Falling Stream climbed up the stairs to gather the last of the supplies into packbaskets.

Alysa returned to the window. The warriors grouped farther down the terrace. Some knelt and folded their arms across their chests. Those were the Trailmen. The Field Folk also knelt; their cause, after all, was the same.

Rainur, Tola, Islean and Poolan stood in the center of the assembly. Islean spoke to the warriors. Her words fell short of Alysa's hearing. Yet she knew that Islean was asking the Forever One to spare all who could be spared and to help in the defeat of the M'raudas.

Alysa knelt on the floor and whispered, breathless, "Please bring all the brave warriors and younglings back safely, Forever One."

Loralle and Obala climbed the stairway. Loralle knelt beside Alysa and put her arm around her. Obala came up behind and watched with them until the last warrior and peltee had stolen down Lower Path into the forest.

The healers slung their packbaskets on their backs, awaiting Obala's lead. "Come," Obala said. "We must not trail too far behind."

Alysa rose, tearful, and hugged her mother farewell. She took up her packbasket and followed Obala and the others down the stairs.

THE BATTLE

In the next morning's pre-dawn, the constant sound of high, churning waterfalls rolled over the steep terraces of Falling Stream Homestead. At the eastern edge of the homestead, cascading curtains of water fell into a deep, rumbling chasm, then smoothed and flowed on a placid southward course.

Slowly coming into view in the early light, the terraces of Falling Stream were steeper and narrower than those of High Point. Ponds high above the homestead were filled with water diverted from calmer places above the falls. The ponds fed rock-lined irrigation ditches that wound their way through the cottage and field terraces.

The design and organization of cottages, barns and shed structures was like that at High Point. However, loose rock was abundant here and was used in place of logs to build walls.

Below the homestead, a deep, wide ridge thrust into the forest and disappeared from view. The ridge overlooked sloping tiers of uninhabited ground. Far below, Rocky Stream's course disappeared among distant, low hills.

The terraces were eerily devoid of people. Normally, Folk would be laboring in the fields as the sun rose; but none were to be seen, nor did any labor in the barnyards. The herds were gathered within the barns. The shutters of all of the cottages and the Great Hall were closed tight.

In one of the lofts closest to the Great Hall, many Trailmen and Folk healers waited, nervous, sitting on cots that would soon cradle the wounded. The healers did not talk. For comfort they listened to the sound of the waterfalls and the bleating and shuffling of animal stock below. Some Folk quietly wept. Stoic Trailmen fussed with bandages while struggling to keep their breath even.

Alysa studied the faces of the people in the loft. She loved each and every one of these good people, Folk and Trailmen alike. She thought about those who would fight in the battle, those she could forever lose from her life: Aryz and Evyn, Islean and Obala. She thought about Orryn and how she would miss his friendship should he not return. The clan still needed Tola's wisdom, so she also wished for his safety. While she thought he had been unfair to her and Orryn, she forgave Tola; she had come to realize that at the time of their altercation, he had responded as he thought best. She also lamented Seda's desperation and hoped that her Sureena and the other younglings would be brought home. Alysa held firmly in her mind the idea that Seda's family would be together again.

For each of them she held special memories and hopes. But most often she worried for Szaren. She so yearned to see him upon his return and make things right!

She struggled with her breath, as it became ragged the nearer the start of battle drew. She stared out the loft window that faced the ridge and closed her eyes. She thought hard: *Forever One, please bring them all home in one piece! And please bring our Sureena and all the younglings back safely!*

She squeezed her eyes tight, trying to hold back tears. But she could not; knowing that the battle may have already begun, they flowed down her face.

Islean softly spoke an order to the warriors just before they reached the edge of the ridge. "Archers, remember to take care with your arrows! Be certain that your targets do not hold a youngling! Spearmen! Do not let one fly if there is any doubt that a youngling is in danger!" All understood, and the caution was passed to the warriors in back.

Tola, Islean, Rainur and Poolan crept to the edge of the ridge and lay on their stomachs. They peered through the mist below as it rose off the stony, sloping ground, waiting until it dissipated enough to give them a clear view. From their vantage point at the top of the ridge, they observed the scene.

Islean motioned the others to disperse along the ridge. Rainur, Marteen, Haraht, Jontif and other leaders guided their ranks to predetermined positions, where they readied their weapons. Many of the archers and spearman climbed trees. Obedient peltees, long ears pricked in excitement, waited by their masters.

A few dark figures moved about the M'rauda camp, the first to rise at dawn. One looked toward the ridge and stared at it for a long moment. Islean, Tola and Poolan lowered their heads and inched back from the edge, holding their breath against the chance that the M'rauda had heard them.

Islean whispered, "We had best make haste!" With that, she rose to give the signal just as the sun crested the distant, rolling hills. She yelled, "For the younglings!" and gave a high-pitched whistle.

Battle cries pierced the early morning quiet as the combined force of Trailmen, Folk and bounding peltees surprised their quarry. They broke through the trees and surrounded the camp, surprising the M'raudas. The beasts jumped to their feet and, for a moment, just stared at the warriors. Then they scattered in all directions. They picked up spears stacked in various places around camp.

Haraht, Kailee and their archers hung upside-down from tree branches along the ridge. They waited just long enough to be certain that none of their targets held younglings and fired several volleys. The hope was that the attack of arrows — sprung before the warriors on the ground met the enemy — would disarm the beasts and bring a quick end to the battle. Some M'raudas fell before they could utter a scream — but not nearly enough.

The spearmen in the trees grabbed vines and swung into the middle of the fray. They dropped down unexpectedly in front of the M'raudas, who were aware only of the advance of warriors on the ground.

Screeches bellowed from the surprised M'raudas' mucous-filled mouths. Both warriors and snarling peltees halted their charge as they came face to face with the beasts. The few witnesses described the M'raudas as ugly. But no one was prepared for how truly hideous they were! None knew that the rag-covered, twisted bodies smelled so foul, or that their skin drooped in thick gray folds upon bodies that were — somehow — descended from their own kin. Slits containing red eyes peered out from faces with distorted proportions, most lacking any real features. Neither did the warriors expect to see additional appendages, such as a third or fourth hand thrusting out from a torso to give triple hold to a spear or wield an additional weapon!

"They are not...real! They cannot be!" someone yelled in horror.

The peltees' ears drooped. They whined and moaned at the assault of the M'raudas' sight and smell.

If the warriors had charged through without hesitation, dashed the two hundred or so M'raudas to the ground before they had found the wits to respond, the battle would have ended almost as soon as it began. That moment of hesitation allowed the lead M'rauda time to shriek a quick order. The M'raudas were better organized than was thought.

It was indeed a frightening order, as the commanding M'rauda issued it not from just one mouth—but from two! A smaller, secondary head with several beady red eyes whirling around to view the confrontation reared itself from the side of the M'rauda's neck. From the smaller head's gaping mouth—which occupied most of what was difficult to even call a face—a discordant, high-pitched squeal accompanied the M'rauda's call to arms.

Rainur, battlerod in hand, yelled, "They are real, you had better know that! Cast out your fear...resume attack!" He surged toward the M'rauda that screeched the order and was met with resistance from several grotesque opponents—and found them also stronger than was expected.

Evyn commanded Trekkar and other peltees within his hearing to attack. With ears pricked high and eyes wide, they jumped onto the M'raudas, who were unprepared for this onslaught. The peltees placed themselves between their masters and the M'raudas. Baring sharp teeth, the peltees grabbed onto crude M'rauda spears and clubs and pulled them away, bit into their ragged clothing and gray flesh, and pounced on them, knocking them to the ground. The advantage of the peltees allowed the warriors to slay many overwhelmed M'raudas.

All along the ridge Trailmen and Folk clashed with M'raudas. Sounds of vicious fighting filled the forest. Many of the beasts fell with wild thrashing and screaming as purple-red blood ran from their carcasses; Folk, Trailmen and peltees fell, too.

During an ambush by three M'raudas on the far side of the ridge, Evyn was speared in the shoulder. Other nearby warriors were engaged in their own fights and could not come to his aid. Despite Trekkar's protection, Evyn went down. Fortunately the peltee's ferocious posturing and snapping jaws kept the M'raudas away. They left Evyn for dead. Trekkar stayed at Evyn's side to ward off any further harm.

Boshe and Panli fought side by side and advanced down the ridge. They worked magnificently together! They thrust their spears in unison at the beasts that approached from downslope, clearing the way for a group of warriors who advanced behind them. Boshe swung his spear at an attacker that ran at him with a stout wooden club. The club hit his spear and broke it. As the beast swung again at the defenseless Boshe's legs as if to break them, Panli jumped in front of him and put the spear clean through the M'rauda. It crashed backward, landing on two others. Boshe grabbed up a rock and he and Panli sprang on the downed beasts to slay them before they could get to their feet. The Traders were joined by several other warriors and continued to cut a swath through their enemy.

Across the ridge, Orryn dashed into the fray holding a spear. Two M'raudas tripped him and he crashed to the ground. Jontif, close behind and also wielding a spear, ended the life of one of the beasts then turned to battle two that came at him from behind. Orryn's spear hit the ground and rolled just out of reach. Before he could get up, a M'rauda jabbed a spear point against his throat. The crude spear was nothing more than a stick with a sharp end; still, it could do what was intended with little effort. The beast taunted Orryn with mucous-filled words apparently intended to instill fear in him. The M'rauda sneered and threatened him. Orryn gulped. At any moment his life could end! Then other beasts started to close in.

The M'rauda moved to thrust. Orryn turned rapidly onto his side and rolled from under the spear, but the ragged point cut long and deep into his cheek. He yelled in pain and jumped to his feet. Blood ran down his face. He stood ready for the continuing attack he was trained to expect. He found himself downslope of the M'rauda. The beast thrust again, this time at his chest. Just in time Orryn dodged the attack and grabbed up his own spear. Yelling in retaliation, he thrust it upward, deep into the beast's chest. The M'rauda wobbled and toppled over, nearly falling on top of Orryn. Now he knew why he was trained to stay upslope! He jumped out of the way. The beast screamed in misery as it crashed to the ground and slid downslope.

Jontif finished dispatching those who attacked him and turned to help Orryn. With a hearty howl he charged at a new group that rushed at them. He swung his spear in a wide, wild arc. They turned and ran off. Jontif chased after them.

Orryn stared down at the M'rauda carcass that nearly fell on him to be certain it was dead. He determined that it was and bent down and punched it in the head. He jumped up, let out a victorious, "Ha!" He dislodged his spear and charged back to the fight, more confident than before.

Farther down the ridge, Rainur bled from several cuts on his bald head, strong arms and chest. The antler tip of his battlerod was broken. He faced three M'raudas at once. One of the hideous beasts, standing at the rear, slurred what seemed to be words of encouragement to the others. Rainur boldly swung his battlerod and shouted at the beasts, "All right, you disgusting walking carcasses...you youngling thieves and nasty, repulsive creatures...you have chosen the right warrior to help you meet your end!" His shouting seemed to perplex them. He advanced and swung his rod hard, hitting the nearest club-bearing M'rauda, sending it careening down the slope and over the edge into the stream far below. The other two M'raudas watched in horror, turning back more fiercely to Rainur. Angered, they screeched at him.

"Ah, ready for contest number two, are you?" He swung hard again and hit the second beast squarely between the eyes. It fell and remained motionless.

Before Rainur could pull his battlerod fully back into position, the third M'rauda jabbed a spear into his leg. Hot anger rose to Rainur's face. He pulled the spear out and yelled, as if the M'rauda could understand, "Vile beast! That hurt!"

Suddenly afraid, the beast turned downslope. Rainur limped behind, blood running down his leg. A peltee, with ears pricked high and leaping with great strides, charged the M'rauda at the same time Rainur shoved the end of his battlerod hard against its back. The peltee jumped up and pushed the beast, which vaulted downslope. This one, too, went over the edge.

Rainur and peltee peered down at the stream. Rainur yelled, "Company for you...you putrid piles of fungus..." He bent down to the peltee and patted him firmly on the back. The peltee's ears softened. "Thank you, my peltee friend! Who belongs to you, eh? We got rid of the leader but we yet have work to do!" Rainur rose and limped up the slope, growling and yelling threats on his way. "Who is next, then? Who is next? We will take you!" The peltee's ears pricked up again as they moved back toward the fray.

Fighting side by side, Haraht and Kailee set down their bows and took up battlerods. They rushed the enemy. A rock pitched hard by a M'rauda hit Kailee on the head. She went down.

"No!" Haraht yelled. She paused, quickly evaluated Kailee's condition, and turned back to the fight. She was fierce. Unstoppable. Shouting in anger, she swung her rod wildly. Every swing struck down a beast. As one after another fell, she jumped on it and thrust her blade into its heart—or where she thought the heart should be. They harmed her best friend! The beasts would pay mightily! It was not long before Haraht was covered in purple-red M'rauda blood.

Szaren fought alongside Jesh and others. He became separated from his group as with spear in hand he and Drongo chased a retreating beast to the far edge of the ridge. Several more M'raudas waited downslope. Szaren found himself surrounded, outnumbered. The foul creatures held spears to his body.

Drongo was uncertain what to do. She seemed to sense that any move she made could bring harm to her master. Her ears remained pricked high as she quietly snarled, watching, waiting.

One beast moved closer to Szaren and with its gray, gnarled fingers grabbed hold of Szaren's spear. He resisted but the M'rauda jerked it forcefully from his hands and threw it on the ground. The beasts jeered and pressed their spears close to Szaren's chest.

Marteen and Orryn—his face, neck and tunic covered with blood from his wound—sprang upon the mess. Orryn stabbed at them with his spear as Marteen poised her bow. A group of warriors followed close behind, shouting with gusto. Drongo took the opportunity to join in and clamped her teeth on a M'rauda's leg.

The beasts scattered, except for the horrible leader. The smaller head sneered and screeched in anger. The beast found a place between Szaren's ribs and thrust its spear, sending Szaren to his knees.

"No!" Marteen roared. Enraged that the unarmed warrior was struck down, Marteen dispatched the M'rauda with not only one, but two arrows between its own ribs. With a stunned look on both its ugly faces, it fell and rolled downslope. Drongo charged off after the retreating M'raudas, and the warriors followed.

Marteen set down her bow to look at Szaren's wound.

Nervously, Orryn said, "Oh, no...not Szaren...what do we do now...?"

"Please, Orryn. I need to think!"

Orryn drew a deep breath, nodded and composed himself. He stood guard against any beasts that might return.

Marteen broke the shaft close to Szaren's body and threw it away as hard as she could. Clenching his teeth, Szaren attempted to rise. "Lay down, Szaren!" she ordered. "Lay down. Be still!"

Szaren moaned and dropped back on the ground. His eyes rolled back and his body went limp.

"Is he...dead?" Orryn asked, continuing to glance around.

"I cannot tell for certain," Marteen answered, "but I think not. We must get Obala to him as soon as possible, or he will be!"

"I'll find her!" Orryn said. He hurried off through the trees, looking about with caution. "Healer! Healer, here!" he commanded through the diminishing sounds of fighting. He saw that very few M'raudas remained standing.

After a few moments, he returned with Obala, Jesh and Jontif, who carried a litter. Staring in disbelief at his friend, Jesh knelt as near as Obala would allow. Islean followed close behind, concerned but remaining quiet while Obala ministered to Szaren. Obala knelt beside him and worked rapidly as Orryn prepared the litter.

Drongo and Vonni ran up, whimpering. Their ears drooped sadly along their faces. Obala glanced at them sternly. They lay down at a respectful distance and remained quiet.

Rainur limped in along with his new peltee friend to help keep watch.

Marteen said, "I will check on the other wounded."

Obala said, "Yes, make note of the locations of those who are the worst. Either I or one of the other healers will be along as soon as we are able."

Marteen nodded and hurried off.

Obala cut Szaren's tunic to expose the wound. From a pouch she produced a tiny wooden flask, poured liquid around the spear shaft, and bandaged his chest. She spoke as she worked. "Forever One, make this brave man whole again, this most cherished of yours who has always believed in the power of your wisdom, who has fought this sun for your younglings. Let him live so that he may fight again, should it be your desire, so that he may rear younglings as brave and forthright as himself." She finished applying her treatment. "There!"

Islean stooped beside Obala and observed Szaren's face. She placed her hand on his cheek. She took a relaxed breath and nodded to Obala.

Obala rose. She said to the men, "Take him to Falling Stream. Carry him quickly but carefully so the shaft is jarred as little as possible. He will not bleed overmuch on the outside as long as the shaft is in place; but he will bleed much on the inside if it moves any deeper. I will be along as soon as I check the condition of the others."

Islean added, "Let them know that I accompany Obala and that we will be up soon to help with the wounded. Alert the Healers that many more will be coming. Tola and Poolan are reviewing conditions on the other side of the ridge. Tell everyone that the battle was a success, despite the injuries…and the losses."

Jesh and Jontif carefully moved Szaren onto the litter and lifted it off the ground.

"I will go!" Haraht said when she came upon the group and saw his condition. She took Jontif's place at the litter, and she, Jesh and the faithful peltees hurried Szaren toward Falling Stream. Jontif ran downslope where Folk and Trailmen searched for more wounded.

Obala called after them, "Let no one else touch Szaren's wound. I will tend to him myself!"

The healers roamed the ridge, applying herbal salves, binding wounds, giving blessings for healing and conveying words of praise to the warriors. Fortunately, the majority of the wounds were minor. Most of the blood that soiled their faces, hands and clothing was the purple-red blood of M'raudas. For those warriors who suffered serious injury, litters were rapidly dispatched to Falling Stream.

Some of the beasts escaped downslope to the cliff bordering Rocky Stream and jumped into the water far below. The warriors who chased after them and watched from the edge did not see any of them surface. Unfortunately, there were many dead strewn about the battleground. Most were M'raudas.

With all the wounded tended to, Islean surveyed the camp. She called, "Has anyone found the younglings yet?"

Rainur limped on his bleeding leg to the center of the M'rauda camp as others scouted the boundaries. He surveyed the area, noting where the beasts slept, ate—and defecated.

He held his nose and thought. As the battle raged, the only sounds to be heard were of weapons clashing, yelling warriors and screaming beasts. Now a new sound came to his ears; the faint whimpering of younglings! His eyes and ears were drawn to a tall, wide pile of hides, or of hides thrown over something, below a rocky outcrop. He limped over to them and pulled a hide off the pile. Beneath were stacked several crude wooden cages. He looked through the slats of one at the top of the stack. Frightened wet eyes looked back at him.

"Ah, moons above!" he exclaimed, breaking the latch off the cage and throwing the lid open. He reached in and picked up a red-haired youngling. Her little smock was filthy, her tiny face and hands soiled. She started to wail and all nearby warriors—dropping their weapons to free their hands—rushed to Rainur. As he held the youngling close, his eyes filled with tears.

Orryn ran up, still bleeding from the cut on his face. "It's Sureena!" he said. "From Falling Stream!" With his sleeve, he wiped what blood he could from his face and took her from Rainur. He held her close. Her crying diminished as she recognized his comforting voice. "Ho, Sureena…you're safe now. You know me…I'm Orryn, precious youngling…quiet now…" He looked inside of her tiny prison. Disgusted, he said, "Oh, look at the nasty rags she had to sleep on!" He looked across the ridge and called, "Aryz! Aryz…it's your Sureena!"

Aryz, making his way upslope, started to run as best he could, straining to see his daughter. Jontif was close behind.

Orryn grinned and held her high. "She is well!"

Aryz let out a roar of relief and thrust a jubilant fist into the air as he hurried up the slope.

Rainur pulled off the rest of the hides and counted, as others ran to the cages. "Ten, eighteen, twenty-eight, thirty…five. Some of these cages must be empty — but open them all!"

It was a command that every able one was glad to oblige. Tola and Poolan rushed in from the other side of the ridge. The warriors unstacked the cages and quickly opened them. They were surprised to find that every cage *did* hold either a male or female youngling between six and twelve moons old.

Nearly all of the younglings began to cry, making such a din that the peltees crowded around, yelping with excitement. They rose up on their hind legs to put their noses closer to the contents of the cages, alternating between pricking and drooping their ears in confusion. Finally the younglings began to quiet in the arms of the warriors, soothed by their tenderness and warmth.

Poolan asked, "In the name of Father Gord'n, where'd they get thirty-five younglings?"

Rainur said, "None of them bear paintings, so they do not belong to the Trailmen."

Marteen quickly checked their condition. With characteristic Trailman's confidence and calm, she said, "They look half starved. But they will survive." She looked into Rainur's eyes. "What in the moons were the M'raudas planning to do with them?"

Boshe and Panli each held younglings. Boshe said, "It would seem they were getting ready to take them somewhere, probably south. That's why they were in these cages. Pitiful!"

Tola asked, "I wonder what in the moons they fed them? Quickly! Warm them in your arms, place the tiny ones inside your tunics. Get some warmth into them!"

Aryz dashed up and took little Sureena from Orryn. He held her at arm's length and looked her over, then snuggled her close. She laughed and said, "Va-Va!"

Surprised, Aryz said, "Those were my youngling's first words!" He hugged her tight and began to weep. "I would never have heard her say them if not for the brave warriors who fought—and died—here today. I'll never forget them!"

Tears sprang to every eye at Aryz's words. Sureena and the other younglings were reclaimed! In every heart, this seemed to justify the cost of the battle. They were quiet, thoughtful, for a long moment.

Jontif wiped his eyes and pointed at the camp. "It looks like they were planning to leave this very sun. Look, there are stacks of pack-bundles beside the cages and at other places around camp; they were all ready to go."

Poolan asked, "But go where? And who do the other younglings belong to?"

Orryn said, suddenly aware of the implications, "Only nine of them belong to us. So there must be other clans we know nothing about, in other places in the mountains—or outside of them! That's the only answer that comes to my mind."

Questions abounded. Where were the homesteads of these other younglings? Did they dwell in the Short Mountains to the south, which were thought to be uninhabited? Were they from the Rolling Territories far to the west, or even beyond? Were the younglings from one clan or tribe, or more than one? How would these younglings be returned to their families, who must be desperately yearning for them?

The answers, for now, would remain a mystery. The younglings needed immediate attention.

Aryz said, "I must take Sureena to her mother. Seda will be...beyond words!"

"Let us get all of them up to Falling Stream," Marteen added. "They need to be fed. And bathed! Poor things..."

Led by Marteen, Orryn and Aryz, the younglings were hurried to Falling Stream. Those whose parents were known would be reunited with them.

Duties remained—the aftermath of battle. Many Folk men who did not take part in the fight arrived from Falling Stream pulling carts filled with digging tools. With picks and shovels, they dug deep holes in the rocky soil. The M'raudas were placed into these and covered over, to be done with and forgotten.

The Trailmen were buried in mounded cairns where they fell. In some of the graves, dead peltees were laid beside their masters. Together, Folk and Trailmen spoke words of gratitude over each cairn. Folk lost in battle would be returned to their homesteads for cremation and sowing over the fields in which they labored.

When the grisly duty was done, the Elders led a solemn throng to Falling Stream. Those spared from death bore the litters of Field Folk who were not—brave warriors all, who gave their lives for the younglings.

Far to the south, over the rolling hills, a thick, dark cloud—a hail storm or even snow—moved over the land. Lightning bursts from the cloud struck the ground. No one seemed to notice. The storm paled in comparison to the tragedies—and the joys—of this sun.

THE SLEEP OF THE WOUNDED

By the third sun after the "Battle at M'rauda Ridge," the majority of Folk warriors had returned to their homesteads. The Folk younglings were reunited with their families.

After the fallen Folk were given a proper final farewell, rejoicing spread through the homesteads. The Folk's own younglings were returned, and the twenty-six orphans of unknown origin were distributed among 'steaders and Trailmen. This fulfilled the dreams of many couples who had not borne younglings. Who knew if their birth parents would ever be found?

The Trailmen were still camped at Falling Stream. They would not leave until they knew the fate of one of their wounded. During these suns, they busied themselves helping the Folk with chores or hunted the forest on the other side of Rocky Stream. At night they gathered around hearthrings near the tumbling waterfalls on the edge of the homestead. Many Folk joined them to listen to their tales. The 'steaders also told some of their individual stories, something they were not accustomed to but found exhilarating all the same. Some Trailmen slept in spare cottage beds, but most erected huts. Few strayed far from the healing barn.

Most of the bandaged and sewn warriors were allowed release by Obala. She also let most of her healing helpers return to other duties. Only two warriors had injuries severe enough to require continued care. Of these, one was Folk. But the deep spear puncture to Evyn's shoulder was responding well to Obala's healing.

Peltee Trekkar stayed at Evyn's side throughout the battle and during his transport from battlefield to healing loft. Peltees were not ordinarily allowed indoors; but Obala allowed him to stay in the loft, as Healers were well aware that the presence of these dedicated creatures often aided their masters in healing. Trekkar sat beside Evyn and rested his head and long, floppy ears on the cot. From sad, yellow eyes he watched over Evyn. Trekkar left Evyn's side only to eat and to relieve himself.

Evyn was propped up in a half-sitting position. Obala sat next to him, helping him finish his meal of hoptail stew. She had spiced it with herbs that aided sleep. Evyn did well holding his own utensils this eve and ate every morsel.

He said sleepily, words broken by yawns, "That was very...very good, Obala...thank you."

"Hush now, Evyn. You must rest."

He blinked, fighting sleep, and whispered, "I wish to go home now..."

She chuckled. "I expect that I will allow you to leave in a sun or two, when you are strong enough to make the hike. But now you must sleep, rebuild your strength."

He smiled a rather silly smile, an effect of the herbs in the stew. No longer able to hold up his eyelids, his head bobbed forward.

Obala set the empty bowl on the table beside his cot. She peeked under his shoulder dressings to check his wound, pleased with the progress. She helped the groggy man settle into his bedding and tucked in his blankets. He closed his eyes, still smiling that silly smile. Obala dimmed the lantern.

She said to Trekkar, "Do not worry, loyal peltee. He will be able to lift sacks of simmel in no time, this Miller of High Point!" The peltee raised his black head off the cot, cocked it as if in understanding, whined, and set it back down.

Obala turned her attention to the second warrior who lay on the other side of the loft. She sighed with guarded sadness. She was not certain that this one—Szaren—would ever walk from the barn. He was still pale, unhearing, unseeing, not feeling the injury to his body. The spear point had deeply penetrated his chest. Obala had extracted the spear point and applied healing compounds; but he had lost much blood. So far it seemed that none of his insides were damaged beyond their ability to mend. Time would reveal his fate. The Trailmen delayed their departure to the Lowlands to wait for him.

Alysa sat on a cot next to him. She rarely left the loft since the battle-wounded were brought in. Joy welled up in her as she discovered that Orryn had not been severely injured and that Evyn's recovery was steady. Sureena and the other younglings were now with their parents. This was the reason for the battle, so it was a major success in that light.

Alysa had helped the Healers tend to the wounded in whatever way was needed, keeping a close eye on Szaren and caring for him as much as Obala allowed. As the suns passed, Obala began to entrust more of his care to Alysa.

Soft lamplight glowed near his head. The weak light allowed Alysa to keep watch for the flutter of dark eyelashes and flash of blue that would signal his return to life. She gently patted Szaren's face with a damp cloth and wiped it over his short, dark-streaked hair.

Drongo also kept vigil. She lay beside Szaren's cot with her nose tucked into her large paws. Her long ears draped on the floor alongside her head. She dozed for short periods at a time, rising between naps to sniff Szaren's face.

Obala was leaving Szaren in Alysa's charge for the evening. Over and above what Obala's care provided, she knew that much healing could result from tender caresses and true caring from one's essence. She learned that Alysa had plenty of both to give Szaren. But she was also concerned for the girl. Obala threw on a cape, preparing to leave. She said, "Yissa, I admire your steadfastness. But I must warn you that when Haraht has finished mourning Kailee, she will return for Szaren. What then?"

Alysa held her gaze on Szaren's face. "I don't know, Obala. I believe that somehow the right words will come."

Obala smiled and squeezed Alysa's shoulder. "Good evening, then. I will return later, after I have stretched my legs and tended to some other duties." She descended the stairs.

Alysa watched Szaren, wishing with all her being to once again see the smile that made her heart leap with joy. She regretted that she wasted her last moments with him by allowing jealousy to interfere with what she firmly believed was true—that Szaren wanted her, and no other.

Eventually, exhaustion overcame her. The soft sounds of the men and peltees breathing and the steady rush of the nearby waterfalls lulled her toward sleep. She dragged her cot against Szaren's, lay down and closed her eyes—just for a moment—and fell asleep.

It was not long before an abrasive voice seeped into Alysa's troubled dreams. "I *said*, it is up to *me* to stay at his side," Haraht growled. "He is, after all, to be my man."

Drongo rose to attention, shook the sleep from her strong body, and whimpered as she looked back and forth from Haraht to Alysa. Drongo sniffed Szaren, lightly licked his cheek, and descended the staircase.

Alysa forced her eyes open and sat up. She looked not at Haraht, but at Szaren, and shook her head. "No, Haraht. You're wrong."

Haraht laughed and clenched her fists. "How can you contend anything that concerns my people? You were not there when our law was made or when I won the right to pair with him. I am a descendant of the Elders, as is Szaren, and you are not!"

"Bloodlines have nothing to do with this, Haraht. You see, I've given this great thought. While it's true you could win his body, it would be impossible for you to truly win *him*. Because his and my essences — which are much deeper than bloodlines — have become intertwined. Szaren has won me, and I him, completely. And not through a tradition of knocking down some challenger and rolling around in the dirt! Your pairing with Szaren, no matter how long it has been planned, won't come to be, Haraht. And if by some odd twist it does — neither of you will be happy."

Haraht stiffened in anger and commanded, "You listen to me, Fielder...stand up!" She raised a fist to Alysa.

Alysa rose. "Go ahead. Strike me. See where it gets you; I can tell you that it'll get you nowhere."

Haraht stood poised for a long moment, clearly intent on striking her. Obviously not seeing any advantage to that, Haraht finally lowered her fist.

Alysa whispered, "Haraht, you must listen to me with an honest heart, which I know you have. I watched you and Szaren the morning we left High Point. I wondered at the time what was taking place between you, why you were so angry at him. But I've reasoned it out. That morning, he released you from your pairing promise, didn't he?"

Haraht hesitated. She sighed and nodded, unwilling to counter Alysa's argument with a lie. Haraht's fierce disposition softened. "That is true. He did break our betrothal. Not that I wanted that. But I cannot lie. That would be of disrespect to him, and to me."

"Thank you, Haraht."

Quickly restoring her brusque demeanor and trying to cover the fact that she had lost this battle, Haraht said, "So you are welcome to him. Or to whatever is left of him!"

"I'm sorry, Haraht. About Szaren. And Kailee."

A tear slid down Haraht's face. She quickly wiped it away, straightened, and leapt down the stairway.

Alysa was truly sorry for Haraht's losses. She believed, however, that Haraht had known the truth for some time: her betrothal to Szaren was no more.

Obala bounced up the steps and removed her cape. She shook light snow off it. "The weather is turning. The tribe grows restless, desiring to return to the Lowlands. But they await word on Szaren's condition before setting out. They wish to take him back with them, even if it means transporting him all the way by litter." She stood at Alysa's side and gazed at him. "I just saw Haraht."

"Yes..." Alysa said, tired.

Obala sighed. "I have seen that there is more between you and Szaren than ever was there between him and Haraht. The truth has a way of manifesting. She has lost much these last few suns, poor girl. But she will rise above it." She bent down to feel Szaren's face. She put her ear to his chest.

Alysa, not wanting to ask but needing to know, said, "He's so quiet and still so cold. How much longer do you think it'll be before he wakes?"

Obala shook her head. "It is difficult to say. His heart beats strong and steady. But he cannot sleep much longer. You must get some sleep yourself, midling." Obala retired to a shadowy corner of the room, removed her boots, lay down on a cot, and spread her cape over herself.

Alysa held vigil until, once again, she gave in to fatigue. Facing Szaren, she settled down on her cot and fell asleep.

Upon the next morning's sunrise, a hand feeble as the early rays of light stroked Alysa's hair. She opened her eyes and saw that Szaren was back! Startled at first, she sat up and took his hand. She caressed his face. He half-raised his eyelids, managed a weak grin, and inhaled deeply.

Drongo rose to her feet and bounced joyfully around the room. She returned to Szaren's cot, licked his cheek, and pricked her ears high in excitement.

Alysa leaned close and looked into Szaren's eyes. She touched her hand to her heart and felt great warmth spread throughout her body. She whispered, "You are the one, Szaren. You are the one!"

AN UNCOMMON JOINING

The air was warm at Greening Moonsfest. Some Folk picked flowers growing along the stream. They adorned each other, sticking blooms into their braids and behind their ears, laughing and singing on their climb to the Tradeground as dusk approached.

Folk and Trailmen younglings spent the afternoon making flower garlands, which graced a circle of flickering lamp poles placed on the Tradeground. The noisy younglings, with hands linked, playfully wove in and out of the circle of lamp poles. On this special eve, the Tradeground would serve as the Joining Circle.

Still more Folk came up Gorge Path, and Trailmen walked across the ancient bridge, the old floor and open holes covered with a plank floor. No longer strangers, Folk and Trailmen greeted one another by name.

Orryn, bearing a long, ragged scar along the left side of his face, stood with Elders Marteen and Poolan. Aryz was with them, one fatherly hand resting on Sureena's head as the thriving wobbly clung to his tunic. She peeked around his legs and stared up at the forest of people gathered there. Aryz nodded in agreement as Orryn, Poolan and Marteen conversed. Nearby, Apprentice Teller Betram listened, watching Orryn with awe.

Poolan said, "That was a very astute statement, Orryn. I believe you're right. We must discover where the parents of the orphans dwell. If they're still alive."

Orryn said, "Oh, I believe they're still alive, Poolan. And that the younglings are not orphans at all, just...not with their parents at this time. We learned how the M'raudas avoided contact with grown Folk and Trailmen. I think we can assume they used the same tactics with the unknown clan to take their younglings. I think their parents are alive and well—somewhere—and probably desperate to know the fate of their wee ones."

Aryz added, "You know, the reason for finding their parents would not only be to reunite them with their younglings, but to form an alliance of some sort, I should think."

"Yes!" Marteen added. "I am keen to learn about them; are they more like Trailmen or Folk?"

"Perhaps..." Orryn said, "perhaps they are not like either of us. Hmm. I wonder, how do they live? What are their dwellings like? What are their beliefs?"

"Do they have knowledge of the Forever One?" Marteen wondered.

Blinking, Orryn regarded his companions. "What *stories* do they tell?"

They stared at each other, suddenly at a loss for words. There was so much for them all to wonder about. Betram, excited by the conversation, inserted himself into the group.

Orryn added, "Finding the parents can be the only resolution to many, many questions."

Thoughtful, Aryz looked down at his Sureena. The wobbly stretched a hand up to him and said, "Va-Va!" He lifted her into his arms. The little redhead squealed with joy as he placed her on his shoulder. She viewed the crowd from high above, clapping her tiny, chubby hands and wiggling in delight. She pointed at the torches and said, "Yook, Va-Va!" and squealed again. They laughed at the sweet youngling's delight.

Bavat and Tach were not far from Orryn, talking with others, accepting congratulatory comments and making little effort to hide the pride they felt as a result of their son's achievement in reaching the status of Full Teller.

Not far from Orryn's parents, Kendira was seated on a bench in the midst of an uncomfortable conversation with Islean. The aged Teller looked up at her and stated with quiet disgust, "After tonight, it'll finally be done; our clan will be forever ruined!"

Amused, Islean asked, "What do you mean, Kendira?"

Kendira spat, "You know very well what I mean! The merging of our people will spoil everything. The Laws of Father Gord'n will become tainted with your wild ways and impractical ideals. The Laws will die, and with them—the Field Folk way of life!"

Islean chuckled and knelt beside her. "Kendira, what you fear will never happen. My people, who are really your people, too, have learned that there are many facets of Folk life that are worthwhile. Otherwise, we would have gone back to the Lowlands immediately after the Battle at M'rauda Ridge without as much as a farewell. Instead, some of us stayed here even through wintertide. This will be the first time the Trailmen have been through the pass early enough to celebrate Greening Moonsfest. Certainly it will be our first celebration of *any* kind with the Folk.

"We can learn much from each other, given a chance, Kendira. And become all the better for it. I think that if Father Gord'n's Laws cannot withstand the discovery of some new ideas and ways of living, then they were not very sound to begin with. This also applies to the laws the Trailmen live by." Islean gestured at the merrily chatting Trailmen and Folk. "Just look how well everyone is getting along. I will wager that there has not been this much excitement in the mountains since our people split three thousand cycles ago!" Kendira grimaced. "Kendira, what can I say that will convince you that both Folk and Trailmen will benefit from our alliance?"

Kendira did not respond, maintaining her anger.

Islean said, "I will confess something to you; something that I have not told even those closest to me. That thing is that it has always been my hope that the tribes would come together. And there was a Folk who shared my dream…"

"Abso, right? Ha!" Kendira sneered, "He was always sneaking off toward the forest. All along I knew he was up to something!"

"Yes, you guessed correctly. But despite his and my influence within our tribes, we could not think of a way to accomplish what Yissa managed all alone to do. It is my belief that the Forever One helped her every step of the way to ensure that things would turn out as they have."

The old Teller said, "I never trusted in the logic of the Forever One. Planning, only tangible planning achieves proper results. You must understand that I've spent sixty-two cycles nurturing and protecting the Laws of Father Gord'n. Sixty-two!"

Maintaining her patience, Islean said, "We all feel that we are right in some way about certain things, Kendira. At least we are of the same mind on that one point." Aware of the darkening sky, Islean rose.

Kendira caught her by the arm and said in a quiet, measured voice, "You are, after all, a very wise woman, Islean. I've decided that we're of the same level of mind; so I will also make a confession. I ask only one thing, however—that you keep these words secret."

Softening to Kendira's change in tone, Islean waited as Kendira continued.

"Long ago, I was as curious as Orryn. On a visit to Falling Stream, I also made the same discovery as he in that hidden room. But I worried about what could happen if the knowledge was discovered by a careless clanfolk. My whole life has been spent protecting our ways, and I've always struggled with the fear that such a discovery would lead to what is happening now! So I wonder and I fear this: if the old arguments that caused the Ancient Ones to hate each other are rekindled, will we in cycles ahead go to battle against each other? Will we destroy each other the way the Ancient Ones did? I've often thought of removing everything in that room and burying what would not burn. But something kept me from doing that. Perhaps knowing that the contents of the room could well be the very last remnants of the ancient world, a once great and wondrous world! When I think of City Infinity, I am awed."

"Why Kendira," Islean smiled, "you *do* have a sentimental bone in your old body!"

"I once did, when I was young."

"It is still there. Please hear me. I know that we will never go to battle against each other. Father Gord'n and Brother Willim no longer exist. And as long as we maintain the best parts of both our ways, accept each other for who we are, I see no reason for us to suffer separation ever again. I would like us, you and me, to work together and help our tribes find ways in which we can mesh." Kendira did not look convinced. "Kendira—please understand that I am not saying that either tribe should give up *anything* in the meshing. But if it happens that in time some choose to dwell with the other tribe, then this was meant to be. It is their choice. I believe that Yissa has helped us to understand this. Will you help, Kendira?"

The Teller asked, "How do we agree on what stories to tell? And who will create them?"

Islean said, "Maybe that would be best left to Orryn, the one who has lived with great awareness and courage through the knowledge of the *true* history. And of course young Betram, who is now moving into your position, will tell both the old and new stories at High Point. Then you may spend the rest of your suns in quietude."

Kendira grimaced at the decision by the Elders a few moons ago that she be retired from her Teller position. Her eyes misted. She turned her head away.

Sensing Kendira's despair, Islean touched her hand and added, "Fear not, Kendira! You will not be completely out of a duty. I am certain that you could continue to do some of the telling, too, as a way to teach your excellent skills to the apprentices. Ah, I know! You must tell the old stories to the Trailmen younglings!"

Kendira's eyes brightened at the prospect of a future for herself, even if it meant telling stories to the Trailmen. She nodded.

Islean looked firmly into her eyes. "One thing is for certain, Kendira; from this point on, we must be honest with each other and with the tribes, in every word that we utter, every tale that we tell. It can hurt no one to speak only truth. Can we make that a new 'law' between us, to speak only truth?"

Kendira closed her eyes, sighed and nodded. "Yes. This we must do. We'll talk more after the ceremony. Agreed?"

"Agreed!" Islean said, nodding in satisfaction. "I must go now." She softly patted Kendira's frail shoulder and rose to make her way through the throng. She went to Tola, who welcomed her to his side.

The slow beat of a flatdrum sounded, and a path cleared for the procession as everyone fell silent. The younglings ceased their play. They found their parents and, understanding the rules of propriety, became quiet.

A Folk flute piped a solemn melody, and a Trailmen plucked a low-pitched strum. Alysa appeared at the top of Gorge Path, dressed in a long, flowing white tunic. The blue beads sewn over its surface sparkled in the lantern light. Her braid was coiled on top of her head. Loralle followed, escorted by Evyn in Abso's stead.

Seda, who looked quite robust and once again with unborn, followed them and walked beside Ellee, who carried the joining sash. Standing around the Tradeground — this night the Joining Circle — everyone strained to watch Alysa's procession.

Szaren crossed the bridge to the Tradeground, accompanied by Jesh. Many other Trailmen followed, some carrying torches high, others patting Szaren on the back in spirited encouragement. Not accustomed to solemnity in any of their celebrations, the Trailmen were as quiet as was possible on this joyous occasion.

Islean smiled at Szaren and embraced him as he walked into the Circle. Dressed in dark-colored hide tunic and trousers, he took his place at Alysa's side. They stared at each other, grinning joyfully.

Tola held up quieting palms and the music stopped. He said, "On this eve of Greening Moonsfest, we're here in the names of Father Gord'n — and the Forever One — to carry out their wish that we go forth and be productive. The couple to be joined will now step forward."

Alysa and Szaren moved a step closer to Tola and Islean. Islean beamed a wide though solemn smile.

Tola asked Szaren, "By what name do you live, and why have you come to this Circle?"

"My name is Szaren of Winding Mountains. I have come to claim Yissa of High Point Homestead to dwell both in my home and in hers until our final farewell, as my wife and the mother of our younglings, should we be so blessed."

Tola lifted his eyes to Loralle and Evyn. "Parents of this young woman, do you wish your daughter to join with Szaren of the Trailmen?"

Alysa looked at her mother and Evyn and was surprised and delighted to see her father's visage just a breath behind them. It had been a long time since he appeared to her. Abso smiled with pride and nodded. His face faded, revealing Orryn's. Orryn nodded and smiled at her. She was delighted that he was happy for her and thankfully smiled back.

Loralle and Evyn joyfully replied, "Yes, it pleases us to give our daughter so that she may live the life that is right for her."

Alysa beamed and turned back to Szaren.

"Bring the sash before us!" Tola rasped. Ellee stepped forward and let the sash unfold. It shimmered in the lantern light as she passed it to Seda, who held it high so that all could see. It was a new sash, with a new stitch repeating from one end to the other. The base cloth was colored deep-green. The stitch—in brilliant golds, browns, reds and blues—was in the likeness of a firestag's head above Winding Mountains.

Tola said, "The sash, patiently created in anticipation of the joining-to-be, is testimony to a woman's diligence and patience, and to the devotion she holds for the man with whom she is joining."

Seda draped the sash onto Alysa's palms and kissed her on the forehead. Seda tried to speak her blessing, but she was too full of happy tears. Alysa nodded, knowing that her friend's wish would be for the happiest life possible.

"You may now say your private vow," Tola said to Alysa.

Alysa looked into Szaren's eyes and said, "Beyond forever, Szaren, my essence is yours!" She wrapped the sash about his waist and knotted it at his side. "This is my charm, the wish that love will continue to grow through everything you do."

Szaren smiled. He reached into a pouch and withdrew a brilliant blue stone captured in a shining metal band. Alysa gasped in delight. As he tied the pendant around her neck, those who were near enough to see it quietly remarked on its beauty. The color contrasted handsomely with the white of her tunic.

The pendant gleamed with the first streaks of moonlight reaching over Winding Mountains; the many stars within the stone shimmered. Craggy Nanthan-kul lifted herself over the peak, shining over the majestic landscape, revealing a luminous beauty never before witnessed from this place by either Folk or Trailmen. Milky Donol-kul appeared moments later, and the trees burst into frosty color as moonslight penetrated delicate buds as far as the eye could see. The sky washed pale-blue, and the stars faded.

Tola said, to Islean's apparent surprise, "For those joined here this eve, as for those joined in the past, the rising of the moons shall seal this joining."

Islean smiled at Tola and repeated, "For those *paired* here this eve, as for those *paired* in the past, the rising of the moons shall seal this *pairing*."

To the surprise of the Folk, the Trailmen responded in delight and began to clap. Everyone burst into laughter and began to talk all at once. Out of the entire joining rite, the last phrase was the only one the Trailmen found to be familiar. The words had changed little over the generations. It was possible that this would be the only similarity found between any Folk and Trailmen ritual. Those words seemed to give them great relief and confirmed that this joining—which some may have been reluctant to completely accept—was right.

Tola and Islean laughed and embraced, glad that the ceremony had ended with a familiarity to all.

The gathering watched as the moons cleared Winding Mountains, the surroundings glowing as never before. A breeze rushed down from the mountains and whisked through the gorge. Szaren pulled Alysa close, and they kissed. Trailmen and Folk cheered the first public kiss exchanged between their people.

The bridge, as if in sunlight, was easy to see as the newly joined pair ran across the gorge and the sparkling waters far below. Friends and loved ones chased after them, singing one mirthful melody after another.

The peltees who waited on the Trailmen side of the gorge joined in, bouncing alongside them as they followed the couple through the forest into Ridge Camp clearing. There, many tables of roasted game, sumptuous foods, drink and desserts were spread.

Szaren led Alysa into his hut. The throng—the largest one ever to observe a joining—surrounded the hut, laughing and singing, teasing the couple for a time. Then the crowd gathered in the center of the camp where they danced and sang and feasted into the night, until long after the moons set. Until the lanterns ran out of oil. And the last song was sung—a new song—about the love and courage of one young woman: Alysa of the Fields!

GLOSSARY OF XUNAR-KUN
People, Terms, Geography, Flora & Fauna

Primary Field Folk of High Point	
Abso (AHB-so)	Alysa's father and mentor
Alysa (Ah-LIH-sah)	Alysa of the Field Folk clan, High Point Homestead
Betram (BET-trehm)	Apprentice Teller
Boshe (BOH-shee)	Major Trader
Dagg (DAHG)	Council Elder
Ellee (El-LEE)	Alysa's little sister
Evyn (EH-vihn)	Major Miller
Kendira (Ken-DIH-rah)	Major Teller, originally from Falling Stream
Levin (LEH-vihn)	Council Elder
Loralle (Lor-AHL-lia)	Alysa's mother, originally from Yellow Cliffs
Marli (MAHR-lee)	Tola's wife, originally from Green Plateau
Panli (PANN-lee)	Lesser Trader
Seda (SEE-dah)	Alysa's best friend
Thad (THAD)	Apprentice Teller
Tola (TOE-lah)	Council Speaker

Primary Field Folk of Falling Stream	
Alvan (AL-vahn)	First Teller and Teacher of the Laws
Aryz (AIR-iz)	Seda's betrothed, Orryn's best friend
Bakar (BAY-car)	Major Teller
Bavat (BAH-vaht)	Orryn's mother, originally from Yellow Cliffs
Father Gord'n (GOR-din)	Founder of the Field Folk clan and First Homestead at Falling Stream
Kahnton (Can-TONE)	Original Elder of Falling Stream
Nonnee (Non-NEE)	Caretaker of Father Gord'n's cottage
Orryn (OR-in)	Apprentice Teller, Alysa's betrothed and Aryz's best friend
Poolan (POO-lahn)	Council Speaker
Sureena (Sur-EE-nah)	Seda's firstborn
Tach (TAHK)	Orryn's father
Yiul (YOOL)	Council Elder

Primary Trailmen	
Brother Willim (WILL-ihm)	Leader of the ancient Trailmen
Callia (Cah-LEE-ah)	Szaren's mother, Staghorn Mountains
Efram (EFF-rahm)	Szaren's father, Winding Mountains
Ferran (FAIR-ron)	Painter, Winding Mountains
Folie (FOH-lee)	3rd Trader, Winding Mountains
Haraht (HAR-raht)	Szaren's betrothed, Far Reach Mountains
Islean (IS-lee-ann)	Szaren's aunt, Chief Elder, Winding Mountains
Jesh (JEHSH)	Hunter/warrior, Szaren's best friend, Far Reach Mountains
Jontif (JON-tiff)	Prominent hunter/warrior, Staghorn Mountains
Kailee (Ki-LEE)	Hunter/warrior, Haraht's best friend, Winding Mountains
Marteen (Mar-TEEN)	Chief Elder, Far Reach Mountains, paired to Rainur
Moronda (Mohr-AHN-dah)	2nd Trader, Winding Mountains
Obala (O-BAH-lah)	High Healer, Far Reach Mountains, paired to Trabo
Qohrlat (COR-laht)	Hunter/warrior, Winding Mountains
Rainur (RAY-nur)	Lead hunter/warrior, Staghorn Mountains, paired to Marteen
Szaren (ZAH-ren)	Warrior, Winding Mountains, Haraht's betrothed
Tibba (TEE-bah)	Painter, Winding Mountains
Trabo (TRAY-boh)	Chief Trader, Winding Mountains, paired to Obala

Terms	
A.C.	After Cat'clysm
Ancient Ones	Those who lived Before Cat'clysm
B.C.	Before Cat'clysm
battlerod	Ornately carved poles used by the warriors in battle
betrothal	Engagement to be joined or paired
Cat'clysm	Time of City Infinity's fall (deriv. cataclysm)
Eve of Moonsrise	Celebration of Trailmen pairing rite; occurs twice each cycle
Fielder	Derogatory Trailmen slang for Field Folk
fieldscript	Written language used by the Folk
final farewell	Death, funeral
firestones	Rough, yellow striking-stones used to start fires
Gathering	When the Folk in each homestead gather to plan events
Joining	Marriage rite of the Folk, held twice each cycle at Moonsfest
joining sash	Embroidered belt created by a betrothed woman

302

Terms	
	and given to her husband at their joining
midling	Child age 14-18
migration	Trailmen journey north and south at greening and leaffall, two suns after Eve of Moonsrise
Moonsfest	Celebration of Folk marriage rite at moonsrise; occurs twice each cycle
moonsrise	When the two moons rise together, twice each cycle
oldenscript	Written language of the Ancient Ones
pairing	Marriage rite of the Trailmen, held at moonsrise, twice each cycle
Pantry	Field Folk building containing free access to community goods
Planting Calendar:	Used by the Folk to plan their lives; represents one cycle
sunstick	= 1/20th of a sun; measured by inserting a stick into the ground and noting the shadow
sun	= 20 sunsticks
moon	= 21 suns
cycle	= 336 suns or 16 moons
seasons:	
greening	Folk: Time to repair equipment, mend fences and irrigation, plant crops Trailmen: Time to migrate north, scout animal trails
summering	Folk: Time to thin, till, pasture animals Trailmen: Time to hunt, gather hides and bone, preserve meat
leaffall	Folk: Time to harvest, amend the soil, preserve the harvest Trailmen: Time to migrate south, transport summering's gains
wintertide	Folk: Time to planning next season, craft goods, persevere Trailmen: Time to gather together in the Lowlands, hunt in the southern mountains
sleep of the wounded	Unconscious state resulting from injury
'steader	Folk slang for Field Folk homesteader
strum	Wooden musical instrument used by Trailmen; twists of taut hide are plucked
tamoree	Complex Folk board game involving many clay playing pieces moved around a series of shapes on a wooden board

Terms

Teller	Folk historian
Telling	Folk stories told by Tellers
Trade	Folk and Trailmen meet twice each cycle, 7 suns after Moonsfest, to trade goods they've grown and crafted (Field Folk) or captured or cured (Trailmen)
Trader	One who conducts Trade
tradesign	Hand gestures used to conduct Trade
Veiled Slayer	Radiation from war
wobbly	Child up to age 3, just learning to walk
youngling	Child age 3-14

Geography

The Bridge	Crosses Rocky Stream at the Tradeground
the City / City Infinity	Now a landmark, the ancient home of Folk and Trailmen
Donol-kul (Doh-nohl-KOOL)	Larger of the two moons, male
Far Path	Path from Yellow Cliffs to Green Plateau
Far Reach Mountains	Eastern mountains some Trailmen migrate to at greening
Gorge Path	Path along Rocky Stream leading from High Point Homestead to the Tradeground
Great Hall	Main building of the Folk where gatherings are held and where crafting takes place
Homesteads: Falling Stream	Southeast homestead, first homestead founded by Father Gord'n
Green Plateau	Southwest homestead
High Point	Northeast homestead
Yellow Cliffs	Northwest homestead
Valley Ridge	South central homestead
The Hunter	Star pattern, Folk name is the Planter
Lakelands	Base of the mountains where runoff collects into many small lakes
Lower Path	Path between High Point and Falling Stream
Lowlands	Where the Trailmen gather for wintertide
Lowlands Camp	Trailmen's central Lowlands camp inhabited mainly at wintertide
M'rauda Ridge	Falling Stream battleground where the M'raudas are defeated
Middle Path	Path from Yellow Cliffs that connects to Ridge Path

Geography

	East
Nanthan-kul (Nahn-than-KOOL)	Smaller of the two moons, female
Ridge Camp	Where the Trailmen camp on their journeys to and from Winding Mountains
Ridge Path East	Path between Green Plateau and Valley Ridge
Ridge Path West	Path between Valley Ridge and Falling Stream; intersects with Middle Path
Roaming Star	Comet that passes overhead during wintertide and summering
Rocky Stream	Stream that demarcates Folk and Trailmen territory
Rolling Territories	Unexplored lands to the west of Folk territory
Sleeping Lands	Dead, highly toxic area surrounding the City
Short Mountains	Hills south of the Homestead territory
Staghorn Mountains	Northeast mountains the Trailmen migrate to at greening
Tabir-sun (TAY-burr-sun)	Sun at the center of the solar system
Tradeground	Where Folk and Trailmen conduct Trade twice each cycle, after Moonsfest
Upper Path	Northern path between High Point and Yellow Cliffs
Winding Mountains	Highest point in view of High Point Homestead
Xunar-kun (Shoo-nar-KOON)	Planet on which Field Folk and Trailmen dwell

Flora & Fauna

briarwood	Hard, reddish wood used for carving
buzzfly	Flying insect
casish hen	Long-legged, domestic Folk fowl
Como (COH-moh)	Ellee's saroo
Drongo (DROHN-go)	Peltee, bonded to Szaren
Feelah	Ellee's saroo
firestag	Large, strong leaping ruminant with broad antlers and shaggy fur
flowerfly	Stinging insects that gather nectar
foya (FOY-ah)	Evergreen tree covered in soft, long, thick leaves
greatclaw	Fiercest creature of the forest, often encountered by the Trailmen and of which many tales are told
greenwing	Greening insect with large, thin iridescent wings
highbush	Firestag's favorite food, has berries
hoptail	Large rodent favored by Trailmen for food

Flora & Fauna	
leaprock lamb	Agile, small-built ruminant the Folk herd for their long white fur and meat
longpiper	Large migratory birds
longtooth	Large, skittish, upright-standing herbivore; very elusive
M'rauda	Distorted beast thought to be extinct (deriv. marauder)
marshdoe	Small, three-toed ruminant
nightchirper	Insect that sings only after dark on cooler nights of leaffall; morphs into greenwings at greening
peltee (PELL-tee)	Trailmen's canine
pricklebush	Tall bush with long thorns
rockhopper	Scaly, three-toed amphibian; mainly blue and green in color
saroo (sa-ROOH)	Furry, agile Folk pets whose main food source is insects
shimmerfish	Long, shiny fish capable of coiling and hiding under rocks
simmel	Staple grain
smartgrass	Tall grass with sharp edges that easily cuts unprotected skin
spicenut	Dark-red nut ground into powder, adds sweetness to food
sweatleaf	Hot herbal drink
swishtail	Water-breathing lizards, capable of running on top of water for short distances
Tahshi (TAH-shee)	Alysa's saroo
Trekkar (TREK-are)	Peltee, bonded to Evyn
udommo (u-DOH-moh)	Bovine domesticated by the Folk for milk and long, curly fur combed from its pelt
Vonni (VAHN-ee)	Peltee, bonded to Jesh
wildberry	Dark-purple bush berries

AUTHOR BIO & CONTACT

Tina Field Howe lives in Corning, New York. This first book in *the Tellings of Xunar-kun Series* won the 2006 Dream Realm Awards for Cover Art. She has published illustrations internationally in several books and other media. In addition to writing stories, poetry and screenplays, Tina has been a freelance communications designer since 1995. She creates everything from web content and graphics to business communications. Although creative in various media all her life, Tina became serious about writing during the 1980s. Tina is available for talks, writing workshops, readings, and signings. Visit her website (see *Further Information & Contact* below) to view her extensive portfolio and to learn more about her books.

The Xunar-kun Science Fiction/Fantasy Series
The TrailFolk of Xunar-kun, Book Two in the Tellings of Xunar-kun Series
We are a part of something greater than ourselves. 6 X 9. 320 pp.
ISBN 978-0-9768585-4-6 Paperback / 978-0-9768585-5-3 Hardcover

The Monx of the Roaming Star, Book Three in the Tellings of Xunar-kun Series
Together we can build a better world.
Coming next!

Other Book by the Author
Snailsworth, a slow little story, a children's picture book
Written and illustrated by the author, this uplifting story is told in both prose and rhyming poetry. Accompanied by rich illustrations and fun characters, it provides quality, enjoyable reading time for children and their adults. 24 pp. ISBN 978-0-9768585-3-9

Further Information & Contact
Web	www.AlysaBooks.com
Email	info@AlysaBooks.com
Phone	607-936-1455
Mail	PO Box 762, Corning, NY 14830, USA

Please inquire about the purchase of autographed copies of the books as well as free full-color Maps of Xunar-kun and the Planting Calendar. Artwork is by the author.

LaVergne, TN USA
29 October 2009
162463LV00010B/68/P